*Tales from
Alfred Hitchcock's
Mystery Magazine*

TALES FROM

ALFRED HITCHCOCK's

MYSTERY MAGAZINE

SELECTED BY

CATHLEEN JORDAN AND
CYNTHIA MANSON

INTRODUCTION BY

CATHLEEN JORDAN

MORROW JUNIOR BOOKS   New York

LIBRARY OF CONGRESS
Library of Congress Cataloging-in-Publication Data

Tales from Alfred Hitchcock's mystery magazine / selected by Cathleen
Jordan and Cynthia Manson ; introduction by Cathleen Jordan.
p. cm.
Summary: A collection of twenty stories of crime, suspense,
mystery, and humor, including "The Batman of Blytheville," "The
Poison Flowers," and "The Dear Departed."
ISBN 0-688-08176-2
1. Detective and mystery stories, American. [1. Mystery and
detective stories.   2. Short stories.]   I. Jordan, Cathleen.
II. Manson, Cynthia.   III. Alfred Hitchcock's mystery magazine.
PZ5.T228   1988

[Fic]—dc19   88-9013
                                                      CIP
                                                       AC

CONTENTS

INTRODUCTION

If you are a regular reader of *Alfred Hitchcock's Mystery Magazine*, you'll have a pretty good idea of what to expect from the stories in this book. If not, let me give you some hints. For one thing, people often think that mysteries and comedy don't go together. After all, murder—or blackmail or theft or whatever—isn't funny; everyone agrees about that. Nonetheless, somehow or other it is possible for humor and crime to go hand in hand in the same pages, and the stories in AHMM— and in this book—are frequently as funny as they are criminous. You'll find a lot to laugh at here.

Second, at AHMM we don't take a narrow view at all about the kinds of stories we include. That is, our offices are open to ghosts and demons and other supernatural folk; even the occasional dragon has gotten through the door. We also let in science fiction, sometimes. We do usually insist that these assorted otherworldly beings come equipped with a story having to do with crime; otherwise, we're pretty much open to all comers. You'll find some of them here, too: by our count, nine of these twenty tales, one of them set on the moon, involve such beings as a household of vampires, a batch of wizards (*and* a dragon, see above), a ghostly dog, and a haunted chair.

Of course, the stories are also often mysteries in the traditional sense; that is, there are plenty of wrongdoers to track down and puzzles to solve. One story is set in Paris, another in London; most of the rest take place in rural or small-town America, sometimes even in the characters' backyards, literally. There are stories for every mood and season—from lazy, hot summer afternoons to the traditional sleazy big-city atmosphere of a private eye's lodgings, to chill Christmas afternoons. Nearly all the stories present young people in a prominent way, boys and girls both, of all ages. The stories weren't written *for* young people, though—they were written for everyone—so if you like the book, you might recommend it to your adult friends and relatives.

Unless, of course, you don't want *your* copy to disappear into *their* libraries.

Cathleen Jordan
EDITOR
Alfred Hitchcock's Mystery Magazine

MYSTERIOUS WAYS

RICHARD F. McGONEGAL

randpa had style. His reputation for spectacular entrances and grand exits was well deserved. But perhaps the grandest exit he ever made was at his own funeral.

His second-grandest exit had come only a few days earlier, when he drove his Barnes Construction Company truck off the Old Post Road, careened down a forty-foot cliff, and departed from earthly life.

Grandpa's plunge rippled shock waves through the community, even if it wasn't wholly unexpected. His daughters—including my mom—and the few townsfolk who were his elders had lectured him repeatedly about how his hard drinking and wild driving would be the death of him. But Grandpa, with customary aplomb, shrugged off their warnings.

The crowd that gathered at the Humansville Baptist Church to pay their final respects and to hear the Reverend William Robert Williford's eulogy was a testament to Grandpa's stature. I was only nine years old at the time, but the events remain vivid even now.

Grandma was there, of course, and Mom and Dad, and my mercenary Aunt Brigetta, whose profuse weeping was spawned by her knowledge that Grandpa had died on the verge of becoming wealthy. It was no secret in and around Humansville that Grandpa's company was the odds-on favorite to win the lucrative government contracts being sought locally for work at the U. S. air base under construction twenty miles south of town. All of Grandpa's employees were in attendance, including his construction foreman, Pete Myers, and his business manager, Jimmy George Lowe. They—along with my dad and the other three sons-in-law—had been selected to serve as pallbearers. Even Roy Crum, whom Grandpa hadn't spoken to for more than ten years, came to the funeral. There had been bad blood between them from the day Grandpa gave Roy the boot, and it escalated over the years as Roy's construction company grew larger and more competitive.

People from surrounding towns also turned out, packing the large sanctuary of the church Grandpa had rebuilt nearly two decades ago, after a tornado demolished the original structure. The only people conspicuously absent were my Aunt Molly and Aunt Eleanor, who were back at my grandparents' house preparing the food and setting out plates, silverware, and cups for what I referred to as the "funeral party."

"We gather here today," Reverend Williford began, his booming voice echoing from the rafters and quieting the congregation, "to pay our respects to a man who will live forever in the history of our proud community."

He paused and waited for silence to settle. "For although Luther Leroy Barnes has ascended to the portals of heaven and has been welcomed to the peace and tranquillity of life eternal by the Lord our God, he also remains forever with us. He remains in our thoughts, he remains in our memories, and"—again Reverend Williford paused for effect—"he remains in our hearts."

The reverend surveyed the crowd with a solemn gaze and leaned forward in the pulpit. "What kind of man was Luther Barnes?" he asked, knitting his brows quizzically and warming to his own rhetoric. "He was a loving husband"—he paused— "and father"—he paused again—"and grandfather." I looked over and saw that Grandma and Mom were beginning to sob quietly, dabbing at their eyes with wrinkled tissues. Aunt Brigetta, who had gotten quite a head start, was now weeping convulsively.

"He was," Reverend Williford continued in dramatic fashion, "a good neighbor and a good friend. He was a man who could be taken at his word; a man of kindness, generosity, and honor.

"But he was more than that. Much more. My words are too poor to convey the richness of his deeds, but I will try to do justice to those deeds—deeds that speak so eloquently of the measure of this man." Reverend Williford made a measured sweep of his arm above the coffin before him.

"Not long after I received the call to return to this, my hometown"—and he extended his arms as if to embrace his audience—"and to shepherd this congregation, our house of worship was destroyed by a great natural force.

"And so it was that I went to Luther—a man I had known since I was a boy—and asked if he would help rebuild the church. And do you know what he said to me? He said, 'Jesus Christ, Billy Bob, I hope they taught you more in seminary school than how to reach into someone else's pockets.' "

I giggled, drawing a glare from Mom, but a quiet chuckle amongst the congregation saved me from further retribution.

"Coming from anyone else," Reverend Williford said with a smile that reached to his eyes, "those words would be blasphemy. But coming from Luther Barnes, they meant, 'I would be honored to help rebuild the house of the Lord.' "

I squirmed around on the wooden bench, looked back at Randy and Ricky Crutchfield, and saw that they were becoming as impatient as I was. We were looking forward to the funeral party, the rare opportunity to have soda and cake and, afterward, to play hide-and-seek, or red light, green light. A slap on my hands from Mom brought me around.

"And so he did," Reverend Williford said with quiet compassion, "and so he did. This house of worship where we have gathered together these past nineteen years, and where we gather today, was built with his hands, with the sweat from his brow, and, yes, with the money from his pocket.

"Not a single dime," the reverend said, his voice rising anew, "not one thin dime would he accept from the church coffers.

"And when we were finished . . ." He paused. ". . . When we were through, we stood together and looked at this glorious new edifice, this magnificent new home for the Lord our God, and Luther Barnes said to me, 'Jesus Christ, Billy Bob, if I'da known it was gonna come out this nice, I'da built it for myself.'

"And I said to him, 'If I couldn't see the love in your heart for the Lord, I'd step away to avoid being burned by the bolt of lightning that would most certainly strike you down.'

"That was the kind of man Luther Barnes was—a man who could not be measured by his words, nor by mine, but only by his deeds. For his love of God, and of his fellow man, ran so deep that it was not easily seen on the surface. But to those of us who knew him, his love was as visible as the stars on a cloudless night, as visible as our fertile fields in the summer sunlight, as visible as the guiding hand of the Lord our God in our daily lives."

I twisted around again on the bench and watched Randy and Ricky Crutchfield surreptitiously elbowing each other until all three of us received slaps from our respective moms.

Despite our signals of impatience, Reverend Williford was not about to abbreviate his eulogy, not by a long shot. He talked some more about Grandpa, painting a colorful but accurate portrait, warts and all. After bringing all the women in the congregation to tears, he embarked on what Grandpa always called "a long-winded, fire-and-brimstone finale that would scare the bejesus out of Gabriel."

I was getting my hands slapped for the fourth time, for fidgeting, when the pallbearers finally stood and lifted Grandpa's coffin. Led by Reverend Williford, the procession adjourned from the sanctuary and proceeded across the road to the parish cemetery.

It was a warm, muddy March day, and the recent snowmelt that saturated the ground permeated my newly polished shoes. The sky was so dark and low it seemed to lie on my shoulders like a wet sack of grain, and the wind swirled and ripped at my jacket and tousled my hair. Reverend Williford took his place at the head of the coffin and began reading, raising his voice progressively louder against the competition from the wind, which was rattling tree branches and howling to be heard.

" 'The Lord is my shepherd; I shall not want,' " he read, pinching the pages of his Bible.

The sky seemed to be undulating overhead, pressing its greenish-gray weight lower and lower.

" 'He maketh me to lie down in green pastures: he leadeth me beside the still waters.' "

The wind whipped itself into a frenzy, like a runaway freight train rampaging through the fields.

" 'He restoreth my soul: he leadeth me in the paths of . . .' "

"Tornado," yelled someone behind me.

We all turned, almost in unison, and saw the twister churning up trees and shrubs and spitting out splintered fragments as it carved a vicious path toward the cemetery. The group scattered. In an instant, Dad swept me up in his arms and, along with Mom and Grandma and most of the others, ran back to the church. I watched over his shoulder as the tornado gathered up a half dozen headstones, then snatched the coffin and carried Grandpa away.

It was minutes before most of the people realized what had happened. Fear lingered and, mixed with the newfound confusion as word spread that the coffin had been swiped, the congregation fell dumbstruck. Whispers became a drone, interrupted by shrieks and cries, until Reverend Williford called out in a loud, commanding voice: "Everybody, please, please, back into the sanctuary."

The reverend conferred with my grandma, my parents, and my aunts and uncles as the congregation slowly filed back inside the church. Sheriff Glover, who had been talking frantically on the radio in his patrol car, approached and conversed in whispers with Reverend Williford for a few minutes before we, too, returned to our seats in the sanctuary.

As soon as everyone was settled, the sheriff informed the group that he had been in contact with headquarters in Humansville and no other tornado sightings or damage reports had been received. He added that he and his deputies would begin a search immediately for what he called "the property in question."

As the sheriff hurried from the building, Reverend Williford slowly ascended to the pulpit and led the congregation in a prayer "for divine guidance from the Lord our God."

Silence reigned in the sanctuary for what seemed like minutes after the prayer ended, before Reverend Williford spoke again. "Perhaps the only shock greater than the tragic accident that ended Luther Barnes's life on earth is the abrupt manner in which his body just now was plucked by natural forces as it was about to be interred in its resting place."

He paused and stared at the group, obviously gathering his thoughts. "But we must remember that although his body has been taken, his soul has already ascended to join the legions of true believers in the halls of heaven. We must remember, too, that the Lord does indeed move in mysterious ways. I believe, and I know you share this belief, that God, who moves the forces of nature, is responsible for this event. We must trust in the Lord our God." He paused. "We must trust that what has happened is as it should be."

Buoyed by Reverend Williford's encouraging words, we repaired to the funeral party—a party Randy and Ricky Crutchfield and I all agreed was unlike any we'd ever attended. Condolences were uttered with awkward smiles, and conversations were punctuated by long pauses. The people moved about and offered handshakes and kisses with a mannequinlike stiffness, then circled the food table with uncomfortable reticence.

After treating ourselves to two helpings of soda and cake, Randy and Ricky Crutchfield and I went outside to play, but not before I received a stern admonition from Grandma to stay off the porch roof, my favorite place for hide-and-seek. "Your grandpa was fixing the supports before he died, and I don't know how safe it is," she said. Luckily, Randy and Ricky hadn't heard her give away my secret spot.

Once outdoors, Randy and I quickly agreed that Ricky, the youngest, would be "it" first, and while he covered his eyes and began counting, we scattered. Randy headed for the shrubs near the garage, and I shinnied up the large oak tree beside the back porch. Despite my temptation to slide onto the porch roof and lie down completely out of sight until Ricky strayed far from "home," I heeded Grandma's warning. I nestled into the wide crook of branches at roof level and drew my knees up to my chin. Even though the storm had passed and the sky had cleared, I knew I would be hard to spot in the rapidly approaching twilight.

"Ninety-eight, ninety-nine, a hunnerd, ready or not, here I come," Ricky called out as he darted away to search for us. As I craned my neck in an attempt to see where he had gone, I heard the screen door to the back porch fall shut, followed by the sound of footsteps and a dull squeak as the porch swing settled.

"It's creepy, Roy," said a voice I recognized. It belonged to Grandpa's business manager, Jimmy George Lowe. "I mean, I helped carry his coffin."

"Don't go gettin' weird on me," said a second voice, which I guessed to be Roy Crum's. "That's the only reason I came out here."

"What d'ya mean?" Jimmy George asked, his voice unsteady.

"I was afraid you might start gettin' weird on me," Roy said. "Just remember. You and I are in this together."

"How d'ya figure?" Jimmy George said, sounding more frightened. "I didn't do nothin'."

"You did plenty," Roy said adamantly. "You agreed to inflate the Barnes bid for my promisin' you fifteen percent once I got the contracts. That's conspiracy, buddy boy."

"Yeah, okay. But it ain't murder. I didn't tamper with the brakes."

"Shut your mouth. Are you crazy?" Roy said. He sounded both angry and fearful. "Listen, buddy boy. You were the one who told me when he'd be travelin' the Old Post Road, and that's conspiracy, too. Conspiracy to commit murder."

"But I didn't know you . . ."

"Didn't know what?" Roy interrupted. "You think for a minute he wouldn't have found out about the bid? It had to be done. But lemme tell you somethin'. If I fall, I'm takin' you with me, and there ain't no jury nowhere that's gonna think you didn't know what was goin' on."

"But I didn't . . . I mean . . . I don't know," Jimmy George whimpered. I could hear him sobbing quietly.

"Shut up and get yourself together," Roy said. "You hear? You fall apart and we lose everything. You'll get no money, you'll go to prison—maybe even the gas chamber. You want that?"

"I'da been . . . I'da been all right," Jimmy George stammered, "once they'd put him in the ground."

"He's dead, dammit," Roy said. "He's dead and he can't hurt us. Everybody thinks it was an accident. Nobody's investigating. We're home free unless you start to . . ."

Crack.

The voices stopped.

Crack.

I looked up and saw the coffin balanced precariously on two branches directly above the porch roof, its dark shape silhouetted against the deep blue of the early-evening sky.

Crack.

Down it came, branches and all, smashing onto the roof. The supports collapsed inward like broken twigs, and the whole works—roof, branches, and coffin—fell with a sudden deadly scream.

Once again, Grandpa had made a spectacular entrance.

We all gathered the next day to bury him, and we gathered two days after that to bury Jimmy George and Roy.

And Randy and Ricky and I had soda and cake three times in the space of one week. Mysterious ways, indeed.

RICHARD F. McGONEGAL is a resident of Jefferson City, Missouri, where he is employed as managing editor for the News Tribune Company. A native of Middlesex, New Jersey, he holds two degrees in English literature: a bachelor of arts degree from Rutgers University in New Jersey and a master's from the University of Virginia. Following graduation, he joined the News Tribune Company, where he worked as both reporter and editor during his twelve years as a journalist.

GOING TO MEET TERRY

RICK HILLS

I t was August, it was Sunday morning, and it was hot. Nathan woke quickly; he had things to do. He had to get out of the house without waking anyone, and he had to go meet Terry.

Barefoot and bareback was how Nathan felt today, so he wore only the jeans his mother hated most. He crept down the carpeted stairway that led to the front door and to freedom, making sure to tiptoe on the outside of each stair. The less-traveled carpet pleased his bare feet. And Nathan knew that this was the only way to walk the steps without the old wood underneath creaking its usual creak and waking his parents. Sunday morning meant they'd sleep late, which also meant there'd be no note for Nathan, no list of household chores he'd be expected to do before he could leave the house.

He made it through the heavy front door without a sound. The screen door's rusted spring groaned with reluctance as he opened it just wide enough to get through, but then it slipped from his grasp and slammed shut with a tattletale bang. Nathan stopped, breathless for a second, straining his ears for any commotion inside the house. When he didn't hear anything, he turned and walked like an Indian across the wooden porch and leapt the three porch steps down to the grass. As he landed he thought to himself, "All right! I made it!"

Back in his parents' bedroom, his mother stirred from her sleep and asked his father, "Did you hear something, dear?"

"Go back to sleep," his father answered. "It was just Nathan going out the front door."

Nathan's bare feet hit the front-yard grass like flat stones skipping across smooth water. His nostrils filled with the smell of morning mist before the sun gets to it. The warm moist air was quite a change from the all-night coolness of the house, and Nathan's skin goose-pimpled to get used to it. The feeling of getting away from something surrounded him as he kicked his way through the cool morning dew, yesterday's grass clippings clinging to his wet feet. The sidewalk was still cool in the elm shadows that covered every front yard on his block. Nathan looked back over his shoulder to watch his wet footprints gradually fade into dry as the cement soaked up each of his steps. *I'm the only one who knows where I am right now,* Nathan thought to himself. The feeling of freedom that buzzed around his head found a home in his legs, and he was off and running. It seemed the fastest he'd ever run, but it didn't seem to take any effort. Down the block he went, past Stimml's, past Johnson's, then Kennedy's, and finally he came to a stop in front of the big house on the corner, The-House-With-No-Men. There was a great-grandmother, a grandmother, a mother, and her daughter—but no men. The house was well-kept, spotless, and a little bit scary. Nathan glanced up the two steep terraces to the house and caught a glimpse of the old woman who constantly sat in her wheelchair, staring out across the broad front porch from behind a huge picture window. Nathan had heard from the older kids in the neighborhood that she couldn't walk, but Nathan had never even seen her move. She always sat the same way, in the same place, staring, staring all day long. But it was too nice a day and Nathan was feeling too good to waste his time thinking about the old woman. He crossed the street in front of The-House-With-No-Men.

Nathan walked on slowly, acting like he didn't know where he was going, but knowing all the time. The sidewalk stretched out in front of him for a while and then was cut in two by some railroad tracks. Nathan didn't know where they came from, but he knew they ended up at Bodie's Lumberyard, where his older brother worked Saturdays for all the pop he could drink and to shape up his muscles for high school football. The sidewalk picked up again on the other side of the tracks, and it wasn't long before it turned into a concrete footbridge crossing over The Crick. Somewhere down below the foot-bridge was where he'd meet Terry. And if Terry wasn't there yet, he would be soon.

Nathan walked out onto the footbridge and looked down into the murky water below. This was the favorite place of the neighborhood; this was The Crick. Almost all of its banks were steep, slippery mud, overgrown with patches of itchweed and stickerbushes. But here, the banks had been built from great chunks of stone block to keep them from caving in. On one of the blocks you could barely make out the number 1896, chiseled into it long ago but worn smooth over the years. Just below that, the cracks between the blocks made a natural ladder you could dig your bare toes into and climb down the wall to the sandbars and the water's edge. The stone walls made it feel like an open-air room with a stream running through the middle. The water flowed in under a street bridge, over rocks and broken tiles, and gouged through ever-changing sandbars filled with half-buried tin cans and an old bicycle rim. Then it slipped quietly into a large washed-out pool with more tiles on the bottom. The tiles were flat and slick, nearly impossible to keep from slipping on with wet feet. But on the steeper sides of the banks, where they rose up out of the water, some of the tiles had broken off or worn away, leaving iron bars exposed. These were the only handholds across the tiles. The places where there were no handholds were the places you just couldn't go.

The cool Crick air puffed up now and then, hitting Nathan in the face, bringing with it a damp, clinging smell of stagnant water and sewage. The stagnant water came from upstream, the sewage from a cement tunnel cut back like a cave into the sheer stone wall. The older kids said it ran under the street six or seven blocks up to the Municipal Hospital. There was always water running out of it, and once Nathan had seen bits of blood-soaked cloth floating by—hospital bandages, he and Terry had decided—so all the younger kids took it for granted that the older kids knew what they were talking about. The smell was ripe, and it amazed Nathan how it never bothered the kids but always bothered the parents. The Crick was so much fun because it was strictly forbidden ("You're going to catch polio down there, you know that, don't you?" is what Nathan's father constantly told him), and it was the smell that always gave you away and usually got you grounded for a week. The smell was such a sure thing that if you really wanted a fight, all you had to do was splash somebody on purpose.

Nathan leaned out over the the guardrail and stared at his reflection below. Then he watched a ball of white spit ease slowly from his lips. Finally it fell, as he watched the spit and its reflection race toward each other, colliding with a splat on the surface of the water, sending rings out, breaking up his reflection. *Maybe that's why Terry isn't here yet,* Nathan thought to himself. *Maybe Irv caught him yesterday and he's grounded for a week.* Nathan didn't like Terry's oldest brother, Irv. Ever since Terry's dad left, Irv had been acting like a big shot.

Nathan spit again but didn't wait for it to hit the water. *Well, either he's coming or he's not,* Nathan thought as he turned away from the railing. *I can't wait for him all day.*

Nathan sat on top of the stone wall where the crawlway started and dangled his legs over the edge, the dark mouth of the storm sewer opening up and gently trickling its water out into the pool just below him. The time didn't seem right to crawl down yet, so he picked up some loose pebbles and killed time tossing them into the water, first kerplunking them out in the middle of the pool and then eye-dropping them like a bombardier straight down into the storm-sewer stream. Nathan heard something close and spun around quickly to see if it was Terry sneaking up behind him. The Big Joke at The Crick was to pretend that you were going to push your buddy off the wall, and, sitting the way he was, Nathan was an easy target for the fake push from behind. But there was no sign of Terry. Nathan remembered how the fake pushes sometimes scared you into laughing, sometimes scared you into being mad. He searched for Terry again when he heard the noise again, only to see a squirrel scratching his way up the bark of a gnarled oak tree. Nathan laughed at himself for the false alarm and went back to pebbling. Staring at the water made him daydream, and as he listened to the different gurgles and rushings of Crick water, the sounds took over his ears and seemed so loud inside his head that he was aware of nothing else. Then he thought he heard something else from The

Crick, first very faint and very low. A far-away moaning that built on itself, getting louder and more painful, and then an all-out howl, filled with hurt and despair, was in The Crick— and it was coming down and out of the storm sewer! Nathan's breath quickened as the howl echoed and died out of the opening, and when it was gone he wasn't sure if he had really heard it at all. But there it was again, a low, damp rumbling of a moan this time, becoming almost a growl that made Nathan instinctively pull his legs up to safety. He spun around to see if anyone passing by might have heard it, too. But no one else was around; the streets and sidewalks were deserted. The instant of silence after the sewer noise was soon filled, was almost crashed in on by the rush of water noise. Nathan saw something move about a block away and recognized a dog, dancing excitedly in the gutter, his nose popping in and out of one of the sewer grates. The dog's body jerked as if he were barking, and then the sound echoed down and out of the sewer opening once again. "Lousy dog!" Nathan muttered to himself. "Probably chased a rat down the sewer and now can't do anything but bark about it." Nathan watched as the dog jumped back from the curb, then bounded up into The-House-With-No-Men's yard, its nose close to the ground, stopping to double-check some smell and then zigzagging on to the next smell until he wandered out of sight. Nathan took a deep breath and exhaled it slowly, feeling himself relax. He turned back to The Crick, but for some reason something seemed wrong. Nathan felt, in a sudden flash, that he should leave The Crick, that he should go home. But then it passed. *For crying out loud,* he thought to himself, *it's only The Crick.*

Nathan started down the crawlway to The Crick below. Climbing down was harder than climbing up, and the hardest part of climbing down was the first step. Nathan had to turn around so his back was to The Crick, then lower himself over the edge until he could rest all his weight on his stomach. He slowly let himself down, and then down again, stretching his legs as far down the wall as they could go. He looked off in the distance at nothing, his mind instead watching the unseen wall below, his bare toes searching for that first toehold big enough to hold his weight and allow him to work his way down the crevices to The Crick's edge. Once off the wall, he sat on some rocks and picked rock grit off his belly. Nathan wouldn't admit it, but the climb always scared him. No matter how many times he went up or down the wall, he was glad when the climb was over.

The climb down was short, but what a difference it made. The gentle puffs of cool air that escaped from The Crick up top were now a constant breeze, closer to a cold, damp wind. The water sounds seemed too loud for such slow-running water, and the steep walls all but cut out any direct sunlight. The wind, the water, and the walls blotted out the real world and left Nathan the only one in a world all his own. The only intrusion was the rare passing of a car over the street bridge, and then the rumbling that took place was more like captured thunder than a car passing by. Nathan could remember spending days in a row in The Crick without one person walking the short footbridge. A feeling of being totally free swept over him and, in its wake, a feeling of being totally alone. "I wonder what the hell is keeping Terry?" he said to the water. His pleasure from swearing like the older kids helped soothe his irritation at his friend.

Nathan mechanically rolled his pants legs up over his knees and started for the water. He chose a shallow spot with mostly sand on the bottom and waded a few quick steps out toward the nearest sandbar. He was careful not to stub his foot on any of the underwater rocks, both for his feet's sake and because he didn't want to disturb the rocks. He knew that if there were any crawdaddys around, that's where they'd be. Nathan wasn't exactly afraid of crawdaddys. He hunted them all the time with Terry. But when he was alone, he'd just as soon leave the crawdads alone.

When he reached the sandbar, the wet sand sponged down under his weight, and then each footprint seeped full of water. Nathan was still thinking crawdaddys. He remembered the time he and Terry had caught a bunch of them and hollowed out an arena in one of the sandbars. Then they put all the crawdads in the center and watched them fight each other, pushing the ones that tried to crawl out back into the fight. For some reason, Terry had decided to inch his way across the steep tiles to find some more. Just for a joke, Nathan waited until Terry reached the steepest part, the place where you had your hands full just staying in one place. Then he quickly picked up the biggest crawdad and, holding it at arm's length from his body, yelled, "Hey, Terry! Catch!" Terry looked up in time to see the crawdad leave Nathan's hand, but he couldn't dodge the throw without slipping off the tiles. He stood there frozen, watching the crawdaddy arc across the pool and land squarely on his chest. Nathan was waiting for the fun but got more than he expected. Instead of bounding off Terry's chest, the crawdad somehow hooked onto his shirt and clung there. Terry panicked at seeing the claws stuck to him, screamed, flailed at his shirt to knock the crawdad off his chest, and lost his footing. He slid down the tiles, trying to catch himself all the way, and finally went into the water up to his waist, the crawdad falling harmlessly into the water in front of him. Nathan was so surprised that his first laugh came out as a hard cough. Then he remembered the look on Terry's face and laughed until he laughed himself out, saying now and then, "You should have seen your face!" and "You've got to admit, Terry, it *was* funny!" But Terry wouldn't admit anything, and he sure didn't laugh. Yeah, there'd almost been a big fight over that one.

*   *   *

Nathan's daydreaming vanished and his whole body jerked before he realized what was going on. There it was again, that same low, pain-filled moan, rolling down from up inside the storm sewer. "Goddamn dog!" Nathan said quickly, so as to scare away his fear. The howl started again, but instead of dragging on and on, it stopped short, each echo of the stopping making the silence seem louder and louder. "That didn't scare me, just surprised me," he said, not being able to take his eyes off the black mouth of the tunnel. The harder he stared into the darkness, the more it seemed to draw him toward it. A tightness swelled up from his stomach as he started slowly toward the opening. *I don't know,* Nathan thought to himself, *maybe there is something in there. Maybe*—And then the air around him exploded with thundering rumbles as a car passed over the street bridge. Nathan wanted to run everywhere at once and so couldn't move at all. "For crying out loud, what's got into you!" Nathan scolded himself. "First a dog and now a car. You big baby!" He took a couple of deep breaths. Then he glanced all around The Crick to remind himself of where he was. He even looked directly overhead, as if to make sure the lazy clouds were still drifting along in the late summer sky. But then his eyes wandered back to the black hole of the tunnel, as he had known they would eventually. And he also knew he would have to go into the storm sewer. Any reason for not going in there now would simply be a lie.

Nathan didn't hesitate at the opening, except to crouch down to keep from bumping his head as he ducked into the dark. The first thing he noticed was the cold, clammy dampness that clung to his skin like a wet T-shirt on a cold night. There was a steady wind coming down the sewer, but all it brought was the smell of stale air and sewage. Nathan stopped a few steps into the tunnel to let his eyes adjust to the sudden darkness that crowded in around him. He strained to see deeper into the black, but black was all he saw. All the outside sounds had disappeared, and in their place was a silence only dark places have, broken by the slow-running stream and a distant dripping, echoing from somewhere deep in the blindness ahead.

Nathan worked his way farther and farther into the tunnel, and the farther he went, the darker it got. Every step took him away from the light outside and into the blackness. He began stumbling over things he couldn't see, and the wind played tricks on his ears. He kept telling himself he'd get used to the staleness, but the air smelled just as bad as it had at first. Whenever he thought he heard something move, he stopped dead, holding his breath. But all he heard was the running water and the drip . . . drip . . . dripping up ahead. Nathan glanced over his shoulder and, with the help of the faint light from the opening, saw that the tunnel behind him was empty. But when he turned to look in front of him, all he saw was blackness. It was time to push on. He hadn't gone in far enough yet to be able to turn around and walk back out. "If this is all the farther I was going in, I may as well have not come in at all," he told the walls. Then he made a deal with himself. "I'll go in at least to the first sewer grate, the one where I saw the dog."

Nathan continued on, deeper into the sewer. He walked along the edge of the tunnel, partly to keep out of the water running down the middle and partly to touch the wall every so often. The wall was damp; but it gave him a sense of security, a sense of where he was in the darkness, to touch it every few steps. With each step, the tunnel seemed to be closing in on him. The bottom was no longer dry along the edges but had thick, cold mud all the way over to the wall. It was deep enough that as Nathan stepped on it, it held his weight momentarily and then he broke through the wet crust, the slime oozing through his toes and climbing up over his foot to his ankle. Broken rocks embedded in the mud and along the concrete bottom sometimes slid by his feet, sometimes jabbed into them. He thought he was bent over enough, but he kept bumping his head on the low ceiling. Cobwebs would suddenly land on his face and string out over his bare shoulders. When the first web hit him, he lurched upright, banging his head hard on the concrete. As he tried to rub away the pain, he felt his hair matted with dirt and web. After that, the cobwebs just made him angry and, with his anger, he felt more courage. He felt like attacking the sewer; he felt he had the sewer whipped.

Up ahead, Nathan was finally able to see a faint light. *There's my sewer grate,* he thought, glad to be headed out of the dark instead of into it. He looked back toward the opening, but it had disappeared in the darkness. The only light was up ahead, barely visible, spilling down from the street next to The-House-With-No-Men. *This sewer ain't so bad,* he thought. *Piece of cake. Wait until Terry*—but his thoughts were stopped when he heard a loud splash up ahead. And before he could be sure if he heard a splash or not, another howl came rolling down the sewer, and then another right behind the first. Even before the echoes had a chance to die, Nathan knew what to do next. "I've had it with that dog," he muttered out loud. "Time someone taught him a lesson!"

What light there was from the sewer grate allowed Nathan to shuffle quickly through the mud, almost running, hunched over, the mud sucking at each foot and splashing up his legs. As he went closer and closer to the opening, the howls became louder and louder, tumbling over and over each other on down the tunnel behind him. But there was no place for fear in Nathan. All he could think about was reaching the sewer grate, screaming up at the dog on the street, and scaring the daylights out of him. *Who knows,* it occurred to Nathan, *I might get lucky and he'll run in front of a car.* Nathan was glad for the howling because it meant the dog would still be there where he could scare him. Nathan jumped into the light and started his scream—but it never left his throat. The grate was empty. No dog, no nothing. The echoes left the sewer. The only sounds were the running water, the dripping, and Nathan's heavy breathing. He stared up at the empty grate in disbelief. "He couldn't have run away that fast. How could he get away so fast?" he asked the grate. The water trickled by beneath his feet.

Nathan sat on his haunches, his head down, trying to catch his breath. He was still wondering about the dog, so he didn't have time to look at what his eyes were already seeing. Gradually he focused in on the spot where he'd been looking, and what he saw made him instinctively slosh backward a few steps. Footprints! Barefoot footprints in the mud, leading back even farther into the darkness. He went to them, compared them with his own, and suddenly the dog was the farthest thing from his mind. *Somebody else is in the sewer. Somebody else is back there.* Nathan wanted to run, to get as far away as possible, but his legs wouldn't move. Then he heard it again; the moaning was starting all over again. He shot his eyes up to the grate, but it was still empty. The moaning came again, but this time he knew where it came from—from out of the blackness, echoing from deeper in the sewer. The moaning was softer than before, a tired, worn-out moan that trailed off almost into sobbing. Fear took a hold on his stomach and gave it a hard twist, making his entire body go tight. Suddenly there wasn't enough air in the tunnel and he had to grab the front of his jeans to keep from wetting them. The sobs came down the tunnel again at him and he felt exposed, standing in the dim light from the grate above. Anything in the darkness could see him without being seen. He thrashed through the mud, a few steps deeper into the sewer, and waited. Nothing. Thoughts flashed through Nathan like popcorn cooking over a high flame. *Should I yell? Or shouldn't I? Maybe they don't know I'm here. Maybe I could get away. If I yell, they'll find me. What if they're hurt? What if they want to hurt me?* That last one struck home, and Nathan had turned to head back out of the tunnel, out of the blackness, when he was stopped by the moaning once more. "Help. Somebody. Help." The words came out slow and weak, hardly loud enough to cause an echo. Nathan squinted into the darkness, cupped a hand to his mouth, and shouted. "Hello! Is anybody there . . . anybody there . . . anybody there" rolled up and down the sewer, the words banging louder and longer than Nathan had wanted. Then the silence took over what seemed forever, and finally Nathan heard weeping in the distance, some gasps, and then the long, hard howl again, slamming down the sewer walls, rushing over him, making his body shake and bringing an unexpected whimper from his lips. "Hang on, I'm coming . . . coming . . . coming . . ." and Nathan forced himself to move deeper and deeper into the sewer where he thought the cries were coming from.

Once past the street grate, the sewer returned just as stale, just as cold, and just as black as before. Nathan continued farther into the blackness, stopping now and then to listen to see how much farther he had to go. He finally heard some movement up ahead of him and stopped. It was coming toward him out of the darkness. Closer and closer he could hear the mud move, and then the claws dug into his foot as a ball of wet fur grazed his leg and whatever it was squealed as it splashed its way through the muck behind him and on down the sewer. It all happened so fast that Nathan's heart didn't start pounding until the animal was already past him. "Take it easy," he told himself. "Whatever that was is just as scared as you are."

A spark of light flickered twice against the wall somewhere down in the darkness and then went out. "Do you have matches . . . matches . . . matches . . ." Nathan shouted. But no answer. A couple of steps farther and Nathan saw another flicker, only closer, and then all was black again. "I think I see you . . . see you . . . see you . . . Light another one . . . nother one . . . nother one. . . ." But again no answer.

Nathan had never been this far back in the sewer, only the older kids had. He wished his older brother were there right now. Nathan struggled on, trying to find good footing where he couldn't see a thing. He kept touching the wall for support and aiming toward where he last saw the flicker of light. He reached out for the wall again, but it wasn't there. Nathan didn't think he had slipped that far out into the middle of the tunnel, but he took another step toward where the wall should be and still found nothing. He swung his arm in a slow, wide arc through the blackness, and finally his hand struck cement. But it was a corner of a wall, the one he'd been touching all along, and then another one headed off to his left. *Another tunnel off this one?* Keeping his hand on the new wall, Nathan carefully took a step into the new tunnel. He waited a moment, listened, then took another step. He started his next step but kicked something large and wet lying on the tunnel floor. A bright flash of light exploded in his face, and a wet, slippery hand reached up and grabbed Nathan by the leg, squeezing hard, digging its nails into his flesh. He kicked out frantically, trying to break away, as his ears were filled with that same howl, roaring up from whatever had hold of him. Nathan's own scream joined the howl, and he felt his head begin to spin. The howling died away, and as it did, the book of matches that had been ignited all at once burned down to a candlelike flame. Nathan's eyes adjusted to the lesser light, but what he saw made him shake his head back and forth, sobbing, "No! No! It can't be!" There, lying at Nathan's feet, in a pool of filth and blood, one trembling hand holding the flickering book of matches, his other hand, caked with blood, grasping desperately at Nathan's leg, was Terry, his eyes looking helplessly up at Nathan through pain and blood and sewage.

"Terry! Aw hell, Terry. What's happened to you?"

Terry coughed, and Nathan saw red spit ooze out of the corner of his mouth. "Help. Someone, please," Terry hissed through clenched teeth. "Don't let her get me. Not again."

"Terry! It's me, Nathan. What happened?"

"Nathan? You found me. Oh God, you found me. . . ." Terry gasped for breath as Nathan felt Terry's hand lose its grip on his leg. As he started to slide into the sewer water, Nathan grabbed him by the bloodstained shirt and tried to drag him into a sitting position.

"Oh God! Don't touch me!" Terry said through his pain. "I'm hurt, Nathan. She hurt me real bad."

"Who did, Terry, who hurt you?"

"The old lady. The old lady—oh God, she hurt me bad." The flickering of the matchbook dimmed. Nathan couldn't tell where the filth stopped and the blood began.

"What old lady, Terry?"

Terry ran his free hand across his face, streaking a watery red that ran down his cheeks. In between heavy breaths, he spit out the words in short, choppy bursts. "The old lady . . . in the wheelchair . . . at The-House-With-No-Men. . . . She can walk, Nathan. This tunnel is a passage . . . a secret passage. . . . Oh, Nathan, she can walk!"

"Secret passage? What secret passage, Terry?"

Terry coughed again, struggling to talk. "I waited for you, Nathan. . . . I waited for you. . . . But you didn't come."

"What secret passage!"

"I found a door down here . . . into her basement. She caught me, Nathan. She outran me. . . . Hurt me real bad. Go get help . . . before she comes back."

"Come on, Terry, I'll get you out of here," and Nathan started to drag Terry to his feet. Terry's body jerked hard, and another doglike howl escaped his lips, a howl starting low in his throat and then forced out hard, like trying to blow out a hundred candles at once. Then he lay quiet while the moan echoed its way down the sewer. "I can't move. But she'll be back. . . . She's coming back for me."

"Where is she now?"

"She went back to her cellar. Go before . . . before she gets you!" The matches burned out, and blackness rushed in on both of them. Nathan couldn't even see Terry, although he still had hold of his arm.

"Terry! Terry! Are you all right?"

"Go, Nathan. . . . I hear something! She's coming back!" and Nathan felt Terry push him out toward the main sewer.

"I'm going, Terry," Nathan whispered back to the darkness. "I'm going, but I'll be right back," and he searched frantically for the cement corner that would tell him he was in the main tunnel. As soon as he found it, he ran as fast as the mud and the dark and being hunched over would allow, one hand held out for the wall. Suddenly another howl came down the sewer, stopping Nathan as if the mud had turned to glue. He heard voices and slowly looked back into the blackness to where they were coming from. Now there was only one voice, high-pitched like screeching tires or fingernails on a blackboard. Then a light appeared back where he'd left Terry; it looked like a flashlight, not the beam of light but the leftover light from around the edges. It glowed out of the secret tunnel, forming a dim curtain of light across the sewer. An old lady's laugh came out from where Terry was lying and rushed down the sewer past Nathan. "Well, well, well. How's my little intruder doing? My little sewer rat, crawling around near my cellar, eh?"

"No! I wasn't doing anything, honest!"

"I think my little rat is lying to me, eh? I think it's time you see the rest of my cellar. I'll show you what I do to filthy, lying little sewer rats, heh heh. . . . Wait a minute—what's this I see? Had a visitor while I was gone, eh? Another little intruder?" Nathan caught his breath and crouched even lower.

"You know what I think, little sewer rat? I think you need someone to keep you company in my cellar." Nathan's legs ached from being bent so long. He couldn't take his eyes off the dim glow of the light back deep in the sewer. The light had started getting brighter and brighter, the beam moving out toward the main sewer. *If that light turns the corner,* Nathan thought, *I'm as good as dead.* But the light moved back to the way it was before, and then the old lady's voice came again. "Yes, yes, yes. You are a mess, my little boy." Nathan's head was on fire. *Leave him alone, leave him alone!* his mind screamed at her. From down the tunnel he heard, "Your little friend can't be far away." Nathan started moving as carefully and as quietly as he could. His foot shlucked up out of the mud, no louder than a whisper, but Nathan felt cheated by being that careful and still making so much noise. "It's time, it's time, eh?" came the old woman's voice. "But first, my sweet little rat, I think I'll just—" and Terry's most bloodcurdling scream yet roared out of the silence, the howl catching Nathan off guard as his feet went out from under him in the slippery blackness. Nathan fell hard on his backside in the cold slime. The tunnel was overflowing with sound. The echo of Terry's scream was still banging down the sewer, and then "Ah heh heh heh!" surrounded Nathan and seemed as if it would never leave. Trying to regain his feet in the greaselike mud, Nathan saw the light bouncing down the secret tunnel, swinging back and forth like whoever was carrying it was running, and then it was in the middle of the main sewer, shining directly at Nathan, the instant brightness blinding him. "Neh heh heh heh," came from behind the blindness. "Is this my other little rat? Just stay right where you are, and I'll come and get you, eh?" Nathan finally found his feet and used them like never before. Hunched low and leaning forward—there was no time to touch the wall now—he raced down the middle of the sewer, the mud sucking at his feet, trying to hold him back. "Neh heh heh heh heh" rushed up from behind him and then past him just as fast, rolling over and over, losing itself out ahead in the darkness. The light from the flashlight danced crazily on his back, the walls, and the ceiling. He looked back, but all he could see was the bright ball of light jerking back and forth, getting closer and closer. But the light also helped him see a little bit in front of him, allowed him to see where to run, what to jump. And there up ahead was the dim light from the open sewer grate. He could yell, somebody would hear him! Nathan was running too fast to stop under the grate, his feet slipping out from under him as they were, and he slid through the mud under the opening above. Even before he stopped sliding, Nathan regained his balance, scrambled back into the light, put his face as close to the opening as he could, and screamed, "Help! Somebody! Help! Help!" He spun around and looked back up the tunnel, but the light was gone. He listened for footsteps, but the only sound was his own echo, way off down the sewer—a faint, distant "Help . . . help . . . help. . . ." Then the echo was gone, and in its place was, first, the silence, then the sound of running water, and then the drip . . . drip . . . dripping.

Nathan breathed as deeply as he could, trying to take in what fresh air the grate had to offer. Still no sounds of her. He looked down at his mud-covered body and scared himself to see how fast he was breathing. He listened hard to the silence and peered first into the blackness from where he had come and then into the blackness where he would have to go. Still no sound. "Maybe she's gone," he thought. "That's it. My yelling scared her back to her cellar. . . ." He listened again. Nothing. Then he heard it. It sounded like two words, very low, like an echo coming out of nowhere, and then again, this time louder but still soft. He could hear the words, "Nay—thon . . . Nay—thon . . ." sounding like a sad, sad song. It was getting louder, or closer—Nathan couldn't tell. "Nay—thon . . . Nay—ay—thon," and then, "Neh heh heh heh!"

Nathan ducked low and ran back into the blackness. Without the flashlight, it was like running with your eyes closed. The mud continued to tug at his feet; cobwebs clung to his mouth, choking him as he ran. His legs ached, threatened to give out with every stride. His back hurt with each jolt, and his lungs felt as if they would burst, but still he pushed himself faster and faster. Something caught his foot and he went down sharply on one knee, the mud giving way so the concrete floor bit deeply into his skin. He rolled over and looked back just in time to see a hunched-over form fly through the dim light under the grate and then become a shadow, lumbering closer and closer, gaining on him all the time. He scrambled to his feet again and dived on into the darkness. "Less than a block," he kept telling himself. "I'm almost to The Crick." "Neh heh heh heh" came again and again down the sewer, the sound reaching for his neck, pulling at his mind, trying to drag him down. He couldn't hold back anymore and started crying, gasping and weeping at the same time as he stumbled his way through the dark. Finally the dim light appeared in front of him—the opening! The Crick! The outside!

The shadow behind him wasn't gaining anymore. Judging by the sloshing sounds and heavy breathing, it must have been as tired from the chase as Nathan. The light grew brighter and brighter; he could make out the entire opening now. He could see The Crick outside, getting closer and closer with each step. Nathan pushed even harder and then flew out of the sewer like a rock from a slingshot. He automatically shielded his eyes from the sudden daylight, straightened up, threw his head back, and sucked in the fresh air through his tears. He could hear heavy breathing and splashing footsteps coming after him, closer and closer, louder with each splash. Glancing up and down The Crick, Nathan saw the rock crawlway and headed across the tiles toward it. Slipping but not falling, he reached the first handholds as the breathing and the foot splashing became louder and louder. His muddied toes slipped once, twice, and finally took hold in the crack in the stone wall, but between the crying and the running and the falling, he was too weak to pull himself up any farther. The foot splashing was out of the sewer now and directly below him. Nathan used all of his remaining strength and started pulling himself slowly, ever so slowly, upward, up out of The Crick. Upward and upward his body crept toward the next handhold, his fingers just inches away, clawing, clawing, when he felt a cold, slimy hand clamp hard onto his bare leg from down below.

"Gotcha!"

Nathan clung to the wall, too exhausted to pull himself free, too terrified to let himself back down to what was waiting for him below. His strength was gone. He forced himself to look back down over his shoulder to see what held him so tightly. There, beneath him on the tiles, covered with mud and filth and carrying a flashlight, was Terry, with the kind of grin on his face that Nathan didn't like one bit. "Gotcha, Nathan," he laughed, "and man, did I get you!" Terry let go of Nathan's leg, set his flashlight down, and went to the water's edge. Nathan let himself down slowly, then plopped down on a rock, staring at Terry and too numb to speak. "Whew, what a mess," Terry said, washing his arms in the pool of The Crick. "But even if Irv whips me, it was worth it. You should have seen your face," and Terry laughed a tired laugh. Nathan sat catching his breath. He looked at how muddy he was, then over at Terry's flashlight, then at Terry. The blood didn't look so much like blood in the daylight, and Nathan noticed as

Terry washed it off his arms that it came off clean, with no cuts or gashes on Terry at all. It was all beginning to sink in on Nathan. "Terry, you didn't—"

"I sure did," said Terry, the tired grin still there. "It was great!" Terry was excited over his victory and wanted to enjoy it a little longer. "What scared you the most, Nathan? The ketchup I poured all over myself or my howls? I thought my howls were pretty good. Or was it the secret passageway? I was afraid you'd see it was a dead end—but you were too busy to even look."

"I knew there wasn't any secret passageway."

"Sure you did, Nathan. Sure you did." Terry laughed quietly to himself as he remembered something else. "You know, you almost kicked my flashlight when you were trying to get me to stand up. I thought for a while you were't going to fall for it, that you'd turn chicken and go back out. But it turned out better than I ever expected. God, I'd give anything to see you screaming bloody murder out of that sewer grate again. I couldn't stop from laughing, I almost gave it away." And thinking about laughing made Terry laugh again.

Nathan felt the anger building up inside him. The thought of pushing Terry into The Crick crossed his mind, but he was too tired for a fight.

"Say something, Nathan."

"Why should I? All you'll do is laugh."

"Why not, Nathan? That's what jokes are for!" Terry went on, flicking his hands to dry the crick water off them. "It's no different from the Fake Push or when you threw the craw-dad at me."

Nathan got up slowly and climbed up out of The Crick. When he reached the top he looked down at Terry. "A joke? You call that a joke? That was a *crappy* thing to do, Terry. And you're a bastard for doing it!"

"Ah, come on, Nathan, don't get mad. A joke's a joke. Remember what you always say. You got to admit, Nathan, it *was* funny."

"It was still a crappy thing to do," and Nathan turned and headed home. The last thing Nathan heard from The Crick was Terry's voice, high and squeaky, going "Neh heh heh heh" and then breaking out laughing in his own laugh.

Nathan walked home slowly, his head held down, his eyes watching his feet and the pavement. The hot asphalt didn't bother him, he didn't have the time for that. He kept going over and over in his mind what had happened in the sewer. "My little sewer rat!" he mocked and had to smile a little to himself. By the time he reached the corner he guessed he probably did look pretty funny screaming up out of a sewer. He felt his energy coming back. Nathan stopped in front of The-House-With-No-Men, and there was the old lady in her wheelchair, still sitting in the same place, still staring out across the porch. He couldn't tell if she was looking at him or not. Then he decided she must be. To think that he had thought this old woman was chasing him through the sewer made him smile and he waved up at her. She smiled back and nodded her head toward him the way old people do. He turned toward his house, wondering how he would get cleaned up without his parents finding out. *That bastard probably got me grounded for a month*, he thought to himself. *But I got to admit, it was* kind *of funny.*

RICK HILLS *was born and lives in Iowa City, Iowa, where he graduated from the Iowa Writers' Workshop in 1973. His stories have appeared in* Alfred Hitchcock's Mystery Magazine.

UPON REFLECTION

ELLIOTT CAPON

L ike most vampires, Darren Meier was very unhappy.

Scratch that; like *all* vampires, Darren Meier was very unhappy. The leering, sadistic count of the movies, the master conniver who reveled in the taking of blood, was one of the most heinous of myths perpetrated by Hollywood on an unsuspecting public. Being a vampire was a miserable way to live . . . er, to unlive. The lust for blood is not the healthy desire of, say, a young man for the company of a young woman, or the need of two tired feet to soak themselves in a hot tub. It is a repulsive need, akin to nothing less than the worst depths of alcoholism or heroin addiction, when the compulsion exceeds the actual act of satiation.

Blood simply does not taste very good, and like others of

his ilk, Darren was always nauseated by the little *crack* sound when his teeth pierced the skin, by the way the jugular pulsed against his gums, by his act of violating the privacy of a sleeping or entranced person. There was more to his unhappiness, of course: the whole business of being undead. By all rights, a man drained of his blood, as Darren had been himself seven years ago when he had been attacked, should have been peaceably buried, his body now a pile of calcium dust, his soul . . . his soul *somewhere*. Instead, he was forced to hide from the light of the sun day after day, year after year, to be dragged out of his hiding place by his hated compulsion.

If it weren't for the rap sessions, Darren felt he'd have gone mad years ago.

Oh yes, the rap sessions. Darren Meier was by no means the only vampire in the world, far from it. As a matter of fact, he lived in a rather large old house in a northern suburb of New York City with three—count 'em—three other vampires: Ed and Phil and Annie. Neither Ed nor Phil nor Annie nor Darren wore black cloaks or tuxedos or stiff white shirts; they all wore jeans and knit tops and shorts on warm summer evenings. And they all hated being vampires. But there was nothing they could do about it.

Darren was the last one "home" on this particular night, getting in about forty minutes before dawn. They always sat up as long as possible, to work things out as much as they could before retiring for the day. They didn't *sleep* in their darkened bedrooms, you know, and, very usually, comforting words by a peer helped them get through the hours of solitude.

"What kept you?" Ed asked when Darren finally got in.

"You're not going to believe this," Darren said, "but I was chased by the police."

"What?" Phil and Annie both said, while Ed asked, "How come?"

"I took it from a guy who had a flat tire on Route 15,"

Darren said. They always referred to their noxious practice as "taking it." Darren shook his head. He had joined the ranks of the undead back in 1977 and still wore his hair longer than your average CPA. "Except that he must've already called for help and had got back to the car when I found him. Just as I finished, a cop car shows up, and bang, I'm off into the woods, and they're off after me. Took me an hour and a half to circle around here."

"I don't know why you haunt the back roads," Annie sniffed. "*I* always head into the city. You can hide better in a city, and you can be more discreet about whom you have to lift." They always called their act of accosting a potential victim "lifting."

"Yeah," Phil said, "Darren'd look great perched under a lamp post with a 'come hither' look." The guys laughed, but Annie didn't think it was too funny. Having to lift by pretending to be a prostitute was an indignity that added insult to injury.

The conversation continued for a while longer, wandering here and there, until Ed said, almost to himself, "I think I turned someone tonight." When they drained a victim completely, with the result of making that someone become a vampire himself, they referred to it as "turning" him.

"Oh no," Annie said. "You promised you'd be careful."

"I didn't take that much," Ed said sharply, biting out each word. "Someone must've gotten to her before me. Short, heavyset black girl, about twenty, curly hair, in the hospital for a tonsillectomy?" The other three shook their heads. "You think there's someone else working the neighborhood?" Darren asked.

After a few moments of desultory conversation, Phil glanced at his watch and said, "Hey, it's almost bedtime." They always referred to dawn as "bedtime." "Let's go nappy-bye."

The house they lived in was somewhat post-Revolutionary

War, somewhat pre-Civil War. It had fourteen rooms and was built as a house should be built. The living room, where they held their nightly talks, was a lofty cavern with a fireplace at one end and a huge mirror at the other. The fireplace was never used because, having no human needs as such, they were never cold. Timed lights went on and off, and, as Phil had been a wealthy man when he had been turned himself, the place was legally owned. As far as anyone knew, it was occupied by quiet, keep-to-themselves people.

The mirror—well, that was another story. Vampires, as everyone knows, and in this instance Hollywood was telling the truth, cast no reflection. There were no lights at the end of the room where the hundred-year-old-plus, ornately framed mirror hung, so it was easy for them to avoid looking at it when they used the living room. It might have been an old spider web, repulsive but not doing any harm, so they weren't compelled to remove it, or even desirous of doing so. In truth, they ignored the thing.

Except for Darren. Every night—that is, morning—before retreating to his bed (coffins were so passé), he would make sure that he stood in front of the mirror. That Darren was human was debatable, but that he once had been was undeniable, and in the human breast, hope springs eternal. Every day Darren stood in front of the mirror, knowing he would see no reflection, but hoping, begging (praying?), that one day he would see a reflection, he would see himself again after seven years and that would mean that the curse of vampirism was removed from him.

This night, as usual, he stood up, walked sixteen paces to the other end of the room, and stood in front of the mirror. There was the fireplace, cold and dark. The chair that Annie was just getting out of—but not Annie. There was the painting they called "Uncle Jim," which had come with the house. There was every speck of dust on the mantelpiece. There was . . . there was everything else in the room but him.

With a sigh, Darren turned away from the mirror.

There was a loud knocking at the front door.

They froze.

The knocking became a pounding.

Darren's first thought was that the police had somehow traced him home.

"Please!" someone yelled from the outside. "Before the sun comes up! Let me in!"

Before the sun comes up? What cop is afraid of the sun?

Since Phil's money had bought the place, he was titular leader of the group. "Open the door," he told Ed.

Hesitantly, Ed crossed the room and the foyer, unlocked and pulled open the heavy front door.

A man entered—fell—inside. He looked more like a movie vampire than did the others. Tall, thin, very pale; a few drops of dried blood on his shirt. He was gasping, the open mouth revealing the pointed canines.

"Who the hell are you?" asked Ed.

"Name's Leo," the stranger gasped. "No time to talk. Sun's coming up. Can you hide me?"

With eight bedrooms, it was the easiest thing in the world to give this Leo a bed. Darren, Annie, Phil, and Ed went to their own rooms and puzzled over the events of the strange evening in their own private darkness. When they got up for their night's wanderings, Leo had already gone. But early the next morning, when they were gathered for their usual tête-à-tête à tête-à-tête, there was a rather polite knock at the front door. Ed opened it again, cautiously, and there stood Leo, a little more kempt, a lot calmer. "May I come in?" he asked.

They pulled another old overstuffed chair in front of the dead fireplace and invited Leo to sit down.

All four were pale, but Darren and his friends had been

turned in the late 1970s, when they were all less than thirty years of age. Leo had obviously been well into his fifties when his vampiric career started, and his life to that point had obviously been no bed of roses. The others looked like pictures of health compared to him.

"Forty years I've been at this," he told them. "Wait a minute, what year is this? It is? Forty-one, then. Forty-one years I've been living this life, if you can call it that. Forty-one years I'm hiding in a shack near the track over by Mann's Ferry . . . and last night some hooligans decide to burn it down, just for fun."

"Hooligans?" Annie asked. "You mean punks."

Leo managed a sort of smile. "Thank you, young lady. Slang does change so, you know."

"Why . . . what made you . . . how'd you . . ." Darren stumbled over his words.

"I've known about you kids for two years at least," Leo said. "But there was never any need to, uh, socialize. Misery does not necessarily love company."

"We find the sense of community helpful," said Phil. "We're horribly cursed, and it helps to maintain sanity to talk about it."

Ed had a thoughtful look. "Say, Leo, had you taken a short, heavyset black girl in Lakeview Hospital, with—"

"The tonsillectomy?" Leo finished. "Yes. Yes, that was me. Why?"

"How come we've never run across your work before?" Darren asked.

"Whom do you kids—what did Ed say, *take?*—usually?"

Darren looked for stranded motorists, kids in lovers' lanes, solitary hitchhikers; Annie worked the prostitute gambit in New York; Phil cruised the gay-bar scene in both New York and nearby White Plains; Ed liked to try his luck at hospitals, all-night fast food places, and the like. Only rarely did they turn anyone, and the non-turned victims, being placed in a miasmic trance at the time of the initial bite, never remembered having been lifted. A comfortable MO was the key to success. Leo nodded.

"My usual, uh, prey, is older ladies. A little charm, a little smooch, and then . . . *voilà.*" He shuddered. "That's why we've never crossed paths before. But I've known you were here, like I said, for about two years. When you've been at it as long as I have—well, you know."

Ed was still upset about the black girl. "What were you doing in the hospital in the first place?"

Leo's smile became an embarrassed grin. "Things haven't been so good lately, so I was . . . I was going to rob the blood bank. I've done it before, in emergencies. Not as good as, as—you know—but it does satisfy the craving. I saw the girl in the hall, all alone, and so . . ." He raised his hands.

It was Annie who brought up the question all of them had been looking for a polite way to ask. "Do you need a place to stay?"

Leo looked at her with all the charm a vampire could muster. "Yes, dear, I do. Do you mind?"

"How could we mind?" Phil asked. "You're welcome to stay."

It was nearing dawn, so they got up to go to bed. Again, Darren walked in front of the mirror, again he stared into it. There was the dead fireplace, the five seemingly empty chairs in front of it, the dust on the mantelpiece, but no Darren. With his usual sigh, he went to bed.

They gave Leo a set of keys and showed him where the fresh linen was kept, and that was all that was needed. A week went by, a week that, given the unusual circumstances under which they lived, went normally, unremarkably. Leo didn't usually get home until almost dawn and couldn't sit in on their postsatiation conversations; even so, they kept his chair in the circle, an almost welcome reminder that they were even less alone than before, that there was another suf-ferer of their peculiar curse.

On the eighth night after Leo's arrival, one Virginia Farmer went out on a date with her fairly steady boyfriend, one Brian Crane. A discussion that needn't concern us turned into an argument, which escalated into a fight, the denouement of which had Virginia leaving Brian's car in high dudgeon on a rather dark piece of County Road 119. She was so angry she didn't hear the footsteps behind her, and of course, when Darren took her, she didn't remember anything of the attack.

Such rare good luck had Darren home by midnight, a good three or four hours before any of the others were expected. Having to spend all the daylight hours in an immobile but conscious state, Darren was in no mood to merely sit quietly and ruminate until his companions got back; he had to do something. There were no books and no TV in the house.

It suddenly occurred to him that it had been years since he had explored this great big old house of theirs.

There is really no word in the English language to indicate extremely mild surprise, but if there were, it would describe Darren's feeling when he opened the door that led to the basement stairs. He knew it had been years since anyone had gone down there, but the hinges didn't squeak at all. Surely, after five or six years of neglect, there would have been *some* noise . . . ? The light switch, which had been installed some-time in the 1940s but hadn't been used since the late seventies, flicked on with no problem, revealing what Darren had figured it would: the basement. He had no strong memories of the place, but everything seemed to look as it should have. A few old steamer trunks, covered with dust and cobwebs; an old couch, left over from previous owners, tattered and filthy; a few rotting two-by-fours in a corner; a stack of eight or ten cardboard boxes, piled neatly; some yellowing *Life* magazines on a stained and pitted ex-coffee table. . . .

Those cardboard cartons. That stack against the far wall. They weren't covered with dust. They weren't wrinkled and seamed and cracked in the corners.

They were new.

Darren pulled the top one open. It was full of clear plastic packages of what seemed to be white powder. He tore open another box. The same. He lifted one of the packages out, hefting it, squeezing it, kneading it. It was either heroin or cocaine, of that he was sure. It didn't matter which. But . . . who? How? He whispered something he hadn't even thought in seven years.

"My God."

He put the drugs back and closed the boxes. He slowly went back upstairs to the living room—the center, essentially, of whatever normal universe he still managed to cling to.

Somebody was using their house as a drug warehouse. Assuming each package was a kilo and that there were twelve bags in each box, times eight boxes, ninety-six kilos, two hundred eleven point two pounds, a pound of that stuff worth what, fifty, a hundred thousand dollars? There was a fantastic fortune down there.

But who was *somebody*? The windows were locked, the doors were kept locked—no one from the outside could get in. It had to be one of them. But *how*? And *why*? What use had a vampire for money? When did whoever it was find the time to do this?

The three-letter torturers—HOW, WHO, WHY—chased after each other in his head, over and over and around and around, till he felt he was going crazy. With a violence he hadn't used in seven years, he viciously kicked at the nearest chair, knocking it out of the circle and onto its back.

That calmed him. He bent over to pick it up, and as he straightened, he happened to look into the mirror at the other end of the room. The chair dropped out of his hands and crashed back onto the floor.

Now it was clear.

Phil remarked that this was the only time Darren had been the first one back. Their conversation ran the usual gamut through the predawn hours until Leo made his usual almost-dawn appearance. Darren invited him to sit down and chat for a minute, which, with a glance at his watch, Leo did.

The five were sitting in their circle of chairs, making small talk, when Darren said, "It's always fascinated me how we don't cast reflections in mirrors."

Ed shrugged. "That part is no more fascinating than any other."

"No," said Darren, "I mean, it's unique." He got up out of his chair and slowly crossed the room. "I mean, look at this big old mirror. Everything that has light refracting off it in the room—the walls, the furniture, the fireplace—everything but us is reflected in here." He was standing right in front of it, facing it, and they could see the room reflected around him. They saw the chairs they were sitting in, of course, but not themselves.

"Is there a point, Darren?" Leo asked. "It's getting late."

"Oh yes," said Darren. "There's a point." He shot out a hand, grabbed the ornate frame at the base, and shoved the mirror sideways. Although it now hung wildly askew, the reflected picture did not change.

"You'd think," Darren said, "that when a mirror is moved, it would reflect what's in front of it, not what it's used to reflecting."

Nobody moved, rigid with confusion. Darren heaved the

mirror off the wall and threw it to the floor, where it landed not with the crash of breaking glass but with the whuff of canvas striking wood.

"It's a painting," he said. "How'd you do it, Leo?"

Within a second, Leo was up, his back to the fireplace, a large crucifix in his hand. "Very good, Darren," he said. "Very commendable."

"What is going *on?*" Annie asked, her voice perilously close to a whine.

"Leo is not a vampire," Darren said, to three *What!*'s.

"I was down in the basement before," Darren continued, "and I found a large quantity of drugs, newly placed there."

"Heroin," Leo said. "About three million dollars' worth."

"I knew it had to be one of us," Darren said, "because no one else could get in here. Then I knocked over a chair and noticed that the reflection in the mirror didn't *reflect* the new position of that chair. Somebody had substituted a perfect painting of the room—as it would look after we added a fifth chair for Leo. Now, who would want to substitute a painting for a mirror? Obviously, someone who would reflect a mirror image. Someone who is not a vampire. Right, Leo?"

Leo nodded. "Absolutely correct, Darren, absolutely correct. As I told you, I knew you were here. A big old house that no one comes near, inhabitants who sleep all day, who couldn't go to the police in the most dire of circumstances . . . what better place for a warehouse for my merchandising operation?"

"But how did you . . . the painting . . . ?" Phil stammered.

"Remember the first night I showed up?" Leo asked him. "Right at the crack of dawn? In the confusion, you never noticed that I cast a reflection. I had done my homework. I knew what this room looked like, less a few details, so I spent the rest of that day finishing my masterpiece." He pointed with his free hand to the painting on the floor. "I'm pretty good, I think, but drug smuggling pays so much better than selling original oils."

"And at night?" asked Annie.

"At night, I'd go home and sleep, making sure I got here just before dawn. During the day, while you all . . . rested . . . I'd go about my business. Since we'd only see each other for five or ten minutes a day, all I'd have to do would be to keep this room looking the same. Oh, and a midnight attack with a hypodermic on a likely victim with a tonsillectomy— remember, Ed?—just iced the cake. Ingenious of me, no?"

"What now?" Darren asked quietly.

Leo looked at his watch. "It's about four minutes to dawn. I'll just hold this little cross in front of me till you're forced to retire, and then, well, I guess today's the day I transact a small sale of some goods I've been storing in your basement. After that, it's adios."

"No," Darren said, slowly crossing the room.

Leo pushed back against the mantelpiece, holding the crucifix out in front of him as far as he could stretch his arm.

"This'll hold you off!" he cried.

Phil and Ed and Annie had gotten up and were moving slowly toward him.

"No," Darren said again. "You've seen too many movies. The cross does not deter us."

Leo had time for one last yell.

That night, at their rap session, it was Ed who voiced what they all wanted to say: that while satiating the compulsion on an unconscious person satisfied their strange craving, attacking a helpless victim while he screamed with fear was fun. Lots and lots of *fun*.

ELLIOTT CAPON was born and grew up in Brooklyn. He received a bachelor of arts degree in English from the City University of New York and has earned credit toward a master's in business administration from Long Island University. He now lives in suburban New Jersey, where he is pursuing his writing career.

BRIDEY'S CALLER

JUDITH O'NEILL

When the mail came this morning, I walked out to get it. The letter from my cousin Nellie was full of chatty family news about her children and grandchildren and questions about mine. I smiled as I strolled back up to the house, reading. And then she casually mentioned, in relating current town happenings, that "old Bridey" had died. I had to sit down suddenly on the steps.

When I was very young, almost forty years ago now, I used to go and stay with my grandparents in Helenwood, Kansas, for long weeks in the summer. I loved it there. I was the oldest—by four years—of all my cousins who lived in or around Helenwood. So during the time I was there, I was Miss Queen Bee. My cousin Nellie and I were especially close. She lived on a farm just outside the tiny town, and during my stays she would be brought in to keep me company. She was an adoring little girl, with dark curly hair and big brown eyes. And because she was so very gifted at worshiping, she was, for years, by far my favorite cousin.

My grandparents did not live on a farm, but coming as I did from the "big city" of St. Joseph, just across the river, their place seemed very rural to me. These were my mother's parents—the sober, honest, almost severe side of the family—as opposed to my father's side, which is another story altogether.

The very order of everything in my grandparents' Helenwood home appealed to me. All of my remembering years, I had been a part of that old white house set back from the dusty street. Helenwood had only one paved street. Actually it was the highway that ran through town, but it was referred to as "Main Street" and housed the post office, a grocery store, and, farther along, the red brick school (kindergarten through twelfth grade). My grandparents' home was three blocks away from the highway, back where the houses were separated by huge, tree-shaded, flat lawns. There were no sidewalks anywhere in town. In winter when the snow melted or in spring when the rains came and the river rose, you stayed indoors as much as you could.

Summers were dry and hot, and my mother would drive me over the arched, narrow bridge from St. Joe and deliver me to my grandparents. Nellie would already be there, and we would set about exploring. We did a lot of "exploring" because there wasn't much else to do. We walked everywhere, from the creek to the Missouri River, up to the highway and the post office, talking, talking.

But our favorite place, only four houses up the street from my grandparents' house, was Bridey's. Bridget was her name, and I'm not sure we ever knew her last name; everyone referred to her as Bridey, and so did we. She was a tall, thin woman, with gray hair pulled back in a bun and gray eyes. I remember they were gray because she was one of the few people I ever knew whose eyes were exactly the same color as her hair. She had a small three-room house, and the front room she had set up as a country store. Straight back from that was her bedroom and then the kitchen at the back. The "bathroom" was out on the back path, surrounded by vines and trees. It was all very neat and clean. She had a door shutting off her bedroom/sitting room, but in the summer all the doors stood open to let a breeze through so that when you walked into her store, you could look right back through the bedroom and kitchen to the back porch.

But Nellie and I were not very interested in what Bridey had in the back rooms. What she had in the front room was what we went for—that long, oval, zinc washtub set up on short sawhorses and filled with huge chunks of ice and floating bottles of soda pop. Leaning against that icy tub, fishing around for your favorite soda, was the coldest you could get in Helenwood in the summer. It is hard for people now to understand the effort and energy we had to put into keeping cool in those days. Nowadays it is just as hot in Kansas, but you can escape into air conditioning. Then you couldn't escape the heat. Even at night, when breezes turn cool in other places, in Kansas a hot wind blows up across Texas and Oklahoma and fries you. It is a sweet-smelling wind, and if it doesn't blow you can poach in your own sweat, but it doesn't really cool you. No, in those days there was no way to escape the heat except to jump in the creek or the river, but there was always my grandmother's fear of polio. So mostly we just tried to find ways to bear it, and that led us to spend a lot of time at Bridey's, leaning against the soda tub. She was never short or impatient with us; she let us lean and play in the water. She didn't pay special attention to us and we, in our turn, were polite, not making a mess or noise. As "Emmitt and Louise's grandchildren," we were conscious of a certain amount of responsibility. We behaved ourselves so as not to reflect badly on our elders. I'm not sure how they managed that bit of psychological control. I don't think they ever *told* us that—it was something we just knew. Nellie loved grape soda above all else, and I was overly fond of cream soda. Even then, I appreciated that Bridey kept the tub well stocked. When my whole arm finally became numb, I would fish a bottle out and pop it open with the opener tied by a string to the tub handle. Then I would lean back against the tub and slug that first icy gulp down my hot, dry throat.

I always thought it was an oversized zinc washtub; but it was very long for that and when I thought about it later— and believe me I did think *a lot* about it later—I thought maybe it had been a trough for horses to drink out of at one time. I have seen them from time to time in antique shops since then, and they always make me a little sick at my stomach.

Bridey lived alone, and while there were all kinds of Sunday laws in Kansas in those days, she would open her door about ten in the morning on Sunday and, if you went by, she would sell you whatever you wanted. But in our eyes Bridey had a fault. This was her Sunday caller. Every Sunday, about two P.M., Bridey's caller would come. He drove across the bridge from St. Joe, down onto the shaded streets of Helenwood, and around to the back of Bridey's. He never parked in front, always in back, under the trees there. Why, I can't imagine, as everyone in town could see his car in back as well as if he had parked it in front. Then he would get out of his car—a short, energetic, good-looking man in a dark suit and hat— and walk to the back door and go in. Shortly thereafter, Bridey would close her front door and her back door and no longer be available for business. Somewhere about five P.M., her caller would depart the way he had come, out the back, into his car, down the streets, and out of Helenwood to the bridge, not to be seen again until the next Sunday. I had broodingly watched this coming and going from my grandfather's grape arbor countless Sundays.

Of course Nellie and I were affronted by this because Bridey's was *never* closed. If she was there, day or night, she was open and there was easy access to the soda tub. And it seemed that the hottest and thirstiest we ever got was between two and five on Sunday afternoons. I was vaguely aware that my grandmother was affronted by this, too; but I could not fathom her giving a whit about the soda tub and she rarely ran out of things just as she needed them, so I couldn't put my finger on the cause of her displeasure. She liked Bridey, I knew; Grandma had known her all of her life. She would sometimes go and sit on Bridey's porch when she was passing on her way to or from the post office and they would talk. But when the Sunday closings came up, she would frown and get testy. My grandfather got a big kick out of it. Once, as we sat at Sunday dinner, Nellie and I were again complaining, of course, and Nellie—being as blunt and repetitive as any six-year-old—asked, for about the five-hundredth time that summer, "Why does she close every Sunday like this?" and my grandmother snapped, "Because she has a caller, you know that, now eat those mashed potatoes."

I was a little perplexed by this behavior myself. *We* didn't go around closing all our doors and keeping people out when we had company. "But why does she close the doors?" I asked, musing. "It must be hot in there."

My grandfather laughed. "I bet," he said.

"Emmitt, Emmitt!" my grandmother warned sharply.

But my grandfather was enjoying himself now and teasing my red-faced grandmother. It was seldom that I had seen her blush. "I think," he said, laughing at her, "that Bridey takes a little after-dinner nap."

My grandmother threw her fork down on the table and glared at him. "Emmitt, that's just about enough!"

He was laughing so hard now he had to take his glasses off and wipe his eyes with a napkin. And while he was doing this, Nellie said in her self-righteous little way, "But isn't it rude of Bridey to take a nap while her caller is there?"

My grandfather started choking and had to leave the table, and my grandmother turned on Nellie and me and told us in no uncertain terms that other people's manners were not our business and we had plenty to do to mind our *own* manners, and it was *very* bad manners to be so nosy about other people's lives and how they conducted them.

That was my tenth summer. It stands out clearly in my mind for many reasons. For one, it was the most incredibly hot summer I have ever lived through. Everyone talked about nothing but the weather and the crops and the lack of rain, and Nellie and I consumed a prodigious amount of soda. Second, I was at my grandparents' all summer for the first time ever, and the reason for that is the third, but far most important, reason I remember that summer. At the very beginning of it, just after school was out, my mother had a nervous breakdown. Up until the previous Christmas, I had never suspected she had a nerve in her body. She was always a happy, fun person with laughing eyes. To this day when I think of her, I remember those laughing brown eyes. Well, they weren't laughing that year. My father had fallen in love with someone else, she had told me just before Christmas. Just like that, my happy-go-lucky, handsome, generous father was gone. Gone with someone else. There's a lot about that Christmas I don't remember. I remember my mother sitting very still at the dining-room table in our house in St. Joe, with the snow falling outside the window behind her, and telling me he had gone. I had never even heard them argue. We would get used to it, my mother said bleakly. We would go on with our lives and they would be different, but we would get used to it. I knew my mother must still reside somewhere in that body, but I couldn't see her at all in the dead brown eyes and the bleached white face.

I went to my grandparents' the day school was out, and my mother went to the hospital.

My grandparents were sick with worry. They didn't talk about it to me much, but they talked *to* me a lot more. They seemed to go out of their way, both of them, to explain the whys of things and idiosyncrasies of the people in town. "Look at poor Cynthia Jenkins," my grandmother would say, "she lost both her parents in a flood when she was very young, and she's turned out all right." That sort of thing. I learned a lot about people in Helenwood I hadn't previously known as my grandparents gently pointed out one survivor after another. And somewhere in that summer I learned that Bridget was one of these—her father dead when she was less than three years old, her mother had married a man with four children, and it came out (from my grandfather, I'm sure) that the Sunday caller was one of these stepbrothers, a *married* stepbrother, my grandmother snorted.

We all suffered into August, one brilliant, blazing day after another. We woke up drenched, unable to cheat nature out of even a few minutes' early morning coolness, moved sluggishly through the day, and sank exhausted into the already heated sheets at dusk. It was that kind of a day the Sunday I was hanging around the grape arbor waiting for Bridey to open up. It was about time for her caller to leave, so I strolled up through the three backyards separating ours from hers. Yes, the car was still there, under the trees at the back of her yard. The back door was still shut. Standing well away from the trunk of the tree to catch even the hot wind and feeling it dry the perspiration on my face and bare arms and scorch my eyes, I waited impatiently for Bridey's caller to leave. And, waiting, I went to sit in the thick, green grass along the stone foundation of her little house where the breeze always seemed cooler.

And I heard Bridey crying. I don't think I purposely sat right under her bedroom window. I was just searching for the coolest spot around and that looked like it, on the shady side of the house, the grass deep and green and bending in the wind. But there I was, right under her open bedroom window. I should have crawled away, but the sobbing was so close I was afraid she would see me. She cried out in a low, strangled voice, "Don't, please don't, Ray, don't say you're going for good." She was crying so frantically and wildly that I was mesmerized there, scrunched up against the rough stone of the foundation. I could hear his voice as he answered her, but not his words. She began to beg. I cannot, writing here, relay to you the utter desperation and grief in those low pleas, nor their effect on me. It was Bridey's voice, strangled and harsh in terror and hurt and desolation, begging, begging. It was my voice, and my mother's voice. And I, who had taken the news of my own father's departure stoically and my mother's breakdown grimly but dry-eyed, rose from the grass sightlessly and ran along the side of the house, back into the trees, and down into my grandfather's grape arbor.

I threw myself on the ground under the heavy green leaves and clutched the grass there in my hands and wrenched and tore it out of the ground and beat the earth with my fists. But none of it helped and, just like an earthen dam gives way, so did I. I shut my eyes as tight as I could, but I could feel the flood coming, the terrible bitter tears of irreplaceable loss ripping out my heart, and then the dam gave way.

When the weeping was all over and I had rolled onto my

back to stare up through the grape leaves at the bright sky, I marveled that there could have been that much water in me. And then I thought about Bridey. Now I know that he must have been everything to her. For twenty years, she must have lived for those short Sunday afternoons. Three precious hours of his time a week.

My grandfather was asleep on the recliner on the front porch, his iced tea sitting on the porch floor, all its ice long melted. My grandmother and Nellie were napping, too, when I went into the house. Nellie in her white, little-girl cotton slip on the big bed we shared, her dark curls stuck wetly to her forehead. I went into the bathroom, washed my face and combed my hair, and wandered down to join my grandfather on the porch.

And then the young people from the Baptist church came swinging down the street, led by the new minister. They had been calling on the sick and widowed and just plain backslidden. Dressed in their Sunday best, they looked hot and bedraggled and sweaty. The girls' hair was wet and hanging down their faces. They frowned against the sun. The boys had on their suit coats and looked like they wanted to die.

"We'll stop for a cool drink at Bridey's," the new minister said. "We'll try to get her to open a little early."

So of course I tagged along. The minister, being new, had obviously not yet caught on to the significance of the car's being there, but everyone else in the group had, because they craned their necks to glance toward the back. It was still there; but the young people, looking uncomfortable as the new minister walked up onto the porch and banged on the door, weren't about to tell him. I didn't have the words to tell him with. I stood in the shade with the others while he knocked and called. He came back shaking his head. "Guess she's not going to open," he smiled apologetically. "Let's go back to the parsonage for iced tea." And they went off.

I stood there, loath to put forth the effort to get myself back to my grandparents' house, loath to put forth any effort at all, and saw Sheriff Mills come out of his house three houses farther down the road and start toward me. Sheriff Mills had company every Sunday. Mrs. Mills had brothers all over the place, and they all gathered with wives and families every week. I knew them, but they didn't have kids my age.

"Afternoon, missy," Sheriff Mills said. He was a big, broad, older man, and he called all women under twenty "missy." "Miss Bridey not open yet?" he asked, surprised, consulting his watch.

I shook my head. He glanced around at the back. "Hmm . . ." he said. Sheriff Mills was not new in town. He turned back to look down the street toward his house. "Well," he said, "it's getting on toward six, and Mother needs milk to get supper on." He glanced behind the house again, hesitated, and mounted the steps.

I guess she had to open when she saw who it was. She didn't look all that different from the way she had earlier that day. Maybe her eyes were a little puffy, but that was all. Her hair was in the bun, not a wisp escaping, her plain face pale but calm.

"I'm real sorry about this, Bridey," the sheriff said, stepping into the store and explaining his quandary. We both refrained from glancing into the back room. As Bridey was getting the milk from the big white icebox, I scooted past the sheriff and went to the soda tub. I was fishing around for a cream soda and I could hear her and Sheriff Mills talking, but I wasn't paying any attention, really.

The water felt *so* good. I was barefooted, and I remember there was a lot of cold water on the dark wood floor. I found my cream soda and clasped it as it bobbed among the huge chunks of ice and the other bottles. Then the ice and the bottles floated apart, and I looked down into the face of Bridey's caller. He had blue eyes, I remember—very blue. He seemed to be gazing up past me to the ceiling. Then the ice and the bottles floated together again and covered his face.

I thought for a second that I was having heat stroke. My grandmother had talked about it endlessly and warned us time and again to stay out of the sun. She had had it once, when she was young; and when we asked her what it was like, she said you got sick to your stomach and dizzy and disoriented. I thought "disoriented" must mean seeing things.

I clutched my cream soda and moved it slowly back and forth in the water to clear some space. The ice and the bottles slid apart again, and there he was. He seemed to be lying on the bottom of the long tub staring up through the water, his curly hair waving gently over his forehead.

I took out my soda and let the chunks of ice float back together, and I turned to look at Bridey. She was staring over the sheriff's shoulder as he dug in his pockets and rattled on. We looked at each other. Sheriff Mills turned and saw me and said, "I see you got your soda, missy," or something inane like that and went right on talking to Bridey. Bridey just stared at me. I think now of all the things I could have done. She must have been waiting for me to scream or faint or just say, "Look here, Sheriff Mills, at Bridey's caller in the soda tub."

I didn't do any of those things. I just walked across the small room, laid my dime on the linoleum-topped counter, and walked out. I remember the tough burnt grass on my bare feet as I crossed the yards. I remember my grandpa still asleep on the porch when I came up onto it. I remember going in and sitting on a chair at the kitchen table and drinking my cream soda while my grandmother moved slowly around in the heat, starting to lay things out for a cold dinner. I don't remember at all just when I started to breathe again.

I don't know what she finally did with him. I don't know how she killed him or got him in the tub. Now that I'm older and have thought of the details of it, one crazy question that keeps popping into my mind is: how did she keep him on the bottom of the tub? Bodies float, don't they?

I don't know how she got rid of the car or how she explained it all. They found the car way out by Krug Park in St. Joe across the river, my grandmother told me. It was a big scandal in Helenwood—how Bridey's caller had disappeared. And Bridey went right on living there, running her little store. I can't say that she was especially nice to me after that. She had never been *not* nice to me. We were just more aware of each other. She had to know that I knew. I wasn't four or five. I was ten. She had seen me see him.

I wonder now at how she must have waited. Maybe she thought I would tell my grandparents, or my mother when she finally got well, or a school friend when school started. It's strange that it never crossed my mind to fear her. I could have easily disappeared down a well or in the river.

I didn't see a great deal of her after that summer. My mother took me back home in time to start sixth grade in September. My father moved up to Mound City, and I began to spend summers with him and his new family. Two years later we moved to St. Louis and my mother remarried. So when I was in Helenwood, it was usually en route to my father's or just coming back from his place, so I was there for only a few days at a time. And then, of course, I grew up and had my own life.

Bridey lived there all the rest of her life in that little three-room house. She never had another caller. She would sit out on her porch in the evenings and she didn't close anymore on Sunday afternoons. Sometimes, when Nellie and I were teenagers, before I could drive Grandpa's car over to St. Joe, we would stroll down to Bridey's.

Nellie would still get her grape pop, but I never drank another bottle of cream soda. I had switched to ice-cream bars; and if anyone noticed, they thought it was more nutritional, anyway.

Bridey would take our money and exchange pleasantries, asking me about St. Louis, how I liked school there, and how my mother was getting on. I answered politely. We kept our eyes neutral. I never saw anything in hers aside from the polite curiosity she had always had, and I kept mine bright and warm and empty.

Of all the questions I have pondered, there is one I never had to ask myself. Why didn't I tell? Why didn't I run screaming out of the store to my grandmother and fall fainting against her, babbling and hysterical? You must know the answer to that one.

Any other summer maybe I would have. But that summer, after all, I knew all about men leaving you.

JUDITH O'NEILL was born and grew up in the Midwest, with a brief odyssey to attend first and second grade in Brooklyn, New York. She attended the University of Kansas and graduated from the University of Pittsburgh. She has taught primary school in Kansas, Pennsylvania, Maryland, and the Dominican Republic, where she was a Peace Corps volunteer during the 1960s. She has published articles and short stories in Quill, The *University of Kansas' Literary Magazine,* Ellery Queen's Mystery Magazine, Alfred Hitchcock's Mystery Magazine, *and* Woman's World. *She has two stories in* Through the Saloon Doors, *a collection of short stories compiled by The Washington Expatriates Press of Washington, D.C., and one in an anthology,* Ellery Queen's Grand Slam. *Ms. O'Neill now resides in Georgia, where she works with the Oxford Book Store in Atlanta.*

LOVE ALWAYS, MAMA

MAGGIE WAGNER-HANKINS

I brought your mail up," I tell Kate as I come through the door into her tiny apartment. The place smells like cinnamon and baked apples, and I take a deep breath. The smell is money in the bank.

"Thanks, Trish. Just dump it on the table." She barely looks up from the goo she's kneading into bread dough, dough destined to become Auntie May's Wholly Good Oatmeal Bread.

Together, Kate and I are Auntie May. She's the one who does the baking, I'm the one who sells.

There shouldn't be anything for the business in her mail because we had gotten the post office box, but I still thumb through the half dozen envelopes. It looks as if Kate's on as many mailing lists as I am.

"I think you should buy the siding," I tell her, and then stop as I come to a pale pink envelope exuding an elusive scent—roses, I think. "Hmmm."

"Grab a pot holder and make yourself useful," she tells me. "Muffins are done in"—she glances at the timer—"twenty seconds."

When the *ding* sounds, I'm at the ready, and out come twenty-four of Auntie May's Marvelous Muffins—this batch the apple spice variety.

"Perfection!" I breathe in a noseful.

"Of course. Auntie May has very high standards." She is still kneading, but the dough now looks like dough instead of ooze. "Okay, slide that next batch in and set the timer for twenty-seven minutes—exactly."

"You're lucky I came along," I tell her, feeling a little like Dr. Frankenstein's assistant as I carefully slide the muffins into the oven and set the timer for precisely twenty-seven minutes.

"I'd have managed," she says, and although there's a smile on her face, I know she speaks the truth. I've seen her put together a seven-course meal for six without missing a beat.

"Anything interesting?" she asks, gesturing toward the mail.

I pick up the stack again. "Let's see—bill, junk, junk, bill, sweepstakes entry—be sure to send that in, Kate." She never does. "Junk. And *this.*" I swish the rosy envelope under her nose. "Easter card, perhaps?"

She glances up, mildly interested, checks the handwriting, and halts in mid-knead. For an instant her face lights up in a quiet smile, then she goes back to her kneading. "It's from my mother," she says.

Now it's my turn to stop. "I thought your mother was dead."

"She is," says Kate, thumping the oatmeal-colored dough down onto the kneading board.

Another few seconds' delay, and then my brain is functioning again. "So this is from—your stepmother."

"No, from my mother." I see now she's glancing at me from the corner of one eye, and there's a playful twinkle there.

"Okay, a riddle," I say. "So what's the answer?"

"It's not a riddle. It's really from my mother." At last the dough is ready. She plops it into a greased bowl, swirls it around so the top is greased too, and puts a cloth over the whole business, leaving it to rise. "My *dead* mother. She writes letters and sends me cards and things quite often. Through a medium."

This time the delay is longer as I try to gather my wits, which seem to have scattered to the far corners of the apartment. Presently, I drag them back and find a smile. Still, my mouth can't decide whether it should be a "that's a good joke, Kate" smile or a "Kate, you've been working a little too hard" smile. It tries to be both and ends up being sappy.

With my brain telling me not to take this too seriously, and Kate's expression telling me she's taking it very seriously indeed, I search for something to say. Being the practical type, I finally settle for "Kate, doesn't it seem a little implausible for the dead to communicate with the living, especially on a regular basis?"

"Not really. My mother told me before she died that she'd be in touch. I had no doubt she meant it. I didn't know how, but when you're six, you don't question your parents."

"But you're not six anymore."

"I don't have to be. She's been true to her word. Boy, has she! You should see the stacks of stuff I've gotten from her in the past twenty years."

I, of course, am having a horrible time with this and am grasping at straws. "Kate, are you sure your mother really died?"

"Positive."

"She didn't just maybe go away and—"

"Abandon me? Sorry, but I saw her lying in her casket.

Believe me, she was dead." She smiles, and I can't help wondering how she can talk about this in the same tone she uses when discussing whether to use more ginger in the muffins.

Seeming to read my mind, something she's been good at almost since we met over a year earlier, she says, "I know it sounds crazy. But it's just one of those things you either accept or drive yourself nuts trying to figure out. I prefer to accept it. Because what other possibility is there?"

I can think of a few, but I don't want to mention them just now. Instead, I say, "Well, aren't you going to open it?"

She finishes washing the sticky dough off her hands, pours us both coffee, and I trail her into the dining-room section of the studio apartment, feeling no compunction about reading over her shoulder.

The card has flowers all over the front and the words "Happy Easter to a Beautiful Daughter."

She opens it and reads aloud, " 'Dearest Kitten, Another Easter and you're lovelier than ever.' " Smiling indulgently, she shakes her head. " 'I'm glad your business is starting to take off. You and your friend Trish have worked hard and deserve it.' " I have to admit, hearing my own name in this letter sends a tiny stab of cold down the back of my neck. " 'Don't forget to recreate once in a while, and keep taking your vitamins. Love always, Mama.' "

All I can say is, "She sounds like a mother."

Kate smiles, and her smile is a lot of things—amused, loving, even a little sad—but one thing it isn't is incredulous. It's clear she finds nothing disconcerting or surprising about any of this. But then, she's got about twenty years on me in getting used to it.

"You really don't believe it's her, do you?" she asks.

"I'm having a little trouble with it. Why haven't you ever mentioned it before?"

"For precisely this reason. I didn't want to upset you."

"Then why tell me now?" Part of me is wishing I hadn't brought up the mail.

"Because you brought up the mail. Besides, you asked."

We sit there for a few minutes, each busy with our coffee cups and our thoughts. I can't keep my eyes off the envelope. Finally, the words have to come.

"Kate, I'm not trying to be a wet blanket, but could I ask— how you can be so certain it's her, and not just someone who felt sorry for you after your mother died and tried to spare you the grief? With the best of intentions, of course."

There was that self-assured smile again. "Trisha, you believe what you want. I can't really expect you to believe this. But I know it's her. I can't explain it, I just know."

Not able to give up quite so easily, I grab the envelope, ready to prove a point, and sigh in dismay. The postmark, which I was sure would be from here in Springfield, is from Bridgeway, a little over a hundred miles to the south of us.

When Kate goes out to check the muffins, I follow her and pour more coffee. "Suppose," I begin tentatively, "it really *is* your mother. Doesn't it bother you to be—I don't know— *watched* all the time? Do you ever feel like you have any privacy?"

"She doesn't watch me all the time. She's given me pro- gressively more privacy as I've grown older, in proportion to what a mother would give you if she were alive. When I was a little girl, I got the feeling she was around more." She laughs. "Especially when I was up to no good. But now she doesn't seem to intrude any more than a living mother would. Maybe even less." I'm sure she's referring to my own mother, who lives four blocks from me and knows what I have for dinner every evening.

Suddenly, the weirdness of the whole thing gets to me, and I turn to Kate, unable to keep the laugh out of my voice. "Tell me the truth," I say. "You act as if this were the most normal thing in the world. But honestly, doesn't it seem a little—bizarre?"

She breaks out laughing, and for a minute I think she's going to admit that the whole thing is just a joke. Instead, she says, "Honestly? Yes, it's very bizarre. But I've had twenty years to get used to it."

Three weeks pass, and I'm still not used to it. But it's something Kate and I have managed to keep out of our conversations. It's clear to both of us that we're not going to reach a meeting of the minds. At first I watch Kate for signs of—I don't know how to put it except bluntly—having only one oar in the water, but she seems as normal as ever so I finally just give up wondering about it. If she gets any more letters or cards, she doesn't mention it, and I don't bring her mail up for her anymore.

Then in October, about the time the leaves are at their most glorious but will soon start to fade, I notice a change in Kate. At first, it's just a sort of melancholy around the eyes. I chalk it up to winter's approach. But when she starts leaving ingredients out of Auntie May's various baked goods, I begin to worry. This is not the Kate I know.

Finally I ask her. She tells me there's nothing wrong.

"Is it because we've expanded too quickly?" I ask her. We've moved the operation into a small store next to a popcorn and candy shop, with whom we share a kitchen.

"No."

"Want to talk about it?"

"No."

"You look like you're coming down with something. Kate, you're not pregnant, are you?"

"No!" It's the first time I've seen her smile in a week.

"What then? Come on, you can tell Auntie May."

"I thought *I* was Auntie May," she says with the beginnings of a grin.

"Then we're the same person and should have no secrets from each other. So come on, what's the matter?"

She hesitates a moment, then sits down. It's as if the act has released something that's been bottled up for ages, and she starts to cry.

"It's my mother."

Uh-oh. Why am I not surprised?

"What'd she do, tell you I'm a bad influence on you?" The joke falls flat, and I could kick myself for even trying to make jokes just now.

"I haven't heard from her in three months. I didn't—get a birthday card from her."

Her birthday was September twentieth. I remember because we (and presumably our dates) woke up with horrible hangovers on September twenty-first, swearing off ouzo forever.

"Trisha, she's never missed sending me a birthday card." She shakes her head, and suddenly I can see her at six, when she got the news that her mother was dead. I just want to hug her. "It's like she's—died all over again."

I can think of nothing to say.

Then as she sits there, staring forlornly at her hands, I get an idea.

"Kate, don't you think it's time we tried to find the medium? She might be able to shed some light on this, you know."

Instant hope takes hold in her eyes, and I thank God I've said the right thing. "Of course. She'd know." Then she seems to sink again. "Only I have no idea where to find her. Mama never told me whom she was transmitting through."

But it's all we have, and I'm not about to let it slip through my fingers. "Bridgeway isn't that big. We'll find her."

In fact, though I don't have the heart to tell her just yet, I have a sneaking suspicion it won't be hard to find our medium. All we have to do is look in the obituary section of the Bridgeway newspaper between sometime in July, when Kate got her last letter, and September twentieth.

Bridgeway is a small, friendly town, the sort I sometimes fantasize about my mother's retiring to. One week after Kate and I have "the conversation," we are here, ready to search for Madame X. On the drive up I've told Kate my theory, and she has at least listened. Now she's recapping it as we pull out of the motel where we've left our stuff and head for the office of the Bridgeway *Times.*

"You really think some old woman took me on as a sort of—charity project—and now she's dead and that's why I'm not getting any more—messages?"

"I don't know, Kate. All I know is if that *is* what happened, it wouldn't seem any stranger than what *you* think it's been all this time."

"But how could someone this far away know all that stuff about me?"

"Who knows? Maybe she used to live next door to you when you were a kid or something. Maybe she has relatives in Springfield to keep her posted on what you're doing. I don't know. But it's at least worth checking out."

"I can't argue with that," she says. Much of the fight has gone out of her. I grow angrier by the minute at this interfering "medium" and her twenty years of good intentions.

The newspaper office is small, clean, and bustling, but the back room with its files is quiet, and we set out on our mission. It doesn't take long. Forty minutes later, we've been through the obituaries in three months' worth of weekly papers, taking down names, ages, and addresses.

Back at the motel, we sort through the names. Maybe I'm guilty of stereotyping, but I put all the women over sixty at the top of the list. I don't think it was a man, and I don't think it was anyone young. We have nine names to start on.

"Now what?" asks Kate.

"Now we go to these houses and see if anyone is there who lived with these people and who might know something."

"You think they're going to tell us, even if they know?"

"Why not?"

She shrugs. "I guess it's worth a try."

Well worth a try, as it turns out. Six names down, and we come to a huge old house that looks as if it's right out of an Alfred Hitchcock movie. I get a feeling about it, but I don't get too excited. I'm not noted for having psychic ability.

Still, when a little old lady with gray hair and a sweet smile answers the door and then does a double take when she sees Kate, I have to admit my stomach turns a flip.

The eager blue eyes grow wide. "Kate," she says. All of a sudden I feel like running.

Of course we don't run. We go in.

In a few minutes the old lady, Ruth Morehouse, has given us the details of her sister Betty's death. "Quick, it was. One minute she was in the prime of health; the next, she'd keeled over of a heart attack."

"I'm sorry," I say.

"Don't be," she assures me. "Best way to go. I'm kind of hoping for it myself." We give a brief explanation of why we're here. She smiles knowingly and says, "Please come this way. I think you'll want to see Betty's room."

"Shrine" is a more appropriate word.

The room is almost dark until Ruth raises the shades, flooding the place with sunshine. It's apparently remained untouched since Betty's death a little over two months earlier, and it's filled with Kate. It's pretty clear to me that I've been right all along.

I feel rather than hear the breath go out of Kate.

We are drawn to the memorabilia. Sketches of Kate, some framed and all quite good, dot the dresser and desk. "My sister was an artist, too," Ruth says by way of explanation, then leaves us alone in the room. There are Kate clippings on a bulletin board at one side of a brass bed. One from when she won the bake-off two years ago. One announcing her engagement (broken a month later) to a local banker. One of her when she was twelve and won the spelling bee for her school district. A few with her name on a list of honor-roll students. Even the article announcing the opening of Auntie May's.

Kate sees the stationery before I do. She walks to the desk and lovingly picks up the box, which is obviously very familiar to her. There is a gold rose etched on pale peach paper.

She looks at it for a long moment, then puts it down. "*Mother* always loved roses," she says softly, and it is clear that she means, "Mother loved roses, *too.*" She has accepted the truth. I wonder if she feels she has lost two mothers.

I go to her and put my arm around her, but there don't seem to be any words. I guess none are needed. She puts her head down and cries for a long time.

When we go out, finally, Ruth is waiting with tea. Though neither of us wants to stay, she is persistent, and she *has* opened her home to us, so we sit down and drink tea and nibble at shortbread cookies.

"My sister really was a talented psychic," she offers without asking. "She helped many people."

"I'm sure she did," I say. "Did she ever live in Springfield?" I expect to hear that she used to live in the same neighborhood as Kate, or went to the same church or something. But Ruth shakes her head.

"Spent her whole life here. Sometimes she talked of going there, though. She said she'd like to see you, Kate—in person, that is—before her time came. Shame she never made it. She really did love you."

Kate shakes her head. "How did she—find out about me in the first place? If it wasn't through my mother, I mean?"

"Who's to say it wasn't?" Ruth asks. "As I said, she had the gift. Perhaps your mother did communicate with her."

And then Kate remembers something. "Bridgeway. Yes, I knew there was something familiar about the name of this town. My mother had a cousin who lived down here. But— she died at least a year before Mama did. We came here to the funeral. I remember because I was in kindergarten and I had to leave early that day, and I didn't want to because we were going to tour a bakery."

But though at first the thought seems to offer a way out of her confusion, Kate finishes by saying, "But I don't see how that could have any bearing on this."

Finally, with the tea drunk and nothing more to say, we thank Ruth Morehouse and drive back to the motel.

The last thing Kate says before we get in the car to leave this town is, "It just doesn't make sense."

Still, in the weeks that follow, she starts to act a little more like her old self again. The grief is there, but she's trying to work through it, to put it behind her. It's an old grief, one that she should have been allowed when she was six years old. Instead it has been delayed for twenty years, and now it's a far more complicated thing than it should have been.

But Kate is strong. The zing comes back to her baking. We get more business and she jumps in with both feet. We even have to hire a third person to help with paperwork and distribution. And all the while Kate progresses.

At last, just before Thanksgiving, the day comes when she

bursts into the shop, the old Kate, wearing her glad smile once more. There is a twinkle in her eye as she looks around the shop, sizing up the day's work.

"I'm glad Jody's not in yet," she says, reaching into her purse. She's even got *me* smiling, despite the fact that it's only six o'clock in the morning and I've had just one cup of coffee. "I want to show you something."

She pulls out a lavender envelope and hands it to me. "Look at the card," she says, and I slide it out, curious.

An elf sits on a toadstool surrounded by roses, his chin in his hands. Over him are the words "A Belated Birthday Wish."

I try not to jump to conclusions, but I can't seem to stop the tremor that runs through me as I open the card, skipping the verse and going to the large, somehow familiar script.

Dearest Kitten,

I'm so sorry this is late. You have no idea how hard it is to find a receptive vessel on the spur of the moment. I hope your birthday was the best yet, and I'm very pleased to see things taking off for Auntie May's. Betty Morehouse sends her love. Have a Happy Thanksgiving!

Love always, Mama.

MAGGIE WAGNER-HANKINS *has been writing fiction since she was nine years old. Her early and continuing fascination with and research into the realm of metaphysics have supplied her with most of her story and book ideas. She lives in Missouri and has written three novels, numerous short stories, and several picture books.*

THE BATMAN
OF BLYTHEVILLE

ROBERT LOY

W hat do you want to be when you grow up?"

No kid ever graduates from grammar school without having had to answer that question a few thousand times. As I remember it, I was in the second grade the first time it was posed to me. My grandmother was staying at our house over the Christmas holidays, and one night while my parents were at a dinner party, the duty of playing the host fell to my seven-year-old hands.

To start off the evening's entertainment, I led my grandmother on a tour through the back pages of the Sears catalogue, carefully pointing out which of the wondrous toys and games on exhibit there were not already occupants of my toy box. I did this because I knew from Christmases past that if

I did not spell out exactly what I wanted she would probably go out and buy me a lot of silly and useless presents—stuff like clothes.

I was willing to give her the benefit of the doubt and assume she did this from well-meant but misguided intentions and not just to torture me. Still, there was no point in taking chances; and so I let her know pretty plainly that this year I wanted models and pellet guns, not mittens and underwear. She said nothing, but she communicated to me by way of that mystic telepathy little boys and grandmothers share that she got the message. I nestled farther down in her lap while visions of air rifles danced in my head.

"How do you like school this year?" she asked.

"Okay," I responded, in that conversation-killing style of second-graders.

"What do you want to be when you grow up?"

I had never thought about that before. I was seven years old; the future, beyond the next game of hide-and-seek, did not overly concern me. But I wanted to give her an answer, especially now that we had come to an understanding on the subject of Christmas presents.

"I want to be Batman," I told her.

My grandmother smiled softly to herself and said, "Well, I think that's just fine." But I could tell she was thinking, *Isn't he the cutest little thing?* That's what grown-ups always thought when you tried to talk to them seriously.

But it was Christmastime and so I forgave her.

My contemporaries were also being queried as to their future employment plans, and the next day it was the favored topic of debate at the local playground. When I had told my grandmother the previous night that I wanted to be Batman, it was mainly because I couldn't think of anything else on the spur of the moment. After being sent to bed, however, I decided to do a little research on what, exactly, "caped crusaderhood" entailed. I hauled out my stack of Detective Comics and my flashlight, pulled the covers up over my head, and read and reread, taking mental notes all the while on exactly what Batman was expected to accomplish in a typical workday.

What I discovered excited and amazed me. Batman's job was to beat up bad guys, rescue pretty girls, crack horrible jokes, and, generally, scare the heck out of people. My definition of the perfect occupation. I had chosen wisely. The message my heart tapped out to my brain was that I had a calling, a grand one.

I realized just *how* grand as I listened to the other kids discussing their career aspirations. Next to my destiny as a masked vigilante, their employment ideals were positively prosaic. Most of the girls wanted to be mommies (this was back in preliberated days), and a few planned to become nurses or—of all things—teachers. The boys' aims were only slightly more interesting. They all wanted to be firemen, policemen, or spies—except Arnold, the neighborhood bully, who planned to become a professional wrestler. As I listened to them recite the merits of their various ambitions, I silently weighed their ideals against my goal of life as a Batman. It was no contest. Being a Batman was more rewarding on all counts: more exciting than fighting fires, more dangerous than espionage, and with a much snazzier uniform than the police department's. When my turn came, I was ready to tell them all about it.

"I'm going to be a Batman when I grow up," I said, and then waited for the adulation I knew would come when they realized that a future superhero was in their midst.

But the only reaction was from Arnold, and it was not adulatory.

"Ahhhh, you baldheaded baby," he said, "there ain't no such thing as Batman."

"Baldheaded baby" was the worst insult there was in the

backyards and playgrounds of Blytheville, Arkansas. Many was the time that I, like every other kid in the neighborhood, had come home crying like Judgment Day because that foul epithet had been applied to me. My mother could never understand why it upset me so. No grown-up ever could. There is no curse in the adult language that can rival "baldheaded baby" for inflicting pain and indignity on the receiver.

"There is so a Batman," I informed him.

"There is not!"

"Is so!"

"Is not!"

"Is so!"

"Is not!"

This clever colloquy could have gone on all afternoon, and I wouldn't have minded if it had. I just did not want to allow Arnold to shift the method of settling this dispute from phraseology to fisticuffs, his favorite means of self-expression.

"Prove it," Arnold challenged, and then again compared my appearance to that of a hairless infant.

"I will," I told him.

"Do it, then."

"All right," I said, "if Batman's not real, then how come they call it *Detective* Comics? Huh? How come?"

Against such a brilliant display of second-grade logic, I honestly expected Arnold to throw in the towel. As it turned out, I wasn't even close. What he actually threw was more like a right hook. He hit me three more times before I, deciding to get in some blows of my own, hit the ground. The other kids formed a circle around us and chanted: "Fight! Fight!" which was unnecessary since Arnold and I both knew what it was.

"Get up," Arnold said. It sounded like a dumb idea to me. What I wanted to do was dig myself a hole and burrow my way back home. But then I remembered what my parents had told me, about how Arnold's mother was dead and how he lived alone with his dad, who was hardly ever home. They told me I should always try to be especially nice to Arnold. So, because Arnold wanted me to, I stood up. He immediately knocked me right back down.

"Get up! Get up and fight!" This was Arnold's one concession to the Marquis of Queensberry: he would not punch your face in while you were down on the ground. I was thankful for that. I took inventory of my injuries and found there were no serious ones, nothing broken or bleeding. I was thankful for that, too; but the audience was disappointed. They had interrupted their games and abandoned the seesaws and jungle gyms to watch this violent spectacle, and they felt cheated when they saw that my eyes weren't black and my teeth were still in my mouth. They were restless, and some of them joined Arnold in urging me to stand up and get punched out again. A couple of them even tried to force me to my feet. Anyone who believes that people are more compassionate than in the days when they cheerfully watched Christians being fed to the lions should pay a visit to their local playground.

As I sat there, I thought of something else my mother and father had told me: any infraction of the rules would be reported to Santa Claus, who would shorten my pile of presents accordingly. Fighting definitely qualified as an infraction. Obviously, I couldn't be nice to Arnold, which required my playing punching bag, and please Santa Claus, who frowned on fighting, at the same time.

"Get up!" Arnold insisted. "Stand up and fight!"

At this point I had no battle scars to take home, so there was no way for my parents, and subsequently Santa Claus, to find out about this scuffle. Although I knew it would result in a significant loss of playground prestige, I decided to quit while there were still no black marks by my name up at the North Pole. I chose not to stand and fight but to sit and refrain from fighting. It was not a popular decision. Eventually, however, Arnold got tired of waiting and plodded off to enjoy another of his hobbies—smashing bullfrogs with a brick—and the bloodthirsty crowd went back to its games.

Finally I trudged home, bowed but unbloody.

Christmas morning came, and with it my reward for suffering indignity at the balled-up hands of Arnold. Mom, Dad, and Santa—all ignorant of the playground incident—showered me with gifts. I got almost everything I asked for. The only thing missing was the air rifle.

I had no complaints, though. Also missing were the hated "functional" presents, and in their place was neat, fun stuff. Even my grandmother did not let me down. We compromised. She got me clothes again—a suit, in fact. But what a suit! A gray sweat shirt with a gold circle on the chest, on which was painted the silhouette of a bat in flight; a wide yellow belt with a couple of million secret compartments; and black shorts over a pair of leggings that ended in hard-soled blue boots. Accessories included gloves, mask (pointy ears and all), and, best of all, a magnificent dark-blue cape—as big, scary, and mysterious as the night sky. This was no cheap Halloween costume but a genuine Batman suit, complete with sharp ridges on the gloves. I abandoned my other presents, put on the suit, dashed up to my parents' room, and stood before their full-length mirror.

The awesome image of the Batman was what I saw reflected. Oh, it was still recognizable as me, I suppose. The real Batman is taller than three feet eleven inches, and his ribs don't stick out when he is in costume; but I was nonetheless transfigured. The nobility and heroism I carried beneath the cumbersome facade of childhood were now on the outside for all the world to see. If it was not a sight to make "strong men quiver with fear," it at least made me shiver with delight. I practiced

Batmanlike scowls and jumped up and down to make the cape unfurl.

"How does it fit?" My dad had entered the room and was watching me while I watched the mirror.

"Great," I answered, without taking my eyes off the fearsome masked man in front of me.

"Bobby and Jenny are outside waiting for you. Why don't you go show them your new costume?"

I looked at my father. I looked back to the mirror; a skinny seven-year-old boy in a Batman suit stared sadly back at me. The majesty of the costume had flown on little bat wings out the window, leaving me to feel ridiculous and alone.

Bobby and Jenny were brother and sister, new kids on the block. They had not been present that day at the playground when Arnold tried to beat the innocence out of me. They had not been laughing and calling me a baldheaded bat baby ever since like the other kids. I had never mentioned Batman to either of them. I was afraid if they too laughed at my dream, my dream would die.

"Tell them I'll be out as soon as I change clothes," I instructed my father.

"Why? Don't you like your Batman costume?" he asked.

"Yessir, but it's cold outside."

I raced to my room and peeled off the gloves and mask. In keeping with my usual method of housekeeping, I tossed them into a corner. They landed on my stack of Detective Comics. The beautiful drawing on the cover of the top comic book, depicting Batman grappling with his insane arch foe, the Joker, disappeared under a tangled wad of dark fabric.

For the first time in my life, I experienced doubt. Was there a Batman? I didn't know. Could there be? I didn't know that, either. But I had read enough of his exploits and seen enough of the real world to know that there *should* be a Batman. We needed a man who did not allow his sense of justice and fairness to be overcome by advancing cynicism. I needed him. I did not want to grow up into an adult world where the price of admission was my belief in heroes. I needed to know there was someone bigger than me, bigger than anybody, watching over us. Not God. Oh, I believed He was up there watching us, but He seemed content just to spectate. God never came swinging down on a bat rope when a mugger in the park—or a bully in the playground—threatened you.

I couldn't present myself in this costume to Bobby and Jenny. Yet when I tried to untie the cape, I experienced another new emotion—self-disgust. I felt like a traitor. So I did what Bruce Wayne, the Batman in the comic books, did. I put my regular clothes on over the costume and crammed the gloves and mask in my pocket. My heroism and nobility once again safely hidden, I walked outside to meet my friends.

We went to the park, a boring place with absolutely nothing to recommend itself to kids, just benches and unclimbable trees. Bobby and Jenny wanted to go to the playground, but I wasn't up to revisiting Waterloo so soon. Our conversation revolved around what each of us had found under the tree that morning.

"What else did you get?" Jenny asked me as we all sat down on a dry spot under an old oak. She looked up at me with an interested smile, and I felt myself getting even warmer than I already was under all those layers of fabric.

"Ah, stuff," I said. "You know, lots of stuff." Jenny's smile always made me self-conscious and tongue-tied.

"I got a doll—a Baby Go Wet-Wet—and some toys, but mostly I got new clothes," she told me.

"Me, too," her brother, Bobby, chimed in. "I got new shirts, new trousers, new socks."

I shook my head in commiseration. "Gee, that's too bad. I'm really sorry."

"Why?" asked Bobby. "Clothing is what I asked Mr. Claus to bring me."

I tried to catch his eye to see if he was joking, but his glasses were so thick all I saw were two black pupils as big around as Cadillac tires.

"Really?"

"Oh, yes. He brought me this sweater, in fact. Didn't you notice it was new?"

"Yeah," I lied, "yeah, I did, it's nice." My social circle had been reduced to this duo and I wanted to keep both of them, but sometimes with Bobby I wondered if I weren't better off as a pariah. His scholarly prissiness offended me. He reminded me somewhat of Clark Kent, and I knew good and well there was no Superman suit under those new duds he was so proud of.

I certainly had no problem liking his sister, however. I liked Jenny to the point of distraction. I had never had a girlfriend before, so I didn't know if the light-headedness I experienced in her presence was due to puppy love or iron-poor blood.

"Have you ever seen Santa Claus?" asked Jenny. I had a suave, sophisticated answer, but unfortunately it blew away when she batted her eyelashes at me.

"I wonder how he gets to everybody's house in one night like that?" She looked hopefully up at me, as though she expected me to explain that eternal mystery. More than anything in the world I wished I could.

"It's simple, Sis," Bobby told her. "Mr. Claus travels faster than light."

To my dismay, Jenny turned her adoring gaze from me to her brother. I did not know why, because what he had said sounded like nonsense to me. Still, it had evidently impressed her, so I set out to redeem myself by exposing the fallacy in his theory.

"Of course he goes faster than light. Everybody knows that.

I mean, he's always finished by the time the sun comes up. I figure it's because he goes real, real fast and skips all the bad people's houses."

I looked at Jenny. I knew a truly scientific explanation like mine was bound to turn her head. But I was too late. Her head had already been turned. She was watching an approaching figure top the ridge.

"Who is that?" she asked. "I've never seen him before."

I had. Coming straight toward us, looking like a muscle-bound Grinch, was my old friend Arnold.

Bobby never saw him coming. He pushed his glasses up his nose and kept on lecturing. "The speed of light is one hundred and eighty-six thousand miles a second. I'm sure you'll agree that's real, real fast. Still, when you consider the entire rest of the year is spent in preparation for that one night, the task is not as amazing as it first appears."

"What ain't amazin'?" In his own inimitable style, Arnold joined the conversation. I was staring down at the ground, hoping, ostrichlike, that if I didn't see Arnold he wouldn't see me.

"We were discussing Santa Claus's feat," Bobby explained.

"Yeah? Well, Santa Claus ain't got no feet, and you know why?"

"What? I mean why?"

"Cuz there ain't no Santa Claus. That's why," Arnold growled.

I could have, and probably should have, warned Bobby. The poor fool took Arnold's comment as an invitation to debate. I still had my head in the sand, but I could feel Jenny's eyes burning a hole in me, imploring me to save her brother.

"Interesting theory," said Bobby. "But how do you explain the evidence—the gifts, the consumed milk and cookies?"

"Big words," Arnold said. "I guess you think big words make you a big man. But you ain't nothing but a baldheaded baby, just like this guy."

The next thing I knew, a huge hand grabbed the front of my parka and pulled me skyward. There was a moment of shock before I realized I had left the planet of my birth. I hung there suspended, face-to-ugly-face with Arnold.

"You're a baldheaded bat baby, ain't you?"

I gurgled something in reply. Owing to the fact that Arnold's paw was wrapped around my throat, I was speechless—not to mention breathless—and faint. He relaxed his grip and I stood, wobbly, on my feet.

"I beat you up good the other day, didn't I?"

I nodded.

I was, in many ways, a naive child, but not naive enough to think that Arnold asked me that question to see if I knew the answer. I knew, even more than he did, how "good" he had beaten me. No, he asked that question because he wanted to impress somebody, and I realized with a feeling of horror and shame that it had to be Jenny. Arnold had assaulted my dreams and now he was trying to steal my girl.

"Do you know what you are?" he asked.

I was silent. I knew I was risking another right hook, but I refused to play straight man at my own public humiliation.

"You're not Batman—you're Chickenman." His face crinkled up into something ghastly, the first time I'd ever seen Arnold smile.

"There ain't no Batman, is there, Chickenman?"

Again I was silent.

"Is there, Chickenman?" Arnold gave me a close-up view of his right fist. Each knuckle was as big as my head.

"No," I mumbled, hoping Jenny wouldn't hear me or see that my face was on fire.

"Now, Chickenman, tell your buddy Big Words there ain't no Santa Claus, neither."

I looked at Bobby. He was studying me impassively, like I was a bug under a microscope or something. I could tell he had no idea what was going on. Then I saw Jenny. She knew exactly what was happening. The look she gave me hurt a lot more than one of Arnold's right hooks. At that moment, as I watched her eyes fill with tears, I felt far too small to hold all the precious agony she was causing in me—but I wanted it all. There was no room for any other emotion, not even fear.

"There is too a Santa Claus," I screamed at Arnold, tears running down my cheeks, "*and* a Batman, you big ape! You big baldheaded baby ape!"

And then I ran. I hoped Arnold would chase me and leave Bobby and—especially—Jenny alone. It didn't work.

"Run, Chickenman," Arnold hollered after me. "Run on back to the hen house. I'll take care of your buddy Big Words."

I ran. I ran from Jenny's eyes, Jenny's tears. Not from Arnold's fists—avoiding them was an unexpected fringe benefit. I tried to take comfort from the fact that Arnold was not going to beat *me* up, not today anyway. Or had he already?

He had forced me to deny Batman, something he had not been able to accomplish in our first battle. And maybe he was right—maybe there was no Batman. Certainly no one had swooped down and rescued me, cracking corny jokes while effortlessly defeating Arnold. No masked avenger was behind me to save Jenny's virtue and Bobby's hide. If only I were bigger. If only I were grown up.

By now Arnold was probably rearranging Bobby's facial features. Bobby had his faults, but he was my friend and I was responsible for what was happening to him. I had no idea what Arnold would do to Jenny. He might beat her up, too. But he might do something worse, like kiss her. He might kiss her *and* beat her up. Whatever he did, I knew that the look Jenny would give me when we next met would be infinitely more painful than the one I was now running from.

It hit me that even if I ran home and cried everything out

to Mom, she couldn't make this mess "all better" the way she used to. And then I faced that moment that comes in every life—the beginning of the end of childhood. I realized that everything I was running from—Jenny and that look and the pain that went with it, a "good" beating from Arnold, the responsibility for Bobby's beating—none of it could I escape. No matter which way I ran, I would be running straight toward them. And since I was running that way anyway . . .

I dashed behind the park men's room. I had been a fool to expect someone to swoop down and rescue me. By the same token, I had been a fool to doubt the existence of Batman. How could I have forgotten? He was there with me the whole time. I tore off my parka and let him out to spread his wings. I pulled the mask and gloves out of my pocket and put them on. I kicked off my trousers.

The world looked strangely different in some indefinable way when I first saw it through my eyeholes. I did not stop to ponder it, though. I took a big gulp of air and ran. In the right direction this time.

I don't know which was pounding harder—my heart in my chest or my boots on the grass. The wind whistled its approval and the cape unfurled splendidly behind me. I felt like I could run forever. Run? I could fly.

Then I saw them. Arnold was merrily punching away at Bobby's face. Jenny was flailing her little fists on the bully's back in an ineffectual effort to make him stop. She was the first to see me. Her fists deflated and fell to her sides. She turned into a statue.

I kept running.

It was several seconds before Arnold even noticed that Jenny was no longer attacking his flank. When the realization finally sank in, he let go of Bobby, turned, and followed Jenny's gaze. All three of them forgot themselves at the fearsome sight of a genuine Batman swooping down the hill. Arnold and

Jenny stood motionless in wide-eyed amazement. Bobby, who had lost his glasses in the fight with Arnold, stared up in squint-eyed bewilderment.

I kept running. I knew if I stopped to think about what I was doing I'd chicken out. Then I'd really be in trouble, because I'd picked up so much speed zooming down the hill I couldn't have stopped if I wanted to. I just kept coming, and when I ran headlong into Arnold's chest he hit the ground with a blow that must have measured a good 7.4 on the Richter scale. I stumbled a few feet and then skidded on my belly. Quickly I disentangled myself from my cape and hopped up. Everything was black! I was blind! I hurriedly adjusted my eyeholes, and my vision returned.

Arnold was lying on the ground, seemingly not very anxious to get up right away. He was clutching his stomach and trying to figure out what had happened. I knew how he felt, but I was not sympathetic.

"Get up, Arnold," I heard myself say. Somewhere in the back of my mind I wondered if I hadn't made a mistake calling him by his first name like that. I didn't want to jeopardize my secret identity. We Batmen had to be careful about such things. I flexed my biceps, hoping the sight of that puny but formidably arrayed muscle would cover up my faux pas.

Arnold found his feet and stood up.

"Who am I?" I asked, giving him one of my best Batman scowls.

"You're crazy," he said, and drew back his fist. I ducked and delivered a sharp jab to his stomach. Bruce Wayne himself would have been proud of such a move.

"Now who am I?" I shouted. I turned slightly so that Jenny, if she were still standing in the spot I'd last seen her, would get my full profile.

"Batman," Arnold moaned.

"You *bat* I am. You *batt*er believe it!" If I hadn't been so busy trying to look menacing, I would have burst out laughing. Everything was falling into place. Even the extremely corny jokes came easy.

Next on the agenda was dispatching this villain for good. I couldn't very well haul him off to jail like Batman did with his vanquished foes, Arkansas officials being reluctant to imprison second-graders. So I did the next best thing.

"You better get out of here," I snarled at the villain, "before I have to *bat* you around some more." Since this was the big moment, and I wanted to get it over with while we were still under the spell of the Batman, I scowled, flexed my biceps, gestured at my utility belt, *and* whooshed my cape around. It worked. Arnold left. Fast.

I watched him go and then allowed myself to breathe for the first time since I had abandoned my street clothes and my childhood back at the rest room. When Arnold was out of sight, I turned and looked around. Bobby was on his hands and knees fumbling around for his glasses. It was safe to assume he had missed the whole glorious episode. Ah, but Jenny— Jenny had seen it all. She was gazing up at me with something closely akin to rapture. I felt as uncomfortable as I had when her eyes were full of scorn—until I remembered we Batmen have nerves of steel. I gave her a grim little smile as if to say: "Think nothing of it. Danger is my business."

She stood on her tiptoes and whispered in my ear, "I know who you are."

I was horrified.

"No you don't," I said. "No one knows my secret identity."

She giggled. "You're my hero, that's who you are."

All of a sudden I realized I did not know what I was supposed to do next. The stories in the comic books always ended here, with the bad guys taken care of and the maiden all full of gratitude and adoration. Batman would probably have disappeared into the night to tackle more bad guys. But it was still early afternoon in Blytheville, Arkansas, and as far as I knew there were no more bad guys. So I gave the grateful maiden my gloved hand and walked her home.

ROBERT LOY *was born in Norfolk, Virginia, and lives on the sunny side of the Mason-Dixon line. A devout vegetarian, he is interested in reading, animal rights, chess, and the Boston Red Sox.*

THE GIRL
IN THE
ORANGE BERET

LEE RUSSELL

J edson Waite stood breathing in the damp earth odors of fall. No leaves had turned, but already the sun's rays through the trees slanted differently. A bird chirped from the hedge. Gina, in her second-hand Fiat and the orange sweater knitted by her mother, had just driven down the driveway and, defiantly alone, off to college, never really to return.

His wife's voice drifted from a side window. "I'd planned just a cold lunch. I had no idea it had turned so chilly."

"Okay by me. Want any help?"

"No."

He wandered back to the patio, where empty coffee cups sat on the metal-mesh table. Young Jed had returned to Princeton the day before. Whole lives, whole persons who might never have existed had things gone differently on just one day in Paris twenty years before. He felt appalled that the crucial life choices and chances present themselves so early—not to the capable mature, perhaps desperately needing them, but to the unformed, inexperienced young. He had wanted an orderly life and he had had one, marred only by an errant blip here and there. And heretofore the beep of a foreign car or a glimpse of bittersweet orange had nudged him merely into brief, pleasant nostalgia and not, as now, into a full shocking recognition of what he had once blundered into; of what had once been possible, and perhaps still was for all he knew; and of how the flow of life—broad and slow, allowing time for deciding, for correcting mistakes, for going back to do what has been left undone—can suddenly narrow and rush between gorge walls, allowing no time to think, no margin for error, and no going back.

Back then, it had been northern sunshine, a sidewalk café, and traffic racketing across the Place de l'Opéra. He had sat, long legs cramped under a small table, feeling sick after three Cinzanos and two *limonades*, embarrassed at having sat too long over these, and both annoyed and uneasy at finding himself being watched, past a raised newspaper, by a thickset man against the far café wall. But all that had ceased to matter as, with the passing quarter hours, the certainty had grown that Griselle was not going to come.

He, a small-town Iowan who had just managed medical school on the insurance left by his mother, then this budgeted trip, this last fling before settling into public health service, had aspired to a five-foot-nine enchantress with silky, wheat-colored hair and sea-green eyes. Among the August throng of Americans heading for American Express around the corner, nothing remotely like Griselle had appeared in the last three hours. Nothing like her had ever appeared in Jed's life before, or was likely, he had known, ever to appear in it again.

When, in a drift of silky gray-green, she had first crossed the ship's dining salon the preceding June, he had looked, along with every other dining male, but never considered trying for her. He had read her as East, Miss So-and-So's School, some New York glamor job, and Money. Later, however, leaning on a mezzanine rail to watch the dancing below, he had seen her alone at a floorside table, and something about her bright, open face seen in profile—some slight droop to the mouth corner, perhaps—had caught at his heart. The band had played, taken a break, and resumed, and still she sat, quiet, erect, slim arms on the white cloth. He had straightened slowly from the rail, then skimmed down the open, curving stairs. For *her* he *did* have something to offer, on a dance floor, anyway—his six foot two inches of height.

They had danced that night and the next and the next; and, although there were other vacationing students in Second Class—beneficiaries, like himself, of convention cancellations—for the whole crossing he had had her to himself.

Days, they had played shipboard games—she in what his mother would have called "beautifully unobtrusive clothes," topped, however, by a downy, vividly orange beret—or lain, wrapped against the Atlantic chill, watching gray water swell against gray skies and talking trifles, the wind seeming to catch up her laughter and toss it out to sea. Nights, they had danced and spoken scarcely at all. Then the last night out, the weather having turned balmy, they had strolled out late and stood watching the moon path shimmer on the dark, heaving water. She had spoken of her parents' air crash. Insurance had seen her through school, too; engineering school, Jed was astonished to learn. And he, holding his voice steady, had told of his mother's last year of agony and of how it had torn him into a daily death to watch helplessly the sufferings of the woman who had been his whole family since his father deserted them sixteen years before. They had previously discovered interests in common, passing over those not held in common; and it had seemed a final bond that neither had brothers or sisters or any close family or, in fact, any "home" anyplace, anymore. Each had left his few possessions with a classmate resident in his college town.

Off the dance floor, he had touched her only accidentally or protectively as they climbed shifting companionways or strolled on unsteady decks. Something had warned him: "Don't grab." But, on that moonlit deck, her shadowed eyes had invited and her lips leaving his had trembled. She had insisted, however, that after their three days in Paris each go his planned way.

"I think this is important, but we could be wrong. We could sink and never surface till too late. We're neither of us casual persons. Let's see how we feel in August."

They had exchanged itineraries and she herself had set the date: noon, Café de la Paix, August twenty-fourth, the day of her return sailing, two weeks before his own. He had never for one moment doubted that she would come.

Throughout his travels, he had accumulated Griselle's picture postcards in his side jacket pockets. He now again drew out the last six—the thickset man still watching—and for the third time in as many hours read her last: "Remember: noon, August 24th, Café de la Paix. So much to tell—some funny, some odd, but all wonderful. You the same, I'm sure. Till then and there. Missed you terribly. Griselle."

He pressed his hands against the table edge, then repocketed the cards, rose, tipped his chair against the table, and walked back and up to the lounge. To the chic attendant, he gave the phone number of the small Left Bank hotel they had stayed at in June, then, although in no doubt, asked her the date.

"August twenty-fourth, monsieur."

"And the time?"

"Three thirty-seven."

"And there is only one Café de la Paix? I mean, there isn't a chain or anything?"

"Chain" had to be explained, but finally, masking obvious shock, she assured him that there was only one and this was it.

The thickset man, newspaper in hand, arrived at the attendant's counter as he, Jed, entered his assigned booth. Mechanics completed, he heard the voice of the hotel owner's elegant young nephew:

"Hallo. Ici l'Hotel des Lilas."

Jed suppressed his irritation at the voice. "Hello. This is Jed Waite. I stayed with you—"

"Ah, yes. The friend of Mademoiselle Griselle Adams."

There had also been the way he had looked at Griselle and what Jed had surmised he had been saying to her in his too rapid French as they picked up or dropped off keys.

"Is Miss Adams there?"

"No, Monsieur Waite. Miss Adams is not yet returned."

"But you expect her?"

"Yes, monsieur."

"Today?"

"Yes. From Spain. But only to collect the *baggage* she left with us last June."

"You still have her suitcase? A large green one?"

"But of course!"

"Well, all right then. Thanks."

Attendant-assisted, he then made a series of calls—while the thickset man phoned from the next booth. His own current hotel—the Lilas had been booked full—reported no messages. Griselle's steamship office reported her booking uncanceled and her boat train to leave at five. Then, after reaching three wrong train depots, he heard someone at the right one assure him that the Hendaya Express had indeed arrived on time and intact.

He returned to his table and signaled his waiter—Alain, he had heard him called—and asked what he owed. He paid, overtipped, stepped out into the sunlight, and stood with the sidewalk flow dividing around him. He had not thought past the moment of seeing Griselle. The thickset man was hurriedly paying off *his* waiter. A cab pulled up and discharged a passenger. Jed stepped into it and gave the driver the Lilas address.

In the small, dark, cool lobby, the nephew was sorting mail at his counter desk.

"Ah, Monsieur Waite." The look seemed meant to be both quizzical and knowing. "No, mademoiselle is still not arrived. Yes, one still expects her. And yes, we still have her *baggage*. I have had it brought up and here, as you can see, it is." He indicated the large gray-green case standing by his desk.

Jed thanked him and crossed to sit on the creaking wicker divan. He took a fingered copy of *Réalités* from the matching table, leafed through it, and put it back. He lit a Gaulois, feeling the rough throat heat, and began to feel hungry. He had eaten nothing since his seven A.M. croissant. He smoked three Gauloises to the finger-searing ends, watched the outside door open occasionally to admit returning guests, then began seeing, in his mind's eye, Griselle arriving before the café, searching for him with puzzled eyes, and turning away. He returned to the counter desk, pushed across a coin, and asked the nephew to get him Alain at the Café de la Paix.

Delays followed misunderstandings, but finally Alain was saying, "I regret, monsieur, but no mademoiselle as you describe has arrived. None."

To his shock and shame, hunger was now gnawing at him, and visions of thick ham and cheese on crusty French bread displaced those of Griselle. He could smell and taste the food.

No matter what had happened, Griselle was going to miss her boat train, so there was no telling how long it might be before she arrived. He had not asked whether there was a second Hendaya Express or a second boat train. He asked the nephew for paper, scribbled: "Be right back. Please, please wait, no matter what. Jed," and handed the note across.

"For Miss Adams. In case she comes before I get back."

The workman's café where they had breakfasted in June was just around the corner. A sandwich could not take more than three minutes. He stepped out, swung right, and knocked stumbling into the thickset man from the café. Hurrying on, he threw back a curt "sorry" and reflected that if he, Jed, were being staked out as a rich American pickpocket or holdup prospect, somebody was going to be very disappointed.

At the café, the fat-stomached proprietor set the sandwich he ordered immediately onto the counter, but the thick bread had to be chewed. Jed chewed and swallowed and waved off beer, coffee, and wine. Then change had to be sent out for. When he finally reentered the hotel, Griselle's suitcase no longer sat by the desk.

He felt his pulse race. "She's here! Where?"

The nephew's glance met his and slid away.

"Did she take a room? Which room?"

"I am sorry, monsieur, but the instant you departed—"

Jed had already reached the foot of the stairs.

"—mademoiselle arrived, retrieved her *baggage,* and—"

Jed swung around. "You mean she's come and gone!"

"Unhappily, yes."

"But didn't you give her my note?"

"But certainly! But she was with friends. They had a car waiting—"

Jed glanced at his watch, then ran out to the narrow street, where, however, only a girl on a motor scooter and a *boulangère* sweeping her doorway moved. He sprinted to the boulevard

and there found a cab. "*Gare*—the boat-train station! *Vite!*"
His feet pressed against the cab floor all the way.

As he ran into the station, its clock showed four fifty-eight.
"Boat train! Boat train!" he called, and persons obligingly
pointed. He was stopped, however, and directed to buy a
platform ticket. He did so, and turning, ticket in hand, heard
the train, or some train, beep its departure.

When he reached the platform, the train was already moving. He strode, trotted, then ran alongside, looking desperately into windows, although Griselle need not, of course, be
by a window. Then the train was passing him and he stopped.
Faces, faces, faces, then the crazy orange beret, the swing of
autumn hair—and the sea-green eyes looking through him as
if he did not exist. The sound and the rush of air across his
face increased as the train gathered speed. The last coach
clattered by and, too late, he knew he should have jumped
onto the train. But, at the moment of passing, she had turned
to the man opposite her, and the little whatever-it-had-been
that had caught at his heart whenever she turned her head
had been gone.

Jed wandered back to the station proper. He fought back
his anguish and felt numb. The flash of her passing replayed
itself again and again until gradually the flat face of the man
opposite her grew, displacing hers. An ordinary face, yet wrong—
and unaccountably familiar. It stayed with him until, as he
emerged onto the busy boulevard, he recalled walking in West
Berlin in July. He had felt uneasy and impelled to swing
around, and when he had done so, it had been that face, he
felt sure, he had seen fading back into the sidewalk crowd.

On the corner across and ahead was the large, red, mirror-
columned café at which he and Griselle had once lunched.
He was not hungry and did not want a drink but started toward
it, and, just as traffic intervened, saw across the boulevard his
thickset café man and a taller one in lightweight oatmeal

tweed. They were parting, but both also headed toward the café. Anger flared briefly. If this man was, for whatever inconceivable reason, watching and following him, he was doing it with contemptuous carelessness. Jed had already learned that confrontations abroad, however, lead only to language difficulties and denials. The thickset man reached the sidewalk café and sat down at the first table. Jed continued to the intersection, crossed, and took a corner table near the sidewalk newspaper kiosk, behind the first row of mirrored columns. The tweed-suited man had already rounded the corner, and in a column mirror, Jed saw him sitting at the far side-street end of the café.

Jed ordered a beer and felt again the anguish waiting to engulf him. He watched rendezvous achieved, while around him other solitaries sipped and read or watched the diminishing traffic while waiting for it to be time to eat. He pulled out Griselle's last six scenic-view cards again and read them in sequence, this time not as a lover but with attention to what they were saying. He found no hint, no warning, nothing but travel data and miss-you's, however, until, on the third from last, his attention was caught by ". . . on the Spanish Steps the same intense man as on the Palma boat," and, on the next to last, "So far my erratic path has recrossed with that of three different men. Peculiar—creepy even—but none my type, so don't worry. Small world and all that."

Just faces reseen. Faces. Offered a copy of either Griselle's passport photo or her graduation photo, he had chosen the latter. He did not pull it out. Instead, he thought about re-seeing faces. Tourists do go to the same places. He reached into his other side jacket pocket for Griselle's earlier five cards and felt only fuzz and space. He searched through all his pockets and re-counted the six cards on the table. His waiter started forward, and Jed waved him back. Beyond him, the thickset man was dining. In the column mirror, Jed saw the tweed-suited one drop his glance to his newspaper and aperitif.

He could not have lost those cards. He had not had them out in days, and his pockets were deep and flapped. The thickset man was overtly watching—the man he had knocked into outside the Lilas. Or had it been the other way around? Jed felt inside his jacket and touched wallet and passport. No one would pick pockets for postcards. But then no pickpocket would expect postcards. He tried to remember what had been on them. Nothing of significance, he felt sure, any more than there had been on these last six. Nevertheless, he put the six inside with his passport and wallet. A busboy cleared Thickset's table, and a waiter served cheese and fruit. In the column mirror, Tweedsuit was now openly watching. Jed felt squeezed between them and suppressed the urge to bolt. Could Tweedsuit be spelling Thickset while Thickset ate? Dinner, Jed understood, was important to the French. But were these men French? Somehow, he felt not. In any case, and respectable as they looked, he did not, it now occurred to him, want to lead them back to his hotel. He motioned for a menu. Hunger was returning, and better to be free of that, and these men, before the postponed but inevitable flood of really knowing that Griselle was gone.

He ordered substantially and ate slowly, needing but not interested in the food. Thickset was served coffee and brandy; Tweedsuit, another aperitif. Somewhere the sun set, and the street lamp by the newspaper kiosk came on. By dessert, he had not outsat them, and to his other disinclinations was added that of having either of them behind him on dark streets. The changing café clientele added to his disquiet. He wanted to leave, but alone. Then, considering a washroom trip—would he be followed?—he remembered this tourist café's curious concession to Anglo-Saxon modesty.

It had two descending stairways, marked, respectively, "Dames" and "Messieurs," but dames and messieurs parted decorously only to find themselves again face-to-face as both stairways ended below at the same landing. However, even if these men did not know this, the thickset one sat closer to the men's stairway than did Jed, and, whatever Jed did, one man could follow and the other wait.

Nevertheless, feeling impelled to act, Jed slipped franc notes inconspicuously onto the table, rose, and strolled to the kiosk, so obviously to buy a newspaper that neither the men nor the waiter was perturbed. Staying in Tweedsuit's view, he edged out of his waiter's sight and delayed over his purchase until the waiter hurried to his table, showed relief at finding money, and, since the café was now filling up, snapped his fingers for the table to be cleared at once. Two teenaged girls grabbed the desirable table. Jed stepped back and saw the thickset man stop struggling to get his chair back from his table. Jed took a new table, nearer the men's stairs, from which he could not see Tweedsuit in a mirror, which meant that Tweedsuit could not see him.

Before he could order, Tweedsuit, carrying his newspaper folded, passed on the side street. He faced right to turn at the boulevard corner; then, perhaps at a signal from Thickset, crossed instead and continued along the narrow way toward the Seine.

Momentarily, Thickset was watching his receding back. Jed rose and strode to the men's stairs, seeing, at last glimpse, Thickset again trying to push away a table pulled too close. Once below his line of view, Jed took the steps two at a time, down to the landing, then halfway up the ladies' stairs, where he waited for the sound of steps descending. Then he ran the rest of the way up and out, dodged across the boulevard and side street, and entered the first open shop. He slipped behind a rack of books, took up the first book to hand, and holding it open, watched and waited while his pulse and breathing calmed.

A customer came in. Another left. Finally Jed stepped cautiously out to the darkening boulevard. No familiar persons in view. And none on the side street as he turned onto it. Just occasional couples, twilight strollers, hand in hand or arms about waists or shoulders, as he followed the only route he felt sure of to the Seine and his hotel. These were the streets and this the time of day that he and Griselle had most loved.

He reached the dusk-blue Seine and glanced back. He crossed and, on the quay, slowed abruptly to fade back among other walkers as he saw Tweedsuit ahead. His pulse picked up at this prospect of playing hunter instead of hunted. Tweedsuit, accustomed to being always follower, never followed, or having already assured himself that he was not being followed, never looked around. Jed felt a shaming, never-before-felt sense of power. But at the vast, traffic-swirling Place de la Concorde, he lost him. Playing stalker had, he knew, been only another tactic to delay feeling his loss. Nevertheless, as he walked up the Champs-Elysées, he glanced into each brightly lit café and up and down all side streets. Occasionally, he looked behind him. Then, up one side street, he saw Tweedsuit entering an indoor café. He came right back out, and Jed, having already turned onto the street, stood wavering between whether to get back around the corner or stay put or advance and risk encounter. A cab turned onto the otherwise empty street. Tweedsuit hailed it and got in and it drove off.

That ended that game, but Jed continued to the café and, through its window, saw three unoccupied tables—the bar hid most of the rest of the café. At one, a newspaper lay on a chair. Tweedsuit had not been carrying his newspaper when he came out but had had ample time at the mirror-columned café to finish it. As Jed started to turn away, a patron going to the bar jarred the chair, and from the newspaper's folds emerged the corner of a brightly colored scenic view. Jed reached for the door, but before he touched it a large, roughly dressed man, who had approached silently, pushed by him, entered, and tipped a chair at that table. Jed, still outside, let the door close. The man fetched his drink, sat down, hooked a foot around a leg of the chair holding the newspaper, and began edging it closer and glancing at the paper—gradually appropriating it. Finally, he tossed down the rest of his drink, took up the paper, and rose. Jed moved to a closed shop several doors distant, propped a foot on a low windowsill, and unnecessarily retied a shoelace. The burly man emerged and strode back to the Champs-Elysées. Jed followed, passed around the Place de la Concorde again, and then, in a dark, deserted area below the Jeu de Paume, lost the man and simultaneously panicked at what he had been doing. This type might not be at all amiable about finding himself being followed.

Jed walked on, however, and, rounding a corner, again saw the man ahead. He paced him, staying well back, and became aware that although the man did not look back he was proceeding evasively. He crossed and recrossed streets, stopped and started abruptly and twice circumambulated blocks, then entered the park. Suddenly ahead was the Seine and its sole footbridge, empty of pedestrians. Jed had to fall back farther and wait until the man had crossed. Then he followed swiftly, closing in for fear of losing him in the warren of dark streets behind the Beaux Arts. Entering that dark maze, he felt a chill inside. Even if this man did have Griselle's postcards, did it matter why he had them? He, Jed, had no plan for getting them back and none for what to do if this man swung around to challenge him or disappeared into a doorway, then sprang out. But the man now seemed to be homing. Jed turned cautiously into one last, dark, alleylike street in time to see ahead a large iron door swinging shut in a wall. He sprinted silently and caught it before it latched. He heard an exchange in French, one voice possibly female, then another door closing, and stood asking himself again what he thought he was doing. At the entrance to the street a dark car appeared, blocking it. Jed stepped through the doorway and saw, sitting against the building wall, a bulbous concierge, wine bottle uptilted to her mouth. It was go on or go back. Calling "*troisième*" in, he hoped, an assured voice, he passed before she could lower her bottle, and, as her startled, semifocused gaze followed him, headed for the only visible door and pushed it, hoping it did not lead to broom closet or cellar.

It was heavy and weighted, and he caught it and eased it shut behind him. Before the darkness had become total, he had seen that he stood in a stone stairwell without windows or light switches or fixtures. Footsteps mounted overhead. Since they continued, the brief, faint light he had let in must have gone unnoticed. Should he go farther? Perhaps a flight or two. He slipped off his shoes and immediately felt at a still further disadvantage and knew that this precaution was unnecessary on stone. However, he found himself unwilling to sit down on steps he could not see, and unable to balance on one foot in the dark. Shoes in left hand, he groped forward with his right and encountered a wooden railing that did not creak but gave alarmingly. He shifted the shoes and, with his left hand, touched a dank, invisible wall. Hand-trailing this and encountering textures and substances he dared not guess at, he mounted the spiraling stairs as swiftly and silently as possible.

Every other flight had a landing midway. On the others, the steps, curling round, narrowed to treacherously pointed wedges. No light or sound came from behind any door—if there were doors. The building seemed uninhabited, possibly condemned. Unless he caught up, the man above could disappear into an apartment and he, Jed, would never know which. What he was going to do when and if he did know, he had no idea. And if challenged by *anyone* on this stairway, he had no explanation. Furthermore, he could not foresee how many men might be in the apartment that was his destination, and he was, of course, unarmed, while feeling sure, without evidence, that the man climbing steadily above was not. Did he plan to knock and say, "Sorry to trouble you, but I think you have some postcards of mine"?

Common sense was about to turn him around and take him quickly back down and out and away when he heard a clink of keys and, by listening for it, the clicks of a door opening and shutting above. The top floor, he felt sure, and hurried on toward it; that is, felt his way rapidly up and up to a midfloor landing where the stairs ended abruptly against a wall. His stiffening arms kept him from bumping clangingly into what his hands told him was a bolted iron ladder. Certain that he was now alone in the stairwell, he lit his lighter. A once-black-painted, rusting, flaking ladder rose against the wall to a bolted trapdoor in the ceiling—access, probably, to an attic for making roof repairs. To his left was a knobless door. In the dark again, he felt over this door, then pushed it open and stepped inside, onto a sloping, slippery surface, and felt one sock grow damp. The door sprang shut behind him. He flicked on his lighter again. He seemed to be in a large, tiled shower without faucets or shower head. The door did have an inside knob. He stepped back out and a door below opened, flooding the landing and the half flight to it in dim light. He remembered having heard of a public convenience called "Turkish" and realized that this was no place to hide. Panic said "run" without suggesting where. Voices came from below. He grabbed at and mounted the ladder, sturdier than it had looked, and felt overhead for the trapdoor bolt, then froze. Judging by the ladder, this bolt, unpulled probably for forty years, would be rusted or painted tight or would shriek at being disturbed. But it was moving silently and smoothly and he felt oil on his hands. Equally silently and easily, he pushed up the trapdoor. Then he stepped up two rungs and caught himself as cool air hit his face and he saw, past a steeply pitched roof, a spread of night sky and other Parisian roofs.

The roof tiles looked slippery and loose. For the first time in his life he felt vertigo. He retraced his steps, lowered the trap, and slid in the bolt. Had he created a noticeable draft? Below him the stairwell swung with shadows as someone with a flashlight mounted to the landing. Caught at the ladder top, fully visible to anyone who threw a light and looked up high enough, he watched the burly man he had recently been following, top and side and then back view, reach the landing and disappear into the tiled facility. Both he and his flashlight would be facing Jed when he emerged and, since that cubicle contained neither washbasins nor lights nor mirrors, Jed had only seconds to get down and away.

He let himself rapidly down the ladder, turned, and stepped lightly down the half flight. To his right, just off the stairwell, was an apartment door, ajar, and, beyond that, light but no sound. The door above opened and the flashlight again swung banister shadows onto the walls. From far below came the sound of a new set of footsteps mounting the stairs. The possibly empty, temporarily empty apartment was the only place to go. Jed slipped in—glimpsing in the lighted room at the end of its hall a table holding a typewriter before a wall of shelves—and plunged through an open doorway to his left. The room, a small bedroom, was not unoccupied. Dim light, reflected, via hall walls, from the living room, showed someone, back turned, on the bed—a girl in petticoat and bra, wrists tied behind her and to her tied ankles and both tied to the bed rail. She twisted her head around and there, above the taped mouth, were the autumn hair and sea-green eyes. Jed moved toward her, but the mounting and descending men had met and were entering, talking in a language Jed did not recognize. Jed dived under the bed and, there being no hanging bedclothes, rolled to the far wall. Trousered legs passed the bedroom doorway. Through the walls came the screech of a stiff faucet, the sound of water running, and the faucet screech again. The reflected light brightened, and Jed heard a rustle of paper, then the typewriter clacking.

He rolled out and stood up, feeling humiliated. A hero would have struck with a blunt instrument—what blunt instrument?—from behind the door—this door opened out, not in. But what mattered was that here was Griselle—somehow not on that departing train, not lost to him forever. Grab her and run. He bent to the knots, but they defied his short nails. He stripped off his jacket to cover her, but the jacket covered also the knots. When she seemed to whimper, he dropped to hold her and heard, too late, the squeak of old springs. He froze and listened. The typewriter clattered on. Rage surged at seeing Griselle like this, and without thinking how it would hurt, he stripped the tape from her mouth.

She did not cry out, and the typewriter clacking continued. The typing man would be facing straight down the hall to the front door, and there were two men now, armed almost certainly. The best Jed could do would be to free Griselle and delay the men while she ran. Someone could come to check on her at any moment. He worked feverishly on the ankle knots, not thinking that without freed hands she could never make it down those dark, winding stairs and that her legs might be numb. The ankle cord was so intertwined with the wrist cord that finally he had to switch to the latter. He picked at those knots, near Griselle's lovely, longer nails that could have worked at them so much more effectively, for what seemed an eternity. Then, as the cord loosened abruptly, a knock came on the apartment door. He could only push Griselle down to her original position and himself dive under the bed again, at a complete moral and physical disadvantage if discovered. The typewriter had stopped. Trousered legs passed.

The hall door clicked open, then shut. Two more sets of legs followed the first back toward the living room. Four men, now, at least. The light brightened further. The men were talking in French and occasionally in the unidentified language. Jed crawled out and again attacked the knots, not listening but only grateful for conversation to cover any noise he could not help making.

Griselle shook and rubbed her freed hands. Jed slid her arms into his jacket sleeves, then freed her from the bed frame. They both worked on ankle knots. He had loosened one when a changed intonation and the scrape of chairs on a wooden floor unmistakably indicated departures. How many were going? How many staying? No way to know, and in any case someone surely would check out the bedroom. With silent apology, he took Griselle up in a fireman's lift—he had to keep one hand free—glanced toward the lighted room—the visible men stood, backs turned—and slipped to the hall and out, leaving the door ajar to supply some light.

Carefully but rapidly he felt his way down the winding stairs, ready to run, in spite of the risk of falling at the first sound or flash of stronger light from above. His left foot slid on a worn step. He caught himself and realized that he did not have on his shoes. He had no idea where he had left them. The stairs seemed endless. Down and around. Twice, in spite of care, he scraped Griselle's bare feet against the rough wall and once, at a turn where he had to stay wide of the apexes of the wedge-shaped steps, he banged her head into it. But the whole flight down seemed uncannily soundless and there was still no sound of pursuit, although his shoes must be lying in plain view somewhere and he had not had the wits to shut the bedroom door.

Don't let anyone, he found himself saying silently, *tell you that fleeing downstairs is easier than up. Up may take your wind, but down gets you in the knees and risks plunging you immediately to your destination.* Just as his knees started to buckle, he stepped down to a step that was not down. Recovering, he felt for and found the outside door, pulled it open, and, still bearing Griselle on his shoulder, ran past the astonished-looking, drunken concierge, out through the wall door, down the street to the corner, and on and into the first lighted place—a *tabac* café.

"Call the police! *Gendarmes!*"

The startled proprietor reached for his bar phone, and male customers came forward and took Griselle from him. Someone slid a chair behind his knees. Then, in less time than seemed possible, Griselle was lying untied and covered on a chaise in a back room and he, who had managed to get up and follow, sat beside her, one hand on her arm, a filled cognac glass in the other. Police, in and out of uniform, filled the room. Jed, too exhausted to attempt French, gave his few facts in English, which seemed to suffice. Griselle did the same, and her facts were even fewer. As police arrived and departed, everyone asked or answered in French or English without noticing any lapse in communication. Then four men were thrust into the room—the three Jed had followed or been followed by and the flat-faced man on the train. Jed felt Griselle's arm move under his hand.

"Are these the men?" a businessman-looking detective, who had been quietly present all along, asked.

Jed said, "Yes," and Griselle nodded. The men were taken out, and the detective pulled up a chair. Speaking slowly but clearly in English, he said to Griselle:

"Do not be alarmed. You yourself are safe, and the other young lady will be taken off your boat at Southampton."

Jed interrupted. "What 'other young lady'?"

The detective turned. "Well, when you and Miss Adams

feel able to again ascend those stairs, perhaps your views on things we found in that apartment will answer all our questions."

"You can't ask Miss Adams to go back to that place!"

Griselle pushed up higher on the chaise. "No, I'm all right. My legs are usable again and the hypo has worn off—the one they gave me in that cab I thought I was so lucky to get at the station this morning. I'm starving, but that can wait. I'd like to get this over with—and to know what it was all about. Why kidnap me? I have no money or family. But they had my name. There was no mistake in identity."

A woman brought in sandwiches; then a policewoman brought Griselle's dress and both their shoes. The men returned to the café proper, where Jed put on his shoes and offered to pay for the brandies and sandwiches, which offer was refused. When Griselle had dressed, they all got into police cars and returned to astonish the drinking concierge once more. Jed's knees protested but did take him back up those stairs.

For the first time, he saw the full apartment living room with its sagging couch, two easy chairs, and two straight chairs by the desk table before the wall of shelves. File cabinets stood against the right end wall. Printed cloth on a string covered the one window. The wall shelves held oversized books and magazinelike publications standing book fashion. File folders lay on the table, and clipped to the inside covers of the two open ones were photos—one a copy of Griselle's graduation picture but on flimsy paper and the other a similar print of his own graduation photo. But the detective directed them to the shelves. "Perhaps you can tell us what these are?"

Jed recognized them instantly. "Yearbooks."

"American college yearbooks," Griselle added.

There were hundreds—thick, thin, hardbound, loose-leaf—arranged alphabetically by state. Jed took down his and Griselle's and opened them to where their brief write-ups would be. Both biographies were circled in red, and both pictures were missing—neatly slit out. The detective motioned them to sit down and pushed the open file folders before them. The top page in each seemed to contain a more extensive biography in French and, blocked out in the upper right-hand corner, a list in English of basic facts: name, description, birth date, college, major, and profession-to-be. Then followed this identical information about each:

> *Parents deceased.*
> *No siblings, siblings of parents, or other close relatives.*
> *No permanent home.*
> *No old or close friends.*
> *No, or lapsed, connection with former "hometown."*
> *Career choice: government service.*

Only the last lines differed. His read: "Physical type, except for height, easy to duplicate." Hers read: "Physical type unusual." But below this had been stamped:

QUALIFIED SUBSTITUTE

FOUND AND TRAINED

and below that, in red:

SUBSTITUTION ARRANGED

Early shadows had crept onto the lawn. Jed stood up as his wife called, "Well, the food's finally ready. Are you coming in, or shall I bring it out?"

"Out." Jed started in to help and met her carrying the tray. Slim in slacks and sweater almost the same pale green as her eyes, her autumn hair tied back out of her way, she was still beautiful, and as she turned her head toward a calling bird, his breath caught.

"Do you still have that orange beret?"

"That—? The angora? Oh, yes. Very carefully wrapped and put away upstairs."

LEE RUSSELL *spent her early years in Pittsburgh but attended high school in a small Ohio town and earned a bachelor of arts degree in French from Ohio State. She later obtained a certificate in junior engineering from Rutgers University in New Jersey. She is a member of the Mystery Writers of America and of Mensa and was formerly the editor of* The Mensa Bulletin.

THE EYE
WENT BY

ROB KANTNER

Y ou're a private detective, right?" Carole said.

"Sixteen hundred dollars!" Pat Sajak said. "What do you want to do now?"

"I'll spin," said the contestant.

"Okay," Sajak said doubtfully as the contestant bent to the wheel.

I pried my eyes away from the TV and looked at Carole. "You know I'm a private detective. So what?"

She flattened her paperback on her stomach and slid into a half-upright position on the sofa. "Detectives are supposed to be *exciting*," she said.

"Says who?"

The contestant asked for an M. Sajak gave his regrets. The

next contestant spun the wheel to the claps and cheers of the audience. I looked back at Carole, who was giving me a dark stare. "Says all the books and the movies," she answered.

"Oh, them."

"Yeah, *them!* I've been reading a lot of these books lately, and—"

"Maybe you'll pass along some pointers sometime." I looked back at the screen just in time to see the wheel hit BANK-RUPT.

"And," she went on, *"these* detectives are *always* doing exciting things. Solving mysteries, apprehending criminals, righting wrongs. Then I look at you, lying there on the La-Z-Boy, cigar in one hand, beer can in the other, feet up in the air with a big toe poking through—"

"You making some point here?"

She turned and sat straight on the sofa and crossed one mile of tanned leg over the other. "I don't know. I invite you over for the evening, and what do we do? Sit around, *that's* what we do."

"Hey, I'm not particular. Find me a nice tasty little crime and we'll fool around with it, kid." I grinned. "Beggars can't be choosers."

"I'm no beggar!"

I snorted. "I didn't mean you. I meant—"

"Beggars can't be choosers!" the contestant squealed.

"You got it!" Sajak trilled as the orchestra played and the audience applauded.

"I got it before *she* did," I muttered.

Carole did her sarcastic one-hand clap. Will Somers, Carole's stocky, blond six-year-old, trotted into the living room. "Ben, can you help me, ole buddy?"

I should mention here that Will isn't my kid, he's Carole's. And Carole, who'd been a steady squeeze for a while, wasn't anymore. We had a platonic relationship based on mutual need. She lawyered for me, I did fixing for her. Service for service, no cash changing hands; just two more cogs in the great underground economy.

"What do you need, Will?" I asked him.

"Can you read me this book?" Will asked, advancing on me shyly.

"Sure, kid." I hadn't seen Will much that evening; besides, the contestant was choosing her prizes, and I just knew she'd end up with the life-size porcelain dog.

Will handed me the book. I knew the blue cover well— *The Fly Went By*, by Doctor Seuss. I knew the story even better, having read it to Will about eight zillion times. A kid gets involved in a chase, with a whole sequence of connecting episodes. About as much like real life as the detective thrillers Carole reads. Will could never seem to get enough of it. He'd sit there and listen to me read, nodding, mouthing the words, eyes bright and face happy, innocently secure in the predictable. The essence of entertainment.

"Gentlemen," Carole said. We looked at her. "First, if you don't mind, an errand. We need milk."

"Ohhhh," Will said.

"No problem," I answered, aware that I was almost done with the last beer in inventory. "Take care of it right quick. Have to pick up some gas, too. I'm running on fumes."

"Can I go with you?" Will asked.

"I don't care. You care?" I asked Carole.

"I don't care. But, Ben?" I squinted at her as I rose. "Just a *small* candy bar. And don't do any lollygagging out there."

I held out my hand to Will, who took it. "Just going for milk," I said to Carole. "Routine. Like you say: boring, boring, boring."

"Can I have a treat at the store?" Will asked.

"We'll see." I answered absently because I'd become interested in the gold Toyota Corona ahead of us. There was a couple in the front seat, and in the early evening light I could see that they were having an argument. The man drove, the woman rode shotgun, and they looked at each other more than straight ahead, tossing silent shouts back and forth. I kept my '71 Mustang front bumper hard up on the Toyota, watching the occupants intently.

"Maybe some bubble gum," Will said.

"Sure, fella." The woman in the Toyota lunged at the driver, smacking him on the side of the head. The driver grabbed her permed hair with his right hand, pulled her toward him, then jammed her head hard against the passenger side window. I gripped the Mustang wheel harder. "Jesus Christ!"

"What, Ben?" Will asked.

Red reflected blip-blip-blip in my rearview mirror. I tossed a glance over my shoulder. Cycle cop. I pulled over, slowing, praying for him to zip past me. He did not oblige, just followed me down as we slowed to the curb. I shut off the engine, popped open the glove compartment, and dug for the paperwork as the cop propped his bike on its kickstand and swaggered toward my Mustang. "We got trouble, Will," I said.

"Oh no," the boy answered.

The young, fresh-faced, helmeted policeman leaned against my Mustang. "Okay, let's see it," he said.

I handed over license and registration and proof of insurance. He squinted at it, then looked at me. "You know I gotcha doing fifty in a thirty-five."

The Toyota was long gone. I frowned up at the cop. "So, like, guilty as charged. I can take the weight. Write me up and let's be done with it."

" 'Preciate your cooperation. Lemme go pester the computer. I'll be right with you." He started back toward his cycle but had made only ten feet when an old rusted station wagon blasted past us, sideswiping a VW bug parked innocently across the street from me. The next thing I heard was the cop's cycle fire up. He cruised up to my car, hollered "Drive more careful next time," tossed my paperwork at me, and shot past like a bullet after the station wagon.

"What happened?" Will asked.

"There is a God, my boy," I answered, as I put the Mustang in gear and gunned up the street.

Will sat on his knees in the bucket seat, peering over the dashboard. "What's the policeman doing?"

"He's going to catch that bad guy there. Watch." I was doing nearly fifty on the side street, trying to keep up with the cop, who in turn gained fast on the rusted station wagon, flasher blinking. The station wagon did not slow down. The cop, who drove the bike with the flamboyance of a rookie, swerved left and pulled up alongside the wagon. They rode side by side like that for a second; then the wagon, without slowing, pulled left, crowding the bike, forcing it closer, closer, closer to the left-hand berm till the cop, who didn't have the sense to slow down or speed up, shot off the street onto the shoulder and down into the grassy ditch. Even so, he probably wouldn't have lost it if he hadn't stood on his brakes. The bike slewed sideways and then down in the shaggy weeds, the cop flying the other way head over heels like a cowboy who'd been shot off his horse.

I slowed slightly as we reached him. The cop was crawling shakily to his feet, apparently uninjured except maybe for his pride. I hollered out the window, "I'll get him for ya," slammed my shifter into second, and popped the clutch. The Mustang catapulted forward with a long scream of rubber and hurtled forward, pressing us back into our bucket seats.

"We gonna catch him, Ben?" Will asked excitedly.

"Yes, sir. Friend to law enforcement everywhere," I muttered.

The station wagon hung a right. I did the same, faster,

thanks to my racing suspension, and charged up, gaining on him. We entered an older residential area, with cars parked sporadically on both sides of the street. The wagon heedlessly slalomed back and forth, dodging cars. I stayed with him grimly, sure that he couldn't keep it up for long, and he didn't. He tried to shoot a four-way stop ahead of a pickup truck, just barely missed being broadsided, and had just recovered from that when he suddenly had to jink right to avoid being hit by a car backing out of a driveway. His outboard tires slammed the sharp stone curb on the right and then jumped it and mowed down three mailboxes in rapid sequence, gaining fast on a Hertz rental truck parked peacefully at the curb by a vacant lot. His right front tire, apparently damaged by the curb, chose that moment to let go, and the station wagon lost control completely, going into a smoky sideways spin, which ended when he plowed into the rental truck.

I geared down, squealed to a stop at the curb, fifty feet back of the collision, shut off the motor, retrieved my .45 automatic from its clip beneath the bucket seat, and threw open the door. The wagon's driver's-side door was open, and a young skinny permhead was racing like a track star into the vacant lot, which was empty except for weeds and a forest of Detroit Edison electrical towers. "Stay put," I hollered to Will, and jumped out of the Mustang and took off running after the perp. A hundred yards into the race I knew it was no good. The perp was twenty years younger, was in better shape, and had adrenaline to fuel him. Arms and legs pumping, he gained steadily, then took a ten-foot chain link fence with a scrambling climb and effortless drop like he'd been doing it all his life. I skidded to a stop in the weeds as the perp ran on and was engulfed by a thick stand of trees. My .45 hung heavy and useless in my hand. No matter how tempting it is, I don't whack a man just because he drives like a maniac.

Panting, I hoofed heavily back toward the Mustang. Will

had disobeyed my orders and was walking hesitantly toward the station wagon, which sat on two flats, steaming, married to the back of the rental truck. "Get back in the car, kiddo," I hollered.

Will looked at me, and I thought he said, "Baby crying."

"Back in the *car*, damn it!"

"Baby crying!" Will shouted back.

I trotted to him and, from somewhere in the wagon, heard a thin wailing. Holding Will back with one hand, I opened the back door. The evening light was rapidly fading, but I had no trouble seeing the securely belted child seat, the little booties waving in the air, and the tiny, toothless, teary-eyed baby face wailing plaintively at me.

"Is it a boy or a girl?" Will asked from the back seat as we drove.

"Boy, I guess. Wearing a blue shirt. Haven't researched it further." Though, judging from the smell, I'd have to pretty soon.

The baby's crying had tailed off to an occasional breathy wail. I heard Will say, "Nice baby." Then: "What're we gonna do, Ben?"

"Find a phone," I said, hanging a right on a four-lane commercial street. "There's a name and phone number stenciled on the baby seat there. Must be the mother."

"Why'd that man run away from him?"

"No idea." A self-service gas station hove into sight on the left. "We'll drop on in here, top off the tank, and make our call from here. Okay, Will?"

"I have to go to the bathroom."

"We'll take care of that, too." I wheeled the Mustang in and stopped at the pump island next to high-test. As I got out, a young dark-skinned man in denims strolled out of the building toward me. "Fill it up for you, sir?"

"Thought this was self-serve."

"Happy to oblige," he grinned.

Miracles never cease. Nobody's pumped my gas since Nixon was in. "Suit yourself. Got a phone here?"

"Busted. Sorry."He pulled the nozzle from the pump, hit the switch, opened my gas cap, stuck the nozzle in, and started to fill. "Try up the street."

"Okay." Will climbed out of the Mustang behind me. "Round the side, I guess," I told him. He nodded and walked away. I leaned against the fender and glanced through the back window at the baby. He lay there in his car seat, mouth agape, staring around, mostly quiet now. Tough kid.

"Where's your boy going?" the attendant asked me.

"The head," I answered offhand.

The pump shut off. The attendant withdrew the nozzle and snapped it back into the pump. I hauled out my wallet and was picking through the bills in search of a sawbuck when I saw that the attendant was walking away. "Gas free, too?" I called.

He didn't look back or respond, just walked purposefully to a newish Chevy Nova parked in front of the station office and got in.

"Hey. Hey, Jack. Where are you going?"

He fired up the motor, squealed back, then shot forward and swerved out of the lot onto the crowded street.

I held my wallet, staring dumbly after him, then swiveled and stared at the station office. Empty. What the hell, guy fills my tank and then splits. I had no time to puzzle it further because just then Will appeared around the corner of the station, walking stiff-legged, eyes saucerlike, mouth moving soundlessly. I instinctively started for him and found my voice. "What's up, Will?"

The boy raised a big fist and jabbed his finger back the way he'd come. "A man! In there, by the pee pot!" he managed.

I moved faster. "What man?"

"In there, Ben! You gotta help!"

I reached the boy, almost ordered him to stay put, then changed my mind and took him with me to the half-open men's room door, from which issued a black work shoe topped by a white sock.

For having been robbed, pistol-whipped, drop-kicked, gagged, and left hog-tied around the men's room commode, the gas station attendant was pretty damn arrogant. When I'd released him, he refused to let me use the station phone. He refused my offer to wait around to give the cops my story. He shrugged off my solicitous comments with a sneer. This was the eighth time he'd been robbed, and relieved of the smallest take yet, only twenty-two bucks. It was routine for him, probably rating a casual mention on his job description. He didn't even call the police, just reported the event to his corporate office and then lighted a cigarette and stood fidgety and obnoxious, plainly desiring my immediate departure, behaving as though I was the one who committed the crime instead of the one who freed him from his wire and adhesive-tape bonds on the soiled, stinking men's room floor.

I loaded Will into the Mustang and motored up the street, bound for a grocery store. Will sat in the back, excitedly telling the gurgling baby the whole story. I sat in the front, planning my strategy. Call the phone number from the baby's car seat, get an address. Pick up the milk and beer I'd started out for. Go to the address and drop off the baby and then head the hell back to Carole's house, where we'd be safe.

The light was about gone when we reached the grocery store. I parked in the crowded lot, hoisted the baby out of his car seat, and carried him with one arm while holding Will's hand with my free one as we headed for the entrance. The baby felt toothpick light, soft and warm, totally trusting as he cooed and whispered nonsense to the side of my face. Will looked up at me and smiled confidently. Six-year-olds trust you, too.

The entranceway to the store was deserted except for a trio of young men, the oldest maybe seventeen, dressed uniformly in dark tight pants, tight white shirts open to the solar plexus, gold chains shining against their brown skins. One of them, the biggest, sauntered toward me as we reached the sidewalk. "Hey, man, do me a favor," he said snottily, half blocking my way.

I stopped and dropped Will's hand. "Not tonight, pal. Go screw."

"Now ain't *that* some way to talk," he sneered, jamming his hands meaningfully into his pockets. "Want you should fetch us out here a six of PBR tallboys, that's all."

"You're not old enough, wise guy."

He drew himself up straight and nudged me hard with his shoulder, eyes narrowing. "Old enough," he answered. His partners spread out, circling us. "Old enough, you read me? Whaddya say?"

I smiled. "Oh, sure, you seem like a reasonable enough sort to me. Excuse me just a second." I held the baby down and out to Will, who extended his arms. "Can you handle this, Will?"

"Sure, Ben," Will said. He took the baby, jaw set, eyes fixed fearfully on the others.

I grinned. "Knew I could count on you, guy." Then I turned to the leader. "I suppose you got something lethal in that pocket, huh, bro?"

"Lethal enough."

"Mind if I see for myself?" I grabbed the kid's floppy white shirt collar and gave it a hundred-eighty-degree twist, pulling him toward me roughly. At the same time I thrust my other hand middle-knuckle-deep into his pants pocket, gripped it hard, and tore it off.

The clasped switchblade clattered out onto the sidewalk, accompanied by a rain of change. I said, "Oh no, a deadly weapon," tightened my grip on his shirt collar, and gave him my best short-armed left jab, square on the nose.

He screamed through a spray of blood. I threw him back against the grocery store wall and faced the others just as one darted toward Will. He stopped in freeze frame. I fixed him with a stare. "You move one step closer to that child and I'll run you down and stomp you. I swear I will."

The leader wheezed and moaned on the sidewalk behind me. The punk ahead of me raised his hands and shrugged. I held my hands out to Will, who handed me the baby. I cuddled him against me and took Will's hand. "I better not see you later, gentlemen," I said, and led Will into the grocery.

The milk was no problem. Neither was the beer. The problem was my phone call, which I attempted from a public phone at the front of the store. The number kept ringing busy. I must have tried twenty times in ten minutes, with no success. Finally I got smart and looked up the woman's last name—Evans—in the book. There was an Evans with the correct number at an address just a few blocks away. I'd just finished writing it down when I noticed a disturbance by the checkout counters.

A tall, clean-cut young blond guy was passing the checkouts, carrying a case of cigarette cartons toward the automatic doors. One of the bag boys straightened from his work, stared at him, then yelled, "Hey, stop! You haven't paid for that!"

The blond crouched into a trot, headed at maximum speed for the exit. The bag boy knocked aside a couple of old ladies and gave the blond a clumsy, full-body tackle. They went to the floor, and the case of cigarettes hopped away, landing against a freestanding display of canned corn. The blond, stronger, more agile, more motivated, regained his leverage first and braced the slighter bag boy and throat-punched him. The bag boy gagged but did not relinquish his half nelson on the blond.

The crowd of customers and grocery employees stood frozen, shell-shocked, gape-mouthed. One of the cashiers found her voice. "Somebody help him."

I was already handing the baby to Will, who had the presence of mind to hang on tight. I threw myself at the grappling pair and slammed into the blond, managing to get a good grip on his longish hair. He kneed the bag boy back from him, slipped me easily, and came up with an uppercut to my chin that rang my gong with an almost audible sound. I went back and down, butt colliding hard with the unforgiving tile floor. The blond turned clumsily to make good his escape, but I managed to trip him, and he skidded down, sliding toward the door. He skittered up immediately, with all the advantage. I was headed up from all fours, firing up the rockets again, when the blond, unaccountably, came hurtling back past me into the vegetable display, sending it over with a crash of canned corn. He lay there, eyes open but unfocused, as I lurched to my feet and looked toward the entrance while the onlookers exhaled all at once.

There, grimacing with pain, rubbing his fist, stood the white-shirted kid from outside. His right-hand pants pocket flapped free where I'd ripped it. His nose was bent, his upper lip was black with drying blood, his eyes were pinched, but he grinned at me snottily. "Not bad, huh, bro?"

"Why?" I managed.

"My brother," he said, staring down at the moaning shoplifter. "I've told him and *told* him not to commit no crimes."

Customers were moving all at once, most of them intent on escape. I went to Will and took the baby back as Will picked up the grocery bag. We met the punk at the door, and at my instructions Will gave him the six-pack of beer we'd bought.

The baby's address was on a narrow, curbless side street about six blocks from the store. I drove at a fast crawl, squinting at the house numbers in the near darkness. I wanted to be done with this. The baby had been pretty good so far, but he was starting to fuss and whine. Probably needed feeding or changing or something, damned if I could tell; I don't know nothing about babies, birthin' 'em or anything else.

Will perched on his knees on the bucket seat next to me, leaning forward, eyes intent. "We almost there, Ben?"

"Gotta be one of these on the right." I slowed. "Yep, that's it, praise be . . . oh, bloody hell!"

A boxy, silver Ford Escort wagon had backed out of the driveway and was tearing up the street away from me. I scanned the flat-roofed, single-story brick house it had left. The correct address, all right. No lights on. Place was deserted, and whoever lived there was taking off up the street in the Escort, nearly out of sight now.

"Buckle up, Will," I said grimly, popped the clutch, and gunned the engine.

The Escort was long out of sight, having rounded a corner. I followed as fast as I could, ignoring the 25-mph speed limit. I caught sight of it again as it made a right on a larger artery. By the time I made that corner, I had gained quite a bit. There were no cars between us. I began flashing my brights and honking my horn as I closed on the Escort, trying to catch its attention. Half a block ahead was a railroad crossing, and as we approached, the warning lights began to flash, the bells began to clang, and the blinking gates started down.

"Okay, Will, we got 'em cornered," I said.

The Escort slowed to a halt, then lurched left and started around the gate. Off to the right a dissonant train whistle blared. Some distance yet, but could be coming fast. As the Escort rolled onto the rails it twisted right to go around the other gate, but it never made it.

It stopped there, dead on the tracks, as I screeched to a halt at the crossing.

Over the rumbling of the Mustang motor I could hear the whine of the Escort's starter motor. The driver, apparently alone, hunched over the wheel. The train whistle issued again. I ripped open my door and jumped out. "Stay put, Will," I hollered, then trotted toward the Escort as the driver climbed out clumsily.

She was a short young butterball with long black hair rubber-banded back into a ponytail. In the bleaching light of the Mustang's headlights, her eyes were enormous, her face corpse-pale. "It needs a tune-up!" she wailed. "I've been meaning to get around to it!"

The train horn sounded again. I could smell gas. "Flooded. Get yourself off these tracks, Mrs. Evans."

She started toward me, blinking. "You know me?"

"No, but I've got your kid back there in the car." I went to the Escort and opened the driver's door. "*Other* side of the tracks!" I snapped. "I can't push your car back the way you came."

She froze. "My baby! My little Charlie! How'd you—"

"Never mind." I reached into the Escort, fiddled the stick into neutral, and, leaning on the door frame, began to push.

"I want him!" she screamed. "Get him for me! My ex snatched him right out of the nursery. I'd left him alone for just a second—"

I released the car, having moved it about one foot. "Okay. You get yourself to the other side there, well back." I dodged the flashing gate and ran back to the Mustang. Will had the passenger seat pulled forward, enabling me to squeeze the baby carrier out of the back. I ran back over the tracks to where Mrs. Evans waited. Tears as big as marbles ran down her round face as I handed her the baby. "Oh, thank you, thank you," she sniffed, looking down at him. I was halfway back to the Escort when I heard her say, "Didn't you even *change* him?"

The train horn screamed and the engine's headlight caught me as it rounded a curve, churning hard. I resumed my position at the driver's side of the car and leaned with all my strength against the door frame, rocking the car back and forth, back and forth. The train horn screamed again and the Escort broke loose and rolled off the tracks. I gave it one last vindictive push; then, as it rolled slowly to a stop on the other side, I dived headlong back over the tracks and under the gate, sliding hard on the coarse gravelly asphalt as the train, with one last vicious scream, reached the crossing.

I climbed clumsily to my feet and limped to the Mustang and fell in the driver's side. I was sore and scraped and revved up with adrenaline. Will for once paid no attention to the freight cars chugging by; he was beaming at me with admiration. "You beat the train!"

"Reckon so." I leaned back in the bucket seat and lighted a short cork-tipped cigar and smoked it silently as we waited, and waited, and waited. Finally the caboose came and went and the gates lifted. The young butterball, and her baby, and her Escort, were gone. Naturally.

We'd almost reached Carole's house when, lo and behold, the gold Toyota appeared ahead of us.

Almost immediately I saw the driver backhand his companion across the face. She got hold of his free arm and bent to it and seemed to bite it. The Toyota swerved and nearly jumped the curb. I fell back from it, just to play it safe, and felt Will's eyes on me.

"Aren't you going to do something?" he asked hesitantly.

"Nope."

Will looked ahead at the Toyota, then back at me. "But they're fighting."

"Let 'em." I glanced at him. "We done took care of our share of problems, Will. For one night, anyhow."

The Toyota made a sudden left-hand turn from the right-hand lane and disappeared. A few seconds later Will broke the silence.

"I was scared."

"Really? Sure didn't act like it."

"That little . . . and the man in the bathroom . . . and those bad men at the store . . ."

I swerved into the parking lot of a Jesse James convenience store, parked, reached out a hand, and squeezed his shoulder roughly. "They couldn't hurt us," I said. "I wouldn't let them."

"I was scared."

I breathed deeply, searching for simple words. "What it is, Will, is, there's bad people all over the place. Always have been, always will be. Don't ask me why, I'm not that smart. But what I do know is that if you're lucky enough to be big and strong and halfway bright, you got a duty to stop the bad people and help the good people because a lot of the good people aren't strong enough to be able to help themselves."

"I was scared."

I looked at him for a long moment. "Well, so was I." I grinned. "The trick is never to let anyone realize it."

Carole, face dark and unreadable, met us at the door. We trooped past her into the living room. The game show was, of course, long over. And from the looks of the VCR it was clear that Carole hadn't taped the bonus round for me. Rats.

"So what's the story, fellows?" Carole asked finally.

"Had to get gas," I answered.

"Stuck by a train, too," the carefully coached Will said.

"You've been gone a whole *hour*, fellows," Carole said in her patented glass-cutter tone.

"Just another boring errand," I said airily, and went into the kitchen to put the milk away. When I returned to the living room, Will was sitting on the couch next to his mother, holding his book. "Can you read this to me now, Ben?"

The Fly Went By again. "Read it? I feel like we just *lived* it."

"What?" Carole asked darkly.

"Later, Carole, okay? Later."

I sat down and read Will the book. After that we put Will to bed. Back in the living room, I assumed the position in the La-Z-Boy and stretched my legs and lighted a cigar, trying to get interested in a New York City private detective with no visible means of support. Carole disappeared into the kitchen, came back with a hefty shot of Jack Daniels Black, handed it to me, then sat on the couch, crossed her legs, crossed her arms, smiled with utter certainty, and said: "Spill it, Ben."

Here goes nothing. I began the story, keeping it light and casual, hoping she'd still be speaking to me when I finished.

ROB KANTNER was born in Ohio, reared in Georgia, and now lives in the Detroit area. A graduate of Eastern Michigan University, he works as an advertising executive. His first short story, "C Is for Cookie," appeared in Alfred Hitchcock's Mystery Magazine in 1982. Since then, some twenty-five of his short stories, many featuring Detroit private detective Ben Perkins, have appeared there and elsewhere. His first Perkins novel, The Back-Door Man, was published by Bantam Books in 1986. Its sequel, The Harder They Hit, appeared in 1987. Dirty Work, the third novel in the series, published in 1988, will be followed by Hell's Only Half Full in 1989. Kantner has been honored by the Private Eye Writers of America with five nominations for their Shamus award, and in 1986 was awarded the Shamus for best short story of the year ("Fly Away Home") as well as the Shamus for best paperback novel of the year (The Back-Door Man).

WESTERN WIND

JANET O'DANIEL

*T*he girl lay on her side, closed her eyes, and listened to the rain. The hay in the shed smelled sweet around her. One of nature's more inspired treats for the senses—dry, fragrant hay and summer rain on a shed roof. And so it would have seemed now except that she was tied, her hands bound with soft bridle rope. Her jaw was sore, her whole head throbbing. The shed door was locked on the outside with a padlock. She had heard it click.

"Standing with reluctant feet where the brook and river meet." That was what her mother had said about her. It has to do with growing up, she had told Margaret. *But I was never going to grow up,* Margaret thought, remembering. *I never wanted to. Maybe now I never will.*

He said I was already grown. "Let her be, she's grown up, for God's sake." He said that over and over. "She's a woman now, Grace." I hated him right from the first, she thought.

Yet it was odd how far removed she felt from it all now. She could still remember the last day, weeks ago, when it had been peaceful and safe. If I'd known that was the last good day, she thought, would I have appreciated it more? Would I have done anything different?

She could see herself, or the girl she had been then, as she led the last two horses down the slope late that afternoon, into the pasture where the grass was tall and bright green with early summer growth. She could see herself sliding the loose leads from around their necks and slapping the horses through the gate, closing it behind them and fastening it with a loop of wire. Then she had walked along the line of fence that fronted the dirt road, examining it. Tomorrow, she remembered thinking, she would go over the rest of it—that part where the woods began. Danger could come from the woods.

She had had great faith in fences then.

She had turned back up the path after that, heading toward the house and stable. All the paths were part of the route the riders took—"Miles of Scenic Trails," according to the sign at the end of the dirt road where the country road met it.

"We should repaint that," Grace, her mother, would often say, looking critically at the sign. "It's badly faded." And Margaret, feeling uneasy, would say, "It's all right, though, isn't it? I mean, people know where we are."

Grace would shrug and push back the light hair that had blown across her face. "I suppose . . . "

At the top of the path Margaret had paused, that last day, to look back down the slope at the eight horses in the lower meadow. They stood knee-deep in grass, heads lowering to it, tails switching. Then she turned toward the house. It was small and, like the sign, in need of paint. Its clapboards had

grown gray. The red rambler at the back door hid the propane
tanks. Margaret opened the door, a wood-frame screen door
with a spring to pull it shut and a hook to fasten it. It made
a squeak when she entered.

"What's that smell?" she demanded.

"An omelet," her mother said. "I put herbs in it. And we
still have asparagus. I picked strawberries today, too, so we'll
have biscuit shortcake."

"I'm starved."

Grace smiled at her. She was wearing a white apron over
her red shirt and her jeans, and her face was pink from the
heat of the stove. Her blonde hair was pulled back and tied
with a red ribbon. Grace was at her best when cooking—
perhaps, Margaret thought, because it was the thing she liked
best.

Margaret looked around the kitchen, which was painted
yellow and was the safest place she knew. Yellow was the safest
of all colors, she thought. They had painted it the year before,
almost as soon as Grandfather's funeral was over. "I hate the
smell of the stuff!" the old man had railed at them from his
sickbed when they had suggested painting it earlier. "Go ahead,
if you want to kill me." So of course they had not. But after
he was dead months later, and after the neighbors had left—
strangers with polite, staring faces—they had hurried to change
their clothes and get out the paint that had been put aside.
They had worked far into the night on it, and when they had
finished had cleared a corner of the sheet-covered table and
eaten baked beans and coleslaw and lemon layer cake with
seven-minute icing, all donated by those same neighbors.

"Not much imagination," Grace had commented, "but very
kind of them." And they had grinned together, feeling their
freedom.

On that last safe day, they sat across from each other over
the blue-and-white tablecloth and ate the yellow omelet and

tender asparagus stalks. As she ate, Margaret counted the cookbooks that stood on a shelf to the right of the sink. There were fourteen of them—all greasy, all thumbed. At the end of the shelf was a book of poetry. Often Grace read from it, standing beside the stove and stirring. Sometimes she read aloud, when she knew the poem was one that Margaret would like—especially those that were apt to have horses in them. Alfred Noyes, for instance: "Back he spurred like a madman, shrieking a curse to the sky" was a line Margaret loved. And Walter de la Mare's "The Listeners" ("'Is there anybody there?' said the Traveller"), which always made the small hairs on her arms stand up.

"I have to go to the feed store tomorrow," Grace said. "So you'll have to stay home and wait for Mr. Pearce. It's his day."

"All right." Margaret did not mind Mr. Pearce, the blacksmith. He was one of the safe ones, an old man with strong knotty hands and startling false teeth. He came each month and looked after the horses' feet.

"When you get your license that's going to be your job, going for the feed, Miss Maggie," Grace said, smiling at her. "If the truck holds out that long."

Margaret's heart lurched as she prayed the truck would hold together because they needed it so badly, and then prayed it would explode and fly apart one day as it stood parked beside the stable, because getting a license meant taking a test—sitting beside some critical stranger who would judge her.

"Ready for shortcake?" Grace asked.

The biscuits were little white puffs with butter melting over them, and the strawberries were rubies. Over the top they put sweet cream that they had to scoop out of the pitcher with a spoon.

The day had had a perfection about it, from the horses in the new grass to the jeweled shortcake. *Nothing that could have been improved upon,* Margaret thought. It was only after that that the danger came.

She remembered that she had brought the horses up from the field early the next morning to have them ready for Mr. Pearce.

"I won't be long," Grace had said, climbing into the truck.

Margaret nodded and waved her off, watching the truck all the way down the dirt road to the county hardtop. When the noise of the motor had died away, she could hear only the grainy chewing of the eight horses behind her in their stalls, where all eight heads were bent to their feed boxes. That, and the circling cry of the wind.

I wouldn't live except on a hilltop, Margaret thought.

Presently she took a fork and barrow and went through the stable's rear door into the riding ring. Beginners and small children used the ring, and it was where Grace gave lessons. Margaret scooped manure and raked the hard earth into tidiness. She had just finished the job when she heard the blacksmith's truck rattling up the road. His truck was as old as their own but in better repair. "My nephew keeps after it," old Mr. Pearce had explained to them. "I only know about horses." It was one of the reasons she did not mind him.

Margaret hurried out to the front of the stable. The truck had already pulled up, and the door was opening. Something about that door opening struck Margaret with a chill. It was too abrupt, too businesslike. Mr. Pearce always edged out of his truck in a cautious, old-man way. She stood rigid and watched as a stranger got down and turned to her.

"Morning," he said.

"Morning," Margaret answered, but she was not sure she spoke aloud. The stranger was a tall man, broad-chested and bulging in his worn jeans and plaid shirt. He wore run-over boots and a Western hat, which he took off now and tossed back into the truck. He had light brown hair, thinning a little at the temples, but she thought that he was not old, even so.

"Where's Mr. Pearce?" she whispered.

He gave her a curious look. "He died—didn't you hear? I'm his nephew, Eddie James. I been trying to keep up with his calls."

She gasped. "But he was here last month!"

His gray eyes went over her, looking cold and dangerous. "Well, he died since last month."

"We didn't hear."

"Yeah. Well." He went around to the back of the truck, opened the tailgate, and pulled the anvil forward to rest on it. "How many horses you got—eight, is it?"

"Yes. Eight."

"Any problems?"

"No. I don't know. I guess not."

His eyebrows went up, and he reached into his shirt pocket for a package of gum. "Well? You want to start bringing 'em out?" He took two sticks of gum and unwrapped them, jammed them both in his mouth, and then made a gesture with the package toward her. She shook her head and fled into the stable.

He had a portable radio on the seat of the truck, and as he worked he listened to country music, humming along with it and shifting the gum about in his mouth.

"This fella looks pretty good," he said of Royal, the black gelding that was Margaret's own horse. "You the one keeps his feet clean?"

"Yes."

"Been hurt though. What happened to his leg? Barbed wire?"

"He put his foot through it."

"Ooh doggies. Looks like it was pretty tore up. You have to have the vet for him?"

"We fixed it."

"Who's we?"

"My mother and I."

"You two run this place?"

"Yes."

"No daddy?"

"No." She hated letting him in on their secrets.

"I come here from Texas last year," he said. "Come for a visit and stayed on, helping Uncle Ned. Then I got me a little business going—repairing cars and like that. Little shop out back is all. Then he died on me. I don't know. Might stay on here, might go back home." He trimmed, cut, pounded. The morning, which had been so silent, with only the wind and the horses, had grown nervous with sound. The clanking, metal on metal, the snap of his gum, the blare of the radio. "One more heartache doesn't matter, I still love you—"

He was an intrusion, filling all the space around him. She would rake up after he was finished, Margaret thought. Clear away all the callused hoof trimmings and scraps, then rake over the tire tracks, too, to erase him.

Grace was not surprised, when she returned, to see the stranger there.

"They told me in the feed store," she said. "I'm so sorry about Mr. Pearce." She gave Margaret a quick, anxious look.

Eddie James told her about Texas and about his shop. "Might stay on, I don't know. Might go back."

The wind was blowing a loose strand of hair across Grace's cheek. She caught at it and gave a little laugh. "Is it hard to decide?"

"Yeah. Well, right now, see, I'm trying to do two jobs." He was looking at the strand of hair.

He was done in four hours; it was faster than old Mr. Pearce had worked. "I'll write you a check," Grace said.

"No hurry. I'll help you unload those feed bags."

"Oh—goodness, we can do that."

"They're fifty pounds each!" he said. "That's no job for a woman."

Margaret shrank back into the shadows as he began taking the feed bags out of the truck, lifting them easily and swinging them down, ripping them open, and emptying them into the big metal drums in the feed room. He filled the stable with his huge shoulders, his powerful swinging arms. Each time he came through the doorway, he blotted out the light for an instant.

"You two could sure use some help around this place," he said.

That afternoon, Margaret rode Royal out to the edge of the field where the woods were. The fence seemed sound enough, but beer cans had been tossed there. There were new houses on the tract over beyond the woods. Boys rode dirt bikes there—she heard their noise all day sometimes. *And they drink beer in our woods,* she thought, and shivered.

That evening as they sat at the kitchen table, Grace said, "Sometimes I think we're too much in the habit of being to ourselves up here. I guess we got that way when we had Grandpa to take care of." Some hard kernel of loyalty seemed to keep her from saying what they both knew—that her father had been miserly and righteous. The only good thing about him had been his love of his horses. And that had not begun to make up for all the rest. *It wasn't that he was ever really mean to me,* Margaret thought. *It was the way he treated* her— *the things he said to her. "You sure fixed it up real good for me. Fixed it so I can't never hold my head up again when I go into town. You took care of that, all right—"*

"I think we're fine just the way we are," Margaret said quickly.

In the night she was thirsty and went to the kitchen for a drink. When she turned away from the sink, she saw that Grace had left her book of poetry on the counter lying open, resting on its limp and overworked spine. Margaret carried it to the night-light stuck in the wall socket. In the dim light she read, "Western wind, when wilt thou blow, that the small rain down can rain? Christ, that my love were in my arms, and I in my bed again!"

She closed the book carefully and put it on the shelf.

Eddie James was back in mid-July. This time he was in a battered blue van.

"What happened to the truck?" Grace asked.

"Got sold right out from under me, along with the house and the property—everything. All but the tools. New owners come in yesterday."

"Who sold it?"

"Uncle Ned's daughter in California. Did it through an agent here. It all went to her, even though she never cared a damn for him when he was alive—even to write. So I'm heading home to Texas. Just thought I'd stop and see to your horses before I left."

"That was very kind of you," Grace said.

Later Margaret saddled Royal and left the two of them examining the latch on the riding-ring gate. "I'll put a stronger bolt through there," Eddie James was saying. Margaret rode Royal down the hill and across the fields, following the riding trails all the way to the small stream that cut across their property. When she thought she had been gone long enough, she went back. The blue van was still parked by the stable.

She found Grace standing at the stove, beating hollandaise

with a whisk. She wore a blue cotton skirt and sandals and her hair was loose around her shoulders. Her bare legs looked long and brown. Margaret stared at her.

"I asked Eddie to stay for dinner," Grace said. "He did so many things to help. He fixed Starfire's door so it works beautifully. He's having a look at the pump now."

Margaret went into her own room without speaking. She changed into a clean T-shirt and brushed her hair so fiercely her scalp hurt. Later that night she lay awake long after she had gone to bed, hearing the voices, waiting for the sound of the van starting up, but it never came.

"He's going to give us a hand—just for a while," Grace said in the morning as Margaret went to the window and looked out. The van was still there, still parked in the same spot. "He can sleep out there—" Margaret spun around and Grace looked quickly at her coffee cup.

"Where is he now?"

"Repainting the sign," Grace said.

Eddie James seemed to fill every private corner of their lives after that. It was Eddie who was responsible for the new horses coming to board. He had heard about three of them owned by people in the big housing tract. Their owners had been delighted to find stabling so close. "And you got those empty stalls just sitting there," Eddie had pointed out. "You could get a hundred and fifty a month easy for the three—maybe two hundred. Pay your whole feed bill—especially if your grass holds out good over the summer."

They took riders daily now instead of only on weekends. "Why not?" Eddie had said, and had added it to the sign. "Daily 8–5." Many who came were strangers, city people adventuring in the country or newly moved into the area. Margaret watched with scorn as they mounted and thrust their toes down in the stirrups instead of up, their two hands clutching at the reins, their shoulders hunched. Eddie James would smile his country-boy smile at them. "I just wonder, ma'am, if you wouldn't feel a little more sure of yourself if you was to have a couple of lessons. Ten dollars an hour, and you'd be surprised—I hope you don't mind my mentioning it—"

They never minded. They smiled back at him as he adjusted their stirrups, and they signed up for lessons.

One day Margaret arrived at the stable to find that he had rented out Royal. "That's my horse!" she shouted. "You had no business letting somebody ride him!"

"Why not? Has to earn his keep, doesn't he? Same as the rest?" And when Royal came back, sweating and winded, "It don't hurt a horse to sweat, kid. Just walk him out. He'll be all right."

Once a party came, renting six horses and asking for a guide. Grace took them over the trails and kept an eye on the in-experienced riders. When they returned, she was in the lead, sitting her horse lightly, laughing and talking, a little wind blowing her hair about and pressing her shirt over her breasts. Eddie James was watching her, too, Margaret saw.

The customers who came to ride were featureless—white blurred faces without identities. It was easy to keep them that way, Margaret discovered. All she had to do was squint a little and focus on a spot just past their heads. It was the same method she used when she disposed of a dead mouse or bird that the cat had left. All the voices were the same, gooselike, gabbling. Laughter was tinny or rasping—never real.

Then one day she noticed someone. Saw him in three dimensions, saw that he had depth and flesh and substance— a man leaning against the hitching rail outside the stable, where riders mounted and dismounted. He stood with his weight on one foot, his arms folded in front of him. He was looking at her.

"Hi there," he said, and smiled.

She saw a yellow haze around him—like sunlight. And safety.

"Hi," she answered, or thought she did.

"I didn't want to disturb you," he said. "You were far away somewhere."

She said nothing, and he gave a faint shrug. "Most people do too much talking anyway, don't they?"

She busied herself picking up a lead rope that someone had tossed down, but she was feeling an inner excitement at what he had said, at the revelation it implied. Someone else who knew what she knew. He did not seem to mind when she did not answer.

"I bet you're the one I should ask about a horse," he said. "You look to me as if you'd know. Which one should I pick to ride?" He glanced at three horses tied in a grassy corner a short distance away. Margaret's look flew to Royal, who was brought out daily with the others now, much as she hated it.

"The black?" he said lightly. "It's the one I would have picked, too. He's a handsome fellow." He paused and turned back to her. "He's your horse, isn't he?"

Margaret looked at him. His eyes were blue—deep and soft. His yellow hair curled around his ears and fell across his fore-head. "Yes," she said, sure this time that she spoke aloud. "He's mine."

Grace came hurrying over then. "I'm so sorry to keep you waiting, Mr.—Beckwith, is it?"

"Yes—Tom, please." The blue eyes turned to Grace and lingered there.

"I didn't mean to keep you waiting, but those last two riders needed some reassurance. You've read the rules posted on the door? No galloping the horses, no reckless riding. And you're familiar with the trails? I always mention these things the first time—" She broke off apologetically, and he raised a hand.

"Perfectly okay," he said. "And I didn't mind the wait. This young lady and I were talking."

Grace glanced at Margaret, startled, and Margaret said quickly, as if it were a normal thing, "He's going out on Royal."

From then on Margaret saw it all as a big square. In books, she knew, such matters were often described as triangles—two men and a woman—but this was different because there was a fourth angle, with her sitting at its apex, watching the other three, Tom Beckwith, Grace, and Eddie James. And there could be no mistaking it; from that first day when she had seen Tom's look following every move Grace made, it was obvious he was in love with her. Once it would have terrified Margaret with its implications of passion, surging blood, and dark desire, all conspiring to violate the separateness of their lives. But Tom Beckwith was different. From the first she had known that he was not one of the others.

He came often to ride—several times a week—and always he found time to chat with her before going out on Royal. He had less chance to talk to Grace, and that was because of a looming, proprietary manner that Eddie James had adopted. He could see the situation, too, Margaret guessed. He'd have been blind not to. At every turning Eddie managed to insinuate himself between Tom and Grace. "I'll lengthen those stirrups on Royal," he would say curtly. Or, "Mrs. Miller's waiting for her lesson, you know." *As if it were his stable and Grace his hired hand*, Margaret thought angrily.

One morning she heard Eddie's voice as soon as she woke up. Its powerful, insistent tones overrode Grace's quiet ones. They were in the kitchen; Margaret could hear cups touching saucers. She got up and dressed, listening.

"If you're going to make the place pay, you oughta have another couple of horses. Blossom's reliable but she's getting old. Foxy's a good horse, only he needs an expert to control him—you can't give him to a kid. And when a crowd shows up on a weekend, you have to turn some away."

Margaret edged into the kitchen and slipped into her place at the table. Grace threw her a quick smile. Then she returned to Eddie, but listening, not speaking. Her eyes were troubled and restless.

"You're making enough money now to swing it," he said, ignoring Margaret. His heavy muscles filled his plaid shirt. Small hairs grew on the backs of his fingers. Margaret stared at them as he lifted his cup and drank. She heard him swallow. "Why the hell not do a little investing? Why don't we take a trip over to Martingale Farm? See what old man Martin's got for sale? His reputation's good, what I hear."

Grace looked worried. "I just don't know. Maybe I should. But I worry about spending the money."

"It's an investment. To make the place more profitable."

"We don't care about profit!" Margaret burst out.

Eddie's mouth drew to one side as he looked her up and down. "Oh, don't you now. That's real good to know when the taxes and the electric bills come due."

Grace said gently, "Margaret doesn't understand all that."

"Why not?" he demanded. "She's old enough to. She's damned near a grown woman."

"She just means—it's our home. And we don't care about making a lot of money. Just staying as we are." Grace's eyes apologized, pleaded with him.

"Well, how long can you do that? How long will those eight horses last? Any business, you got to make investment." He clanked his cup into its saucer. "Look, how about this? Why don't we ride over there to Martingale Farm tomorrow and spend some time looking around—we won't rush it. Maybe we don't even decide right off." He hesitated, then added, "We could take in a movie in Dorset before we come home.

You never go anywhere. She can handle the stable for one afternoon, can't she?" He jerked his head toward Margaret. She felt, at the gesture, reduced to a cipher.

Grace's mouth was growing tight with worry. "She could, of course, but I wouldn't want to leave her here alone."

"Why the hell not?" he exploded. "Isn't she sixteen or damned near it? My God, I was working on a road construction gang when I was sixteen. Why couldn't she manage for one afternoon?"

But Grace was shaking her head, and the tight knot that had formed inside Margaret began to untangle itself. Grace would never leave her.

"What the hell are you scared of?" he asked. Then, more calmly, "Oh, Jesus, all right then. Let her come with us. You can call up and cancel the riders for one day."

"No! I don't want to come!" Margaret shouted. She thought of being crowded into the cab of the truck with that voice, those bulging thighs, those huge rough hands with their hairy fingers.

There was silence for a moment. Then he said, still ignoring Margaret, "It's time she got to know something about the world. She's scared as a rabbit."

Grace looked beaten. Margaret's heart ached for her.

"You stop it!" she cried out. Grace put out a hand to silence her.

"I do appreciate all you've done, Eddie," Grace said. "And you're probably right about the horses, too. Wouldn't you go for me and look at them? We'll talk about all those other things another time. I just can't do everything at once. It's going to take me a little time to change."

The word *change* had a clanging, ominous sound. Contemplating it, Margaret lost a bit of the conversation. Then she heard Eddie say, "All right, I'll go. I'll look them over, at least."

"Thank you, Eddie." There was more talk, but she lost that, too, in the wonder of what she saw ahead. A whole day without Eddie James's presence.

Later, as she was making her bed, Grace came into her room.

"You mustn't mind what Eddie says," she began. "He means it for the best."

Margaret pulled the spread up over the pillows, and Grace went around to the other side to help. "He sees things a little differently from the way we do, that's all."

"A little," Margaret said, and would have said more except that she did not want to add to Grace's unhappiness. What does it matter how he sees things? she wanted to ask. They came around to the foot of the bed and Grace hugged her. "You're my little cricket," she said. "And the trouble is you're standing with reluctant feet."

"What's that mean?"

"You know—it's from a poem I read you once. 'Standing with reluctant feet where the brook and river meet.' It's about growing up."

"Oh, that."

"Yes—but things do change, baby. It can't be stopped." The worry still lingered in her voice and her eyes. Margaret wondered if it would be difficult to kill Eddie James. She began to think how it might be done.

That afternoon she took Royal out and went for a ride down the slope, along the dirt road, all the way to the woods. It was some time since she had checked the fence there. She looked for breaks and weak spots and evidence of intrusion. She was relieved to see that it looked safe still. When she turned back, a shadowy form loomed up in front of her and her heart thumped with fright.

"Hey there!" A cheerful voice, no rough edge, not threatening.

"Oh." She felt the panic subside. "I didn't know you were riding today."

"Last-minute impulse," Tom Beckwith explained.

"I'd have left Royal behind for you if I'd known."

"That's all right. He's your horse, not mine. Blossom's okay—not too spirited, but a good old girl." He patted the horse's neck. He sat easily, one hand holding the reins loosely, one resting on his thigh. They turned back together and started along the road, walking their horses, and for a time did not speak. Margaret thought, *I can bear it, being with him. He doesn't mind my not talking every minute.* After a long time he said, "Is that one of your special places—in the woods there?"

She kept her eyes on Royal's ears. "No. I don't like it much in there. But I go to look around and see that the fence is okay."

"Why wouldn't it be?"

"They ride dirt bikes in the woods there—they've made trails. Boys—you know."

"Boys from your school?"

"I don't know. Maybe. I don't have much to do with the kids at school." She glanced at him and saw that he was looking around at the roadside, thick with dusty Queen Anne's lace, purple loosestrife, and tall mullein spires, and then beyond to where the hills rolled back and two hawks soared and glided.

"You live in your own world, don't you?" he said softly. "I don't blame you—it's a beautiful one."

She did not answer, but she knew he understood. No one but Grace had ever understood.

Presently he said, still in that quiet way, "Does that fellow Eddie live at your place?"

"He has a van, out by the stable. He lives there." She did not mention the footsteps at night.

"Is he a sort of hired man?"

"Yes, sort of."

"I wondered because he seems to—take charge a lot. I mean, he's always around."

Margaret knew what he was saying. Someone like Tom, unused to pushing himself forward, would find it hard to get past Eddie James's muscular presence. She was quite certain that if only he could, he and Grace would get along—they were the same sort of person. For a moment she thought of the three of them, Tom, Grace, and Margaret, living on the hilltop in the little house, caring for the horses, watching the seasons come and go. Surprisingly, it seemed not such a bad picture.

"He'll be away tomorrow," she said suddenly. She could feel his sharpening attention. "He's leaving early for the Martingale Farm over past Dorset, to look at horses."

"I see," he said.

In the night she heard a door opening and closing, heard the footsteps, the low voices. She turned her head into the pillow and pulled the covers up, wanting to shut them out. Wanting even more not to look at the wall that separated her room from Grace's, for fear she might see through it.

There was reassurance in the morning. A clear yellow sunrise full of shining and glitter, the world reborn, all omens good. She made her bed before going in to breakfast, taking particular care to square the blankets at the corners, to place the pillows straight, making it all true and safe. By the time she finished, she heard the pickup truck leaving, and only then did she go out to the kitchen.

That was only this morning, Margaret thought, twisting as she lay on the floor of the shed. How many hours ago? She had lost track, but she knew it was today. She moved her bound wrists painfully and thought of that neat bed, still unslept-in. The rain was coming harder now, not gently but with force, pounding on the shed roof. Wind was driving it, and there was still thunder. She could no longer see lightning because the window in the shed was covered with stacked bales of hay.

She could feel the swelling in her face where his fist had struck her.

Tom Beckwith had arrived earlier than usual that morning. "You two seem to have your hands full," he said. His face had a smiling, eager look. "Instead of riding, maybe I'll stick around and help out." Grace assured him it was not necessary, but he did anyway. All day he was there, leading horses in and out, helping riders to mount, adjusting stirrups, talking in his quiet way. He was a reassuring presence, lending a hand with anything that needed doing, and always anticipating it. There was a smooth, seamless quality about the day. It seemed to Margaret a blessed relief to be without Eddie's hulking presence, the rasp and abrasion of his voice.

It was after five when the last riders left. Grace and Tom leaned against the hitching rail and Margaret stood in the stable doorway, all of them watching the shadows grow longer. It was a soft afternoon, turning lavender now, with gold on the rims of the clouds. Margaret willed it to stop in a freeze frame and for the pickup bearing Eddie James never to turn up the road toward the house.

"How about a ride before we put the horses away?" Tom suggested. "Just us three?"

Margaret's look went quickly to Grace. She saw the hesitation, knew that Grace, too, was thinking about the truck and Eddie. Then Grace's chin tilted slightly upward and she laughed and said, "Why not? That would be fun."

"I'm too tired," Margaret said quickly. "But you two go. I'll get started with the feeding and watering."

"You sure, Maggie?" Grace said, but not putting up much argument, and Tom said, "We won't be long."

Margaret watched them as they rode off down the slope, across the dirt road in the direction of the creek. There was a big willow that grew there near the water and a soft grassy place under it. Sometimes Margaret rode Royal there, walking him into the water to let him drink. Watching now, she saw how close together their two horses stayed. She started unsaddling the other six, brushing them, fetching feed in buckets, finally leading them down to the pasture and closing the gate on them. It was odd, she reflected, how she didn't mind sharing Grace with him. Perhaps it was because he never made her feel left out.

She was back at the house when she saw them returning, still far away, two small figures in the twilight. At the same moment, she heard the distant roar of the pickup coming in from the county road turnoff. She stood at the screen door and watched the dust move along the dirt road and up the slope to the house. A thumping panic started up inside her, but satisfaction was mixed with it; she had helped engineer something that Eddie James could do nothing about. She watched as the truck pulled up and he got out. Then she retreated from the doorway and busied herself getting a drink at the sink while he came banging in, dusty and sweaty. He let the screen door slam shut behind him.

"Hi, kid." He gave her a curt nod and looked around the kitchen. "Where is she?" he said. Not even using her name. She. He crossed to the refrigerator and opened it, took out a can of beer, and slammed the door shut. He plucked off the can's metal tab and tossed it on the counter. Then he tipped the can up and drank. "Where's your ma?" he asked.

"She went riding."

"By herself?"

"No, not by herself." He had not seen them, then. Something sang in Margaret's ears. "With that Tom Beckwith."

He paused, the beer can in his hand, and stared at her. Then he moved to the screen door and looked out into the dusky young evening. His free hand rested on his hip. She saw him watching, saw the look of his body change slowly, all the muscles of his back growing rigid. The hand that was on his hip turned into a clenched fist. Margaret slid open the drawer near the sink and took out a kitchen knife, the one Grace always took care to sharpen. She slipped it under her shirt and went on looking out the window. She saw what he had seen—Grace and Tom moving into the stable yard, unsaddling their horses and feeding them, then leading them down the slope to the pasture. They returned and she heard Grace's laugh, then the sound of a car starting up.

Grace avoided looking directly at Eddie as she entered the kitchen and moved to the sink to wash up and then to tie on her apron. "Goodness, but we were busy today," she said. "How did it go over at Martingale? Did you see anything good?"

He went to the refrigerator for another can of beer, not answering. The tab clinked on the counter and he said, "What was that guy doing hanging around here?"

"Just helping out. He gave us a hand with the riders this afternoon."

"Then stuck around to get paid."

Grace's cheeks flamed red, but she did not answer.

"I don't like him hanging around you," he said.

It hung in the air between them, sharp as a blade, sharp as the knife wedged precariously under Margaret's shirt, but Grace did not take it up. Instead she said mildly, "For goodness sake,

Eddie. He was just being helpful, that's all."

Margaret felt as if her body would burst and fly in all directions, but she held it in. She imagined her blade stabbing Eddie James to the heart.

"I don't trust guys like him," he muttered, but Grace said quickly, "Tell me about the horses."

Margaret saw the muscles of his jaw working as he clenched it tight, but after a time he said stiffly, "Well, there was a couple there I thought didn't look too bad—"

The precarious peace lasted through the meal, but something was building, Margaret thought. And in the night air something was building, too. Heavy, sluggish currents moved in through the screen door. Grace turned on the small kitchen radio. There was music and then a voice, talking of fronts shifting, of rain, heavy at times, and of locally intense thunderstorms.

"I'd better bring the horses up from the field," Margaret said.

Eddie, leaning over his plate, said through his chewing, "A little rain won't hurt 'em."

"Roy's afraid of thunder and lightning. That time he ran his leg into the barbed wire it was thundering and he was scared."

"We should have replaced that bit of fence," Grace said worriedly. "It's no good around horses—"

"Well, if he's got any sense he's learned his lesson," Eddie said. "Not that horses are very bright about anything but food. Finish your supper, kid."

Margaret cast a look of helpless rage at Grace, but Grace only gave a tiny shake of her head.

The argument came later, and Margaret could hear snatches of it through the wall. "A guy like that . . . making a fool of yourself . . . if you can't see. . . ." And then a lot of swearing. Presently there was a slamming of doors and then the sound of a motor starting up. But not the pickup, Margaret noticed. The van. Was he leaving then—maybe for good? Something inside her buzzed and soared at the thought. She crept out of bed, feeling the heavy air of the building storm, hearing the thunder that crept closer.

She dressed quickly, pulling on her jeans and T-shirt. After a moment's hesitation, she stuck the knife in her belt. No matter how much she might will him to be gone for good, he might come back. She had to be ready. If she hurried, she could beat the rain, bring Royal up from the pasture and have him safe in the barn before it started. As she passed her mother's door she heard a small sob, but she ignored it. Things would soon be right again. Things gibbered and gnawed in the dark, but morning made them right again.

She crept out of the house quietly and ran down the slope. The night was dark, waiting for the storm. When the lightning flashed, it became a bleached-out moonscape. She felt strong and full of purpose and unafraid of the storm. There was nothing in it that could hurt her. Down at the corner of the field, just inside the gate, stood the small shed where hay was stored. She would stop there and pick up a lead rope. Roy would be impossible to manage without one.

The padlock was hanging open, the door slightly ajar. Had she left it that way earlier? She tried to remember. But the storm was coming closer; she had to hurry. She pushed into the shed and reached in the dark for the hook where the lead ropes hung. A hand closed over hers. She gave a small, gasping scream. Thunder swallowed the sound.

"Margaret!"

She stopped struggling; the hand released her.

"Tom?"

"I'm sorry I frightened you. I didn't know who it was coming in."

"Oh." She felt weak and shaky from fright. "Is something

wrong? How come you're here?"

"I was worried about you and your mother. Are you all right?"

"Yes. Why? What do you mean?"

"I saw him leave in that van of his—going like hell. I came back because I was afraid he might be sore about today—about my being here. I was afraid he might—do something. What about you? What did you come out for?"

"I'm going to bring Royal in before the storm hits." She reached up again for the rope.

"Wait," he said.

"I have to hurry. It's starting to rain." She took down the rope and started out the door. His hand shot out and grabbed her wrist. She stared at him curiously, but in the dark she could not make out his features. "I have to go," she said stubbornly.

"Wait. I have to think for a minute," he said. Lightning flashed, and she saw his face. Calm and thoughtful. "I have to decide how to do this. And I have to be sure he's coming back. He's got to get the blame for it."

"The blame—for what?" she whispered. Dryness crept up in her throat.

"For killing you. It's got to look right."

Another flash of light showed his face plainly—not twisted with hate, not dark with anger. Bland and calm as ever. But thoughtful. He was figuring out a problem. Margaret trembled with sudden cold. She made a lunge for the open doorway, but he was too quick for her. He slammed it shut and held her by both wrists. The rope she had been holding fell to the floor. He let her go and leaned over to pick it up. As he did so, Margaret grabbed the knife from her belt and struck out with it. She heard his startled yell of pain, but she knew by the way it felt that the knife slid along his neck harmlessly, making no more than a shallow gash. He seized her and struck her hard with his clenched fist. The blow landed on her jaw and stunned her for a moment, long enough for him to wrap the rope around her tightly and bind her arms together behind her back. He flung her down on the floor. Her head hit hard against it. She heard the door close, the padlock click. The sound of the rain grew faint, then stopped.

She awoke to fear, but she had done that often before. Only at once, in the moment of waking, she knew that this time was different. For several minutes she lay there, hearing the storm again, feeling sore, and in a curious, disconnected way trying to remember why this was different. A stickiness of blood on her cheek told her. This time it was real.

Memory crowded in as she tried to trace back to the beginning, to when it all started. Days and incidents slid by, ending with Eddie James's voice that evening, talking to Grace. "I don't trust guys like him . . . making a fool of yourself . . . if you can't see . . ."

Had Eddie seen?

Over the drumming of the rain she heard another sound, the steady approach of footsteps, then the click of the padlock. The door was pushed open, and he was back. He stepped over her calmly, sat down on a bale of hay, and lighted a cigarette. He sat there smoking in the dark, and Margaret watched in frightened fascination as the small glowing tip of the cigarette reflected off his features. She saw why he had left. He was holding a shotgun across his knees. He must have gone to his car to fetch it; she had not even noticed the car earlier. Now he sat there waiting.

"That son of a bitch is taking his time," he said at last.

"Maybe he's not coming back," she said. "He took his van. Maybe he's gone for good." She bit her swollen lip. Should she have said that? Was he less apt to hurt them with Eddie gone?

"Oh no. He's just gone out for a few beers. He'll be back for more of what he's been getting." Bitterness had crept into his tone. "I can wait. I'll take him first, then you. It'll look as if I tried to come to your rescue." He paused. "This whole thing would have been a snap without the two of you," he went on then, almost conversationally. "I don't know which one's worse—that beer-guzzling cowboy or you with your scared-mouse act. You're about one step from the nuthouse, you know that, kid?"

She could feel his eyes on her, smell the smoke from his cigarette. He said thoughtfully, "I could have handled a good-looking woman with a valuable piece of property. Hell, that's a cinch—I've done it before. Even the other guy wasn't fair competition—goddamned cowboy. But you. You were a real problem. You came first with her. I could see that. And you'd never want to get rid of this broken-down farm, no matter how good the offer was. Hell, you know what this place is worth? Development going on all around you?" His tone was almost conversational again, as if he were about to cite figures.

Margaret, her eyes used to the dark now, looked around the tiny shed. Her head was pounding. A long-handled shovel stood by the door; some loops of baling wire hung over a nail. Nothing else except for the hay stacked against the wall. Nothing that would help, and nothing that she could reach anyway. Her knife was gone; he had taken that. She moved painfully. He had wrapped her as tight as a sausage, only the rope he had used was the plump, slippery, nylon one she had planned to use to lead Royal back. It held a knot poorly. She worked at it clumsily while he sat there smoking.

"What if he doesn't come back?" she asked at last.

"I'll think of something." He dropped his cigarette on the floor and let it ignite a small clump of straw before stamping it out with the heel of his boot. "A fire would do. Lightning."

Margaret could feel sweat, cold and clammy, starting out over her whole body. The knot was looser, but it still held. She was afraid to try harder for fear he would hear.

From a distance came the sound of a motor. Eddie James's van coming from the county road. But he would turn up the drive to the house. He would never know she was in the shed with Tom. She held her breath, listening. Tom heard it, too. He got up from the bale where he had been sitting. He held the shotgun in his left hand. With his right he pulled the door open a crack and looked out. Then he shut it again and turned, pulling down the bales from where they were stacked, tossing them this way and that. Awkwardly, because he was doing it with one hand, not letting go of the shotgun. Some of the bales came tumbling against her. The wire binding of one ripped along her forearm. She hardly noticed. She worked quickly at the rope that held her wrists.

He had uncovered the small window that faced the meadow. It was hinged at one side. He undid the catch and yanked at the handle to open it. It stuck, and she heard him swear and give it another wrench. This time it opened. Cool damp air flooded in from outside. She could not hear the van now. Had it gone up the slope to the house already? She saw Tom Beckwith at the window. It was just at the level of his chest. Slowly he raised the shotgun, steadied it on the window frame, and lowered his head to take aim. There was an unaccustomed light beyond him, as if the meadow were illuminated. Then through the storm, distantly, she heard Eddie's voice. "Come on, boy! Hold still, boy!" The little hut exploded with sound as Tom fired. Margaret yanked wildly at the rope holding her, felt it slide away. At the same moment she heard the pounding of hooves galloping past the shed and out through the gate. She scrambled to her feet, not caring, suddenly, whether he heard. But now his attention was focused outside. She could see over his shoulder, see that the field was flooded with light from the van, which had been parked at the gate. Halfway across the field, picked out by the headlights' glare, she could see Eddie. He was bent over, one knee resting on the ground, a lead rope trailing from his hand. He tried to straighten himself. There was blood seeping through his wet shirt. The man in the shed leaned forward to take aim again. Margaret got to her feet and reached for the long-handled shovel that leaned against the wall. She held it by the end of the handle and swung it in a huge arc, putting all her strength behind it. It caught him at the back of the head. He toppled over a bale of hay and lay still. She grabbed the shotgun and ran toward the field. Eddie had staggered to his feet and was stumbling toward her.

Between them they fastened Tom Beckwith's wrists and ankles with baling wire, but by the time they had finished she could tell Eddie's strength had run out.

"We've got to get you to a doctor," Margaret said nervously. "You're bleeding pretty bad."

"I don't think he hit anything important inside," he gasped, but his breathing was shallow and labored as if it hurt.

"Sit here," she said, and propped him as well as she could among the hay bales, trying all the while to pull safety around her, to think all her safest thoughts. About living in a house on a hilltop, sitting in a yellow kitchen, checking the fence daily to make sure it was holding.

All games.

"Get up to the house," he said. "Call the sheriff."

"All right. My mother can drive you to the hospital."

"You'll have to wait here for the sheriff."

Fear buzzed in her ears. Her throat had gone dry. "Okay," she breathed. "Okay. I'll wait." But could she? Could she bear to stay here alone in the night, in the storm? She darted a frightened look at the bound man. With him?

"Hang onto that gun," Eddie said. "Not that this guy's going anywhere, but hang onto it anyway."

"I will," she said. There was something astonishing in his assumption that she could manage.

"You came back to get Roy in," she whispered.

"Yeah, well—" He attempted a shrug and winced.

"And you knew about him—about Tom?"

"Oh, hell, kid," he said softly, "it's not so hard to spot a con man. And I wasn't so damned smart. I didn't take him for a killer."

Other words, unspoken, lay between them in the dark shed, jumbled in a random heap like Scrabble tiles. She wondered if they would ever be able to put them in order. She heard him gasp faintly, "Ooh doggies—"

"I'll get help," she said, suddenly frantic with haste. She ran out of the shed and up the slope, bending against the rain, clutching the shotgun. She heard Royal pawing at the barn door, saw the outside light come on at the house. Grace appeared, raincoat thrown on over her nightgown. She was looking around anxiously.

"Maggie?" she called out. "What's wrong?"

"I'm here," Margaret called out. "I'm okay." And then, in a firmer, stronger voice, taking charge, "I'm all right."

JANET O'DANIEL, a former reporter and newspaper editor, is a native of Ithaca and now lives in Nyack, New York. She is the author or co-author of ten novels, including O Genesee, The

Cliff Hangers, Garrett's Crossing, *and* A Part for Addie. *She has also collaborated on several romances, and her short fiction has appeared in a number of magazines, including* Yankee, Woman's World, *and* Alfred Hitchcock's Mystery Magazine.

OUR LITTLE
RED SHOVELS

DAVID HOLMSTROM

E dith Joan was not a sister who drew much currency out of the bank of her affections. Mean-eyed and superior, she used to stand over me in the backyard with her arms crossed and say quietly, "You look like a squirrel, a weasel, or both."

I was seven years younger than Edith Joan, a mere eight-year-old, necessarily independent because of the recent death of my mother. I was learning quickly that to be loved was a benefit bestowed on me only by a few adults. And a partially blind kid named Buzzy.

Edith Joan and I lived in a big white house with a comforting green lawn as plush as Christmas. The trees, too, were bushy and green. A wide stream ran by the back part of our lot. "I do not look like a weasel," I said to Edith Joan, hurt but defiant. "Good," she would say, her chin up, "don't let anybody malign you, not even me."

When she came home from school in the afternoons I was usually in the backyard digging holes or playing circus. I imagined a big circus ring with elephants, tigers, horses with plumes, and brown bears all circling on bright red-and-blue cloth at my command. My whip was a stick with a cord tied to it, and I cracked it expertly.

If Buzzy were there, seated behind glasses as thick as two full moons, I would describe each animal to him between cracks, my voice building until I imagined breathless adoration from a surrounding crowd. Each person paid eight-fifty to get in, thereby making me rich and famous.

The beautiful bareback rider—the sweet and lithesome Gorgeous MaComber—was my dead mother, the bejeweled star of the biggest show on Earth. "Hi, Mom," I whispered in between cracks. "Do you remember me?"

If it was circus I was playing when Edith Joan came home from high school, I stopped playing. Prearranged signals from me to Buzzy would end the show. Edith Joan was not one for make-believe or pictures of giants done with crayons. "Freaks," yelled Edith Joan, standing on the back porch with a diet drink in her hand, holding the door open. She looked at us across the lawn and under the trees and said, "You two are freaks." I was too far away to see if her lip curled.

If I was digging holes when she arrived, I would keep on digging. This momentarily inflamed her. "Are you digging to bury or digging to uncover?" she yelled and shook her head. "You are one stupid kid," she said. Why did she dislike me so? What had I done to be regarded so terribly? It was impossible to like her at age fifteen. She would be intolerable at twenty.

The digging became an area of concern for my father. At

the dinner table he would look at me with squinted teddy-bear eyes and say, "Tommy, honey, is this digging for a real reason or just to fill and unfill a boy's time?"

I had a reason then. I was lonely for a purpose of my own, and somehow it was satisfying to take that little red shovel, feel my foot push it in the earth, and bend and lift and dump the loamy earth in a pile. And then do it again and again. I was no longer neutral. Digging was power, all of my little body doing something with a friendly shovel that said, "Let's chew the earth together, Tommy."

"I'm just digging," I said lightly to my father. "I like it just the way Edith Joan likes to smoke." She was too clever to react.

"Edith Joan," said Daddy angrily, scraping up the last of the mashed potatoes, "I know you are not smoking cigarettes or any other substance and that is the way it should be and will be."

"He's lying," she said at me, collecting the dishes as Mildred came into the room.

"Nobody smoking nothing around here," Mildred said, bringing in three plates of apple pie. "I got a nose that still smells anything two days later. Cigarettes, anything that can be lit, I got holy permission not to miss it."

But I knew Edith Joan smoked. At night she sat in her bathroom naked with the fan on and smoked cigarettes and marijuana and tossed the butts down the toilet. She also looked at pictures of men with no clothes on. And she looked at herself in the mirror for hours.

Mildred put apple pie in front of me and grazed my head with her hand. This gnarly, loose-jointed woman who lived in a big room off the kitchen with a porch filled with flowers loved me. Mean as Edith Joan was, Mildred loved Edith Joan, too. I learned later that my father paid Mildred double what she would have received at any other house in Evanston.

When Buzzy asked his parents for a shovel for his birthday, my father got a phone call, then a visit from Buzzy's father. "Show us what you do," said my father as he and I and Buzzy and Buzzy's father stood by my digging ground. I took my little red shovel and I dug. I dug about four shovelfuls, annoyed that with adults watching, I had no power over the earth. I could feel power being sucked out of me into them. So I stopped digging.

"I don't see anything wrong with this," said Buzzy's father, standing there in his pin-striped banker's suit. "The Buzzer could use a little shoulder and back exercise," he said, smiling, his pink hand resting on Buzzy's shoulder. Buzzy was no weakling. He couldn't do sports because he couldn't follow balls with his eyes. He was no weakling. On his birthday Buzzy got a little red shovel with a white ribbon around it.

Edith Joan mocked us. She called us crazy. "Why don't you guys play with trucks or baseballs like real boys?" she said to us one day after coming home from school. "You guys are crazy."

Mildred encouraged us. "Make some patterns," she said after walking across the lawn and around the trees to the bare place where we dug. She wiped her freckled hands on her aprons. "Make me a square, then a circle. . . ."

Excited, we made a huge circle, a double circle with the inside circle being the holes and the outer circle the small piles of earth. "Now a figure eight . . ." said Mildred, her face beaming, her bony old legs moving slowly back to the kitchen.

It was on one of those early summer afternoons, in the speckled shade of the trees, that Buzzy and I stood side by side, our hands callused and tough, and he said, "Let's dig down . . . really down far. . . ." His feeble eyes were big and grotesque. We were not tired of digging, just tired of the limitations of the surface.

"How far?" I asked.

"All the way to Hell. . . ."

We laughed and started digging.

The basic principles of earth engineering caught up with us quickly; several cave-ins led us to pieces of plywood for side braces. At the four-foot level we stopped and held a meeting.

"We need buckets," I said, "to haul the dirt to the stream."

"Why?" asked Buzzy.

"Big piles of brown earth would tell Edith Joan what we are doing."

From then on, laboriously and tediously, we hauled bucket after bucket of dirt to the stream and flung it into the water. Three afternoons later we camouflaged the entrance with boxes, boards, and earth. No one knew we were on our way to Hell, not even Edith Joan.

We started in June and mixed our digging with circus playing, with reading, with bike riding, with camping out at night in the backyard, all the games and fun of summer.

Edith Joan slept until noon or later and, when she did get up, was on the phone or watching television. She argued all the time with my father and ignored Mildred's request to clean up her room. One day she dyed her short hair blonde with a black streak on the left side. When she saw me she either called me a "freak" or ignored me. Once she ran away for two nights but came back.

By July, Buzzy and I had reached the twenty-foot level and had built a six-foot-square room at the ten-foot level. The vertical tunnel was three feet in diameter. A rope ladder was our access to the bottom, and we hauled the buckets up with a pulley system. For lights we used candles and flashlights. What kept us going was the secrecy, power, and grandeur of what we were doing.

"You boys still digging out there?" asked Mildred when she made lunch for Buzzy and me one day. We were seated at the kitchen table, feeling our calluses. Complaining that her legs ached too much, Mildred wasn't able to walk across the lawn to the trees and see us dig. "Yes," I answered. Buzzy looked at me. "Yes, we dig every once in a while."

"Edith Joan sure needs to dig at something," Mildred said under her breath. She sat down at the table with a sigh, a cup of coffee in her hand. "That girl's gonna be the death of your father."

"Why?" I asked. "What's she doing now?"

"Stealing money, shoplifting." Mildred shook her head. "Child's got everything but sense. Stole some jewelry. Stole some money. This ain't no teenage phase, either. She's going to hell, if you ask me. . . ."

Buzzy dropped his fork.

"She's stealing things?" I asked in disbelief.

"Everybody's doing it, she says. Girl has everything. Big house. Clothes. Good father. And what's she doing? Stealing cheap jewelry because everybody's doing it. Child's going to hell, if you ask me. . . ."

Buzzy and I finished our meal in silence, then excused ourselves. On our way across the lawn to the hole, Buzzy said in shock, "Is Edith Joan going to get there before we do?"

"I don't know."

"How does she know how to get there?"

"I don't know."

"How close are we?"

"I don't know."

We dug every other day until the end of July. At the thirty-foot level our enthusiasm began to wane. The hole was becoming cold and dank. We had to wear sweaters at that level while, outside, the sun kept the temperature in the high eighties. "Maybe there isn't a Hell," said Buzzy.

Then on August second, while I was digging and Buzzy was hauling up the bucket by the pulley, I noticed all three candles flickering. I stopped digging and stood perfectly still in order not to create air currents. In the gray, earthy coldness, I felt my stomach tighten. The candles continued to flicker. Somehow air was now gently pushing itself into the hole, moving around me and rising up to the surface.

"Buzzy," I yelled. "Come down."

It took him several minutes to descend the rope ladder but, when he reached the bottom, I said, "I think we're close."

"Close to what?" The thickness and curved surface of his glasses reflected a hundred yellow candle flames. I couldn't see his eyes.

"Hell," I whispered.

"Wow!" he said.

We dug slowly, pushing the dirt behind us. It was simply too tight an area for anything but side-by-side digging on our knees with our hands. Then, without any warning, the earth gave way beneath us. "Yeeoow!" we yelled. Like two bags, we fell about six feet into a brightly lit room and were caught in a springy, soft net.

A man in a red sweat shirt carefully lowered the net and said, "We thought you might give up. But here you are at last." He had gray hair, an impish smile, and blue eyes. "Come sit down." He peered at us as we disentangled ourselves from the net and stood on the wooden floor. To the right was a door, to the left a wide sofa strewn with red, white, and blue pillows. I looked up. Above us was the bottom of the hole and a ceiling of domed earth reinforced by wooden beams.

"Well, boys, welcome to Hell," he said as we sat down. "Actually, this isn't really Main Hell. This is a midwestern tributary of Hell." He smiled and leaned forward. "You are to be congratulated for a truly amazing job of digging. We didn't think two eight-year-old boys could do it. But the hole is superb, straight, well-dug, and here you are." He rubbed his hands together, then raised one finger and said, "Slight problem. Hell is closed to visitors."

Buzzy said, "How far is Main Hell?"

"Quite far, straight down." He leaned to his left and picked up a briefcase next to the sofa and opened it and took out a pile of folders.

"Through that door?" asked Buzzy, pointing to the door.

"Through the door," said the man.

We stared at the door and imagined the agony of a fiery, eternal Hell bubbling and boiling behind it.

"Sir," I said, "would you mind if I asked if you are the Devil?"

"Not at all. I'm not the Devil. I'm a regional adviser to the Devil." He smiled again. This time I saw the black and red fire burning deep in his eyes. He also had a peculiar smell about him, somewhat like rope or hair being burned.

He opened one of the files and said, "Edith Joan. I can make a deal on Edith Joan, but neither of you nor any other members of your families are due here at all."

He thumbed through pages, wrinkled his nose, and said, "Edith Joan has before her the possibility of a hellish life— drug addiction, abortions, alcoholism, three failed marriages, two major car accidents, countless lies, blasphemy, excessive greed, and virtually endless jealousy. In addition she will run over a kitten."

Poor Edith Joan, I thought. *If only our mother hadn't died.* The man looked at me. "No, no," he said, "everybody comes to Hell all on their own. No excuses of any kind. You earn it or you don't."

I was amazed that he could read my thoughts.

"What's blasphemy?" asked Buzzy.

"Swearing against God."

Buzzy covered his eyes and began to shake. "Let's go home now."

The man grinned. "Tommy," he said, "I want to reward your hard work and imagination in getting here. Let me make you an offer. It will save your father a lot of grief. You bring

Edith Joan down here and we'll put her to work. She'll have a taste of Hell for three weeks. Sometimes we can work re-markable transformations and save space for the truly corrupt."

He leaned forward. "Quite frankly, Hell is overcrowded these days, and I'm authorized to stem the flow just about any way I can. If Edith Joan fumbles through Hell's initiation and fails, we'll send her back after three weeks. She'll avoid a hellish life. She'll be transformed, pale and thin maybe, but wiser, loving, and infinitely patient. Your father will probably cry with joy."

"What will she do while she's here?"

"Ah, she will commit truly despicable acts of collective and individual self-indulgence and cruelty. She will do and think deliciously vile things beyond your imagination. If she can't do them easily and quickly, we don't want her."

"And she'll come back and lead a good life and not call me a freak, a squirrel, or a weasel?"

"Practically guaranteed."

"And she won't smoke anymore in the bathroom?"

"She will hate smoke."

How could I be wrong for myself, for my dad, or for her? If she likes Hell, good riddance. If she doesn't, she'll come back pale and thin but wiser, loving, and infinitely patient.

"Okay," I said, "I'll get her down here."

"A deal." He held out his pink hand. I shook it.

"Edith Joan?"

She was seated in front of the television in the family room, leg over the armchair, her hand applying bright blue paint to her toenails. She wore a white T-shirt and faded black pants. She smelled of cigarettes and a thousand crushed flowers. "What's up, freak?"

I came around and sat on the floor next to the chair. "I was wondering if you know what gold looks like?" I said in a tone of great seriousness. "I don't mean a gold bracelet or ring, but a vein of raw gold in the ground. Do you know what it looks like?"

"Why, freak?" She had finished her left foot and was starting on the big toe of her right foot.

"Well, I don't know if I should tell you."

She looked at me, her black-lined eyes covering me with disdain. "Don't tell me, freak." She went back to her toes.

"I have to ask you, I guess. I can't ask Dad because I don't want him to know what I've done." I paused. "You promise you won't tell him?"

She turned to me again. "Just tell me or go away, weasel," she said angrily.

"Okay," I said. "Buzzy and I dug a hole in the backyard, a really deep hole. You have to use a rope ladder to get to the bottom. And down at the bottom we dug into this vein of dull, heavy stuff that looks like gold. But I don't know what raw gold looks like. All I know is that this stuff is kind of heavy and it might be gold but I don't know. And I can't tell Dad because the hole is really deep and he'll get mad because I dug the hole. But if it is gold . . ."

"You want me to go down the hole, don't you?" she said, smiling as if she had caught me. "You and Buzzy have some kind of trick waiting for me at the bottom, don't you?"

"No, I . . ."

"Why didn't you bring up a piece of it?"

I stammered, "Well, I . . ."

"Show me the hole," she said and stood up.

We walked across the lawn, Edith Joan in her bare feet and me in my sneakers. It was a brilliant day on earth, a fine blue sky mottled by tumbling clouds.

"Where'd you put the dirt from the hole?" she asked suspiciously. *She won't need shoes in Hell, will she?* I thought.

"In the stream," I said.

"How deep is the hole?" she asked.

"About thirty feet."

"Good God, thirty feet!"

She stood over the hole and couldn't believe it. She looked down into the darkness, intrigued and excited, and listened to me innocently describe the possibility of gold. She seemed almost proud that I had done this bizarre thing: her little eight-year-old brother and his bug-eyed friend had actually dug a deep, deep hole into the earth with two little red shovels. And nobody knew it.

"The vein is on the right," I said, "all the way to the bottom. You have to get down on your knees and scrape dirt away. You can't miss it." I held up a flashlight.

She circled the hole. The trees filtered the sun so that her face was shadowed a little. In this light I could see a little of our mother in her face. But Edith Joan had encrusted it with hardness, the way she walked and talked, all encrusted. Hell will knock it out of her, I hoped. She would come back pale and thin, but wiser, loving, and infinitely patient.

"You little devil," she said in conspiracy. She took the flashlight from me. "So help me God, if there is anything down there other than a vein and dirt, you'll be in deep trouble when I come back," she threatened me.

"It's on the right," I said, my hands suddenly a little sweaty. "Scrape away the dirt."

She climbed down the rope ladder without looking up at me. For a few minutes I could see the top of the rope ladder, tied to a nearby tree, wiggling and shaking as she descended. Then it was still.

Buzzy came out from behind another tree, his owl eyes searching for me. He found me and we stood together. Then he looked in the hole. "That was easy," he said.

"No, it wasn't," I said. "She's smart."

We stayed there, looking in the hole. Buzzy squinted and

checked his watch. "Quarter to three," he said. "Give her a half hour to make sure she's gone."

Fifteen minutes later we stretched out on the grass and I described the animals in the circus as they circled the back-yard. But I couldn't muster much enthusiasm at all. I didn't even mention bareback rider Gorgeous MaComber.

I hadn't thought of how the man would get Edith Joan to go with him. Would he grab her and pull her through the door? Or would he smile and lie to her, "Honey, this way leads up," and then she would be on her way down to Hell?

Overhead the clouds bulged and twisted into great backs and shoulders. Mildred called to us. "Any cookie eaters out there?" she yelled from the back porch. We ran and got fist-sized chocolate chip cookies and then lay down on the grass, chewing and watching the clouds.

"She deserves whatever she gets," said Buzzy.

"She'll probably be back," I said, "full of stories."

"Maybe she'll like it there."

After an hour passed, we knew Edith Joan was safely in Hell. Buzzy went home. I stayed there on the grass looking over at the hole every once in a while. Why should I care about her? She never cared about me. She didn't appreciate Earth, either.

I got up, walked over to the hole, untied the end of the rope ladder from the nearby tree, and dropped it to the bottom.

After many years of writing articles and short stories for national magazines and scripts for documentary films, DAVID HOLM-STROM is now the feature editor of the Christian Science Monitor *in Boston. His short stories have appeared in* McCall's, Fantasy & Science Fiction, Campus Life, *and elsewhere. His articles have been published in over forty magazines, including* Travel & Leisure, Reader's Digest, Signature, *and* Americana.

DOUBLE SUBSTITUTION

COLLEEN M. KOBE

rene Everett eyed the Moon Children with professional interest. They seemed to behave much like any other sixth-graders, Earth-born or not. *Well,* she amended, *perhaps they bounce around a bit more.*

She sat behind a new aluminum work desk whose contents did not belong to her, on a chair too stiff for the Moon's slight gravity. She touched her graying hair and smoothed her dark green skirt. The children ignored her, as children always ignored substitute teachers until the last possible moment. They had entered the room one by one, red-faced and breathless; all the children showed surprise when they saw her.

The 0900 bell rang, and Irene rose and crossed to the front of her desk. "I'm Ms. Irene Everett," she announced when the children quieted. "Mr. Brigham became ill last night, so I'm your substitute teacher. I see from his agenda that science is your first class and that you have homework to go over. Please get out your books—"

The classroom door opened, interrupting her. Mare Imbrium High School Principal Walter Barrister stuck his balding, gray head in. Irene had heard he was only forty, but he looked ten years older. "Ms. Everett. So sorry to disturb you, but can I see you out here a moment?"

"Uh, certainly, just a moment." She turned back to her pupils. "Class, I'll be right back. Ahm"—she turned to a plump brunette girl wearing faded coveralls stuffed into knee-high boots—"what's your name?"

"Andrea."

"Well, Andrea, will you be class monitor until I return? This will only take a minute." She walked to the door and glanced behind her. Andrea strode pompously to the front of the room, turned, and folded her arms firmly. Irene closed the door and walked to join the principal, who tapped his foot impatiently.

"What can I do for you, Walter?"

"Just a minute, just a minute." He quietly checked the door. Then, sighing, he took her arm and led her down the hall, slapping his free hand against his thigh compulsively. Two suit-coated gentlemen waited around the corner for them.

"Irene, this is Dick Nguyen and Jerome Kubaki, from Lunar Intelligence." She shook their hands. She smiled. They did not. "It seems we have a rather large problem. Jeez!" Walter exploded suddenly, smacking his hand against the white brick wall. "Why, why, *why* does this have to happen to *me?*" His hands trembled violently as he fumbled for a cigarette. "Always me, always me," he muttered angrily. The shorter of the two men lit the cigarette for him. Walter inhaled and began to cough explosively.

"Take it easy, Walter. Whatever it is, it can't be that bad." Irene awkwardly patted him on the back.

Jerome Kubaki cleared his throat. "Ms. Everett," he said, "we're here because there's a Chameleon in your room."

"What!" Irene exclaimed. "A Chameleon? *Here?* On the *Moon?*" She glanced from Jerome to Dick and back. "Surely there must be some mistake. Really. A Chameleon? How could he get this close to Earth without getting caught? And what for?"

Jerome sighed. Irene noticed absently that his eyes seemed to lack color. *Or maybe that's what they call gray. They match his hair.*

"Our intelligence reports that a small two-man scouter ship made its way through our defenses all the way to Mars," said Jerome. "From there we tracked it to here, although our ships were spread so few and far between that none could intercept it in time. Besides, they still have the faster ships. We're working on that.

"Anyway, they landed last night on the dark side. We found their ship but no traces of the occupants. A lot of good that would do us, even if we had, because when they change their shapes it's tough to tell the difference between them and the real McCoy. Right now, anyway. However. They can't just float through walls, either, at least we don't think they can, so when we got an unauthorized entry on Port Seven here this morning, we knew we were getting close. So. We had the computer check every monitor in every room in this whole damn quadrant and found we had one room with an anomaly: seven people and only six life-readings. Yours. You have a Chameleon in your room."

Irene's knees threatened to buckle. "My God. One of those children—really isn't—and the others . . . What do you plan to do about it?"

"We have one plan, and it depends a lot on you," said Jerome. "We want you to go back in there and figure out which kid is the Chameleon and send it out here."

This time Irene did sag; Walter reached out and grabbed her arm as she fell. "I—you want me to go back in there? But I don't know anything about espionage or Chameleons or deceit or anything! I wouldn't even know where to begin! I'm sure I'd be much more of a hindrance than a hel—"

"Shut up and listen," hissed Walter coldly, squeezing her arm hard. "Just listen to me. You *have* to go back into that room because none of us can."

"Why the hell not?"

"For God's sake, think a minute. Suppose he, or it, or whatever you call them, suppose it decides to turn into some big hungry carnivore with big sharp teeth? Or a cloud of carbon monoxide? He could easily kill us all! No. *We* can't go into the room without arousing suspicion, but *you* can. What we need is some way to figure out which student he's masquerading as and get him to go outside, and then these two guys here can catch him."

"Oh, sure, with what? A vacuum cleaner?"

"That's our business, Ms. Everett," answered Jerome with a tight smile. "As it happens, when the Chameleons assume a body-shape, they also become vulnerable to that body's weaknesses. Now, I doubt if they can turn into a cloud of gas because it would be too hard to get themselves all back together again, but that's mere conjecture. Anyway, when he comes out the door, we can stun him with this"—he lifted his suitcoat enough for her to glimpse a holster with a dark object in it—"and then we'll have our first prisoner of war."

"But how can I figure out which one of those children really—*isn't?*" wailed Irene. "I don't even know what the children are like under ordinary circumstances."

"You don't?" asked Jerome.

"No. I was called in this morning to substitute for Arthur Brigham."

"Wonderful," he groaned.

Irene racked her mind desperately for a way to avoid reentering the classroom. *Calm down,* she told herself. *You think better calm.* "Have you tried calling the kids' parents to find out which ones went to school today?"

"Yes," Jerome said. "All the children left at seven-thirty sharp from their respective homes. It seems there was some kind of a race to get to school, with the winner getting a prize."

"Oh! That's why they were so excited this morning."

"This isn't helping anything," interrupted Walter. "How are we going to get that thing out of there?"

"Well, let's see. Say, why do you suppose he's in a sixth-grade classroom of all places?" wondered Irene. "It seems to me that he could assume the shape of a tree or a bulkhead somewhere and not have to worry about arousing suspicion by breaking character. He wouldn't get caught as easily." Irene turned to Dick Nguyen. "What do you think, Dick?"

Jerome interrupted smoothly. "Dick doesn't speak. He has no vocal cords."

"Oh," said Irene. "Excuse me."

"Perhaps it would help if we went over what we know, and the sooner the better," Jerome continued. "What we know is this. At seven-thirty this morning, all the children left their houses to come here. We know that two children live north of this school, two live west of school, and two live east of school. Each child, however, took a different route to increase his or her chance of winning, and each route was either inside or outside."

"You mean they space walked?" asked Irene.

"No, they didn't space walk, they just walked outside of

the buildings. The ones that walked inside walked through the tunnels and such. Now. At some point during the walk, one of the children was accosted, and the Chameleon took his or her place. But which one? And when? We don't know for sure.

"However, we do have a report of a peculiar sighting," he went on. "A field laborer was bicycling to work near the school this morning when he noticed a child walking through the cornfield. In itself that was nothing unusual, although it's frowned upon, but he noticed something odd about the kid. For one thing, he looked as if he were having trouble walking. Not that walking looked painful, but like it was an effort. And if it was an effort, what was the kid doing out there in the first place? There are any number of easier ways of getting to school."

"The Chameleon," said Irene.

"That's how it looks. He must have already assumed the child's shape and was continuing on the child's way. Apparently they pick up a lot of the host's memories when they assume a shape."

"Boy or girl?" asked Walter.

"Couldn't tell. It was dawn, and with the season-simulators it was too dark to notice much besides that it was a kid. And anyway he probably couldn't see much—the corn gets pretty high by this time of year."

"Can't you just figure out from where the guy saw the kid who it was?" asked Irene. "Surely the sighting was more north than south, or east than west, and you could tell that it must be one or the other."

"No, because just north of the school, all three outside trails converge. From the cornfield south—and it really is a good shortcut to the school—all the kids walk together. If they come via outside.

"We have a time limit, too, I'm afraid," Jerome added after a pause.

"A time limit?" echoed Walter faintly. "Great."

"Yes. We have tentative information that a Chameleon develops strain when he maintains a shape for more than two Earth hours. After that he has to change back to his real shape, which is some sort of a gelatinous blob. It looks harmless but it emits cyanide gas. Deadly to any human nearby."

They were silent a moment. "Is that what happens when they lose consciousness, too?" asked Irene.

Jerome chuckled grimly. "As far as we know. We've never actually witnessed one assume a human shape before. And now, time's wasting. Have you any ideas?"

"I know!" Irene grinned excitedly. "We can just have every child leave the room one at a time and monitor the life-readings in the room! That way when someone leaves and the readings don't change, we'll know that child was the Chameleon."

"Don't be stupid, Irene," Walter snapped. "Don't you think we already thought of that? Why not just announce at the front of the room, 'Hey, Mr. Chameleon, come out, come out, whoever you are'? I *told* you it can change into anything— or *anybody*—it damn well pleases. And as soon as it figures out we're onto him, he will. And *you're* the only one he won't suspect immediately. You *have* to be the one to nail him. Nobody else would stand a chance."

Irene fell silent. "Well," she sighed, "I guess I don't have a whole lot of choice. How much time do we have?"

Jerome glanced at his chrono. "Thirty minutes."

"Thirty minutes," whispered Irene.

"Thirty minutes!" wailed Walter.

With a visible effort, Irene pulled herself together. *It's got to be me. Nobody else can reasonably do this.* "I'll send a child out of the room within the next half hour," she told the men.

"That child will be the Chameleon. Do what you have to then."

Jerome nodded unhappily. "Remember, thirty minutes."

"Remember, Irene," said Walter urgently, "don't believe everything the kids say. You never know which one is the Chameleon, he could be lying."

"Yes, sir."

"And if it looks as if something strange is happening to one of them, act like there's nothing wrong but get the rest the hell out of there." Walter ran his fingers through his hair, leaving it sticking up. "Can you imagine the lawsuits the parents could slap on us? My God."

"Yes, sir."

"And for God's sake, Irene, *don't excite it!*" Walter's face puckered. He bonked his head gently against the white cinder-block wall. "Why me?" he moaned softly. "Why always me?"

Irene turned and walked slowly down the hall. She realized that her palms were sweating and that her heart felt like a tap dancer's foot. *Calm down, Irene.* She paused to take a breath, then, pasting a smile on her face, entered the room.

The chatter in the classroom ceased abruptly. The girl she'd left in charge sat on her desk, arms still crossed. Three names were scrawled on the blackboard. "Ms. Irene, these kids were bad while you were gone," she squealed. She pointed a pudgy finger at the board.

"Oh, huh, Andrea, you baby," scowled one of the two black boys.

"Thank you very much, Andrea," Irene said smoothly. "You may be seated now." The fat girl waddled to her desk and plopped down gracelessly.

"Now that you children know my name, why don't you tell me yours?" Irene continued pleasantly. "Let's go around and introduce ourselves." She looked over her six students.

The children reflected the racial diversity of the lunar colonists. Four boys and two girls occupied two rows of three chairs each; the rear of the small room sported the computer work stations the children used for their classwork. The black boys were identical twins; fortunately, they wore different-colored shirts. The one in the front seat wore blue, and the one behind him was in yellow. She nodded expectantly to the twins.

"I'm Chuck Walkerson," said the twin in the blue shirt.

"And I'm Craig Walkerson," said the twin in yellow.

The chunky brunette smiled in the center chair in the first row, nose high in the air. "I'm Andrea DuPres," she announced.

Behind her sat a frail-looking girl with frizzy blonde hair. She examined her mechanical pencil with a slight frown. She wore an expensive green printed dress. A doll sprawled haphazardly beneath her chair. "I'm Bonnie Broker," she whispered shyly.

The redheaded boy beside Andrea fidgeted in his seat, catching Irene's eye. "I'm Harrison Oliver Snodgrass the Fourth," he announced proudly. "Or Harry."

The last boy, behind Harry, looked up long enough to say, "I'm Rodney King," before he resumed his quiet perusal of his science textbook.

Is your quietness because you have nothing to contribute, wondered Irene, *or because you don't want to attract attention?*

Okay, now. Irene walked slowly around her desk. *Who do I have? Chuck and Craig, Harry, Rod, Bonnie, and Andrea. And one of them is not what he or she appears to be. But which one is the ringer? And how do I trip him up without letting him know?*

"So," she began, "I understand you had some kind of a contest this morning." Several heads nodded. "Just exactly what was it? Was it a relay race?"

"No, it was a get-to-school race," exclaimed Harry. "And I won it!"

Instantly, dissenting voices filled the room. "You did not, you liar," snorted Andrea. "It was a tie between you and Craig."

"Oh, huh," protested Harry. "I was here first! And I get to have a day off next week."

"Look, if he wants so bad to have a day off, let him," said Craig quietly. "The reason I only tied with him was because I—I—" He hesitated.

"You what?" asked Bonnie gently.

He reddened and stared fixedly at his desk top. "Oh, I, uh, I had to go to the rest room." Andrea giggled.

Irene glanced casually over at the coatrack. Three coats hung limply on the coat hooks. One of them was a girl's. She looked back at the children.

"Well, it sure is interesting that someone really did win the contest, anyway," she smiled, realizing how inane that sounded. "How about if we tell each other the routes we took to get here today? I bet maybe we could all get ideas if we think together." *And besides, maybe one of you will give yourself away.* "Now, who wants to go first?"

Silence.

"How about you, Bonnie? What route did you take to get here?"

Bonnie lowered her eyes and shook her head. Irene frowned. "What's the matter? Don't you want to share with us?"

Bonnie glanced up wide-eyed, then hesitated. She stole a look at Harry, who smirked, and shook her head to Irene again.

"Oh, for crying out loud, Bonnie," said Andrea impatiently. "Just *tell* her. It's not a secret."

"No," hissed Bonnie to Andrea.

"Well, then," interrupted Irene smoothly, "how about if you tell us your route, Andrea?"

"Okay. I live, um, north of here. That way." She pointed.

"Or is it that way? Anyway, I walked outside to school today." She crossed her arms and looked around her. "You wanna know why I walked outside? Because my mom says it's quicker because it's always quicker to move in a straight line than in a curved one. And she's right!"

"Oh, yeah? Then why didn't you win?" snickered Craig.

Andrea whirled in her chair. "You shut up, Chuck, you jerk!"

"I didn't say that," protested Chuck.

"Maybe I had a longer way to go than you did," Andrea continued hotly. "Did you ever think of that? Nooo-o-oo."

Bonnie raised her hand.

"Yes?" said Irene.

"Can I go to the rest room?"

Oh, no, thought Irene. She glanced at her chrono. Twenty minutes to go. "Ah, well, Bonnie, we're just about to start some important work, and I really think it would be a better idea if you waited." Irene ground on, ignoring the incredulous looks the children gave her.

"Why don't we get our science books out now?" she continued, reaching behind to pick up her own. The children shuffled in their desks to get their books out.

Though, come to think of it, Irene thought quickly, *there's only one girl's coat, and Andrea has admitted that it's hers. She's wearing boots, and no one corrected her, so I believe her. So Bonnie must have walked to school* inside, *and she can't be the Chameleon.* Irene felt pleased at this unfamiliar chain of logic.

"Sure is getting cool outside at night nowadays, isn't it?" Irene continued cheerfully. "The trees out in the courtyard are even starting to turn colors. Since I see you're studying botany, who can tell me why leaves change colors in the fall? Chuck?"

"Because it gets colder?" he guessed.

"Nooo . . . Anybody else want to try? Rod?"

"Because the plants aren't getting as much light as they're used to," the quiet boy said confidently.

"Right. A drop in temperature happens to accompany the gradual decrease in light every fall. I wonder how cold it is out today?" she said suddenly, inspired. "Would you like to check the temperature for us?"

"Sure." Rod rose and walked to the windowsill upon which the outdoor thermometer perched precariously outside. He looked at it from several angles, frowning. "It's turned so I can't see it." He reached up to the window latch, and before Irene could protest, opened it. The thermometer, freed of support, fell slowly and silently to the ground outside. "Oops."

"Good going, Rod," giggled Andrea. "You're getting almost as good as Harry." Harry stuck his tongue out at her.

Wait a minute, thought Irene suddenly. *Assume that the twins came from one direction, and that one of the coats belongs to them. The girl's coat belongs to Andrea. Could Rod own the third coat? He looks like maybe it'd fit . . . but what if he doesn't live in the same direction as Andrea? But on the other hand, what if he does? Ooh, my aching head. How can anyone think when it's so hot in this room?*

Irene glanced at the clock. Ten minutes.

She surveyed the remaining faces. *Well, one of them has to be it. But which? Andrea, Rod, Chuck, Craig, or Harry? For heaven's sake, maybe I should just come out and ask each child which direction he lives in and hope the Chameleon doesn't catch on—no. I can't assume it's that dumb.* She wiped her sweaty palms inconspicuously—she hoped—on her skirt.

"Open your books to page one hundred twelve. Now, I need a reader. Any volunteers? Chuck?" He nodded and began to read aloud.

"Chapter Two. Plant Research Discoveries. The biggest findings in recent his—history were the disc—discovery of gen—general—" Chuck paused, struggling with the word.

Harry snickered loudly. "Genetics, clowning—no, cloning tech—techniques, and Goober, I mean—" By now Harry was openly chuckling. Chuck glared angrily at him. "Think you're something, don't you, Harry?"

"Hey, when you got it, flaunt it."

"Oh, yeah?" Chuck leaned slowly back in his chair, crossed his arms, and an unpleasant grin spread over his face. "Well, I got something, too. I have a secret. I know why you didn't want to announce your route to school. What'll you do if I tell?"

Harry's grin froze.

"Think you're so smart that you won, huh. Cheater! You cheated. I wasn't gonna say anything, but I am now. I hate it when people make fun of me." Chuck suddenly turned to Irene. "You know how he got here before everybody else?"

"Shut up!" screamed Harry. "Shut up, shut up, shut up!"

Chuck ignored him. "His father drove him in. I saw them."

"Oh yeah? Oh yeah?" Harry stood half out of his seat now. "How do you know, Bigshot? Were you there?"

"Yeah! As a matter of fact, I was. I saw you coming in."

"Well, I didn't see you, and I looked all over the place."

"That's because—" Chuck paused. "That's none of your business," he concluded huffily. "Can I go on reading now?" he asked Irene.

But Harry was not about to let it drop. "I know how you saw me today. You took a shortcut! You cut through the cornfield, and you know no one's supposed to cut through the cornfield!" He turned frantically to Irene. "You heard it, Ms. Irene! Chuck cheated, Chuck cheated!"

"Oh, no, I didn't. He did!" shouted Chuck, stabbing a finger at Craig, who looked up in surprise.

"Now, wait a minute here—"

Andrea rolled her eyes. "Oh, geez, here we go again. It's *always* like this with you two. '*He* did, no, I didn't, *he* did.' "

She turned to Harry. "Hey, Harry, even if one of them did cut through the field—so what? At least *he* doesn't *bother* other people when they walk to school, like *you* do. Why don't you leave poor Bonnie alone? You're driving her crazy. Why do you think she didn't want to say how she got here, anyway? 'Cause she finally found a route that you wouldn't bother her on, that's why. So just knock it off."

So Bonnie and Harry come from the same direction, thought Irene, taking advantage of the noisy opportunity to think. *But I know Bonnie walked inside, so Harry must have walked out- side—except that his father drove him, so he couldn't be the Cha- meleon. So that leaves Andrea, Rod, and the twins. But then Rod must have come from Andrea's direction, and since she walked outside he must have walked inside—and is therefore innocent.*

So now I have three suspects left: Andrea, Chuck, and Craig. And I have five minutes to figure out which one is the Chameleon.

Or, she amended suddenly, *which ones are not.*

Andrea walked outside, I know that. One of the twins also walked outside—and that was Chuck because he spilled the beans on Harry, who admitted Chuck was right—that Harry did cheat. So Craig must be out, because he traveled inside. So now we're down to Andrea versus Chuck.

Sweat trickled down Irene's shirt. *I'm running out of time and ideas, so I'll have to make an educated guess. Walter will kill me. Andrea or Chuck? Would an alien who doesn't wish to be discovered be as loud and brassy as Andrea has been? Would he read as well as Chuck?*

Who the hell knows what motivates an alien?

Abruptly she thought, *Let's let you trap yourself, Alien. You wanna leave? Here's your chance.*

Sharply she clapped her hands twice. "Enough! It's time to continue. But first, ah, I think I've run out of paper clips. I need someone to go to the supply room to get some for me. Any volunteers? Andrea?"

The fat girl shrugged. "Sure, I—"

"I will," cried Bonnie.

"I will, I will!" shouted Chuck. "Let me go!"

"Fine, Chuck, you can go," Irene smiled. Chuck half-ran out of the room. She listened intently as the door closed behind him. Muted shuffling sounds penetrated the door; then she heard a high-pitched, inhuman wail echo down the hall. The children stared fearfully at the door.

"Ms. Irene—?" whispered Andrea. Irene motioned for silence.

After an eternity, the door opened. Walter stuck his head in, just as he had—was it only thirty minutes ago?—and motioned for her to come into the hall.

"We got him," he said dazedly. "I mean, it."

"Great. Um, Andrea, would you—"

"Sure."

"Good, good." Irene followed Walter out into the hall. A gray, windowless, stainless-steel cube reaching to Irene's shoulders dominated the hall just out of sight of the door.

"What's in there now?" Irene asked.

Jerome stood on the other side of the small prison. "The Chameleon. It's in its native form. It is, however, sedated and should remain so for a while. We think."

"No chance of its getting out of there, is there?"

Jerome smiled grimly. "None."

Irene stared at the small prison, then sighed hugely. A great weight rolled off her shoulders. "Have you found Chuck yet? I mean the real one?"

Walter reached for another cigarette. "Yeah, they found him about a hundred meters from the place the worker said. Good place to hide him. In those damn cornfields this time of year, he could have stayed invisible forever. Well, at least for a few more weeks. They just found him five minutes ago. So even if you hadn't figured it out, we knew." Walter snorted.

"Though I don't know what good it would have done us."

"Is he alive?"

"Barely. But the doctor said he should live." Walter exhaled abruptly. "How did you know, anyway? Should I ask? I mean, do I really want to know?"

Irene smiled sweetly. "I just used common, everyday logic, Walter. Have you ever heard of it?"

He scowled thunderously.

"If you gentlemen will excuse me, I have a classroom to care for. It was nice meeting you, Mr. Nguyen, Mr. Kubaki." With that, Irene returned to the familiar business of a substitute teacher.

COLLEEN M. KOBE *was born in Detroit and received a bachelor of science degree in computer science from Michigan Technological University. She now lives in Cedar Rapids, Iowa.*

THE TERRIBLE THREE

THOMASINA WEBER

I t was four o'clock in the afternoon, and the temperature must be a hundred and fifty degrees, thought Jackie, sprawled in the shade of the oak tree in his yard. He felt twenty times older than his twelve years.

Tonight would be *it*, the big blowup. They had been planning it for weeks, because they were bored with pilfering stuff from convenience stores and gas stations. And now Slim, the leader of The Terrible Three, had chosen tonight, even though he knew Jackie could not be there.

"Googie can take your place," Slim had said. "He's tired of being number three man, anyway."

"*Googie!* But he's dumb!"

"He's smart enough not to have to baby-sit his bratty brother."

Googie's father owned a grocery store, and Googie could get all the free cakes and Popsicles he wanted. That was the real reason Slim had picked tonight. He wanted Googie to be second man, and, according to the club rules, you could move up only if the man above you failed to show.

Since Jackie could not face the humiliation of being bumped back to third man, there were only two choices left to him. He could quit The Terrible Three—in which case Slim would spread it all over the neighborhood how Jackie was a mama's boy and Jackie might as well drop dead—or he could show up for the job tonight.

Slim said it was set for ten o'clock. If Bunny would go to bed like other kids, Jackie could sneak out after he was asleep. But every night Bunny would watch TV and scream if anyone tried to put him to bed, and when Mom finally did get him upstairs, he would stay up half the night reading some dumb book from the library.

"Jackie! Come on in and eat."

He shuffled toward the house, wishing Mom would make a real meal once in a while the way Slim's mother did. Slim was always bragging about the roasts they had and the baked chickens and the casseroles, whatever they were. Jackie sometimes wondered if he was making it all up, for everyone in Slim's family was skinny.

"Fix yourself a sandwich," said Mom as Jackie sat down at the table. Bunny was already there, his bright blue eyes seeming even brighter because of his white skin and nearly white hair. "There's peanut butter in the cupboard."

"You can't have any jelly," said Bunny.

"Why not, Bratso?"

"Because I finished it."

"Finished what, Bratso?"

"The stupid jelly."

Jackie looked at his brother's sandwich. "You didn't have to put it on an inch thick."

"Okay, you kids, shut up. You want your father to come home and hear you fighting?"

"Who cares?" said Bunny.

Mom turned back to the sink and slapped a fat hand down on the counter top. "I should have stayed single," she said.

"Mom, do I *have* to sit with Bunny tonight?"

"You bet your sweet life you do! If I don't get out of this house, I'll blow a fuse."

Jackie finished his sandwich in silence, ignoring Bunny's kicks under the table. He looked instead at the wall clock. It said four thirty-five; that meant it was twenty to five. His mother was always saying she was going to have the clock fixed. Just the way she was always going to go on a diet. Jackie swept his crumbs off the table and went to his room.

When his parents left that evening, Bunny was in the living room with the TV turned on full volume. Jackie considered locking his door and climbing out the window, but Bunny would come and pound on the door as he always did, and when nobody opened it, Bunny would know he was gone. When Bratso told Mom and Pop Jackie had sneaked out, they would ground him for a month.

But if Bunny *did* go to sleep . . . Mom kept her sleeping pills in the medicine cabinet. If she could take them, why not Bunny? Sleeping pills only put you to sleep, after all, and a little sleep never hurt anybody. By morning Bunny would be good as new and Jackie would still be the number two man of The Terrible Three.

He did not have to tiptoe into the bathroom, for Bunny could not have heard a bulldozer behind him. Even so, Jackie was nervous and his fingers shook as he opened the bottle of pills and took one out. He put it in his shirt pocket and went back to the living room.

"Hey, Bratso, you want something to drink?" Bunny did not answer, so Jackie shook him roughly and repeated the question.

"Leave me alone!"

Jackie went to the kitchen. He put milk into a small pan and began to heat it. Then he added chocolate syrup and the sleeping pill. He was pouring it into a mug when Bunny spoke behind him.

"I want some."

"Okay," Jackie said, pretending annoyance, "I'll make some more for you."

"I want *that.*"

"That's mine," said Jackie, taking a sip.

Bunny's hand flew up and knocked the mug across the kitchen, splattering its contents all over the floor and the cupboards. "Not anymore, it isn't," said Bunny.

"Boy, wait till I tell Mom what you did!"

"I'll tell her you did it."

And he would, too, thought Jackie bitterly. "You better clean that mess up," he said, pouring more milk into the pan.

"I'm watching TV," said Bunny, marching back to the living room.

Jackie got another pill from the bathroom and made more chocolate milk. He carried it into the living room and, sitting down, took a very tiny sip.

"Where's mine?" asked Bunny.

"I didn't make you any."

"Why not?"

"Because there isn't any more milk." Jackie took another sip, hardly any at all.

A sly look came over Bunny's face. "Do you want me to splash it around again?"

"In the *living room?*"

"I will, if you don't give it to me."

With an exasperated sigh, Jackie handed the mug to his brother, who took one taste and made a face. "You put something rotten in it! You're trying to make me sick!"

"Maybe the milk is sour," said Jackie, managing to get hold of the mug. "I'll pour it down the sink."

"I'm going to tell Mama you tried to make me sick!"

Bunny flung himself down in front of the TV set and Jackie went back to the kitchen. It was nine thirty-five. He would have to arrive five minutes ahead of time in order to secure his place, and since it was a fifteen-minute walk to the library, that meant he had only five minutes in which to figure what to do with Bunny.

He considered sneaking up on him and blindfolding him and tying him up in front of the TV set. He could be back from the job before his parents got home, and he would release Bunny, telling him he himself had been tied up in the kitchen and had only now managed to get loose. It wouldn't work, of course. Bunny might believe him, but his parents wouldn't, and Bratso would be sure to tell them.

Suddenly an idea came to him. Why hadn't he thought of it before? He would take Bunny with him. It was nine-forty. He would have to leave right now if he wanted to get to the library on time.

"Hey, Bunny!" He hurried to the living room. "Do you want to go out with me?"

"Where?" Bunny asked, without taking his eyes from the screen.

"Can't tell you. It's a secret mission."

"I'll bet!"

"No kidding, it really is. You could be the lookout."

"What will you be doing while I'm looking out?"

"Would you believe Slim and Googie and I are going to rob a bank?"

"No."

"That shows you're smart. You don't believe everything you hear."

"What *are* you going to do?"

"I told you, it's a secret."

"You have to tell me if I'm a part of the gang."

"Look, isn't it enough that I'm taking you along?"

"I have to know or I won't go, and when Mama and Papa come home, I'll tell them—"

"Okay, okay." If they ran all the way they could probably reach the library by five minutes to ten. "We're going to blow up the library," he said.

"With a *bomb?*"

"What else, dumb-dumb?"

"Where did you get a bomb?"

"Slim made it."

"Why do you want to blow up the library?"

"For kicks. To wake the town up. Besides, Slim got thrown out of there last month for spitting on the floor."

Bunny's eyes were wide. "You're *really* going to bomb the library?"

"Somebody is, but it won't be us if we don't get going."

"It won't be us," said Bunny.

Jackie stopped halfway to the door. "What do you mean, it won't be us?"

"We're not going."

"You said you wanted to go!"

Bunny was grinning. "You shouldn't believe everything you hear."

"You little rat!"

"You know I'm not allowed to go out after dark. Mama said—"

Jackie grabbed his arm. "You're going whether you like it or not." He twisted the arm until Bunny squealed.

"I'll go! I'll go!"

Jackie started to pull him toward the door. "We'll have to run all the way because of you!"

Bunny dug his heels into the carpet. "Wait! I have to go to the bathroom."

"Holy cow! You've been sitting here all night! Couldn't you—"

"I didn't have to till now."

"Hurry up, then. You've got half a minute and no more." Bunny ran down the hall and slammed the bathroom door. Jackie heard the key in the lock; then Bunny began to laugh.

"Don't believe everything you hear," sang Bunny.

"I'll fix you," said Jackie, shaking with rage. "Just as soon as I get back, you're going to be sorry you ever—"

The explosion rattled the windows, cutting off his words. Jackie sagged. It was too late. He had missed it, and all because of Bratso. He would hate his brother for the rest of his life. With dragging feet, he went back to the kitchen. The clock said nine fifty-five. Then Jackie realized he would not have reached the library in time anyway, for in the hassle with Bunny he had forgotten about their slow-running clock.

Bunny came quietly into the kitchen. "Some bang," he said in an odd voice.

"We missed it because of you, Bratso."

"I didn't believe you," said Bunny, the corners of his mouth starting to droop.

"So you missed the fun."

There were tears in Bunny's eyes. "I liked the library," he said.

The next morning Jackie and Bunny were unusually subdued at the table, each sad for a different reason.

"I don't understand what makes kids do the things they do," said Mom, huge in her flowered wrapper. "It serves them right, those two. Friends of yours, Jackie. Slim and Googie."

"What did they do?" asked Jackie, expecting Bunny to pipe up and say that Jackie was supposed to be in on it and why was he pretending he didn't know anything about it?

"Blew up the library and half of themselves with it."

Jackie's stomach bumped inside him. "They got *hurt?*"

"It's right here in the morning paper. Slim's hands got burned and Googie's face." Jackie's mouth dropped open. "Slim admits making the bomb. He said it was set to go off at ten o'clock."

"It did," said Jackie. "I looked at the clock when I heard the explosion and it said five minutes of, so that meant it was ten o'clock."

"Uh-uh," said his mother, shaking her head. "I had that clock fixed yesterday."

"Then the bomb went off five minutes early?"

"Yes. That's how they got hurt."

Jackie looked at Bunny and wondered if he realized he had accidentally helped Jackie, might even have saved his life. Maybe he would have to stop hating Bunny now.

"Jackie can't have any sweet rolls because I just ate the last one."

But then again, maybe not.

A native of Scotland, THOMASINA WEBER has been writing ever since she was old enough to hold a pencil. She is an instructor of creative writing at Manatee Community College in Bradenton, Florida, and former co-editor of the newsletter of Southeastern Guide Dogs, Inc., in Manatee County.

A SPECIALIST
IN DRAGONS

AL AND MARY KUHFELD

*I*t was a bright and beautiful morning, though it promised to be hot by afternoon. Baron Halfdan of Thorney was riding the fields on his destrier, visiting the peasants and checking on the crops. His pretty daughter Halla rode beside him on her brown mare, keeping him company. Since they were well within his lands, they had dispensed with the usual rattling company of retainers; they were alone together.

There was a sudden leathery flapping, and an enormous blue dragon alighted on the lane in front of them. Before Halfdan could react, the dragon snatched Halla out of her saddle with one large foreclaw. She screamed and kicked violently, but it ignored her. "You're Halfdan?" it hissed smokily.

"Yea! Release the girl, lizard!" roared Halfdan, drawing his sword and kicking his horse forward. He slashed at the dragon's claw, drawing purple blood in a great spurt that stained his beard and tunic, but the dragon ignored that, too. It leaned forward and bit the destrier's head off with a horrible neatness, then rose on its wings with a loud *whap-whap-whap* and disappeared over a copse of alders.

Halfdan untangled himself from the ruin of his stallion, cursing. He was a big man, with more black hair on his body than was really needful or attractive; and the blood dripping off the hem of his yellow tunic did not improve his appearance. He looked around and saw the terrified mare lunging against her reins, caught on a thorn bush a few dozen yards up the lane. He trotted up to her, calmed her, and climbed awkwardly into the unfamiliar woman's saddle. It was indicative of his fury, anxiety, and need to find help quickly that he did so; but he cut across the fields rather than risk being seen riding a mare.

Halfdan hid her behind a neatly whitewashed cottage a few minutes later and went up the path to pound on the door. He glanced down at himself and hoped his gory appearance would not shock Wulfstan. But then Wulfstan was a wizard, probably used to far more horrible sights than a blood-covered mortal.

Halfdan wanted two things: his daughter back, and his sword healed. Already the dragon's blood had begun to eat its way into the metal. Wiping at the blood served only to spread it farther up the blade. Leg-Biter had been his father's sword, and his grandfather's. It was famous for holding its edge through the longest battles, and it was the most valuable weapon the baron owned. He impatiently hammered at the door. What was the use of buying a wizard if he wouldn't answer his door?

Halfdan boldly lifted the latch and went in. The wizard's

raven screeched in alarm and flew to the rafters with a great clattering of wings. "Here, here!" he croaked. "The wizard is out. Have you got an appointment? Take two cups of wine and call on him in the morning."

"None of that, Hugin! Look at this sword! Dragon's blood, fresh from the dragon." The baron waved the weapon in the general direction of the raven. "He stole Halla. Get your master, and get him fast."

Hugin sneezed at the purple smell. He flew higher into the ceiling beams and crouched with his eyes shut.

"Hugin, I bought a very large cat at the fair last week," said Halfdan dangerously. "He's extremely fond of fowl."

"Yes? But my master's conjuring an elemental, and it will take a certain delicacy of approach."

"Delicacy be damned! Fetch him or I'll fetch my cat!"

The bird screamed, "All right, all right, all right!" He swooped down and out an open window. "Humans have no respect for a raven's feelings," he grumbled as he flew off.

The baron sat down and looked about. This was only the second time he'd visited Wulfstan's cottage since he'd acquired him last month. There were two rooms and a half loft. One room was a kitchen, and the other, the bigger, was a clutter of shabby-comfortable furniture, books, and paraphernalia Halfdan intended never to inquire too closely about. He briefly wondered where all the dust had come from; surely there was more than a month's worth?

He was studying a moth-eaten tapestry showing a wizard conjuring up a wind for a sea captain when Wulfstan came bustling in. "Sorry you had to wait. I was doing some lab work on the harvest weather. Your problem is dragons, Hugin said."

"Dragon, Wulfstan. I hope you can do something, and quickly." He displayed his sword, now badly corroded. "I wounded a dragon with this not an hour ago and look at it! And Halla—he took Halla away with him."

"Really?" Wulfstan produced a tablet and stylus from thin air. He was young yet, a very thin man with glowing dark eyes. His dirty blue wizard's gown had a smell of ozone about it and a peculiar pattern of holes burned into the sleeves. Despite the shabby robe—perhaps even because of it—he was the picture of wizardly dignity. "What kind of dragon, my lord? Any special characteristics?"

"He seemed a perfectly ordinary dragon, maybe a bit larger than usual. Blue and silver. Not like those oriental things."

Wulfstan was taking quick notes. "What about your daughter? Did she provoke him?"

The baron thought. Fifteen-year-old Halla had inherited his own imperious temper and was perfectly capable of provoking a dragon if it seemed the thing to do. "No, we didn't see him until he landed. And once he landed there wasn't time. He grabbed her and asked if I were Halfdan."

"Hmmm. So he was specifically after Halla. Uh—is she a virgin, by chance?"

The baron was taken aback. "Of course! I've warned the neighborhood bucks about her. Flaying alive for the first man who so much as kisses her. I'm saving her to marry to Baron Aethelwold." Halfdan combed his beard with his fingers, flinging bits of dried blood in all directions. "Decent sort, he'll treat her okay. But he'll die young of the apoplexy—all his line does—and she'll hold the land. . . ." His eyes had gone dreamy, but he suddenly jerked back to the present. "Why? Is it that important?"

"Halfdan, either the dragon's got a taste for young female flesh, or some wizard sent him after a virgin for a spell he's working. Let's hope for the latter."

The baron looked stricken by simultaneous doses of hope and despair. Wulfstan laid down his tablet with a serious expression. "We'll have to call in a specialist on this."

"Specialist?"

"A specialist in dragons. I'm just a general wizard, fine with elementals, healing magics, and weather. But dragons are a bit beyond me. Fortunately, Marduk of Oxney is very good with dragons, and he lives nearby. He's expensive, but what specialist isn't? I'll call and check if he'll see us right away."

The wizard reached out and took a crystal into his hands. He gazed into it and his body stiffened, became outlined in a faint blue light. He stayed that way for quite a long time. Even a glowing wizard can be a boring sight after a while if glow is all he does; Halfdan sighed and picked up a small silver knife to take a closer look at the runes incised on its blade.

"My lord," the wizard said irritably, "can't you control yourself around blades? Now I'll have to reconsecrate that athame before I can use it again." The baron started, looked guilty, and set the knife down. Wulfstan had stopped glowing and was once more aware of his surroundings.

"What did Marduk say?"

Wulfstan rose and began to strip off his robe, revealing tunic and hose beneath. "He wants us there as soon as possible. You go get us a pair of good horses while I pack some equipment." He began rummaging in a box of old vials; dust rose about him. "Quickly, please!" he said. "Every minute counts."

Within half an hour they were riding down Oxney Road. Baron Halfdan held the stained sword across his pommel, carefully wrapped in virgin wool according to Wulfstan's instructions. As promised, the day had grown hot; and after galloping some distance, they had to pull back into a walk to cool the horses. Halfdan moodily commented that it would have been nice if this expensive specialist could have conjured them into his presence. "I hear there's a wizard over Stowold way who can do that."

"Aelfric of Stowold is a specialist in telekinesis," Wulfstan explained patiently. "He once moved an entire castle for his owner."

"Yes? Well, why didn't you call him? Couldn't be bring Halla back to me?"

Wulfstan smiled grimly. "Yes, my lord. But summoning live persons without harming them is prohibitively expensive. You could sell this barony without meeting his price. I think we'll have to be satisfied with Marduk. Anyway, I'm doing the best I can to smooth this ride. If you'll notice, there's a shower up ahead, wetting down the dust. And see that small white cloud traveling with us, keeping off the sun? If you weren't riding with me, you'd be choking and sweating."

"Yes, sorry. I guess I'm distracted by all this." They continued in silence, each wrapped in his own thoughts. Halfdan was a little surprised at the strength of his distress. After all, Halla was only a girl. She was strong, bright, and witty, like her two brothers now being educated at Earl Edgar's castle. He'd saved Edgar's life in battle a few years ago, and this was Halfdan's price for the favor. The earl had no sons, and his daughters were exceptionally homely. He might have to settle for a baron's son for them.

With such bright prospects, surely Halla was not very important. So why was his heart so heavy? Perhaps because he had felt no great need to exploit her and had allowed himself to know her as a person. And she was a chip off the old block, all right. Poor Aethelwold would probably die years earlier than necessary unless he learned how to handle her. Halfdan smiled, then frowned. First, of course, they'd have to get her back.

Marduk's "cottage" was very nearly a small castle, with a crenellated wall and a high tower from which he could study the stars. To the left of the wall was a church with its graveyard, and to the right a forest; Marduk could gather his bats, toads, and herbs readily. In front of the gate Marduk stood waiting, wearing a robe of Tyrian purple with runes of power

embroidered in threads of all the seven metals—even quick-
silver, which moved and shifted but stayed nonetheless in its
pattern. His long hair was gold and silver, and a small owl
was perched on his shoulder.

Marduk invited them in and treated them to fragrant cups
of something which, while hot, was nevertheless very refresh-
ing. "I think I can help you," he said to Halfdan. "But it will
be expensive."

Halfdan's heart sank. "How much?"

"Five ounces of gold," Marduk said.

"And what do I get for my gold?"

"I'll find out what dragon has your daughter, whether she's
alive, and what he intends to do with her. Then I'll be able
to say more about what the rescue will involve."

Halfdan took five large coins from his purse, which Wulfstan
had insisted he refill before they set out. He gave them to
Marduk, who immediately led them to a large and very impressive hall. Two freshly drawn pentacles were on the floor,
linked by obscure signs in an ancient language. Marduk took
the sword and balanced it upright on its point in the center
of one pentacle; he stood the baron in the center of the other.

"Think of the dragon, every detail you can," the wizard
said; then he froze Halfdan's thought with a quick stab of his
wand. Facing the other pentacle, Marduk made a dozen quick
gestures, at least half of which would have been grounds for
battle if performed by anyone other than a wizard.

A mist formed about the dragon's-blood stain; the rest of
the sword melted into the mist. In the pentacle a tiny dragon
suddenly appeared, hissing and ill-tempered, with a bandage
around its left foreclaw.

"You ain't got nothin' on me!" snarled the creature.

"Speak!" Marduk said. The dragon belched brimstone and
turned its back. Marduk began to chant in a thin dry voice

of unspeakable things. The dragon hunched its shoulders and wrapped its head in its wings.

"Speak!" Marduk said again.

The dragon made a gesture in Marduk's direction that Half-dan found insulting, but Marduk only raised his chant to a higher level. The air in the room turned smoky blue.

In a few moments the dragon, smoking and bubbling like a leaky alembic, cried for mercy. "Lighten up, boss," pleaded the dragon. "I'll talk. I was only following orders. He woulda skinned me alive if I hadn't."

"No sniveling! Who would?"

"It was Zark, boss, Zark of the Golden Tower, he's behind all this. 'Go fetch me the virgin daughter of a ruling noble-man,' he says, and he threatens to stick me in the basement and heat his tower with me for the next three winters if I don't. So I took off and I hang around this tavern and I hear stories about this baron with a kid he won't let a man near, and I wait for him and grab the kid."

"Is the lady alive still?" asked Marduk.

"Well, I think so," whined the dragon. "I didn't stay around once he took her off my hands."

"If he's hurt her—" began Halfdan indignantly.

"Silence!" ordered Marduk. "Why didn't you kill the lady's father when he cut you with his sword?" he asked the dragon.

The dragon hissed like a new horseshoe plunged into cold water. "Zark warned me not to so I didn't, even though he like to took off my hand." The dragon held up the bandaged appendage.

Marduk looked at Wulfstan. "I don't like this," he said. "Zark is extremely powerful."

Wulfstan agreed. "We'll have to tread most carefully."

"Well, perhaps we can inquire further." Marduk made the magical gestures again, in reverse order. There was a tiny shriek from the pentacle as the small dragon melted away, leaving the sword to wobble for a moment, then fall. The stain on it had vanished, and the blade gleamed like new. *That's something, at least,* thought Halfdan.

Halfdan and the two wizards went back into the comfortable living room and Marduk served up more of the hot beverage, which he explained was a brew of roasted mountain berries from a distant land.

"Zark of the Golden Tower is a specialist in war," said Marduk. "I fear for your daughter's safety. His kind of spells tend to use up the ingredients very thoroughly." He thought. "The virgin daughter of a ruling nobleman. That sounds like a conjuring spell."

The baron bowed his head. "Will she die?"

Marduk said simply, "Perhaps it would be best to hope so. Warmongers play with devils and demons. Would you want your daughter to be given as a plaything to one of those?"

Halfdan's heart grew cold. "No, I suppose not." She was young and very pretty, and not a bad sort of creature, for a girl. She sang merrily and rode well, and had taken over many of the more wearisome tasks of running the barony. He'd miss her. "Can't we go take her? Zark's stronghold is only a few leagues from here."

Wulfstan said instantly—he didn't like switching owners too frequently—"No, no; I can't recommend going up against Zark. He's far too good at what he does."

"I agree," said Marduk. "I think we'd better call in a specialist in demons for consultation."

After a quick scan by way of a candle flame, they found that Beo of Lutetia was visiting Aelfric, the telekinesis specialist, so they called on Marduk's crystal and were invited over.

Beo was a splendid sight, if a trifle excessive in dress and manner. He was a short, plump eunuch in a flowing gown of red and gold, green and lavender, brown and blue, depending on which side he presented. He was wearing a turban with a peacock feather held front and center in a golden clasp. Half-dan disliked him on sight. He didn't care for eunuchs, was beginning not to care for specialists. This one looked even more expensive than Marduk.

Marduk introduced Beo as one of the world's greatest prac-titioners in a demanding field. Beo giggled archly and eyed Halfdan's purse.

" 'Demanding' is the word for it," Halfdan murmured to Wulfstan with a groan. "The gods grant this oily clotheshorse knows his business as well as Marduk says."

With Beo was a tall, wild-eyed Arab in a tattered robe. "A colleague of mine," the eunuch said. "Abdul Alhazred, on a pilgrimage gathering material for a book he's writing. He's also a demonologist."

The wizards huddled, muttered, and conjured. Mists with glowing eyes of many colors appeared and dissipated. Under Aelfric's spells, the transparent forms of other wizards appeared and gestured together with Marduk, Beo, and Abdul while Wulfstan watched with sheer enchantment and Halfdan, in a daze, produced gold coins as demanded.

The room darkened and took on a sulfurous odor. More pentacles were drawn, and demons came and went as great thundering invocations were made. Abdul Alhazred performed a conjuration that vaporized fully seven pieces of gold.

At long last windows were opened. Fresh air and late after-noon sunshine stole into the great hall. The five wizards, and Halfdan, were alone. The wizards nodded together and then came over to the baron.

Marduk spoke first. "Zark intends to make a Midsummer's Eve sacrifice of your daughter to the Demon Lord Zabibbo, thus gaining command over all the demons in Zabibbo's legions. It is a long, complex, difficult, demanding conjuration, and none of us would dare attempt it, much less try to stop it. We are a little surprised that even Zark should attempt it. If the sacrifice isn't exactly as advertised, Zabibbo will tear Zark to shreds."

"The dragon was under orders not to damage you," Wulfstan put in, "because the orphan of a nobleman doesn't count. Zabibbo is an extremely particular demon."

"But this is Midsummer's Eve!" groaned Baron Halfdan, covering his face with his hands. "Can't we do something?"

"Well . . ." said Marduk, "you could kill yourself."

"Seeing as how we can't do anything about the virgin end of it," smirked Beo.

Halfdan frowned. "I can't really see how killing myself would be much of a solution," he said.

"Perhaps it's not quite as bad as that," said Wulfstan, producing parchment, quill, and ink from thin air. "I'm only a general practitioner, but I think I have an idea." He explained what must be done.

"That shavetail?" shouted Halfdan. "Never!"

But after a few minutes' thought about the shabby but comfortable castle that would nevermore ring with a merry voice, and a brown mare disconsolate in the stables, he sighed and took the quill in hand. Wulfstan dictated the formula. Fortunately the writing was brief, for Halfdan was more warrior than scholar. He scrawled his signature on the badly blotted page just as the sun was dipping below the horizon.

The instant he pressed his signet ring into the pool of wax, making the document legal, the air was rent with a distant hideous scream that grew louder until the room filled with an agonized orange color. The wizards paled and made furtive gestures. A darkness followed, one that devoured the orange light. A probing angry chill crawled along Halfdan's bones.

But the presence slowly left, and candles pipped into flame in the wall sconces.

A familiar *whap-whap-whap* was heard outside the window, in the courtyard. Halfdan ran to look out.

"Daddy!" shrieked a glad voice. *Whap-whap-whap* went the hurried dragon's wings back over the wall.

"Halla!" he shouted. "Are you well?"

"A little smoky! Daddy, I've had the most interesting time! Wait till you hear!"

Halfdan smiled. Brave child. Good thing the marriage contract was already signed. He'd have to move in with his son-in-law because he'd resigned his barony to his half-brother William in order that Halla no longer be the daughter of a ruler. William wouldn't want him underfoot, with his own ideas of how the barony should be run.

He wondered if Aethelwold would allow him to bring Wulfstan along. It had been the wizard's idea for Halfdan to resign, and a mind capable of such subtleties might prove useful in the years to come. For Halfdan did not intend to sit idle before Aethelwold's fire. . . .

AL KUHFELD is curator of The Bakken in Minneapolis, where he restores old medical and electrical artifacts and designs museum exhibits. MARY KUHFELD works part-time as a secretary and full-time as a writer. She has published two murder mysteries as Mary Monica Pulver.

THE MATCHBOOK DETECTIVE

E.E. AYDELOTTE

One day I am in a state liquor store buying a pack of cigarettes plus some medicine for my landlady (who happens to be the mother of my girlfriend Olive) when I also take some matches from a bowl of the same they have on the counter by the cash register. I do not notice until I get home that inside these matches is a limited offer from the Matchbook Detecting School of Yuma, Arizona, to become a certified correspondence-school private detective.

The detecting business (asserts the inside cover of the matchbook) is expanding daily and has an urgent need for new operatives. It is the growth field for the eighties. To verify this startling fact, all I need do is read the crime page in my local newspaper, says the matchbook.

I do so and find that the matchbook is correct. Crime is on the rise in the U.S. of A., and there is a shortage of trained detection operatives. This I prove with my own newspaper, and so I rush to my savings and loan, withdraw a money order for $87.95, and I am forthwith enrolled in detecting school.

It is difficult and exacting work, this detecting school correspondence course from Yuma, Arizona. Perhaps you have never had to memorize the four stages of decomposition in a corpse, or the complete text of the Detective's Code of Honor, or what the seven warning signs of adultery are. I have, and I can tell you that it is not a picnic situation.

Resolutely I finish the six weeks of travail, and eventually the biggest day of my life occurs—although I am at work and miss it as my landlady signs for the package, which comes first-class mail and contains my inscribed diploma from the Matchbook Detecting School of Yuma, Arizona, along with a genuine copper-plated private detecting badge and a very generous offer to enroll in the postgraduate course (open to Honor Roll students only, of which I find I am a prominent member) for the special discount tuition of $318.75 (regularly $425.00).

Regretfully I forgo the postgraduate course as I am now restricted on funds, having decided to leave my old employment as finished-goods inspector at Mr. Penney's rubber-band factory on the south side. Mr. Penney is somewhat difficult about it, but I stick my resolve in the butter, as they say.

"Warner Digby!" bellows old Mr. Penney. "You've pulled some damn fine boners in your eleven years with me. Yes! I can remember at least a half a dozen triple doozies, like the time you thought you saw—"

"We agreed never to speak of that, Mr. Penney," I interrupt him, "and besides, I paid for the horse out of my own paycheck, which you so helpfully deducted in advance of my offer, and I do think your protest in this situation is based on jealousy."

"Jealousy?" he sputters. Mr. Penney is eighty-three, and he sputters when he becomes enraged, which is a daily occurrence in the rubber-band plant.

"Yes," I admonish him, "jealous of the young women I will be having social intercourse with daily now. You have seen examples of this on television detective shows—which I very well know, having been invited once to view the Super Bowl on your wide screen, although I could not attend because you had me scheduled to work overtime that Sunday."

Mr. Penney sputters and rages, as is his custom, but I am firm in my resolve. I am assisted by my mind's-eye view of the Matchbook Detecting brochure, which displays on its cover a typical private detecting secretary. This is a pneumatic young woman of excessive attributes who smiles fetchingly into the camera. From what the excellent text intimates, a successful private detective may have his pick from dozens of comely applicants for the position of private detecting secretary.

"I shall not be able to purchase a Chevrolet Camaro immediately," I say to Mr. Penney, "which is the customary transportation in my new trade, but I hope soon with the easing of credit restrictions and my own imminent business success to acquire one."

"You cretin!" roars Mr. Penney. Out in the rubber-band shop people stop their work to look toward his office window. "You've been here eleven years and you still don't know the difference between a Number 8 narrow band and a Number 10 wide! Why, inside of a month you'll come crawling back here for your old job, and it might not be here, Digby! I might have found a twelve-year-old who is overqualified but willing to take it on! Why, I—"

There is more such unpleasantness which, if I was to repeat it, would only serve to tire you. I have been one of

Mr. Penney's pets, to admit the truth, and I did not relish telling him the news of my departure, knowing as I did how ungracefully he would take it. He spits when he talks too fast.

The next day I move into my new office and become, officially, a private detecting agent. I am prouder than a peacock with quintuplets.

I choose my new quarters with care, as they must satisfy the complex requirements of the Matchbook Detecting Agent's Pocket Manual. I select an office in an older building (for economy's sake, see manual page 37)—seventy years old, to be exact, and built of brick from the days when *brick* meant something besides a woman's figure, if you follow me. The building is in a location (for easy access to my work environment, see page 112) that detecting sociologists call a "melting pot" district.

This spot is ideal. The block behind me holds the rich wheeler-dealers of the financial world who will be my clients. That avenue has jewelry stores, banks, investment houses, swank restaurants, ritzy clothing stores, and sundry other establishments catering to the monied elite. The block in front of my new office is home to the dregs of humanity, those who will form my natural opponents and who will, in the months ahead, grow to dread my fearless tread (manual page 14). My location is urban renewal in all its glory. I pay the rent in advance and don't have enough left over for even the corpse of a sandwich.

"You can eat at the mission," says my fair Olive, observing just such an institution situated across the street from my new "digs." I suspect Olive fears my new career will lengthen our engagement beyond the six and one-half years at which it already stands. "Olive," as I fondly call her, is a slender girl of scrawny dimensions who, as I explicated prior-wise, is the sole offspring of my landlady and is a particularly unmarried offspring at that.

"I point out to you, my dearest Olive, that, number one, the Fourth Avenue Mission of Faith only serves meals to the destitute and down on their luck, of which I can certainly not be one as long as I uphold the Private Detecting Code of Honor; and two, now that I have opened my office to the public, I am certain to begin my rapid rise as foretold in the Matchbook Detecting Agent's Pocket Manual, which I constantly refer to and trust."

"Huh!" is her pithy reply. Olive has a rather negative streak to her, which is why we are a well-matched couple, opposites attracting as they do.

I, on the other hand, am what the manual calls "an electric force of positive thinking." I am planning to rely on word of mouth throughout the city's financial district and underworld to bring me the business my talents deserve. "Once a success, you may pick your clients from among a clamoring multitude" (manual page 346).

"Should you have complaints, Olive, regarding my choice of career," I say, "I suggest you bring them to your mother's attention, as I would not be availing myself of the growth job of the eighties as I am if it were not for the errand I undertook for her that fateful night, fetching her a fifth of medicinal brandy and her cigarettes, in the accidental acquisition of which the matchbook has benefited me so."

I glance through the sooty front window. "I believe," I say, "that word of mouth is about to deliver my first client."

A young woman of configuration enters. Olive sniffs like she does.

I give our visitor my last dollar.

"What is this?" asks this woman who is destined to be my first client.

I make a sweeping gesture of manliness, like the manual

recommends. (First impressions mean everything.) "It is a custom in the private detecting business to award one's first client a dollar. I am Warner Digby, trained detecting agent. This is my new office, and I am at your service."

My dear fiancée Olive says, "Warner, you big baboon, you've mucked it all up again! You're supposed to frame the first dollar you earn, not give one away! You're hopeless!" And with that broadside my fair fiancée Olive stalks out.

"I think it's a cute custom," says my visitor. She pockets my dollar.

"I must warn you, miss," I say, "my aim is to be the highest-paid detecting agent in this city. Before I accept your commission you must be aware that my fees will be sizable . . . as will be my service to you."

"You mean you *really* have rented this old place?" she asks, drawing her finger in the dust of an ancient desk that sits in the center of the room. The real estate agent has confided to me that the last use of this property was very long ago, as a seedy race-booking establishment.

I draw myself erect. "Perhaps it is not much to look at today, but I intend to bring this old office to a high state of preparedness. I will install venetian blinds so the late afternoon shadows will fall correctly upon the old brick walls, and that neon hotel sign across the street will add nicely to the evening atmosphere. I shall hire a buxom secretary who will wear silk stockings, and when the official police are stumped they shall come to me for succor."

She observes me carefully. "What *exactly* did you say you do?" she asks.

"Why, I am a private detecting agent. I thought you knew." I produce my special imitation-vinyl case, open it with a practiced flip (I have been practicing all morning), and display my official copper-plated badge.

"My!" she says with what I take to be admiration. "Badge

Number 311 from the Matchbook Detecting School of Yuma, Arizona."

"You've heard of it?"

"Of course! Ask anyone in Yuma. All the tourists go there," she says. She smiles and laughs at me. What a nice young woman she is!

"I was an Honor Roll graduate," I admit with careful modesty. I can tell she is impressed.

"Now," I say, getting down to business, as I do not wish to be victim to dinner at the Fourth Avenue Mission of Faith, as my fair Olive has intimated, "what can I do for *you?*"

Just then a burly fellow carrying a pick and a shovel enters my office. I take him, from a long study of the manual and its chapter on criminal types and their distinguishing features, to be a ruffian. Curiously, he seems somehow to be acquainted with my client.

"Who's the mug?" he calls to her. "What a queer-looking bird! What the—is he doon here?"

"You, sir, are a cad, speaking foul language in front of a lady and a citizen and my client." I step forward and, as the manual instructs, firmly present my fists.

"What the—" says the burl, as I plant my "hard left" directly on his chin. My knuckle gives a cracking noise and feels similar, but there is no other distinguishable result.

The burl apparently grasps a wall and flings it at me because I distinctly sense being struck by it twice. My client is talking rapidly. The burl backs off and I regain my feet. The burl and my client go into conference, which I join indiscreetly.

"This," says the girl, gesturing a thumb at me, "is Warner Digby, private eye. He's just finished a mail-order course and has opened his office today."

"So?" says the burl.

"He rented *this* office, you thickheaded ape."

"This office?" says the burl.

"You got it. I think perhaps you ought to go out for a while."

He goes, along with his pick and his shovel.

"Is he a friend of yours?" I ask. She explains that she was once a secretary for a road contractor and she has gotten to know many of the laborers personally and happens to recognize this one when he inadvertently takes a wrong turn into my office.

"Oh," I say with sudden comprehension, "so *that's* why he has those sundry implements. He is a road worker. I could have sworn he is a criminal type. I hope I do not disremember my lessons so rapidly." I remove my manual from its pocket and flip through, searching for the chapter on criminal types.

"I need your help, Mr. Digby," announces my client. I remember my difficulty regarding dinner and replace the manual.

"I am at your service."

She pauses a moment to think. "It is my sister," she says.

"Of course. She has embezzled your inheritance? Or perhaps run off with the chauffeur?"

My client looks at me funny, as if I am a curious specimen. "Yes," she says finally, "how did you know?"

I smug my face. "Training," I say. "I could explain my chain of reasoning to you, if you would like. It will make the simplest deduction of the obvious seem overwhelmingly complex, and—"

"That won't be necessary," she says. "My sister has escaped with my inheritance and the family chauffeur, all that our dear father left us. We are the only children, you know, and our mother passed on years ago. How could Eileen do this to me?"

"When did you last see this harlot?" I ask probingly.

She considers. "This morning at breakfast. She had an airline ticket to Hawaii poking out of the pocket of her robe. Do you think that might mean something?"

"Yes," I say, "to a trained observer such as myself it reveals all. Not a minute to lose, Miss, uh—"

"Cheryl Thompson."

"Yes, Miss Thompson. Now, this may seem confusing to you, being as you are unversed in modern detecting science, but I must be off to the airport at once. Think hard now, and tell me: on your chance perusal of the ticket, did you notice which airline it was written for?"

"Uh . . . no."

"Rats! A setback! It means I'll have to cover both terminals. Oh well, I'm young, well trained, and therefore up to this task."

"My whole future lies in your hands," she says breathlessly.

I kiss her wrist, ever the gallant gentleman (manual page 419), and I rush off through the open door of my office. I am back in two jiffies. "How will I recognize your sister?" I ask.

"Uh . . . she looks just like me," says Miss Cheryl Thompson. "We're twins."

"Yes, I should have known." I run back out the door. Again I return to the office. "Say, Miss Thompson . . ." I inquire hesitantly, ". . . could you advance me bus fare?"

"Certainly," she says in that swell voice of hers. Birds must envy her. She hands me over five dollars. Cash.

I am already making money!

I return late that night. My client, Miss Thompson, is standing in the rear of my office conversing with the same burly man who has previously violated my premises. He has apparently put in a day of heavy labor on his road construction job, as he is covered with grime and is sweating profusely.

"Look here," I say to him firmly, "are you bothering my client?"

Miss Cheryl Thompson turns her generous eyes my way and

says sweetly. "What? Who are . . . oh, it's you. How did you get on at the airport, Mr. Digby?"

I take her out of earshot of the tough-looking burl and give her (as the manual recommends) an "encapsulated synopsis" of my day's activities on her behalf, including detailed observations and an expense account consisting of bus rides both ways and a strawberry milk shake.

" . . . anywhere in either terminal," I say. "I suspect your sister Eileen has fled the country, utilizing misdirection with a false airline ticket she permitted you to view, and is now in Mexico or another Latin hideaway where it will be difficult but not impossible to pursue her. 'The southern climes,' " I quote the manual, " 'traditionally have offered safe haven to the criminal classes when they are forced to flee established authority.' "

"Look, honey," says the burl, addressing Miss Thompson while coming toward me in what I consider a menacing fashion, "let me take care of this mug my way."

As the Detecting Agent's Pocket Manual promises will happen in these situations, realization strikes me.

"You called her 'honey,' " I accuse the burl.

"That's nothing to what I'm about to call you," he growls.

I notice another clue. "Just a moment! What is this?" I demand of the burl. The rear of my office has been damaged. There is a hole the size of a manhole cover in the flooring, and dirt is piled about. The burl's previously mentioned pick and shovel are present. I walk over and examine same. "What have you been burying?" I demand of him sternly.

"Burying?" He laughs heavily. "Why, that tunnel—"

"Shut up," interrupts Miss Thompson. "You talk too much."

The burl snarls something rude to her and jumps my way, drawing back a meaty fist to swing destruction at me. Fortunately, in his anger he steps on the blade of his own shovel, which he has left carelessly about, and the handle springs upward in violation of safety standards, tripping the burl. He falls and strikes his head on the brick wall and is momentarily dazed.

In a wink I have my handcuffs out and have attached same to one wrist of the burl and the other end of the cuffs to one of the pipes of plumbing that run exposed down the left-hand wall of my old office.

In a moment he has regained his senses, but it is too late. *"What the—!"* roars the captured burl. He struggles and struggles, yet he cannot escape. My handcuffs are firmly holding him to the pipe, and he is doomed.

"Now for you, Miss *Eileen* Thompson," I say to the woman.

"But . . . I'm your client. I'm *Cheryl* Thompson," she protests.

"Hah!" I respond. "Who do you think you're dealing with? Your little game is obvious."

"Get the keys for these cuffs from the——!" shouts the burl.

She obeys the burl and comes at me with evil intent. After a brief and disagreeable struggle (she is no match for me, of course), she finds herself bound by my second pair of handcuffs. I fasten her securely alongside her accomplice.

"You had no chance to get away with it," I lecture them. "Your scheme was transparent to me from the moment I returned."

"Whatever you think is going on," says the girl, "I can explain."

"Obviously," I say, "what has happened is that while I am on a wild-goose chase at the airport, which was caused by your clever display of the false ticket at breakfast this morning, you two took advantage of my absence to sneak in here and place Miss Cheryl Thompson under bondage. I don't know yet where you've imprisoned her, but I'm confident I soon will discover that fact and I warn you both that if any harm has come to my client, the law will deal severely with you both."

"Listen to me," pleads the girl.

"No, you listen to me," I say. "You are Cheryl Thompson's twin sister Eileen and this ugly fellow here is your sweetheart, the family chauffeur. This morning when he entered, he struck such fear into Cheryl that she was afraid to reveal to me who he really was and therefore, terrified, she contrived the statement that he was a road worker of her acquaintance. He loitered around outside, and as soon as I departed for the airport, he kidnapped Cheryl so that you, her twin sister Eileen, could take her place. That is why when I returned just now you did not at first recognize me. You are not the same girl who was in here this morning. I, of course, knew at once because among other clues Cheryl is *much* prettier."

"You're nuts!" roars the burl.

"Am I?" I taunt him. "It was your own blunder of calling Eileen by the name 'honey' instead of 'Miss Thompson' or 'Cheryl' that allowed my deductive insight. Miss Cheryl Thompson would never allow a ruffian such as yourself to call her by the familiar name 'honey.' You revealed yourself, mister criminal!"

I walk over to where he is imprisoned. After a brief struggle I remove from his inside pocket a bulging sack. Further examination reveals it to be stuffed with various forms of jewelry.

"This," I say triumphantly, "is obviously the inheritance. Half wasn't enough for you, was it, Eileen? In your greed you craved Cheryl's share also."

I point to the hole in my floor and the dirt piled beside it. "You were burying the inheritance here until the heat blew over, eh? What safer place than under our noses? We'd have looked everywhere in the world except right here.

"Pretty clever," I allow. "It was a plan that would have

fooled most detectives. But you two had the misfortune to go up against an Honor Roll graduate of the Matchbook Detecting School of Yuma, Arizona."

Detective Lieutenant Miller comes in, has a few whispered words with the beat cops (who arrived first), and then examines the arrested parties. "All right," he says, "take them downtown and book them."

"We can't," complains one of the uniformed officers, "because those aren't our handcuffs. They're his," pointing an official finger at myself, "and *he* won't surrender the key. He's some kind of nut, lieutenant."

"You got that right, brother," says the burl, who is handcuffed to the plumbing. "He's a regular loony-tune."

The lieutenant comes over and peruses me in a detecting way. "What's your name, sir?"

"I am Warner Digby," I say proudly, "trained graduate of the Matchbook Detecting School of Yuma, Arizona, at your service."

"Mmmm," says the lieutenant. "Do you know who it is that you have in your handcuffs there, Warner?"

"Certainly," I inform him. "That is Eileen Thompson and the Thompson family chauffeur. I have caught them red-handed absconding with the full inheritance that is rightfully shared by Eileen's sister Cheryl Thompson, the same who is now missing and whom I fear for the safety of. We *must* break their silence and force a confession regarding Cheryl Thompson's whereabouts, lieutenant! Until that is accomplished I will not unlock the handcuffs for which I have hidden the key. My client is in danger and I must consider her interests."

"I keep telling him there *ain't* no Cheryl Thompson," lies the chauffeur. "Sally here made it up to get him out of the office."

"Mmmm," repeats the lieutenant. He paces over to the rear wall and examines the pile of dirt, the shovel, and the pick.

"That's where they tunneled under and broke through to Chamberlain's Jewelry," says the first officer. "The ice they took still has Chamberlain's markings on the boxes."

The second officer says, "These old buildings have common walls, lieutenant, and the back of this office butts up against the back of the jewelry store. Walk around the sidewalk to Broadway and see for yourself, sir. I've been telling old Mr. Chamberlain for years that the circuit alarms on his front door and windows aren't enough. He really needs a motion detector and—"

"Yes, yes," says the lieutenant, waving his hand. "Wait out front, will you, boys?" The two uniformed cops depart. I naturally assume that Lieutenant Miller intends to consult me and is too proud to let mere uniformed officers observe.

"I am at your disposal, sir," I tell him politely. The manual (page 222) suggests a mock-submissive tone in these situations, for his comfort. It isn't easy for a veteran police detective to admit an amateur is his superior, and I am always willing to allow accommodations to his pride, if such are possible without jeopardy to the case.

I give the lieutenant a complete rundown of my day's activities. Lieutenant Miller removes his spectacles and vigorously rubs his hand over his eyes and face. I suppose he has been through a tough day and is tired.

"Warner," he says to me finally, "these two people locked to your toilet are Cincinnati Phil and his girlfriend Sally. They're wanted from here to the Coast for more than two dozen jewelry-store heists.

"I don't know who you think these two are or what you think is going on," continues the lieutenant, "but we need your cooperation. The police department is *asking* for your cooperation. I promise you on my badge as a lieutenant of detectives that if you release them to us you can have all the credit. Think about it, Warner—your name would be in the paper tomorrow—might even make the TV news."

" 'The safety of my client's interests is all the credit I require,' " I say, quoting directly from the Private Detecting Code of Honor.

"Mmmm. . . . Look here, Warner, maybe I could put in a word with old Mr. Chamberlain. When he gets his jewelry back and is told that *you* were the one who single-handedly recovered it, I'm sure he'll be willing to shell out a nice reward," he says. "Just *give me the key to the handcuffs, Warner!*"

"I'm sorry," I say, "but you are mistaken. These criminals are Eileen Thompson and her family chauffeur. They are sweethearts and they have absconded with the family inheritance that is by rights half-owned by Eileen's sister, Miss Cheryl Thompson. Must I draw you a picture, lieutenant?" The manual warns that the official detectives will sometimes be a little slow on the uptake.

I walk back over to my prisoners. I slap the burl across his face. "I knew you were a criminal type the first time I saw you," I say. "I'm asking you one more time, *where* is Cheryl Thompson?"

"Lieutenant," cries the dastardly Eileen, "keep him away from us! He's crazy!"

"Yeah," says the burl, "I don't think he's even got a license. We got our rights, don't we?"

"Is this true, Warner?" asks the lieutenant. "Have you been practicing without a license?"

"Certainly not!" I ejaculate. In a fit of pique I produce my genuine copper-clad Matchbook Detecting School badge. "See!" I cry defiantly. "I am a trained detecting operative!"

Lieutenant Miller glances from the badge to me to the badge

and et cetera. Then he does that thing again where he takes his glasses off and vigorously rubs his hand over his eyes and face. "Brrr," he says, which is an odd thing to say, as it is not cold.

"Look," he says almost gently, "in this state you have to apprentice to a qualified detective or have equivalent government experience for a period of not less than three years before you can even apply for a private detective's license. Have you done that, Warner?"

"The correspondence course didn't mention that requirement," I admit.

The lieutenant goes on, "You see, Warner, you have to be licensed before you can legally work at this game. Why, they can fine you up to five thousand dollars, son!"

I am quite impressed by this information. "You wouldn't report me, would you, lieutenant?"

"I will," says the burl quickly. "Lieutenant, I wanna file a complaint against this guy."

This brings a quick response from Detective Lieutenant Miller. "I'll tell you what you're going to do, Cincinnati Phil. You and your girlfriend Sally are going to go downtown and make a complete confession to us, and you're going to sign it in front of witnesses. Or else . . ."

"Or else what, cop?"

". . . I'll leave you here and let Warner beat the whereabouts of Eileen's sister Cheryl out of you."

"Let me at them, lieutenant!" I say. "I'm your man!"

"Okay, okay!" shouts the burl quickly. You can see how the criminal types fear a man of resolve such as myself.

The lieutenant takes me aside. "C'mon, Warner, if you give me the keys to those cuff links, I'll forget all about your, uh, licensing difficulties. What do you say? I promise we'll rescue Miss Cheryl Thompson and take care of her interests. You don't need to be involved further, and I'll have a word first thing tomorrow with old Mr. Chamberlain about your reward."

So that's the way we decide to work it, Lieutenant Miller and me.

The next afternoon I pull up in front of my rooming house in a brand spanking used 1969 Chevrolet Camaro. It has mag wheels on the driver's side and plaid seat covers all around.

This new vehicle will be extremely useful, as I intend in the months ahead to be excessively busy in my new profession. Word of mouth from old Mr. Chamberlain's satisfied lips must inevitably bring me desperate citizens from the monied classes, seeking my services for recourse of their grievances and solution of their mysteries.

I interpret my agreement with Detective Lieutenant Miller to mean that I now have official permission to proceed in my profession without the formality of licensing by the state. Being unlicensed is an advantage I expect will allow me to move unhindered and unrecognized among the criminal classes while I hunt transgressors.

"Oh, Warner!" shrieks my loyal Olive when she hears of the twenty-one-hundred-dollar check I have just received from old Mr. Chamberlain. "Now we can get *married!*"

Our landlady, who is also Olive's mother and my soon-to-be mother-in-law, is beaming happily and even allows as how I may kiss her (my mother-in-law-to-be is meant) on her wrinkled old cheek. This is not among my lists of desires, but I yield to her wishes for the sake of harmony in the family.

There is still one matter to finish. "You will recall that yesterday," I say severely to Olive, "you made a rude suggestion about my potential income as a trained detecting agent. You inferred I will soon be forced to take my meals among the destitute at the Fourth Avenue Mission of Faith.

"Quite the opposite, however, has occurred. I have been, as you can see, Olive, quite successful, and to impress this fact upon you more fully, I desire to take you out to a fine meal tonight. Wear your best dress and be on the front steps at seven P.M."

The Camaro, my fiancée, and I depart promptly at the appointed hour. Olive wears a pink gown of breathtaking rigidity.

You guessed it, I take her to dine at the Fourth Avenue Mission of Faith. There it is "stew night," and while I personally enjoy the modest meal, I sense that Olive, dressed to the teeth, finds the situation a bit humbling and thus learns a valuable lesson . . .

(. . . as the Matchbook Detecting Agent's Pocket Manual, Chapter 23, "Spousal Relations," page 514, recommends).

E.E. AYDELOTTE currently lives near Seattle and works as a technical writer, preparing user manuals for a software development company.

APPOINTMENT WITH YESTERDAY

HUGH B. CAVE

O n the way back to camp that evening, following an afternoon at the seashore, the red-haired boy said, "You guys go ahead, y'hear? Tommy and I got somethin' to do."

"Like what?" he was asked.

"Like never mind. You'll see. Come on, Tommy."

There was still a good hour of daylight left. This was July on Cape Cod. The redhead and little bespectacled Tommy Hibbert, who always did what the redhead wanted, turned off along a sandy footpath, leaving the other six boys of Cabin One to continue along the forest road. All eight were from a Providence, Rhode Island, boys' club, in camp for a month as part of a program for underprivileged youth.

"Boy, will they be surprised when we turn up with it!" said the redhead, whose name was Mark Watson. At fourteen, he was the oldest in Cabin One and naturally the captain. "The only thing is, we have to make sure old Fowler don't see us."

"Will it be dark when we reach camp?"

"Should be, just about."

"What's the problem, then, Markie?"

"The darned thing's *big*. That's what's the problem."

"Oh."

The path they followed was a link between two dirt roads. One road led from a main highway to the camp on the lake. Where the other came from or went to neither boy knew. All they knew was that in an overgrown field by the side of it stood an old Cape Cod cottage, apparently long abandoned, known to all at the camp as the "haunted house." When you came to Camp Wampanoag and heard about the murder from kids who had been to camp before, you had to visit the place. There was a camp rule against it, but you had to go anyway. It was an initiation, kind of.

Approaching the cottage now, red-haired Mark Watson grinned at his protégé. "You scared, Tommy?"

"Not of the house. Only of what'll happen if old Fowler—"

"I tell you he won't know. By the time he even sees what we got, we'll have it fixed up and painted. We'll just tell him we made it."

"Well . . . okay. If you say so."

They trudged through the tall grass to the front door, which made a noise like a stepped-on cat when Mark pushed it open. Had it screeched that way when the robber opened it that night? Probably not. The house was being lived in then by old Mrs. Lazarus, and the hinges wouldn't have been rusty like now.

"I bet he just opened the door real slow," Mark said. "I bet she never even heard him before he squeezed the trigger. Then, pow!"

"What?"

"That's how it must have happened. He was after the money she was supposed to have stashed away here someplace. He just inched this door open"—Mark read mystery stories and intended to write them someday—"and she was sittin' there in that chair with her back to him, rockin' away all unsuspectin', and he shot her."

"You sure she was *shot*, Markie?"

"Well, I never heard any different."

"Did you ever ask?"

"No, I never asked. Why would I ask, for Pete's sake? What difference does it make, anyway?"

The younger boy sensed he was making the redhead angry. "Well, gee, all right, Markie, I was just wonderin'."

The grit on the old board floor made scrunchy sounds under Mark's shoes as he walked toward the chair, which was the only piece of furniture in the room. For that matter, it was the only thing in the whole house, he knew. The kitchen, the dining room, the two bedrooms upstairs—all were empty now. Halting beside the chair, he looked around while waiting for the other boy to join him. To tell the truth, he felt a little scared.

But there was nothing to be afraid of, he told himself. It was just a grimy old living room in an abandoned cottage. The walls were yellow and dirty, with crazy cracks running every which way through the faded flowers on their peeling paper. What else could you expect?

"Come on, will you?" he urged his companion.

"This is it?" Tommy said on reaching Mark's side.

"This is it. The old lady was sittin' in this when she was killed. Anyway, that's the story." The chair lay on its side, and Mark leaned over to touch it. "See what I mean? How we can fix it up?"

"Not like it was, we can't."

"We can come close. Anyway, it'll be the chair she was murdered in, even if it don't look exactly the same as then." Reaching down, Mark took hold of its one unbroken arm. "Come on, now. Let's get it out of here!"

It was not an easy task for two boys their age and size. The chair was of Cape Cod pine and fairly heavy. Worse, it was bulky. After a number of tries they settled on a way of carrying it between them with one boy holding the arm, the other an edge of the seat, which was intact. Even so, it kept bumping their legs and thighs, and they had to stop often to rest.

Only once were they forced to move off the road to avoid being seen—or "detected," as the future writer of mystery tales would have put it. They were back on the camp road at the time and heard a pickup coming. "Hey!" Mark hissed in alarm. "It could be Fowler!"

But while the director often did drive the pickup, he was not in it when it passed them. At the wheel was Edgar Nesbit, the middle-aged camp handyman, too interested in sipping from a pint bottle to be aware of the two boys crouching beside their stolen rocking chair in the roadside underbrush.

Edgar almost always had a bottle to sip from—a thing Mr. Darren Fowler, with all his snooping, never seemed to find out. The kids knew but liked Edgar well enough to keep quiet about it. Besides, he didn't get drunk; he just drank.

"All right," Mark chortled as they scrambled back onto the road with their burden. "That's one we don't have to watch out for. Now we only have to get past the others." The others, of course, included Fowler, an assistant director, and several counselors.

But, thanks to the chair, their timing turned out to be excellent, and they arrived at the camp just at dark. Five minutes of waiting behind an old sawdust pile—the place had been a sawmill site once—and they were able almost to stroll to their cabin without danger of being seen. In a welter of excitement, their cabin mates crowded around them.

"There it is!" the redhead gloated, propping the broken chair up so it appeared to be almost usable. "Old lady Lazarus was murdered in this, by gosh, and when we go back to Providence, I'm takin' it with me!"

"How?" someone demanded.

"Never mind how. I'll think of somethin'. But when I start writin' my mystery stories, this is the chair I'll be writin' 'em in."

"Writers use typewriters nowadays, Markie. Even computers."

"All right. I'll think 'em *up* in this chair, then. That's the most important thing—thinkin' 'em up!" He gave the chair a prideful pat, which promptly caused it to fall over on its side as it had been in the front room of the haunted house. "But first we got to fix it up. And fast, before anyone sees it and figures out where it came from."

That night the chair lay in a corner of the cabin, half hidden by the end of the double bunk in which the redhead and his protégé, Tommy, slept. In the morning, after breakfast and chores, Mark went to Edgar Nesbit, the camp handyman, to borrow some tools.

"What you want them for?" About fifty, Nesbit had a beard the color of salt and pepper mixed together in a shaker and eyes so bright blue they looked artificial. He'd been born there on the Cape, less than five miles from the camp.

"I'll show you when we get it done."

"You want them right *now*? You skippin' the swim?"

"We went to the ocean yesterday."

"Okay." Nesbit shrugged to show it made no difference to him. Then he produced, on request, a hammer, a saw, a hand drill, nails and screws, and a screwdriver. When asked for scrap wood, he shrugged again and pointed to an assortment of it on the floor of his workshop.

Mark returned to Cabin One laden and triumphant, and by nightfall the chair had two arms instead of one. Next day it acquired a new rocker and new rungs, though in referring to them as "rungs," the future author admitted he might not be using the proper word. "When I write about this someday, which I intend to, I'll look it up. We don't have time now."

The carpentry finished, back he went to Edgar Nesbit to beg some paint.

"Now, what in the world are you kids doing over there in that cabin?" Edgar demanded. "What you want paint for?"

"We'll show you when it's finished. Please, Edgar? Just a small can of enamel?"

"What color?"

"Well—red." That was the proper color for a murder chair, no?

The following day the old rocking chair, rebuilt and painted fire-engine red, was ready for use, though it looked nothing at all like the one old Mrs. Lazarus had been murdered in.

Now began the games.

With little Tommy Hibbert seated in the chair, solemnly staring at the cabin wall while he rocked, Mark showed the others how the murder must have been committed. Going outside and closing the door behind him, he waited, like the mystery-story writer he intended to be, for suspense to build up inside. Then he silently eased the door open, stepped over the threshold, whipped up his right hand, and said, "Pow!"

Tommy obediently slumped forward in the chair and began groaning.

"You say he was after her money?" one of the other boys said.

"That's the story. People in the village said she had a pile of it hidden away in the house somewhere, though she pretended to be poor."

"Where would an old lady like that get a whole lot of money?"

"Well, she was some kind of witch. Like she told fortunes and stuff."

"There's a Lazarus in the Bible," someone said. "Jesus raised him from the dead."

"That was a *man*, dummy. Anyway, this old lady had a pile of money and this guy, whoever he was, was after it."

"Did he find it?"

"Now, that's a stupid question if I ever heard one. How do we know if he found it or not, when we don't even know who he was?"

"They never arrested nobody?"

"Uh-uh." Mark wagged his head. "They never had a clue."

"Didn't they find a bullet or anything?" someone asked. "If he shot her in the back, like you say, the bullet must have stayed in her or gone through into a wall or somethin'."

From the expression on Mark's face, it was plain to see the future writer of mysteries hadn't thought of that and was annoyed with himself. Luckily he was saved from having to think up a reply when little Tommy Hibbert, still in the chair, suddenly voiced an exclamation.

"Hey! It's moving!"

They all looked at him.

"It's moving!" Tommy propelled himself out of the chair as though it had suddenly become electrified. The leap sent him sprawling to his hands and knees on the cabin floor, where he twitched himself around to look at the chair in astonishment.

The chair was slowly rocking. It continued to rock until Mark reached out and stopped it.

"You're a nut," Mark said. "You rocked it yourself, dummy."

"I did not! I was just sittin' there!"

"You rocked it. Anyone sittin' in a rockin' chair rocks it, even without thinkin'."

"I tell you I didn't," Tommy insisted, though less emphatically than before.

"Look." Mark sat in the chair. "I'll show you."

They watched, some standing within arm's reach, some seated on their bunks. The redhead sat in the chair and nothing happened for what seemed a long time, though surely it was less than a minute.

Then the chair began to rock.

"See?" Mark pushed himself out of it. "You don't know you're doin' it, even. But you do it."

Satisfied, they let the matter drop and began discussing a treasure hunt scheduled for the following day. In charge of that event was the one person in camp they unanimously disliked: the assistant director, Joel Abbott. It was Joel, born in a nearby Cape village, who had gruffly warned all of them to stay away from the house from which Mark and Tommy had removed the chair.

"That house is out of bounds to you kids. And I mean it, you hear?" With his fists on his hips and his head thrust forward like a rooster's, he had snarled his ultimatum. "You go snooping around there, and you'll find yourselves taking the next bus back to Providence!"

Question: Should they boycott the treasure hunt to show the assistant director how little they thought of him?

It was a lively discussion.

But Mark, having retired to his lower bunk, did not enter into it. He sat there with his elbows on his knees and his chin on his fists and gazed at the red rocking chair as though it puzzled him.

His protégé, losing interest in the treasure-hunt talk, retired to the bunk above him, leaned over, and said quietly, "Did you, Markie?"

"Did I what?"

"Make it move? Or did it move by itself, like I said?"

"I dunno." The redhead scratched a corner of his mouth. "I don't *think* I made it move, Tommy, but I dunno."

Now for two days the chair stood in the center of the cabin, and the boys took turns sitting in it. Some said it moved of its own accord; others said they were crazy. Around camp, it became known that the boys of Cabin One had finished a carpentry project, building themselves a rocking chair. The director, Mr. Darren Fowler, came and admired it, praising them for their ingenuity. So did the assistant director, Joel Abbott, and the counselors. None of them recognized the chair as the one from the abandoned home of the murdered Mrs. Lazarus.

Finally, one evening just before dark, Edgar Nesbit, the camp handyman, came to see what had been achieved with his tools, lumber, and paint.

"Well, I'll be gosh darned," he said, gazing at the chair in wonder. His breath betrayed the fact that he had been sipping again.

The boys grinned at one another, and one said, "Give it a try, Edgar. It works real good."

"I bet it does." Edgar eased himself down onto it. Then, obviously enjoying himself, he gripped its arms and closed his eyes and began rocking.

Suddenly the chair went all the way back and so did Edgar's head, with something apparently pulling at his hair. His eyes opened wide in bright blue terror and his neck arched up, with his Adam's apple all but popping out of it. And across his neck, just above the Adam's apple, appeared a line of crimson, as though someone had taken a red-ink marking pen and drawn it from under one ear to under the other.

It seemed he tried to scream but couldn't and only made a gurgling, bubbling sound as though his throat had been slashed.

Terrified by what looked like the man's death throes, the boys fled wildly from the cabin. Mark Watson, the future writer of mysteries, was the only one to pause in the doorway and look back.

When they returned with the director and his assistant a few minutes later, the man in the rebuilt rocking chair was dead. The line of red across his throat was already fading. But what was in those brilliant blue eyes would go with him to his grave.

It was terror. Sheer, total, heart-stopping terror.

"This chair!" Mr. Fowler fiercely turned on young Mark Watson. "*Did* you make it as you said you did?"

"N-no, sir. N-not exactly. We made an old one over."

"Where did it come from?"

"The haunted house, sir."

Mr. Fowler turned in triumph to his assistant. "We seem to have solved an old mystery here, don't we? Even to how it happened. He must have opened the cottage door so quietly she didn't hear him. He walked up behind her and grabbed her by the hair and pulled her head back. He cut her throat."

Still staring at the man in the chair, the assistant director slowly nodded.

"All right," Mr. Fowler said then to the occupants of Cabin One. "You boys may use Cabin Four tonight; those lads went home today. Don't touch anything here. Just clear out with what you'll need."

The boys moved to the other cabin and talked in low tones about what had happened. All agreed that somehow the spirit of the murdered witch-woman must have been waiting there in the rocking chair, for revenge. After all, the Lazarus in the Bible had come back from the dead, hadn't he?

The future writer of mysteries was chided for his invention of the gun.

"You and your 'pow!' Ha!"

But the redhead had no time to waste on foolishness. "Never mind that, you dummies. Don't you see what we got here? This proves the killer never found the old lady's money. He wouldn't have been workin' here as a handyman if he did."

Mouths open, they stared at him.

"What we got to do now," he solemnly told them, "is go back to that old house and do some real detective work."

Born in England, HUGH B. CAVE grew up in Massachusetts. His work has appeared in a range of magazines, including The Saturday Evening Post *and* Boys' Life. *He has published thirty books on a variety of subjects, from World War II to travel to young adult novels.*

Several of his novels have been book club selections, and many of his shorter works have been anthologized. A collection of stories called Murgunstrumm and Others *won a World Fantasy Award for Best Collection. Other stories have been dramatized on radio and television. In 1987, he received the Phoenix Award for outstanding achievement by a southern writer (he lived in Florida at the time).*

NO ONE EVER LISTENS

STEPHANIE KAY BENDEL

My name is Tracy Rogers, and I want to report a murder," I said carefully into the telephone.

"Yes, ma'am." The policeman's voice sounded as though he believed me. I was afraid he wouldn't. He asked for my address. "Now, tell me what happened."

I took a deep breath. "My neighbor, Mr. Eddie Huggins, killed his wife and buried her under the rosebushes in his backyard."

There was a long silence. "Miss Rogers, how old are you?"

"Eleven—and a half."

"Oh! And did you *see* Mr. Huggins kill his wife?"

"No," I said truthfully. "But I heard them arguing. And now she's disappeared, and he says she went to visit a sick sister. But he's lying. And I *did* see him bury something!"

"Uh-huh. Okay, Miss Rogers, I'll take care of this for you," the policeman said.

But I heard him chuckle before the line went dead, and I knew he wasn't going to do anything at all. That was the worst thing about being eleven years old. No one ever listened to me.

So I had to figure out what to do about Eddie Huggins all by myself.

Although the Hugginses had lived next door for the past two years, I didn't know very much about them. They kept to themselves. Mrs. Huggins—her first name was Sharon—was tall and slim and had beautiful red hair that tumbled halfway down her back. She always wore tight jeans or short shorts and walked with a little wiggle. Heads turned when she passed. Even Daddy's. Mom once teasingly called him swivelneck, and his face got all red.

Mr. Huggins was older than his wife, and he had a bald head and a big belly. He always scowled, and he smelled of stale cigars if you got near him. I wondered why Sharon married him. As far as I could see, the only thing the Hugginses had in common was that they both hated Mrs. Bailey's cat.

Mrs. Bailey was the Hugginses' neighbor on the other side. A widow, she was cranky and hard of hearing and lived alone with her cat. He was a big orange tom named Merwin, and he often made a ruckus at night—usually from outside the Hugginses' bedroom window. They threw things at him, like shoes and magazines.

But a few weeks ago, Eddie peppered the cat with buckshot, and Mrs. Bailey took him to court. The judge said that Merwin was a public nuisance and Mrs. Bailey was supposed to keep him indoors at night. He also said Eddie had broken the law by firing a shotgun inside the city limits. Eddie had to pay a fine.

That left everybody unhappy. Mrs. Bailey said Eddie was an inhuman monster and begged the judge to lock him up. Eddie shouted—right there in court—that if he ever got his hands on Merwin, he'd kill him.

I think Merwin understood what happened. He still went wherever he pleased during the day, but I noticed that he always detoured around the Hugginses' yard.

Anyhow, my problem began around eight-thirty last Wednesday evening. It was the first week of summer vacation, and I didn't have to worry about homework or early bedtimes. I was walking past the Hugginses' yellow ranch house on my way to the corner store for an ice-cream cone. The evening was warm, and the Hugginses had their windows open.

". . . don't know what in hell you think you're doing! I'm not letting you get away with this!" That was Eddie's voice.

". . . don't give a damn what you think, Eddie!"

". . . if I catch you sneaking out again . . ."

"*Don't touch me!* No, Eddie! Don't—" Sharon's voice sounded real funny just before it broke off.

Then there was a silence. I stopped and listened, but I couldn't hear anything.

I tried to imagine what was happening inside that house. Mom and Daddy fought sometimes. I'd be lying in bed and their angry voices would float up the stairwell. It might go on for a half hour at a time. But I knew Daddy would never *hurt* Mom. And eventually the angry voices would soften and I'd hear an occasional giggle from Mom and a low chuckle from Daddy. And if there was silence after that, I knew mushy things were going on.

But the silence in the Hugginses' house wasn't like that. It was a scary kind of quiet. I got so frightened that I forgot about the ice cream and ran home.

As I entered the house, my sister Mary Ann pounced on me. Mary Ann is fifteen and absolutely gorgeous. Trouble is, she knows it. Right now, her dark eyes were wide with anger. "*You!* You used my nail polish and didn't put the cap on tight! The whole bottle's gotten gummy!"

"Me?" I brushed my hair out of my eyes and stuck out my lower lip at her. "Does this look like I've been using your nail polish?" I held out my hands, showing her my ten bitten fingernails. Then I remembered that I *had* used her polish— to touch up the red paint on my bike. "Ooh, I'm sorry, Mare. I *did* use it. I'll buy you a new bottle tomorrow, right after breakfast, I promise!"

Mary Ann softened. "Well, if you promise! Be sure it's 'Frosted Apple.' " She disappeared into the living room, trailing a cloud of cologne and hair spray. I wondered whether I'd ever be as pretty as Mary Ann.

I forgot all about the Hugginses until the middle of the night, when I woke up without knowing why. I hadn't had a nightmare. My stomach didn't ache. I was lying in the dark, trying to figure out what had awakened me, when I heard a soft, dull thud outside my open window. Then I heard it again.

My second-story window overlooks the Hugginses' backyard. I pushed back the frilly pink curtains Mom had made for me. The moon was just a sliver in the sky, but I could make out Eddie's bulky figure. He was digging up his rosebushes.

I thought it was strange that he wasn't using a flashlight. Even if he had been, no one could have seen him except me. The back of his yard is lined with tall arborvitae, and the windows of Mrs. Bailey's cottage look upon a six-foot fence.

Eddie had already dug a big hole. I watched with my elbows on the windowsill and my chin cupped in my hands. He made the hole deeper and deeper until only the top of his bald head reflected the dim moonlight.

I was wondering how deep he was going to dig when he scrambled out of the hole and went into the house. A minute

later, he reappeared, carrying something wrapped in a dark
blanket. With a shiver, I realized that the something was large
enough to be a person. It was heavy enough, too, because
Eddie was really struggling with it. He staggered across the
yard. Then he dropped it—blanket and all—into the hole
and began covering it with earth.

I had read enough detective stories to know what I was
seeing. Eddie had killed Sharon and was burying her in his
backyard. What other explanation could there be? I stayed at
the window watching until he had reset the last rosebush in
place and carefully tamped the earth around it. When he went
back into his house, I padded down the hall to Mom and
Daddy's room and knocked on the door. "Daddy! Mom! Wake
up!"

Mom opened the door, her eyes puffy with sleep. She was
pulling on her robe. "What's the matter, Tracy?"

"We've got to call the police! Mr. Huggins killed his wife
and buried her in his backyard!"

Mom looked at me for a long moment. Then she looked
back into the bedroom. *"George!"*

Daddy staggered sleepily down the hall to my room and
looked out the window at the rosebushes in Eddie's yard.
"Everything looks normal to me, Trace," he said. "I think
you just had a dream."

"I wasn't dreaming!"

Mom yawned. "Sometimes dreams can seem very real. Better go back to bed, babe."

Mary Ann, globs of night cream on her face, stood in the
doorway. "What's going on?"

"Nothing," Daddy said, running his fingers through his hair.
"Tracy just had a nightmare. She's going back to sleep now."

"But, Daddy!"

He tousled my hair. "Believe me, Trace. This will seem
pretty funny in the morning."

And when I looked out the window again at eight-thirty in the morning, I *did* wonder. There were four rosebushes in the Hugginses' yard. The earth around them looked black and fresh, but they still looked as ordinary as ever. There was nothing to prove that I hadn't dreamed the whole thing.

At breakfast in the sunny kitchen, last night seemed even more unreal. Daddy was already dressed and finishing up his coffee before leaving for the office. Mom, in robe and slippers, poured a glass of orange juice for me. Mary Ann was toying with her eggs. Her hair was still rumpled from sleep, but her mascara and eyeliner were already carefully applied. She grinned at me as I sat down.

"Here she is! Tracy Rogers, girl private eye!"

I glowered at her. "Go ahead and make fun of me! I *know* Eddie buried *something* last night! I saw him!" I sipped my juice, then added, "And I *still* think we should tell the police!"

Mom gave Daddy a funny look and he put down his coffee cup. "Trace, what happened last night was probably a dream. But if you *did* see Eddie bury something, I'll bet it was Mrs. Bailey's cat. She let it out again. I heard it yowling around one o'clock."

"It was a lot bigger than a cat," I insisted. But Daddy was draining the last of his coffee and didn't seem to hear.

Mom set a plate of eggs and toast in front of me. "Eat something, dear. You'll feel better."

"Daddy—"

"Sorry, Trace. I've got to run." He stood up and folded his napkin. "Don't worry. Your imagination's just working overtime. And for Pete's sake, *don't* say anything about this to *anybody!* Huggins'll sue us for slander or something."

He left, and I felt deserted.

"You promised to buy me a new bottle of nail polish," Mary Ann reminded me.

On my way back from the corner store, with Mary Ann's

polish in my hand, I kicked with discouragement at a stick on the sidewalk. It wasn't fair! If I were a grown-up, they'd have listened! They'd probably even have taken Mary Ann seriously. But anything an eleven-year-old said wasn't worth listening to.

When I'd left the house, Mom had asked, "Where are you going?"

"To feed the tigers at the zoo."

"Well, be sure to be back by eleven. We're going to Aunt Vera's for lunch."

It was always like that. Nobody ever listened to a thing I said.

I kept thinking about Eddie. Was it possible I was wrong? Maybe he'd gotten rid of something else in the backyard last night. Maybe Sharon Huggins was perfectly all right. It would be nice to be sure.

I was nearly home when I got an idea. I trotted up the Hugginses' front walk and rang the doorbell. After a moment, Eddie opened the door. His eyes were swollen, his chin was covered with dark stubble, and he smelled of stale cigars.

"Yeah?" he growled.

I held up the nail polish. "I bought this for Mrs. Huggins. My sister borrowed a bottle from her a couple of days ago."

Eddie grabbed the bottle. "Yeah, okay. I'll give it to her." He started to shut the door, but I pushed forward.

"Would—would you ask her if the color is all right? It's not quite the same as the one Mary Ann borrowed. If she doesn't like it, I can exchange it."

Eddie's eyes narrowed for a moment. "She isn't home right now."

"Oh! Well, I can talk to her later. When do you expect her?"

Eddie stared at his hands. His fingernails were dirty. "Actually, she's out of town. You see, she went to stay with her sister in Des Moines. The sister's real sick." He shrugged. "I don't know how long she'll be gone."

A little thrill ran up my spine. "I'm awfully sorry," I said quickly. "I hope her sister gets better."

A minute later, as I mounted the steps of my own home, I realized that Eddie had kept the polish.

"What are you doing?" Mary Ann demanded as I charged up to my room.

"Gotta get some more money for your polish."

"I thought you left to get it a half hour ago!"

"I did, but I lost it. Gotta buy another bottle."

Mary Ann moaned. "Honestly, Tracy! You haven't got a brain in your head!"

"Mrs. Huggins is gone!" I retorted. "Does *that* sound like I'm so dumb? I *told* you something's happened to her!"

"How do you know she's gone?"

I explained.

Mary Ann sniffed. "The only thing that proves is that you've been reading too many drugstore mysteries." She gave me one of her pity-my-little-sister looks. "*Tracy Rogers and the Case of the Planted Wife,*" she teased. "How do you know she *hasn't* gone to Des Moines?"

She was right, of course. A good detective would check that out. Only I didn't know how.

All during the ride to Aunt Vera's house in Middleton and all through lunch, I thought about it.

"Goodness, girl! You're so quiet today!" Aunt Vera, who was a somewhat older and plumper version of Mom, clucked over me. "And you haven't eaten a thing! Don't you feel well?" She shoved a buttered muffin toward me.

I protested, but Mom cut in. "She's all right, Vera. She just didn't sleep well last night."

Aunt Vera turned to me. "Why don't you go upstairs and

lie down while the rest of us visit?" she suggested.

I was glad to be alone. I flopped down on Aunt Vera's big soft bed and stared at the roses on the wallpaper.

If only I could be sure that Sharon wasn't in Des Moines. If I knew the name of Sharon's sister, I could call Des Moines and ask for Sharon. Then I'd know.

Of course, if Sharon *did* answer, it would be pretty embarrassing. What could I say?

I wouldn't have to say anything, I decided. If Sharon answered, I'd just hang up. But then there'd be the long-distance call to explain. And I couldn't very well call collect.

I stared at the pink Princess phone next to Aunt Vera's bed. There was a simpler way. I dialed long-distance information and, a moment later, the operator.

"I want to make a collect call to Riverside," I said. I gave her the number.

"And your name, please?"

"Sharon Huggins," I said sweetly.

"Hello." Eddie's gruff voice came on the line.

"I have a collect call for anyone from Sharon Huggins," the operator said. "Will you accept the charges?"

I heard a gasp at the other end of the line. There was a long silence. Then Eddie said, "Yeah, yeah. Sure."

"Go ahead, ma'am."

I didn't say anything.

"Hello! Hello?" Eddie's voice had changed. It was tight and strained.

"Who in hell is this?" he hissed.

I hung up. My heart was pounding. There couldn't be any mistake now. Eddie had known it wasn't Sharon calling from Des Moines or anywhere else.

"Who were you calling, dear?" Mom was standing in the doorway.

I got up and smoothed out the bedspread. "Dial-a-Prayer." I smiled. There were some advantages to being ignored all the time. "Are we leaving already?"

"I'm afraid so. We have to shop for a new outfit for Mary Ann to wear to the youth dance on Saturday night. Do you feel any better?"

"Yeah, lots. Do I have to go shopping, too?"

"I don't suppose so. Just stay around home, all right?"

A half hour later, from my own front door, I watched Mom back the station wagon out of the driveway. As soon as it was down the street, I called the police.

But the police didn't listen to me, either.

The heck with it, I finally decided. If they won't listen to me, let them find out about Sharon's murder by themselves!

I went up to my room and sat by the window and stared into Eddie's backyard. Sooner or later, somebody'd report Sharon Huggins missing. And sooner or later, they'd dig up those rosebushes, and then I'd laugh at all of them. *I told you so!*

As I watched, the back door of the Huggins house opened and Eddie came out into the yard. He inspected the rosebushes. He walked all around them and carefully poked at the soil with his toe. Then he stood with his hands on his hips and looked around. His bald head slowly turned from one side to the other.

Suddenly, he looked up at my window and saw me. His body stiffened. I sat frozen in horror, feeling like one of the little yellow ducks in the shooting gallery at the carnival.

He knew! He knew I saw him bury Sharon!

I pushed myself away from the window and scrambled downstairs. Mom and Mary Ann wouldn't be back for a couple of hours. Daddy would be even later. I locked the doors and began checking the windows.

What could I do? Eddie might come over and break into

the house. He might kill me, too! There was nowhere I could go. No one was going to listen to me. And even if nothing happened before Mom and Mary Ann came home, I still wasn't safe. Eddie could wait. It might be tomorrow or even next week; but sooner or later he'd catch me! And then—

I felt sick to my stomach as I closed the dining-room window. Outside, on the patio, Merwin was stalking an unsuspecting robin. I rapped on the window. The startled bird fluttered off, and Merwin gave me a dirty look. The nasty thing! Picking on a helpless little bird. He was as bad as Eddie Huggins.

I stopped and stared at the cat through the glass. What if—?

Maybe there was a way to take care of Eddie after all!

With a little coaxing and an open can of tuna that I hoped Mom wouldn't miss, I managed to get Merwin into the house. I wasn't any too soon. As I locked the patio door, I saw that Eddie was coming across his yard, heading for the front of our house. I locked Merwin in my bedroom and went downstairs to the phone.

"Mrs. Bailey?" I shouted into the mouthpiece. "This is Tracy Rogers. There's something you should know. . . ."

Eddie was pounding on the front door. "Hey, kid! Open up! I want to talk to you!"

Then I started shaking. I couldn't stop. My knees got so trembly I had to sit down on the kitchen floor. Eddie kept pounding on the door until the police car pulled up.

A short while later, Mrs. Bailey, Eddie Huggins, two policemen, and I stood in Eddie's backyard.

"He killed my cat!" Mrs. Bailey shrieked. "The girl saw him! Says he buried it right there under those bushes!" She shook a bony fist at Eddie, "You'll pay for this! You wait!"

Eddie was a sickly white. "This is ridiculous!" he sputtered. "I never touched her damned cat!"

One of the officers looked at him. "But you did threaten to kill it. I heard you. In court." He turned to me. "Are you sure you saw him bury the cat?"

I nodded solemnly.

"Then, sir," the officer said to Eddie. "I'm afraid the only way to settle this is to dig. Do we have to get a court order?"

Eddie's shoulders slumped. He shook his head.

"He buried it real deep," I offered helpfully.

By supper time, the news of Sharon Huggins's murder was all over town. Merwin had been returned to his bewildered owner. Mom had to be sedated.

"She saw the whole thing, George! And she's only a baby! My poor little girl!"

Mary Ann sat on the sofa in her new outfit, her eyes dripping with mascara. But no one paid any attention to her. Newspaper people and television reporters with cameras were crowding into the living room. A blonde lady held a microphone in front of me as I told my story.

I really enjoyed it.

They were all listening.

STEPHANIE KAY BENDEL has taught adult education classes in mystery writing, creative writing to gifted elementary school children, and freshman English at the college level. She is the author of Making Crime Pay: A Practical Guide to Mystery Writing *and a romantic thriller,* A Scream Away, *as well as a number of short mystery stories, several of which appeared in Alfred Hitchcock's Mystery Magazine. She now resides in Boulder, Colorado.*

THE MARLEY CASE

LINDA HALDEMAN

We do Christmas right at our house—the holly and the ivy and the manger and the tree. Stockings all hung and an ever-full wassail bowl for thirsty carolers. I use the pronoun "we" editorially, for all this holiday jollity comes your way with the compliments of Joyce and the kids. I'm not much of a celebrator myself and, even in my youth, avoided, when possible, all those cherished tribal rituals.

Some people don't. Joyce, for instance. For years I didn't understand. I thought it was just for the children, all the decking of halls and jingling of bells and harking of herald angels. But as the children grew up, the merry mayhem diminished not at all, and I still find myself in my middle years surrounded by a trio of oversized moppets bandaging boxes in miles of red satin ribbon and spreading tinsel all over everything.

A week before this Christmas just past, I was force-fed a certain minimal dose of spirit when I was carted to the church youth club's annual dramatization of *A Christmas Carol*. This, I must admit, is one of the less objectionable parts of the customary saturnalia. It's not the Royal Shakespeare Company, to be sure, but it certainly is an improvement on the pageants of my childhood, where at least one angel fainted every year and the wise men always forgot their lines. As in everything else seasonal, the family had a considerable stake in this production. Stephanie, in a billowy gauze gown that reminded me painfully of a Sunday School angel's robe, was the Ghost of Christmas Past.

"Long past?" the boy who played Scrooge asked warily.

"No, your past," Steffy replied in a thin, ethereal voice that actually made me, her father, shiver. I have at times envisioned Steffy as a basketball coach or a carnival barker but certainly not as an actress, and not with that voice. Remarkable.

Mark played, of course, Tiny Tim. He's small for his age and is able to project a deceptive air of cherubic innocence.

"God bless us every one," he intoned with the falsetto intensity of a child evangelist. It was a performance that melted poor sentimental old Scrooge's heart. It hardened mine, not just because I could not fully separate Mark smiling sweetly onstage from Mark raising hell at the dinner table, but because I always suspect virtuous children.

We stopped at Mister Donut on the way home. Steffy, no longer ghostly, had a double chocolate doughnut and a cup of hot chocolate. I could almost see the acne pop out. Mark, choosing, it seems, to remain for a while in character, selected something gooey called "angel-filled."

"It's remarkable," said Joyce, "how a great piece like that doesn't date. But then the Christmas spirit doesn't date, either."

"Bah!" I said. "Humbug!"

"Oh, Daddy," Steffy sighed as only an adolescent daughter can.

"You know," I went on. "I've often wondered about one thing. Just as it says: 'Marley was dead: to begin with. There is no doubt whatever about that.' " (I was proud to quote with such perfect accuracy, for the kids were obviously impressed. And how often can a man of my age and shortcomings impress his kids?) "Okay. Marley was dead. But what did he die of?"

"I don't know, probably a stroke or a heart attack," said Joyce. "After all, he was a classic type-A personality."

"Have you considered the possibility of foul play?"

There. I had caught their attention, dropped a curdling dollop of vinegar into their emotional eggnog of peace and goodwill. What fun.

"Oh, I get it," Mark exclaimed in an astounding show of insight, for him. "He could have been murdered."

"Now who would do that?" Joyce laughed.

"Look for a motive."

"Scrooge himself would be a prime suspect," said Steffy. She's quick-witted for a ghost and a sophomore, and she shares my love of detective fiction. "He had a motive. Money. He inherited Marley's half of the business, right?"

"Too obvious," I said. "The obvious suspect is never the real culprit."

"Anyhow," Mark chimed in, "if Scrooge had done him in, why would Marley have come back from the dead to save him? I bet it was good old Tiny Tim, bashed the old skinflint's brains out with his crutch for not paying his father a decent wage."

"Impossible," Steffy snickered. "How old do you think Tiny Tim was, midget? He probably wasn't even born when Marley died. 'Mr. Marley has been dead these seven years,' Scrooge says. Bob Cratchit might not even have worked for Scrooge and Marley then. Faced you, hosehead!"

Occasionally, not often, mind you, but every now and then, your children make you proud.

We celebrate Christmas early now that the children are older, one tradition that I like, for it gets the worst of it out of the way and permits the household to settle back more quickly into the blessed monotony of the midwinter doldrums. It all starts on Christmas Eve, with an extensive caroling tour of the neighborhood, ending up at St. Nicholas (no less) Parish Church in time for Midnight Mass. I don't attend, especially at Christmas, for of all tinsel, liturgical tinsel is the most incongruous.

I was feeling particularly Scroogish about the whole business this year, so I took my dinner, a slapdash hoagie on an undersized bun (fast before feast, I suppose), sought refuge in the den, and did not show my face until the merry revelers were ready to leave. Then I sent them off with a resounding, "Bah! Humbug!" which was greeted with much untoward merriment.

"Oh, Daddy," said Stephanie.

"Don't get into the brandy," Joyce warned.

I waved to them from the doorway, then went back inside the house and watched them from the living-room window until they had turned a corner and could no longer see the house. Then I turned off the string of colored lights that outlined our front porch, pulled the plug on the Christmas tree, and got into the brandy. Not terribly, for brandy gives a vicious hangover, just enough to make me mellow. Once I was sufficiently mellow, I turned out all the other lights and went to bed.

That was a mistake. Sometimes brandy works, and sometimes it backfires. I don't know that it really was the brandy's fault. The house was so empty, so silent. For the last month

I had longed and prayed for silence and solitude, but now that I had it in abundance I found it a hollow and empty state.

And then there was the moon, which had the bad taste to be full on a cloudless cold night. It was a silver-white moon, shining down unshaded on a silver-white earth. Too much, much too much, as if the entire universe had been hung with tinsel. And the light wouldn't stay outside where it belonged; the damned washed-out white light slithered in around gaps in the lined drapes and crawled across the bed to sit glaring on my eyelids and murder sleep. I lay under that light brooding, I don't know why, on the fate of one Jacob Marley, dead nearly a century and a half.

Finally, giving up the struggle, I crept out from under the electric blanket, shrugged on my slippers, and went downstairs. The moonlight followed me, illuminating the stairs and the wide entrance hall. The living-room curtains were sheer and generously invited all the moonlight in the vicinity inside, as to a silver-white open house. The Christmas tree stood before the large bay window looking tacky as only an unlighted Christmas tree can. The trees outside, undecorated even by their own natural foliage, silhouetted by the overpowering moonlight, appeared like black specters, skeletal, ominous. I turned quickly about, went into my study across the hall, closed the door, drew the drapes, and turned on the comfortably warm yellow reading lamp.

The third shelf of the bookcase that lined one wall held a handsome leather-bound set of the complete works of Dickens, an inheritance from my grandfather that I had not bothered for years. I took out the volume titled *Christmas Stories*, settled back in my recliner, opened it, and read aloud softly into the moonlight.

" 'Marley was dead: to begin with. There is no doubt whatever about that.' "

"Amen say I to that," declared a voice deep as the Pit, yet

thin as a breath. I jumped up with a cry, dropping the book. In front of me stood the ghost of Jacob Marley, exactly as Dickens had described it, a tall, stocky man in waistcoat and boots, dragging along with him a large wrought-iron chain to which ledgers, keys, padlocks, purses, and the like were attached every few links, like charms on a bracelet. He was so transparent that I could read through him the titles of my grandfather's set of Dickens on the bookshelf behind him.

"What the hell?" I cried, realizing as the words left my mouth how absurdly un-Dickensian they sounded. The apparition did not crack a smile, prevented perhaps by a strip of white cloth bound around its head from jaw to balding crown.

"Marley, sir," he said. "Jacob Marley."

He offered his transparent hand, and I automatically held my own out to shake, then drew back.

"With all due respect, Mr. Marley," I said, my voice admittedly a little tremulous, "this is very absurd. What do you want with me, anyway? God knows, I keep Christmas. Look at that damned tree out there. It must have a pound of tinsel on it. Do you know that I actually sing along at the elementary school Christmas program sing-along? That's keeping Christmas with a vengeance."

"Keep Christmas in your own way, and let me keep it in mine," the Ghost said illogically.

"By scaring the living daylights out of innocent people in the middle of the night?"

The Ghost sighed. "I am doomed to wander through the world trying to do the good I failed to do in life."

"What possible good could you do me?"

"I would lay you," replied the Ghost.

I said, "Good God," and sat down quickly. My chair of its own will flew back into the reclining position, pitching me back with a jarring thump. I closed my eyes and tried to bring order to my gyrating thoughts. It was possible, of course, that all this time I was safe and asleep under the warmth of the electric blanket and the influence of a slight overdose of brandy, dreaming. Or my subconscious had finally won the battle for my mind, and I was hallucinating in the den, enthroned like some mad king on my recliner, where I couldn't do anyone much harm. But, being a rational person, even in the worst extremity, I expect my hallucinations to be consistent and make sense.

"I think you have that wrong, Jacob," I said very quietly, wondering if it might be wiser to attempt to wake myself rather than waste intellectual energy reasoning with a trick of the right brain. On the other hand, I was a little afraid I would find that I was not asleep at all. "As you are the ghost, I ought to be laying you."

"If you could, I should be most grateful," Marley's Ghost said courteously. "For you see, though you are in the flesh and I in the spirit, we share a common affliction. We do not find rest in the night."

"Well, if someone would turn the moon down, I might be able to get some sleep."

"You walk the night only when the moon is full?" the Ghost asked. "I do not think so."

"Well, a little darkness might help. I don't know why the hell I can't sleep. If the story runs true, you can't rest because you were a miserable, stingy bastard in life, and now you have to go around scaring other miserable, stingy bastards into playing Santa Claus. If that's what you're after here, you certainly picked the wrong house."

"I came here because you thought of me," said Marley's Ghost. "It is the thought of me that keeps you awake. You have asked a question that has never been asked before, not even by he who created me. To lay you is an easy matter; we must simply find the answer to your question."

I looked at the shade in astonishment. "Surely you know what you died of?"

He shook his head. "I exist only to the degree in which I have been thought about. He who created me did not think about the manner of my death; therefore the manner of my death did not exist, at least not until you inquired into it."

"I wasn't all that interested," I grumbled. "I was just making conversation."

"If you were just making conversation, how is it that you do not sleep?"

"Damned if I know."

The Ghost shuddered, causing his chain to roll thuddingly along the carpeting. "My dear sir, I beseech you. Avoid that expression. As it stands, you have aroused my curiosity, and since, for whatever reason, we have both been deprived of our repose this Christmas Eve, we might amusingly and perhaps profitably pass the time exploring the mystery, eh?"

I shrugged. "Why don't you go on without me? I think I'm going to mosey on back to bed."

I got up and started to move past him, but his transparent hand caught my forearm in a remarkably strong grip.

"Come now, my dear fellow, don't be hasty. I cannot travel alone, incorporeal as I am and a very minor ghost at that. I must justify any journey that I make like some otherworldly civil servant, and you could be my justification. Besides, I was a man of business and had not the imagination to solve mysteries. You could be of much assistance."

"And what do I get out of it?"

"Unless I am much mistaken, my dear sir," said Marley's Ghost, "you are not the sort of fellow who sleeps well on an empty belly or an unanswered question. What I offer you is a rare opportunity to travel through time, to observe the world as it was and will never be again. You have in your secret heart longed to be a detective and solve some great mystery;

here is your chance, perhaps your only chance, to fulfill that wish. Corporeal life, believe me, is woefully short. There is much time on this side to regret lost opportunities."

I walked slowly back to the recliner and sat down.

"You probably died of a heart attack or a stroke or—or food poisoning."

"You do not see it that way," said Marley's Ghost, "so that is not the way it will be."

"What do you mean by that?"

"I mean, my dear sir, that you are the author."

He picked up the tooled leather volume from the floor where I had dropped it and handed it to me. I pushed the chair into the reclining position and began to read aloud. The Ghost, leaning on the back of the chair, looked over my shoulder at his own likeness in a reproduction of the original engraving.

" 'Marley was dead: to begin with. There is no doubt whatever about that. The register of his burial was signed by the clergyman, the undertaker, and the chief mourner. Scrooge signed it, and Scrooge's name was good. . . .' "

A reclining chair is not the best place for reading; it is too comfortable. I have often dropped into a doze even while reading some remarkable thriller, so it is not so awfully strange that I did so now. I was startled into wakefulness by the resonant striking of the hour, twelve. That did not seem so awfully strange either, until it occurred to me that we do not have a clock that strikes the hour.

I sat up quickly, jerking the chair upright. The moonlight, it appeared, had taken over my den, touching everything in it with a silver glow of tinsel. And directly in front of me, in the place where old Marley had first appeared, stood my daughter Stephanie, in the billowy Christmas-angel gown, her light brown hair caught in a circlet of holly, a mysterious half smile on her lips. The tinsel moonlight reflected off her in such a way that she appeared to glow.

I struggled to regain my equilibrium.

"Back from Mass already, hon?"

"I am the Ghost of Christmas Past," she said in that voice of wind-rattled icicles that made me shudder.

"My past?" I decided to play along.

"No. Long past. Come, my time is short."

"As is your stature."

I fully expected the usual "Oh, Daddy" but got, instead, an outstretched hand and a calm but firm order.

"Rise! and walk with me!"

"No thanks, hon . . ." I started to say but then saw that the beckoning hand was transparent and slightly iridescent. I shrank back against the Naugahyde upholstery of the chair, my cold, but quite opaque, hands firmly gripping the armrests. "M-must I?"

The apparition, so like yet so unlike my daughter, shook its shining head solemnly, and little sparkles of tinsel floated in the air around it.

"You are under no compulsion and may decline, without retribution, to accompany me. Though it is strange that you would do so, as you are one of the fortunate ones who is spared the painful journey into your own past. What you are being offered is an opportunity offered to few, to visit a past that is not your own, simply for the satisfaction of your curiosity."

"Really? No strings attached? No moral?"

The Spirit's slight smile broadened just a trifle. "Few journeys are made in what you call the 'real world' without something being learned. You will be shown things; what you do with them is your business. The opportunity will not arise again. Come with me now, or close the book forever."

I am a man incapable of passing an open door without peering into the room, so this challenge left me no choice but to accept it. I grasped the Spirit's hand, surprised to find that it felt like solid flesh. Its grip was, indeed, very strong, pulling me up abruptly from my chair and leading me through the den and across the hall to the silver-bathed living room. I can well remember Steffy in the flesh dragging me from the comfort of the den with this same eagerness to see the decorated tree. I saw it now, shining in the moonlight, and it seemed larger, fuller, more brilliant, and, goodness knows, gaudier than it had been before.

"Where are you taking me?" I asked as we hastened toward the bay window.

"London, December 24, 1836." It spoke in the tone and manner of the narrative voice that so often opens cheaply made historical or science fiction films. The date, seven years prior to the publication of *A Christmas Carol,* reminded me all of a sudden of the purpose of my journey.

"Wait, where's old Marley?"

"Right with you, my dear sir."

And there he was indeed, peering over my left shoulder, bandage and all; apparently he had been there, unnoticed, the whole time. Now he grasped my left hand, and together the three of us passed through the bay window's leaded panes. I felt the solid glass brush past me like the strips of a beaded curtain.

I had closed my eyes as I approached the window and did not open them at first when I felt the cold outside air. For one thing, the air itself felt different, damp and chilly rather than sharp and crisp. And all about me was a confusion of noises and smells. So many smells: coal fires smoking, gas fumes, old fish, beer, sewage, sweat, and then, rising above all this, the sweet pungent odor of mince pie. I stood for a moment in wonder, my head raised like that of a hound downwind of a herd of deer, just sniffing. Then I had the strange, vaguely unpleasant sensation of someone passing through me, as if I were a beaded curtain, and I opened my eyes.

I knew at once where I was, for I had been there before,

in the City of London late on a winter afternoon, at a busy intersection just east of those three brooding stone edifices that form the hub around which the ancient city spins: the Bank of England, the Mansion House, and the Royal Exchange. I marveled at how similar the scene was to the one I had enjoyed in my student days, watching schools of office workers crowding down the old streets through the early twilight into underground and railway stations. And yet, as I recovered from the shock of finding myself in that well-remembered spot, I saw it all as very familiar yet marvelously strange.

Leadenhall, that was the name of the street, between two churches—St. Michael Cornhill to the west, its stolid, rectangular, pinnacled tower standing out above everything, and, to the east, St. Andrew Undershaft, the site, it is said, in older times of a gigantic Maypole. It is the churches, the ubiquitous churches, that give the City of London its illusion of timelessness. The London I now stood in was older, dirtier, noiser, and even more charming than the one I had known.

I am a city person, reveling in the urban rush and clutter and racket. But this was almost too much city for even me, noisy beyond belief, with the clatter of donkey carts and hackneys and great, lumbering omnibuses over the stone paving, the shouts of peddlers urging their wares on the passersby, and the intermittent clanging of bells. I counted the chimes of the hour coming from St. Michael's tower with some surprise. It was only three o'clock, yet it was dark enough for the gas lamps to be lighted. The air was thick with an oppressive dark-green smog that penetrated everywhere but softened the roughness of the street life as if wrapping it in gray-green chiffon.

I was finding it difficult to see, a problem the natural inhabitants of the place seemed to have overcome, and blundered into a young woman who materialized suddenly out of the fog, hurrying along the street, a dark knit shawl wrapped around her striped silk gown, a wide-brimmed bonnet shielding her face. I got a look at it, though—a pretty, childlike, bright-eyed face set with a grimness that seemed contrary to its nature. I attempted to excuse myself but realized, when the stack of petticoat rustled right through my astonished leg, that apologies were not just unnecessary, they were downright useless.

I fell in step beside her, curious about where she might be going and why she was so nervous. Invisibility, by the way, is a very useful attribute to have in a crowded city street, especially when trying to keep up with someone who is in a great hurry and doesn't even know you're there. I was enjoying myself thoroughly, drinking in the wonderful grimy aliveness of the city, feeling the rush and the gaiety, observing with delight the sideshow of strange and colorful characters free in their anonymity. I took pleasure now and then—as I hurried through (literally) the crowds—in playing childish "invisible man" games, swinging unseen from a lamp post and passing right through the polished brass "can" of a baked potato vendor stationed on the pavement in the shelter of Whittington Avenue as it leads into the old Leadenhall Market. I must have caused a bit of a breeze, for the coals in the iron fire pot suspended beneath the large, showy receptacle shot up in a sudden surge of orange flame and died down. Then I remembered Marley and the superstition that flames rise in the presence of ghosts.

"Sorry about that," I said over my shoulder but saw only the Ghost of Christmas Past helping the hot-potato man get the conflagration under control before his primitive steam table blew up. Marley had hurried on ahead through the confusion of the great poultry market.

"Where are you going?" I shouted over the racket of hundreds of chickens, turkeys, geese, ducks, and, for all I know, dodos and emus, bewailing their fate in the overcrowded condemned cells of the market, a Dickensian slum for poultry if ever there was one. A group of three or four very dirty, ragged boys hoarsely chanting some tuneless carol passed through me, surrounding the potato vendor in an effort to take advantage of the generosity of his clients and the warmth of his fire.

"My chambers," Marley panted, pointing vaguely toward the street ahead of us. "I lived there, and still do, in a way of speaking, in the wine cellars."

"Nice work if you can get it," I murmured.

I followed the Ghost down a narrow byway along the back wall of a great stone house, relieved to be free of the feathered bedlam of the poultry market. We came out on a street of large, impressive buildings only slightly less congested than the thoroughfare, and Marley's Ghost, apparently oblivious to the chill drizzle of sleet that was beginning to fall from the gunmetal-gray sky and the black city mud splashed up from the street by passing hooves and bare metal wheels, jaywalked joyously across toward a narrow courtyard almost hidden between two buildings. I hesitated a moment before following him into that nineteenth-century rush hour, for I still did not quite trust my bodiless condition.

A light touch on my arm caused me to turn. The Ghost of Christmas Past, disguised as my daughter Stephanie, pointed northward along the side of the great stone house.

"East India House. Torn down in 1862. You ought to have a look at the front portico facing Leadenhall Street. You will have seen something no person living has seen."

That sort of exclusiveness holds little appeal for me. I was much more interested in exploring Marley's wine cellars, but something else facing Leadenhall Street did catch my interest. A nervous young woman in a striped silk dress and a dark shawl and bonnet had just crossed the thoroughfare and was turning north by the soot-stained Gothic church of St. Andrew Undershaft.

"Hey, Marley! Up this way!" I shouted. "I want to see where that girl's going."

He followed me with an obedience I have yet to inspire in the living.

"May I presume to ask why we are stalking this particular person?" he asked when he had caught up.

"I don't know, really. It's just a hunch. Good detectives always follow hunches."

Crossing Leadenhall at that hour was dangerous and indeed all but impossible for ordinary mortals, but we floated easily through hansom cabs and hackney coaches, pie men and holly-decorated donkey carts. We followed the girl northward past aging mansions and half-timbered Elizabethan relics into an area of small shops with living quarters above them.

"Where are we?" I asked Marley.

"Simmery Axe."

St. Mary Axe, I translated. English place names are marvelous and their pronunciations even more marvelous. I couldn't say at first how I happened to know this particular pronunciation, but a song began to run through my head as I trotted up the pavement in pursuit of my hunch.

> *"Oh, my name is John Wellington Wells,*
> *I'm a dealer in magic and spells,*
> *In blessings and curses*
> *And ever-filled purses,*
> *In prophecies, witches and knells."*

Gilbert and Sullivan, wasn't it? I used to know all the words to most of the patter songs when I was younger and could sing, after a fashion. The clatter of the horses and the rhythmic clanging of a muffin man's bell formed an accompaniment, and I sang aloud, safe in the realization that no mortal ear could hear me. Marley, however, regarded me with some pain.

> *"If you want a proud foe to 'make tracks'—*
> *If you'd melt a rich uncle in wax—*
> *You've but to look in*
> *On our resident Djinn,*
> *Number seventy Simmery Axe!"*

Good Lord. I stopped abruptly in front of one of the small shabby shops, for the girl in the bonnet had stopped and was looking uncertainly at it. The stone front was black, as was the door. The bowed windows—meant, I suppose, to display wares—were so soot-begrimed as to appear black as well. The uncertain flicker of candles inside the shop only helped to obscure the view. I looked up. Over door and window in polished brass letters was the name of the shop, with the number 70 set like quotation marks at each end.

70 J. W. WELLS & CO., SORCERERS 70

I started to laugh. The whole thing was so preposterous. I was not used to having such literary dreams. But this was stuff I knew about, and I couldn't let a gaffe like that pass.

"I'm sorry," I said to Christmas Past, who still floated on my right. "You just can't do that."

"I beg your pardon?" said the courteous Spirit.

"Anachronism. Blatant, bald-faced anachronism. Gilbert wrote *The Sorcerer* in 1877. This is supposed to be the London of 1836. Gilbert was born in 1836! Now, how do you explain that away?"

"Elementary," said the Ghost. "It's an old established family firm. The present proprietor is Gilbert's sorcerer's grand-father."

"That's ridiculous. How could the company exist before its author invented it? You can't do that, even in fiction."

"You can do anything in fiction as long as you're consistent," the Ghost explained with a great show of patience. "And once something, a place, a character, is conceived, it acquires an existence of its own—a past, a present, and a future."

I laughed. "What a cop-out. Are you trying to tell me there's no difference between flesh-and-blood historical reality and—and the figment of somebody's imagination?"

"My dear sir," the Spirit replied, "we are all figments of Somebody's imagination."

That's what you get for arguing with a ghost.

I returned to my hunch.

The girl, after taking another quick, frightened look about her, entered the shop, activating a tinkly little bell. I followed, passing through the door after she had closed it, just for the thrill of doing it that way while I could. After all, I'm going to have to open doors for the rest of my life.

The inside of the shop was as dark as the outside, and the soot-saturated fog seemed to have passed through the closed door and filled every crevice. What little I could see through this miasma looked like a combination of old-fashioned hard-ware store and the sort of cheap magic-tricks emporium found on seaside boardwalks between the penny arcade and the bingo parlor. A small, round, bald man wearing a blue herringbone checked waistcoat over a pink shirt looked up from behind a low wooden counter where he sat playing solitaire with a set of ancient tarot cards by the light of a close-trimmed oil lamp. A meager coal fire provided the only other light.

"And what may I do for you, madam?" he asked the girl in a carefully smoothed-down cockney accent. His face was pink, his smile somewhat cherubic; his voice was oily and self-deprecating, a pudgy Uriah Heep.

The girl's hand, when she removed it from her fur muff, was trembling, and her voice was thin and strained with tension.

"I—I've come for the—uh—the effigy."

The proprietor raised his spectacles to the top of his head and looked carefully into her face for perhaps half a minute.

"Ah, yes," he said slowly. "Mr. Scrooge."

He spun around to face a cluttered shelf on the wall behind his desk, although I have no idea how he did it, since the chair did not swivel.

"Ah, here we are. Mr. Scrooge."

He took down a cylindrical package, wrapped in newspaper like an order of chips, and handed it to her. She took it gingerly and stared at it a moment.

"Oh, dear. How dreadful. I don't know how I could do this."

J. W. Wells smiled slightly. "The first time is always the hardest."

"Oh, dear," the girl cried in agitation. "I certainly shan't be doing this again. It's not for me, you know. I never could do such a thing for my own gain. It's for Fred, poor dear Fred. He hasn't a farthing, and it's so dreadfully unfair."

"And if dear Fred 'asn't a farthing, he can't marry you, eh?"

The girl lowered her head. "He hasn't asked me yet."

"He 'asn't? Bless my soul." The little shopkeeper chuckled, catching the girl's hand in a quick, gentle, but firm movement. "Come now, let's see what we 'ave here." He took the package from her hand and spread the palm out under the lamp, raising the wick just a trifle. "Now this is very nice, don't you see? Such a lovely long life line. I see marriage, but not so soon. No matter, it's a very fine hand: happiness, many children, prosperity in due time. Be patient, say the Stars, your time will come."

He released her hand and placed the package back into it.

"A Christmas gift for poor dear Fred. That'll come to five quid, madam, and a bob for the reading. For you. Regular clients I charge 'arf a crown."

"Oh." She fumbled in her muff and pulled out a small purse from which she carefully counted out coins.

"You're sure this is Mr. Scrooge?" she asked, staring at the little package. "Do you know Mr. Scrooge?"

The chuckle was less cherubic, more malevolent. "Know Mr. Scrooge? My dear lady, there's not a chap within the sound of Bow bells that don't know Mr. Scrooge, more's the pity. His chambers being just over the way, I'm privileged betimes to share the street with 'im. 'Mr. Scrooge?' says I and tips me hat. 'Umph,' says he, if he says anything at all. Not a kindly man, our Mr. Scrooge." He leaned over the counter familiarly. "It's a favor we're doing this old town, you and me."

The girl shuddered and drew back. "For Fred," she whispered. "Just for Fred. What do I do with it?"

"Set it in the fire, madam, saying these words . . ." He drew her face close to his and whispered a series of phrases in her ear which I, though I leaned close, could not make out. "You've got that now? Good. Wouldn't you care to have a look at it? It's a marvelous likeness, I must say."

"Oh no. I couldn't bear it. I'd rather not know what he looked—looks like."

She secreted the package in her muff and ran from the shop, the bell on the door tinkling in her wake.

"Thank you very much, and a Merry Christmas to you," the shopkeeper called. "And a Merry Christmas to Fred, the lucky fellow."

I passed through the closed door just as the great bell of St. Andrew Undershaft boomed the hour of four. The sky was dark, what sky could be seen, but the street was bright with torches and gaslights. Marley materialized beside me.

"Who is this Fred?" he asked.

"Scrooge's nephew."

"Oh yes, that dreadfully jolly young fellow who came around to the countinghouse every Christmas Eve, spreading cheer, like marzipan, all over everything. Scrooge assumed he was after his money. But I don't recognize her. Who is she, and what's she up to?"

"She's Scrooge's niece-in-law-to-be, I think. And, if I'm not mistaken, she's attempting to melt a rich uncle in wax, so to speak. Come on."

I pushed through the crowd, for I was losing my hunch. Suddenly there was a diversion on the southwest corner of Leadenhall Street, in front of the brashly neoclassic facade of East India House. Two slightly drunken porters had collided and were now settling the question of right-of-way with bare fists. The nearby market emptied into the street to join the melee. I passed through the center of the mob, having caught sight of a dark bonnet disappearing down Whittington Avenue. Then I saw her standing in front of the brass baked potato can temporarily left untended. She looked around, white-faced, then quickly threw her package onto the glowing coals of the fire pot and fled westward.

By the time I reached the vessel, the paper had burst into yellow flame and shriveled to a blackened crust, and the wax effigy itself was starting to melt. It was a rather horrid sight, as recognizable human features began to run together. Recognizable indeed, for it was a good likeness, a perfect likeness of Jacob Marley.

"Hey!" I called to the girl's rapidly retreating back, forgetting my ghostly state. "You hexed the wrong man!"

The effigy was beginning to melt rapidly, and I put my hand into the pot, attempting to retrieve it. A firm, transparent grip on my wrist prevented me.

"You are free to observe only," said the Ghost of Christmas Past, "not to intervene. The past cannot be altered, even in fiction."

So we stood, three ill-matched specters in the sooty darkness, as snow began to fall lightly over the scene, watching the effigy slowly dissolve and run in rivulets of molten wax around and between the hot coals.

"I don't understand," said Marley's Ghost.

"It's a form of black magic," I explained. "A wax image of the victim is slowly melted with appropriate curses or whatever."

"That bright-eyed, dimpled, fresh-faced child involved in such dark deeds? I find that difficult to comprehend."

"She was driven to it by necessity, I think."

"Oh?" Marley's Ghost was puzzled. "Not by me, surely."

"No. By your partner. She wants to marry Fred, you see, as in time she will and make him very happy. And I suppose in time she will also secretly be glad that her attempt at witchcraft failed. It wasn't her fault, of course, that it did, or the sorcerer's either. Apparently he mistook you for Scrooge. I gather you sometimes answered to the name of Scrooge, as it is written of him: 'Sometimes people . . . called Scrooge Scrooge and sometimes Marley, but he answered to both names: it was all the same to him.' "

Marley's Ghost nodded solemnly, his jaws clacking together under the white bandage.

"We were like that, as it were one person in two bodies. It was also a device for keeping clients guessing. If an unwanted solicitor asked for Mr. Marley, he would be out for the day. I would be Mr. Scrooge. It was something of a game, I venture."

"A game that cost you your life."

Just at that moment, Marley's Ghost gave a gasp and backed into the baked potato can, pointing at something with a trembling finger. Following his gesture, I saw Marley himself, in the flesh, a solid identical twin of my companion of the evening in all aspects except the bandage, stumbling eastward, somewhat unsteady on his feet, as though the curse had already begun to take effect. He tripped on a loose paving stone and fell through me, catching himself on the large round handle of the can. He leaned on it an instant to get his balance and inadvertently looked down into the glowing coals of the fire pot. The effigy had melted from the back of the head forward, and the face now spread over the coals like a projected relief map. I tried to shield Marley from the sight, but of course he saw through me, as many do. With a cry, the poor fellow staggered back, holding his chest, took three steps forward, and fell. We three stood there, helpless in our insubstantiality, and watched a crowd gather around the stricken man, make a corridor for a doctor to come through, and then close up again around him. After a while six strong men, like premature pallbearers, carried the dying man down the street to his chambers. For though some of the bystanders weren't certain whether this was Mr. Scrooge or Mr. Marley, all knew that he was one of those gentlemen and that his home was above the wine cellars and offices in the old dark house in the courtyard off Lime Street.

Chimes sounded again from the tower of St. Andrew's Church. It must be six, I reasoned. The great bell tolled once and fell silent. I waited, straining in the sudden oppressive silence for the bell to go on. But it did not. All was darkness and stillness around me, and I was alone. Where was I now? In Scrooge's dark chambers above the wine cellars and holiday-vacant offices? He could not have been more alone than I was. I sat back, for wherever I was, I was sitting, and wished fervently for companionship, longed to hear the ominous clank of chains, to see some otherworldly luminosity break through the terrible blackness. Then I knew what Scrooge's curse was, and Marley's: to be alone and lonely on Christmas.

In the distance I heard voices, faint but growing stronger— the voices surely of an angel choir sent to redeem my hardened soul. I welcomed it as it drew near.

> *"God rest ye merry, gentlemen,*
> *Let nothing you dismay.*
> *Remember Christ our Savior*
> *Was born on Christmas Day*
> *To save us all from Satan's pow'r*
> *When we were gone astray.*
> *O tidings of comfort and joy!*
> *Comfort and joy! O tidings of comfort and joy!"*

With a rush of comfort and joy, I realized that I was in my recliner in the den and the angelic choir was Joyce and the kids coming from Midnight Mass, strewing vocal tinsel through the dark world as they came.

I stumbled to my feet, groping for a light switch. I must turn the decorations on again before they got back. I had suddenly lost all desire to be mistaken for Scrooge. I felt along the wall, falling into bookcases and knocking over bric-a-brac. The singing was coming closer.

> *"Glad tidings we bring*
> *To you and your kin—*
> *Glad tidings of Christmas*
> *And a Happy New Year!"*

My hand was on the knob, and I pulled the door open. Light, brilliant, festive, many-colored, twinkling, clashing, gaudy Christmas light filled the living room and glowed from the porch. The lights had come on, how or why I did not know, but I thanked the Ghost of Christmas Present, who surely must have been.

The front door burst open, and there were my wife and children, bright and glowing in the light of the outdoor decorations. And I was glad to see them.

Standing like a young orator on the hall carpet, shaking off snow like tinsel, Mark spread out his arms and crowed.

"God bless us every one!"

"Amen say I to that," I answered, turning back to the den just long enough to pick up and carefully close the book that lay on the floor still open to the picture of Marley's Ghost, before I joined the family around the misplaced, overburdened tree in the living room.

"Shall I light the candles?" Joyce asked.

"No, no," I said. "Don't do that. There's light enough already, light enough."

And I kissed her quickly, under the mistletoe.

LINDA HALDEMAN was born in Washington, D. C., and published her first story at the age of twelve. She received her bachelor of arts degree from Loyola University in New Orleans and her master's from Penn State. She is the author of several stories and three novels: Star of the Sea, The Lastborn of Elvinwood, *and* ESBAE: A Winter's Tale. *A number of years spent living in England gave her the material for much of her published work, including "The Marley Case." Haldeman died in January, 1988.*

THE
POISON FLOWERS

ANITA McBRIDE

'**ve thought about it one hundred times. One hundred
times. It happened three years ago, right after my mother
married Al. I was eleven years old, but not a smart
eleven. Just an ordinary kid.

I was glad she married Al and that I could say what my
new father did without making things up. My mother had
explained how my real father's name was on my birth certificate but it wasn't the same as if they'd been married, and
anyway he moved out before I could walk. He's not a part of
this story. When other boys asked where he was, I said the
army. I always pretended she was a Mrs. even though she
claimed I needn't feel that way with women's lib and all.

When my mother married Al, she and I got to leave our dinky little room in Chicago, and we all went up to Al's cottage in Wisconsin.

Cloverdale, long ago, was built as a summer resort, but it isn't much now. The lake is choked with weeds in places. The cottages are built all alike. There was a narrow screened-in porch across the front; I liked sleeping on the iron cot there, and I could run the inside awnings up and down if I wanted to. At night the sky was covered with stars, stars I'd never noticed in Chicago. Inside, we had a space heater in the living room and an old oak dining-room table, some chairs, and a sofa. There was a bedroom and a tiny kitchen with a kerosene stove. Al lived in Cloverdale all year round. Most of the neighbors did, too. Only Mr. and Mrs. Ramsey had a house in the city. He owned Clover Lake and all the cottages.

Across the road from the Ramseys, the Marshes had a truck farm. When we moved in with Al, Mr. Marsh brought over a basket of fresh vegetables, and Mrs. Marsh had put a bouquet of yellow flowers on our table. A welcome to Cloverdale.

The Ramseys' cottage was just around the bend in the lake from where Al lived. Mrs. Ramsey had dark curly hair and used cherry-red lipstick. She wore a white dress sometimes with a red patent-leather belt, and she always smelled like perfume. Al used to raise his eyebrows in a way that made me laugh when I'd mention her.

I have to explain that Al worked at a local factory on the night shift. My mother was on the early day shift, so she was ready to leave when he got home. I know they worked these lonesome hours so that one of them was always home for me.

After Al left for work, my mother and I stayed up for a while, and we would say how lucky we were to be there and how Al was a great guy. I didn't have to be told that he was a mile better than my real father. Pretty soon, we'd go to bed.

But I didn't stay there. I used to get up, real quiet, put on my clothes, sneak out the screen door, and walk down the sandy dirt road in the moonlight.

It was so peaceful and mysterious, that country road, barely wide enough for a car, and I'd creep up on the other cottages and see what I could see. Or hear. This one night when the heavens were sparkling—the Milky Way, the Big Dipper—I was stalking shadows. Al's gray and white old mother cat was running along in front, pausing sometimes to check that I was following, her eyes like neon in the starlight.

I rounded the woods that separated our place from the Ramseys'. Their dark green cottage sat snug in the birch and pine woods with moonlight shining on the lake behind. Mr. Ramsey was a big man and he'd had a bit of bad luck. He'd broken his leg, and so I hadn't been surprised to discover on a previous peek around that Mrs. Ramsey was sleeping on a cot on the screened-in porch just like I did at Al's.

As I started my scouting toward the house, I could hear a muffled laughing, and I got up close to the side of the porch to see what was so funny.

Mrs. Ramsey wasn't alone. A man was crouched on the floor at the head of the bed and he had his head next to hers and they were whispering and laughing, and this is what I heard.

"He said it tasted delicious—" She broke off to laugh, a pretty sound, trying to smother it in the sheet.

"He said the casserole was delicious?" His low murmur of amusement mingled with hers, and I caught the shine of his white teeth. "How does he feel? That stuff's supposed to do a job!"

"He said he loved it." She sure laughed pretty, like music it was. He nuzzled his face into her neck and there was more merriment, but it was snuffed out because there came a sound from the bedroom of bedsprings being disturbed, and then the clatter of Mr. Ramsey's crutches and the hop of his good leg.

"He'll kill us if he sees you," Mrs. Ramsey said. "Oh God!"

The man on the porch squeezed himself in between the head of the bed and the wall. I pressed my face against the screen.

"Who are you talking to? What's going on out here?" Mr. Ramsey said. He was standing in the cottage doorway, looking out at the porch. He looked seven feet tall.

I spoke up. "It's me, Mr. Ramsey," I said.

"Who are you, boy?" His voice rumbled out into the dark night, and Al's cat ran up a pine tree as quick as a wink.

"Wadsworth," I said, taking the poet's middle name. Sometimes it doesn't pay to tell the truth.

Mrs. Ramsey was as still as though she were under a magician's spell, and the man on the floor was just a dark shadow against the wall and half under the bed.

"Is that your last name?"

"Yes, sir," I said, and justified the little white lie because it was the last time I had said a name.

"Your people know you're out?" He made a gagging sound and bent over.

"No, sir." I could see he was real sick.

"You get yourself home, boy, and never come here bothering folks again." He could hardly get the words out.

I beat it, but not before I saw Mrs. Ramsey throw back the sheet and help the poor guy into the cabin.

"Oh, Minnie, oh, Minnie," the old man was saying.

Her body looked as white as milk. I was surprised she could sleep with hardly any clothes on like that. It gets plenty chilly during the night.

The next morning, I saw Mr. Jensen out in back of our house when I went out. Mother had gotten breakfast and gone to work, and Al had come home and eaten what she'd put out for him, and had gone to bed.

Well, I was surprised to see Mr. Jensen, the sun glinting on his shiny black hair. He operated a dance hall about halfway between the resort and the nearest town. I used to walk over there sometimes and buy a candy bar. You could buy candy and cigarettes and play a slot machine there. Mr. Jensen was always hail-fellow-well-met, like they say.

Mr. Jensen looked glad to see me when I came out and walked over to see what he wanted. He wanted to use Al's canoe that was overturned on the beach. The paddles were propped against the house next to Al's fishing poles.

"You're Ralph, aren't you? You look like a smart young one." No one had ever said that to me before, and of course it made me feel good. "Do you think we could borrow your dad's boat for half an hour? I'll give you a dollar to come."

"I don't know." Al had never let me take the canoe. They tip awful easy and I think he was afraid I'd swamp it in the deep water. That means fill it with water, and of course then it would sink.

"Dad's asleep. He just got home from work."

I liked calling Al "Dad." Al liked it, too.

"Well, let's not wake him up." Mr. Jensen gave me a wide smile and picked the paddles ever so gently away from the side of the house.

Just then the doctor's car went by, going toward the Ramseys' house. Carpenter was a nice old guy, retired except for helping his neighbors, and we had only ten cottages.

I felt kind of guilty, but I didn't want to disappoint Mr. Jensen, so I went with him down to the shore where the minnows were chasing each other in the green water near the edge.

"You're a city boy, aren't you?" he said, giving me a friendly look. I recognized then that Mr. Jensen was the man on the porch with Mrs. Ramsey, and I figured he wanted to give me the ridiculously big sum of a dollar for just half an hour in the canoe because he appreciated what I had done for him last night. I gave him a big grin back.

"Did you ever learn to swim?" he asked.

"Learn to swim?" said I, feeling like a smarty-pants. "No, I never learned to swim." Because, you see, I was born knowing how to swim. My mother explained it to me, about there being water in the womb, my natural habitat, and how she dunked me in the YMCA pool when I was an infant and I took off like an eel.

He didn't say I should run back to the house for a life jacket or anything like you might expect, just motioned me into the canoe, and with a few strong strokes, we were in the middle of the lake where it's about five hundred feet wide. He looked this way and that, like he wanted to see if anybody was about, and all of a sudden he began to clown around, rocking the canoe hard, first one way, then the other. I shouted for him to stop—Al would be furious—but over she went and I was in the brown-colored water, and I went down deep, believe me, all the way to the mud bottom.

I came up with my hair all clotted in front of my eyes and I could see Mr. Jensen treading water, looking at me. Well, maybe it was mean but after his goofy, silly behavior I decided to give him a good scare, so I flailed my arms around and kind of gasped for help. He just kept staring, sort of hypnotized, so I let myself sink under the water. When I came up again, he had moved toward the shore, but he'd been waiting, sure enough, for me to come up. This time I just got my eyes above water and sank again. I could see the shadow of the overturned canoe, and I swam underwater toward it and came up under it where I could breathe. I could hardly keep from laughing, but it was a good lesson for Mr. Jensen to learn not to fool around in a canoe.

When I came out from my hiding place, I saw that Mr.

Jensen had gone, probably to spread the alarm for me, and I put the canoe back on the beach and went up to the house. After a while, I woke Al and told him what had happened, except not about last night because he would have said not to go out alone that late. He said I shouldn't have frightened Mr. Jensen like that, but he was mad at him because I'd lost one of my shoes in the water. He said that Mr. Jensen was a damned fool and I should make him give me a dollar. Then he went back to sleep.

When he woke up and I asked him, he said the reason Mr. Jensen hadn't spread the alarm was because he knew I was only fooling. I didn't think so. I thought he felt too guilty, it being all his fault.

That evening we learned that Mr. Ramsey had died. That made me feel bad. After Al left for work and my mother had gone to bed, I lay on the cot and looked up where white clouds were drifting across the moon and I supposed that Mr. Ramsey was up there someplace.

I didn't much like going out that night, but after a while I began to wonder if Mr. Jensen would be there with Mrs. Ramsey. Like Al said, he owed me a dollar. Besides, it was time I let him know that I was still alive. Fun's fun, but you don't have to be mean about it. So I got my shorts and T-shirt back on and an old pair of shoes, and let myself out.

I came up to the Ramsey house scout style, not making a whisper of noise. They were laughing again, like when Mr. Ramsey was taken sick. You know how it is, eavesdroppers never hear any good of themselves, right?

"Someone brought the boat in," Mr. Jensen said.

"He's not much, but you'd think they'd wonder where he is." Mrs. Ramsey must have thought she was being funny, and Mr. Jensen laughed to please her.

"They both work, they probably don't know what the boy is up to half the time," he said.

That's not true. Either one or the other, Al or my mother, is home with me all the time. I got a heavy feeling in my chest and tears in my eyes. Who were they to talk about Al and my mother like that?

That was the end of the conversation. I could see that they were going to hug and kiss and they'd forgotten about me. They thought I was sitting on the muddy bottom of Clover Lake. How do you like that? That's all I meant to them, and after I kept Mr. Ramsey from finding out that Mr. Jensen was there.

I did another mean thing.

I went around to the back of the cottage and let myself into the kitchen and then into the bedroom. Sure enough, Mr. Ramsey's crutches were standing against the wall. I threw myself onto the bed, and the springs let out a wail that I knew would galvanize them out on the porch. Then I grabbed the crutches and made that crutch, hop, crutch, hop sound that I'd heard last night.

I heard the screen door fly open as Mr. Jensen hightailed it away and Mrs. Ramsey started to scream. The screams, a couple of octaves higher than an opera star's, ran along my nerves like a buzz saw. I dropped the crutches before I got to the cottage door and ran out the way I'd come in.

The next afternoon I was sitting on the beach behind our cottage watching a box turtle sunning himself on a log that stuck out of the water. It was real hot and the sky was as blue as those flowers that grow along the wayside. "You don't want to touch those," Mr. Marsh had said. "The green leaves are poisonous, the roots fatal." I never went within touching distance of those flowers, dancing on long stems in a light breeze, the flowers almost purple, they were so blue.

I watched the turtle sunning himself for a long time, and finally I threw a pebble so it splashed about ten feet from him and he slid into the lake so fast he could have given lessons to a rabbit. I loved being at Al's place. I sure didn't want to cause any trouble for him with the neighbors. After a while, I knew I'd have to go over and tell Mrs. Ramsey that I was sorry about the trick I played on Mr. Jensen. I was too ashamed to mention fooling around with her husband's crutches.

The fastest way for me to get to Mrs. Ramsey was to swim over because her beach was right next to Al's, just around the bend of woods. The cool water felt like it was holding me up and parting before me like for the Israelites as I took easy, lazy strokes to carry me around the bend.

There sat Mrs. Ramsey, wearing a few wisps of bathing suit and a wide-brimmed straw hat with a satiny bow tied under her chin. She had a bottle of oil in her white hands, and she was applying it in gentle sweeps up her legs and thighs, like she was loving putting it on. She looked so pretty sitting there that when I got right in front of her, about thirty feet out in the lake, I treaded water so I could watch what she was doing. I swear I meant no harm.

She looked up, like you do sometimes when you sense someone watching, and when her eyes met mine through the hair across my face, her mouth opened and no sound came out, but her eyes rolled up and she fell over backward.

I swam and splashed through the water, my toes finally squishing in the mud until they reached sand, and clambered to her side as fast as I could go, but she was out cold, lying there breathing in a heavy way, and I could see the whites of her eyes through her half-closed lids.

I ran up the sandy track through wild grass and shot right past her cottage, and there was Mr. Marsh across the road, standing in a patch of corn. He was a part-time policeman for Cloverdale, not that we needed one. I ran up to him and threw my arms around his waist. I couldn't talk for a minute or so, I felt so bad.

Mr. Marsh put his arms around my shoulders and got the

whole story out of me, starting with Mrs. Ramsey fainting on the beach, and then going back to my supposed drowning and what I'd heard on my nightly rounds.

That's pretty much the end of my story. Mr. Marsh rode in the ambulance with Mrs. Ramsey to the hospital, and she confessed to him that she and Mr. Jensen had poisoned her husband. They're both in prison now. Mrs. Marsh took me to town and bought me a soda.

My midnight rambles are ended, but often Al takes a stroll down the road under the stars with me before he leaves for work, and my mother bought a telescope and put it on a tripod in the yard.

You might say that this terrible experience was a very bad thing to happen to an impressionable boy. Some people said that. But there was a relative of Mr. Ramsey's who ended up being the poor old guy's heir, which he hadn't expected to be, and this gentleman put a handsome sum of money into the bank for my education. So you see, there's a chance one day I'm going to be really smart.

ANITA McBRIDE grew up in Chicago and now lives in suburban Orland Park, Illinois. She attended Mount Mary College in Milwaukee and Governors State University in Park Forest South, Illinois. She is a member of Friends of American Writers, which honors Midwest writers and those who write about the Midwest.

HUNTING THE TIGER'S EYE

RUTHVEN EARLE-PATRICK

S o far, he had seen no one. Traps, Strategists, Traitors, he had shaken them all. And now he was almost home. Twenty paces to the red oak, fifteen, now five. He stopped short, seized by the idea of a pair of eyes glinting in the thigh-deep grass. Metallic eyes. He looked again, saw no one, and hurried on. The red oak's limb arched over the river to the other side, home. Glancing back one last time, he climbed up and inched his way outward, over the water. At the limb's edge, he sucked in his breath and jumped.

He landed on metal.

Beneath him, the earth splintered like shrapnel. He staggered down to the river and collapsed. Blood was trickling from a small wound on his forehead. He wanted to rise but the earth shifted under him, the sun throbbed, faded. . . .

His first clear thought was the orb. Fumbling with buttons, he dragged a small crystal sphere from his shirt and tried to focus. Streaks of gold fire shot through the emerald iris, winking in daylight. It was whole. He nudged closer to the river, letting it rush over his skull, cooling the slow pulse of pain in his forehead. Closing his eyes, he thought of Peter. He must congratulate this new one. He would never have suspected a Trap at the finish line. As for the next run, there would be plenty of time to teach him what *Victim* meant.

Inside the cave, four boys sat near the fire, watching Peter stash his last colored stone. For a novice, he had won a fair number, at Daryl's expense. Daryl was beginning to get up, clumsily, steadying himself against the wall of the cave. Peter was reminded of an alien not yet used to Earth's gravity. "How's the head?" he said, sounding genuinely concerned.

"Hurts like hell. What did you put in those mines, TNT?"

Peter smiled and tossed a twig in the fire. "It's a military secret. My dad taught me. Thought you'd get a kick out of it." He leaned forward, eyes catching the sudden blaze, burning with the glow of achievement. The younger boys especially were in awe, if also a little frightened.

Daryl roused himself at the mention of Peter's father. "Your dad?" he said casually. "I thought he was confined to a wheelchair." He looked around at the boys. Nobody laughed, but the glow around Peter was gone.

"My father got blasted in the war," he said simply, without embarrassment.

"Yeah. Sure." Again Daryl looked at the others. It was clear whose side they were on. "Didn't everybody's?" he said. Terry and Simon giggled. Jude looked away as if offended. But with Jude, it was hard to tell. "Come on, guys," said Daryl, heading toward the cave entrance. "Mose is still out on the field. Jude, tell the war hero about Friday night." Obediently, the two young ones trailed out behind Daryl.

After the others had gone, Jude sat down beside Peter and said, "You know, for a novice, you sure pack a lot of punch. Why did you set that mine for Daryl? You nearly blew his head off."

"Flatterer," said Peter, with a sarcastic smile. "I barely singed his eyebrows. You wanted a Trap. I set one."

"So your little surprise package earned you a few points. To get ahead in this game takes more than that. You've got to use a little creative intelligence."

"Okay, genius, how come *you're* not running things around here?"

Jude's face relaxed into a grin. "Guess I'm not ambitious. But you are. And besides," he stood up and brushed off his jeans, "Daryl has the orb."

Peter glanced up. "So?"

Jude was already on his way out. He turned back briefly, his face smoothed into innocence. "Right now, that's Daryl's little surprise package. But after Friday, who knows? Show up at the warehouse at nine." And he was gone.

"Peter? Where the devil is that boy?" Mr. Rourke wheeled his chair violently into the piano room.

His wife peered at him over her novel. "Peter isn't here, dear. He left an hour ago for one of his meetings."

Peter's father yanked off his spectacles and aimed them at the baby grand occupying the center of the room. "Three paychecks I spent to collect cobwebs?" He jammed his glasses back into place. "He has no time for anything lately. Including homework."

His wife put down her novel and went over to her husband. "Give him a chance," she said. "Now that he's made a few friends, they might even be doing him some good. You remember the stories he used to tell. Sharks, dragons, dinosaurs. At least now all his characters are human."

Mr. Rourke scowled over his rims. "Some progress," he said.

Peter arrived home just after sunset, pockets jammed with colored stones. He spread them out on the breakfast-nook table, dug a black Magic Marker out of the sewing-machine drawer, and began initialing each one.

When his mother came in and sat down on the bench opposite, he was still working. She eyed the stones. "Gloating over your spoils? What mad dragon were you after this time?"

Peter was indignant. "That's old, Ma. I was a Strategist. Had them all doing the goose step over a mine field. Daryl fell off a tree and set off an explosion that cost him four of these." Peter held up a handful of pink, mottled stones. "They're color-graded, see, depending on how big the job is."

His mother picked up a blue one. "Is this the ultimate?"

Peter looked thoughtful. "No," he said slowly. "The orb is. It's all kinds of colors. That's the one I'm going to get next."

She smiled, amused by his determination, and picked up a few of the other stones. "I think you've done well enough for one afternoon," she said. Then she added casually, almost as an afterthought, "I know one person your father can count on for help with his stories."

Peter took the stones from his mother and began initialing again, distant, absorbed in the task. "No, Mom," he said flatly. "I couldn't help him with that stuff. That's fantasy."

His mother risked a smile. "Then, Peter, there is one other way you could help your father. You remember the present he bought for you?"

There were rustling noises in the other room. Peter lowered his voice. "Mom, *he* bought that thing. What do I want it for? Mozart was a sissy; Beethoven went deaf. What kind of company is that to keep? I'm an army man. You've either got a mission for something or you don't. And I don't have a mission to play the piano."

"Peter—" his mother began.

"Peter?" his father was shouting from the den. "Peter, have you decided to come home?"

Peter looked at his mother, appealing. "Is he going to start on me?"

She reached for her son's arm. "You've had your fun today," she said gently. "Now it's your father's turn."

"Can't he make his own?" said Peter, hotly.

"My own what?" demanded his father, rolling into the kitchen with a stack of sheet music.

"Dinner," said Mrs. Rourke. She saw the pages in his lap. "Oh, look, isn't that 'The Sunken Cathedral'?"

Peter looked vaguely interested. "How did it get sunk? Was it blown up?"

His father's face was a mask of patience. "It sank before bombs were invented. A lost relic it was. Swallowed by time, by the earth." Peter stifled a yawn and began pocketing the pebbles. His father carried on, blithely. "You should be able to master this one, Peter, long before the recital. It's relatively short and not difficult. I'd play it myself to give you an idea—"

"I remember," said Mrs. Rourke, softly. "You played it beautifully. Why don't you try—"

"Alice." His tone cut through her. "The pedal work is vital. I'd rather not spoil it for him."

She nodded. Peter stared at the sheet music, willing it to self-destruct. Again he felt the burden of his father's lost career. Without a word, he pushed the wheelchair toward the piano room while his father chatted about the composer, pointing up a weakness here, an eccentricity there, as he might do with a colorful relative. Peter nodded faintly, from far away, from some distant emerald planet born of his imagination and christened "The Orb."

"Sorry, guys." Daryl came rushing in the back door of the warehouse, apparently fully recovered. He took his seat by the orb. The rest of the boys had already exchanged news and were now shifting impatiently. Only Peter seemed unconcerned about his lateness.

"What kept you?" said Jude.

"My old man," Daryl said, still catching his breath. "He's been getting out of hand lately. Says the club is taking up too much of my time."

Jude snickered. "He must have seen your chemistry marks."

"So what's wrong with a C here and there? He says with marks like these, I'm not going to make it to medical school. Who says I want to? Wants me to be a surgeon, for God's sake. He's the first one I'd operate on."

Jude started rubbing his palms. "Igor, zee operation vas a success, but zee pashunt died."

Peter stared at Daryl long after the joke was forgotten and the group had lapsed into conversation. His expression was dispassionate, analytical, as though Daryl were some odd insect, curious but disposable. Daryl felt the eyes on him. He raised his hand. "Okay. Peter looks anxious to start." There were a few surprised looks. He waited for quiet. "Tonight we'll follow the regular course," he said. "With one exception. My Strategist tells me the Traps have been repositioned. So keep your eyes open. Try to anticipate likely changes. And watch for the Traitor. He'll be any one of us. You've got to judge who to trust, who looks suspicious—Terry?"

Terry, the youngest, was waving his arm. He was a small boy, but intense, and he always played as though his own life were at stake. "How many Coll—Collabraders this time?"

"There'll be two Collaborators. If you find them, they'll get you back faster, safer; but you've got to decide which ones they are. Because just maybe you'll find yourself talking to the wrong one, the Traitor. Their faces won't give them away." Daryl held up a half dozen black hoods with the eyes slit out. "Their voices won't, either. Nothing's real, nothing's one hundred percent certain in this game but you. The Victim will get a head start—three minutes—before we set out. If he makes it back, this yellow one's his." He held up a stone that glittered like fool's gold. "Otherwise, whoever gets the Victim gets it." He passed the stone around.

Jude stole a glance at Peter and said, "What about the orb, Daryl? When does that go up for grabs?"

"Tonight," he said sharply. "Who's ready for it? The orb goes to the first person who demonstrates a little creative intelligence. Anyone who can take Strategy and apply it on the outside. The first person who can expand the game. Are you volunteering, Jude?" Everybody studied Jude.

Jude was silent for a moment, then said darkly, "I'm working on it." The boys laughed, but no one else volunteered.

A few others had questions. While Daryl answered, Peter nudged Simon and whispered, "Who set the Traps tonight?"

Simon's round chin jutted out. "I couldn't tell you, even if I knew." He hesitated, as if debating whether it was safe to go on. "We had a drawing last night for all the positions. Except one."

A sudden fear entered Peter. He leaned closer. "Is that why nobody told me about it?"

Simon shifted nervously, then turned away, suddenly, in a vain attempt to conceal the redness seeping across his cheeks. Peter looked up and discovered the cause of his embarrassment. The others were watching them.

Daryl broke the silence. "Any more questions before you get your head start?"

"What?"

"You're the Guest of Honor tonight."

Peter stared in disbelief. "You keep telling me I'm new at this. Pick somebody else. I'm not ready."

"Peter, we'll die of old age before you're ready. You're going tonight."

Jude pushed him into the center of the group. The rest shone their flashlights in his face. Peter's arm went up, shielding his eyes. "You know the course," Daryl continued. "Around the lagoon, through the old cemetery, across the river, and back home. Now the rest of you, be careful. Because this one's new, he'll be a bit desperate. So make sure he doesn't see you first. Remember—no names, no faces. Okay, Peter. Go! And watch out for the Traitor!"

Jude began the three-minute countdown while Peter ran out the back door, headed for the lagoon. What a change from Strategist, he thought. All he'd had to do before was run the course and keep an eye out for the Victim. Now that he was "It," even pace was critical. When he ran, he worried about anticipating Traps. He slowed down and felt the others gaining. He glanced around. Every bush seemed a camouflage, every step a Trap. Even the night air smelled of panic. And all for a lousy yellow rock. But no, it wasn't just the rock he wanted—they wanted. It was the orb, its tiger's-eye glowing, capturing the dull sun, splitting it into emerald, sapphire, ruby, and diamond. It was a jewel, a weapon of rare worth, secret power. And it made Daryl, its discoverer, the Leader. For now.

"Hey!"

Peter sucked in his breath, stifling a scream.

"Don't go that way!" The voice was a staccato whisper, the face a shadow. "Look!" It threw a handful of stones in the direction Peter had been headed. Instantly, a thick rope net

dropped from a tree. Peter pictured himself pinned underneath. *A Collaborator*, he thought, and breathed a sigh of
relief. "This way! Hurry!" said the voice.

Peter followed, cautious, anxious, yet relieved. His skull
pounded. He wanted time to think, to breathe. Let someone
else make the choices, briefly. *If we can only make it to the
river*, he thought.

They were in the heart of the graveyard now. Stones, crosses,
cracked and crippled by time, leaned into the sunken earth.
Other ancient plots gaped open. His guide kept well ahead of
him, slowing at intervals to see that Peter was still following.
Suddenly he stopped.

"Wait! Ssh! What was that?" The voice was shrill, piercing.

"What?" said Peter, skin prickling. "I didn't hear anything."

"There!" The guide aimed his flashlight at a nearby cross
and the dark mass on top—hollowed eye, pumpkin-lit, blood
spilling out of the socket and the slack gray mouth: a human
head, carved and spitted. Peter turned, wanting to run, but
he fell forward, sprawling into a rectangular pit. A shovelful
of dirt followed him. Then another. Dirt thudded on his face,
in his eyes.

"Traitor!" he screamed, outraged, as the dirt continued to
fall. "Traitor!" he wailed until there was nothing left but
terror. And then the others came.

One by one the heads appeared. One of them—Jude—
grinned as he dangled the rubber Halloween mask over the
pit. They shone their flashights down into Peter's distorted
face, laughing. "Ssh, you'll wake the neighbors, little boy."
Another crooned, "Don't cry, baby, we're coming to get you."
A rope dropped over the side, and as Peter struggled back up,
he heard, among the jibes and whispers, "Don't you think this
got a little out of hand? It's only his first run."

A shrill, piercing whisper hissed, "You've got a lot to learn about tactics." Peter hardly heard the words. It was the sound he listened to. The sound of the Traitor's voice. And it belonged to Daryl.

By the time he was back on the surface, he was himself again. With one exception. He was beginning to understand Strategy. He pushed his way through the group, walking briskly, waiting until he was out of sight to run.

When Daryl and the boys returned to the warehouse, Peter was already there, waiting. In his right hand, he held the orb.

"What are you doing with that?" said Daryl, laughing off his surprise.

Peter laughed back. "Like you said. It's time for a little creative intelligence. I'm going to expand this game."

Peter disappeared through the back door with the orb. Daryl and the boys stared after him. But no one made a move to stop him.

When Peter arrived home, he wanted to slip past his mother, but she saw the strange sphere glowing like a tiger's eye. "Peter," she said, drawn by the colors, "what have you got there?"

"Just the orb I was telling you about," he said casually.

"Just? You must have done something spectacular to lay hands on this one. Tell me about it."

Peter moved past her, an odd light in his eye. "I can't, Mom," he said. "The guys would kill me. Besides, I might have to give it back. This job isn't finished yet."

"Speed up! It's a cathedral, not a funeral parlor. You're forcing it, boy."

"You're a fine one to talk about forcing," Peter muttered, under his breath. "Nothing's worse than a backseat pianist."

Three weeks had gone by. And in those three weeks, he had been chained to the piano in an ivory, unflinching grasp that held no promise of relaxing, ever. He had missed so many meetings that the boys had threatened to expel him. But Peter had the orb. So they could threaten all they wanted. For the moment, it was still his move—small compensation, it sometimes seemed, for the hours he spent riveted to the piano, his father barking commands like a drill sergeant. Still he played. And progressed. Not brilliantly, but steadily, plodding toward completion.

Two days later, he was interrupted by a knock at the front door. It was Jude.

"There's a meeting tonight in Daryl's basement. Can you make it? Or do they still keep you chained to the piano?"

"I'll be there. Don't worry about me."

"I don't." Jude paused, suddenly serious. "But Daryl does. How come you two don't get along?"

Peter looked angry. "What do you want me to do, send him a valentine?"

"Just don't get on the wrong side of him. You're new at this game, Peter. You've got the orb. But does that make you an expert? If that's what you think, you're in for a surprise. You don't know Daryl."

"Daryl doesn't know me, either," he said, impatient now. "Two things I've learned already in this game. Don't trust anybody, including you. And the first principle of attack is surprise. Maybe Daryl's the one with the surprise coming." He moved to close the door.

Jude put his hand out to stop him and stepped inside, his face suddenly rigid, almost a sneer. "You think that's all there is to Strategy? If that's all you've got up your sleeve, you'll find yourself back in the pit."

Peter's eyes flashed. "But that's *not* all," he said, his fingers tightening around the doorknob until the knuckles were white. "This job isn't finished yet, Jude. I've already shown a little 'creative intelligence.' "

"What makes you think so?"

Peter nodded toward the piano room. "Look at the orb."

Jude remained skeptical. Even on the way home he squashed the doubt that crept into his mind, a doubt that surfaced again immediately. More and more the orb looked like some animal eye watching. And never had he seen it glow so red.

Daryl opened the meeting, borrowing a few beers from his father's fridge. "So, Mozart," he said, handing Peter one, "how's your little piece going—what's it called again?"

" 'The Sunken Cathedral.' And don't call me Mozart. It's bad enough the old man thinks I'm Debussy."

Daryl studied Peter through his beer glass. "Pops giving you a hard time?"

Peter chose his words carefully. "No worse than yours," he said. "He doesn't have any crazy ideas about turning me into a brain surgeon, like yours. Mine just squats over me like a drill sergeant."

The boys laughed. Daryl asked, "When's D day?"

"Two weeks."

"Well, you're not hung yet." Daryl continued, casually, "Where's it going to be?"

"At St. James Cathedral. Where I take lessons. Where else would it be?" He spoke sharply, annoyed by the sudden interest.

Daryl rubbed his forehead and laughed. "Knowing you, in a mine field."

Peter smiled. The atmosphere was almost friendly. "Yeah," he said. "That's one cathedral I wouldn't mind sinking. How come your father isn't down here chasing us out of his fridge?"

"Pops had to go to the factory."

"Something come up?"

"Something blew up. One of the gas drums. Some worker smoking on the job, looks like."

"Figures," Peter smiled. Jude looked at him oddly.

After Peter had gone home, Jude sat staring at Daryl, nursing his beer. "What do you think?" he said, after a long silence.

Daryl looked disgusted. "I think they should tattoo a no-smoking sign on the foreman's forehead."

"I don't care what you say. I saw the orb."

"Yeah. But I saw the foreman."

When Peter arrived home that night, his mother opened the front door. It was unusual for her to be up that late.

"Hi, Mom," he said. "What's up?"

"Miss Stark phoned," she said, leading him into the living room. "She said some chemicals had been taken out of the storage room. She wanted to know if you knew anything about it."

Peter slumped casually into a chair beside her. "Not a thing, Ma. What do I want with chemicals?"

"I don't know. She sounded pretty upset."

Peter chuckled. "I wouldn't doubt it," he said. "Old Stark has a fit every time she loses her test tubes. Which is pretty often. You know what the class calls her? Miss Stark Raving Mad. Her problem is she should have retired about a hundred years ago."

Ordinarily she would have laughed along with him. But something was different about her tonight. She continued, in her low, serious tone. "She said one of the students—Jude, I think she called him—said he saw you in the area after school."

"Jude?" Peter's voice cracked. Suddenly he was back on the field, running, keeping a sharp eye out for Traps. He answered coldly. "That creep? He'd turn in his mother if he thought there was anything in it for him."

Still she pursued him. "So you don't know anything about the chemicals then?"

He was impatient with her. "I told you, no. What's the big

deal about a few lousy chemicals, anyway?"

"Ordinarily, nothing. But these, according to Miss Stark, can be used to make explosives."

"Jesus." Peter stood up suddenly. So that was their game. "Like I said, Mom," he said quickly, "she probably put them with her test tubes." He said good night and hurried upstairs.

His mother remained in the living room. She wanted to tell her husband, but tell him what? Peter had mentioned a mine field. That was ridiculous. But if his stories were pure imagination, why the orb? Was it just a variation on the stones—like props for a play? Even if he and his friends were playing a game together, surely it *was* a game. Boys played war games all the time. And anybody could have run off with those chemicals. Peter didn't steal. He made up stories, but that didn't make him a thief. Maybe Miss Stark was a little excitable. Maybe that boy Jude . . .

Late that night, when everyone had gone to bed, she nudged her husband. Somehow, sharing her fears made them seem less formidable. He promised to talk to Peter. At least try.

"Peter!" Mr. Rourke was thumping on the piano so hard the orb teetered over the edge. Peter made a dive for it.

"Watch it, Dad. You nearly broke it." His tone was childishly accusing.

"You and your toys," said his father, responding with resentment of his own. He had tried to be patient. But the afternoon had been long and full of error. It gave the upcoming recital all the charm of an apocalypse. "You need more than good-luck charms to learn this piece. If you'd spend more time rehearsing and less playing those ridiculous games—" There. He had said it. He regretted it instantly.

"They're not ridiculous, Dad. No more ridiculous than the ones you used to play. We're also doing military maneuvers."

The anger went out of him. He spoke with the quiet bitterness of memory. "You don't have to play war games to prove your manhood. There are other ways."

"Like playing the piano?" said Peter acidly. "There's no glory in that."

Mr. Rourke moved his wheelchair forward. It was important to see his son's face. "The men in my outfit called it 'hunting the tiger's eye,' " he said, a bit of the old Irish creeping into his voice. He went on, grimly. "Nobody I knew ever found it and lived."

"But, Dad—"Peter was suddenly enthusiastic—"you were great. The stories you used to tell. Out on the battlefield. Dodging B-52's. Rigging up mines with tin cans and nails. I'll bet they ran the other way when they saw you coming."

His father leaned forward, fixing Peter with his sharp green eyes. "Those were only maneuvers," he said patiently. "We were too far behind the lines to see any real fighting. We were too isolated. Too raw. It was one big training camp that never got tested. That is, until the rains came. And only then by some hideous foul-up."

"But what were you doing playing the piano?" Peter said, the old reproach creeping into his voice.

His father's eyes flashed with irritation. He felt his son had never quite forgiven him for not being wounded on the battlefield. "What else is there to do on a rainy Friday night in a village bar?" he replied angrily. "And who could hear bombers with twenty men singing 'It's a Long Way' in the midst of a downpour? Before we realized what it was, it was on top of us. We ran out into the rain like rats, but it was too late. Bad weather, instrument failure, general hysteria on the pilot's part: It all added up to an honorable discharge. From both professions." He was silent for a moment as if the memory had tired him. Seeing Peter's impatient expression, he smiled wryly. "So much for the tiger's eye," he shrugged, then added,

"So much for my brilliant career as a pianist. But I wasn't the only one. It happened over and over. Young men blown apart in maneuvers before the real show even started." His voice became quiet but no less intense as his large pale hands gripped the sides of his wheelchair. "Peter, what we're doing now, this is a game worth playing, a game you don't win by doing in your opposition. This is a game that celebrates life."

Peter seemed distracted, or at least not wholly convinced. "Then how come I don't feel like celebrating?"

His father nodded, seeming to understand. "Maybe you haven't lost enough. You need time to think. Maybe after practice—"

"Dad, I'm already late for my meeting."

His father stiffened. He glanced at the calendar. "Your recital is in three days." Peter looked at his watch as if to say it was this evening, not three days from now, that concerned him. His father felt suddenly like an intruder. He broke the silence with a plea colored by hurt and anger. "Your reputation as a pianist is at stake here." No response. Again he tried, this time determined to smash, brick by brick, the wall Peter had erected between them. "I have invited personal friends to this performance," he said bitterly. "A standard has been established in this family. A standard which you are invited to uphold."

"Invited?" Peter's voice was savagely quiet. "That implies I was given a choice."

"You were," said his father, withdrawing into a formality more penetrating than rage. "You were given more choices than most. When this recital is over, however, you may abandon your piano playing. I realize, now, how little my assistance has meant."

Peter swiveled around on the bench to face his father. "It's not that, Dad," he said quickly. "I didn't mean—" He searched wildly for an explanation his father would understand, all the while battling against the guilt and anger warring within him. He wanted to stay and fight it out with his father. And he wanted to run. He felt trapped again, outmaneuvered, ashamed. In desperation he turned to the piano. He struck savagely, with a passion that translated as renewed enthusiasm. Chords exploded, recreating the sunken cathedral in all its ruinous glory. As if in sympathy, the orb blazed golden. "Why can't you always play like that?" said his father. The argument was forgotten.

The playing went on, well into the night. Until Jude phoned. "Forget valentines, Peter," he said. "Daryl's father is in the hospital. You wouldn't know anything about the latest fireworks at the factory—would you?"

It was a Trap. Peter recognized it. Probably the rest of them were listening in the background, holding their breath, waiting for an incriminating remark. Now it was his move. He forced the anger out of his voice and spoke calmly. "Why should I know anything? You're the one with the chemicals, in spite of what you told Miss Stark."

There was a pause, followed by background noise. "Stark?" The voice was pierced with irony. "You're coming loose at the seams, Peter. I don't even take chemistry." And he hung up.

In the middle of the night, there came a soft, dull thud outside Peter's window. It was enough to wake him. Enough to remind him that he was still a beginner. While he was sleeping, someone had crept in and stolen the orb. Whatever Jude and the others had started, now, with the orb in their possession, it was their move.

When he got back to sleep, Peter dreamed that he was inside a crypt. And he was falling. Because there was no bottom to this crypt. And he knew at the same time that he was inside something even more threatening. A presence, a power, that encircled even the crypt. A sphere that contained him and watched him and compelled him. It had drawn him toward the pit, pulled him inside and then down. And now he was falling, inside the terrible eye of the orb.

It was the afternoon of the recital. Peter was still struggling with the last few bars.

"Leave it, just leave it!" his father shouted. "If all these weeks of practice haven't hammered it into you, neither will this last-minute fumbling. Play it. That's all. Simply and competently. And make an end of it."

Peter tried again, without anger or impatience. But even with the performance looming, he found it difficult to concentrate. He kept wondering how they were going to strike. And when.

The hall began to fill, mostly with relatives of the performers. The parents all sat in the front row. Mrs. Rourke was scanning the program. "Peter's name comes last," she said, smiling. "That must mean he's the best."

Her husband groaned. "Then I predict a long and painful evening."

Mrs. Rourke was still poking and half seriously scolding her husband when the first performer entered, a small, red-faced girl with wobbly knees. In spite of her terror, she played adequately. A poke in the ribs as the little girl bowed reminded Mr. Rourke of his hasty adjudication. Still he looked thoughtful and stern as, one by one, the rest of the students subjected themselves to his scrutiny. There was only an odd moment or two when his face relaxed and he entered the spirit of the recital. He was waiting for that final moment when his son would enter and make his debut, mediocre as it might be. Still, it would be a beginning. For Mr. Rourke, a new beginning. If the boy were not exactly an inspired performer, he was young and, given time and direction, would progress. But, and this he promised himself, only if his son should choose to.

It was time. Peter went out into the middle of the stage and bowed, peering into the lights. His mother waved. He froze. The pause lasted no more than a second, yet the audience felt the shock. Stage fright, it was generally agreed. Peter's father sensed something deeper. He followed his son's gaze. There in the fourth row—in a group apart—sat Daryl, hands cupping the orb like an offering as the other boys whispered softly, nervously. Jude was the only one absent.

Peter moved toward the piano, stiffly, like a puppet with glass eyes. The image of his son's face remained in Mr. Rourke's mind: the impression of peril, of panic. Then the playing began. So timid, at first, it was scarcely audible. And then one rich chord sounded, and the real playing began. He made the keys sing. His father wondered what had moved him to play like that, as though his very life depended on it. Never had he sensed such intensity. The idea of the orb recurred and haunted him. Again he saw the boy's hands lifting it— like an offering, like a challenge. When the performance ended, he turned to his wife. "Not a brilliant performance, Alice. But it was inspired. Certainly better than any rehearsal. But why did his friend have that orb thing with him?"

"Did he? I didn't notice." She was still wiping her eyes. "For luck, I imagine."

"Well, it worked," he said, still not satisfied. "But I thought it was Peter's."

"Oh, no. It was on loan. He said it was for some job that wasn't finished yet. He wouldn't tell me any more about it."

Peter came forward for his parting bow. The boys whistled and applauded noisily and then, except for Daryl, left the room. Daryl took Mrs. Rourke aside and spoke a few words to her, privately. She returned to her husband, looking pale and anxious, and told him that he was the boy whose father was in the hospital.

"What does he want?" he responded abruptly.

"He wants to speak to me outside. It's about Peter. Can you wait for me?"

Mr. Rourke was annoyed. "Why can't he speak to you here?"

She paused, a little embarrassed. "He has something to show me. He wouldn't say more. . . ." Her voice faded out.

"In front of me?" he demanded.

She kissed his forehead. "I'll just be a minute," she said. And she was gone.

Mr. Rourke sat frowning. Why was he being excluded? What could they possibly say to or show his wife that couldn't include him? Again he went over what his wife had told him about Peter's most recent experiences: the war games, this glowing orb, the missing chemicals. And most recently, the explosion Daryl's father had been in. For the first time, he tried seriously to understand what game it was that Peter's new friends were teaching him. He stayed, puzzling over the pieces as the cathedral emptied and the sound equipment was carried off and only a thin cord remained: crude, makeshift, running from the piano into the orchestra pit. . . . He wheeled himself over casually and peered down into the pit. The pieces were beginning to fit.

Mrs. Rourke found Peter outside the front entrance. She hugged him and slipped her arm through his, proudly, then looked around for the boys. He seemed reluctant to follow her. "Come on, Peter," she said. "I want to show you off." The boys were waving from the far side of the parking lot. Mrs. Rourke and her son went to join them. "Well?" she said, with her arm around Peter. "What did you think of my son's performance?"

Daryl raised the orb, the gold eye of it blazing. "Mrs. Rourke," he said, "I'd say it brought the house down."

Mrs. Rourke jumped at the sound that followed. Her hands flew up by instinct to shield her eyes. It was the piano hall. Stained glass splintered like shrapnel, smoke funneled, while the rest of the cathedral lay quiet and stone-stable, as though waiting for a real apocalypse. She went running toward the cathedral. Peter started after her, but a fierce hand gripped his shoulder and swung him around.

"An eye for an eye, Traitor." It was Daryl. The other boys closed in around him.

"For God's sake," cried Peter, struggling against Daryl's grip. "What are you talking about?"

"My father." Peter was now surrounded by five boys, threatening, apelike. Daryl tightened his grip. "Like Jude said—"

Peter stopped struggling. His whole body went rigid. "You think I was responsible? Because Jude handed you some story to cover himself?"

Daryl's face mirrored his disbelief. "Jude wouldn't—"

Peter broke in, savagely. "Wouldn't he?" He wrenched himself free. "Where is he now, this 'faithful servant' of yours? Right from the start, he played the two of us against each other, hoping one day we'd cancel each other out. And you never realized. You were breeding your own Traitors."

But they had stopped listening. They were all watching the far side entrance to the cathedral. Peter's mother was pushing a wheelchair toward them, her face filled with love and relief. In front of her, spectacles cracked, face blackened, rigid with fury, rode Peter's father.

"Dad!" cried Peter. He started toward his father, then turned, on an impulse, and snatched the orb out of Daryl's hands. "You lose," he said, raising it high like a trophy. "I get to keep the orb. Every last piece of it." Before Daryl, or anyone, could respond, he brought it down on the pavement, blasting it in a hundred thousand splinters of colorless glass. Out of the bottom dropped a circle of paper—color-wheel painted, fluorescent. Rigged to trap light. The rest was plain glass. The boys looked at Daryl, horrified.

"It's a fake," gasped Peter. "Like everything else in your little club. A fake." The boys scattered like rabbits, leaving Daryl to hurry after them.

"Some tiger's eye," said Peter. He kicked his way through the fragments, defiant and free of them, running, running to meet his father.

RUTHVEN EARLE-PATRICK received her master's in English and a teaching degree from the University of Toronto. In addition to teaching high school English and children with learning disabilities, she assisted in a three-year research project on bereavement at Stanford University in California. Her side projects have included a ten-minute clay-animation film and a novel. Currently, she sells real estate in the San Francisco Bay area.

THE
DEAR
DEPARTED

DAN CRAWFORD

always knew her footstep. Or actually, because there was carpet on the floor, I knew the sound of her legs and skirt as she walked. So I knew she was there long before she said anything. "Rebecca?" she said, gently, "Rebecca, are you there?"

"Yes, Aunt Rose," I called back, loud enough for her to hear it. "Yes." I turned around and saw her standing by the butcher-block table. She was wearing her gray outfit, and both pairs of glasses hung around her neck. She looked vaguely worried, as she almost always did.

"I don't like to disturb you, dear," she said. "But there seems to be someone in my room. Things have been moved around, and so on. Would you come look at it?"

I didn't get up. "I know, Aunt Rose," I said. "She, er, works here. She did move some things around, but she told me about them, and I checked to be sure she didn't take anything."

"Oh," she said, not quite reassured. "She does? I see. Yes. Are you sure?"

"Yes, Aunt Rose," I told her.

"My, my," she replied, "works here, you say." She seemed to be fading a little, and I hoped she would continue before Paul heard me.

Of course I had to speak up so she could make out what I was saying, and also of course Paul came bursting in from his workroom. "Are you here again?" he demanded, seeing his aunt. "Go back where you belong!"

Fortunately, he was too far away for her to make out the words, but she could see he was upset. She waved her hand fondly, smiled at me to show that we shared our trials in dealing with this lovable but not entirely sensible child, and vanished.

"Damn it all, what did she want this time?" he demanded, coming up the hall.

"Someone has been in her room, moving things," I answered, demurely.

"I should think so," he snapped, unmoved. Chamois had the misfortune to amble into the room at this point.

"And as for you . . ." Paul began, turning on him.

"Oh, don't pick on the dog," I ordered. I do try to be soothing and understanding, but I'm new at it.

"Oh, it's a dog, is it?" Paul demanded, watching the little black poodle through narrowed eyes. Chamois was headed for the butcher-block table. "I thought it was a large cockroach."

Chamois raised a leg, and Paul stooped down like avenging Jupiter and dealt him a hard slap just behind the head. "And if he doesn't mind his manners, I'm going to get a cat!" Chamois rolled back, looked up at Paul, and wagged his tail. He didn't know what the game was, but he was willing to play. Paul snarled and stormed back to his workroom.

Chamois is Aunt Rose's dog. Paul and I have a basic disagreement about him. I think he's cute. Paul thinks he should be run through a sausage grinder. Of course, he's known Chamois longer than I have.

His Aunt Rose had no children and had lived with Paul and Chamois for twelve years. Then she died. I am not quite sure what happened after that. Paul, who is up on this sort of thing, says that she was so vague by that time that she didn't know quite what to do. Unable to realize that she was dead and buried, she had simply returned to the apartment to live as she always had.

In the ensuing year, he had attended a comic-book convention, where I met him, and so on and so forth. The courtship was fairly normal, thank you, once I learned, on his system of values, I was only 9.5 out of a possible 10. Copperbound books on magic and mysticism came in at 9.65. We were married, and we had just about reached the point at which he trusted me to go into his workroom, escorted by him. It is full of braziers and incense and elderly books and has a not-quite-clean look about it. I do not offer criticism. I have to work up another fifteen-hundredths of a point first.

I had known I was marrying a sorcerer, of course. Paul was too much of a gentleman to let me find it out after the wedding. He even let me watch as he conjured up our rings out of a smoking bowl of water and rue. He said it came from Atlantis and the rings were Atlantean work, too. I believed him. At least I couldn't see "Hong Kong" stamped on them anywhere, and mine never turned my finger green or orange or any other color. And he had no objection to being married like normal people, with a regular license and church ceremony. I had had visions of having to tell my parents to meet us in the cemetery at midnight and bring a shovel.

So I was really not overly upset to find that our bedroom was haunted by Aunt Rose. She was a dear, departed soul, and she had a tendency to appear during daylight, just before lunch and just after supper. This made things easy to arrange.

But Paul found her infuriating, and her little dog, too. I had the presence of mind not to ask why he didn't use his magic to banish her. He had explained to me, while we were dating, that a magician can't do everything he wants to, even if he has the power. I accepted that. It is rather a mature, adult concept, and I'm proud of it. A child assumes that an adult can do lots of things but just won't, out of a sheerly perverse contrariness. As a child, I had planned to move to a jungle, live in a tree, wear leopard skins, and be a friend to all animals. (I don't know where I thought I'd get the leopard skins.) When I got older, I learned about malaria, and passports, and snakes, and so on. Nothing, of course, was stopping me from going off to a jungle; I had just noticed numerous logical reasons not to do so. I think it works that way with magic.

Chamois barked and ran to the door. "Hush!" ordered Paul.

Chamois, of course, did not hush, particularly when someone began to smack the knocker against the door. The sound always drove the little dog frantic.

"I said, 'Hush!' " bellowed Paul, emerging from the workroom again. He swatted the dog away from the door. "This is for me, I think," he said turning the bolt.

"Yes," he went on, pulling the door open. "Dr. Young, is it?"

I went over as a tall man with a briefcase entered. Chamois was still barking. This was unusual, since Chamois seemed to feel that once a person had actually entered the apartment, his responsibility had ended. I grabbed him up, carried him to the bathroom, dropped him into the tub, which was too tall for him to jump out of, and shut the door.

When I got back, Paul was chatting with his visitor. "This is Dr. Young," he told me. "My wife, Rebecca. Dr. Young is what you might call an exorcist. I called to see if he could help with Aunt Rose."

"I thought exorcists only dealt with evil spirits," I said.

"Okay," answered Paul, "then don't call him an exorcist."

"Perhaps it would be better to call me a removal expert," said Dr. Young, smiling. "I take unwanted ghosts away from the spots they haunt. Or, if you want to, you can call me a Ghostbuster, if you promise not to sing." He smiled to show his teeth.

I didn't like him. I can't say why. His suit was clean and pressed, much nicer than any of Paul's suits. His hair was neat and unobjectionable. His teeth were white and even but not white and even enough to be obnoxious. His briefcase had a battered, comfortable look about it, and his shoes were neat but not newly shined. He wore a plain blue tie with a simple tie clasp. He looked like a thousand people you meet on the street.

But there was something about him that made me think of frog claws.

"Now, what I do, Mr. Sangesoxe," he said, turning back to Paul, "is less a matter of exorcism than simple removal. I just take the ghost that's causing you trouble, get it into a bottle like this"—he opened the briefcase and brought out a small green bottle about the size of one of those screw-top bottles that come in six-packs—"and take it away with me."

"What do you do with it then?" I inquired.

"Why, that's a little difficult to explain," said Dr. Young, smiling again.

"And not really any of our business," Paul broke in. "I'll show you the room where she appears most often." He took Dr. Young by the elbow and hurried him toward the bedroom, with the bottle.

I turned to follow, but stopped and looked back at Dr. Young's briefcase. I am not nosy, as a rule (I tell myself), but if I'm going to be a good wife to a sorcerer, I ought to take every opportunity to learn (I told myself). So, making sure that Dr. Young and Paul were out of the hall, I knelt quickly and unlatched the briefcase.

I didn't learn much there. There were two long rods, a bundle of leaves, and three neat rows of empty bottles, held in place with straps. I was reaching down to open a bottle, to see if it was really empty, when I was suddenly hit by one of those fierce, hot itches. You know the kind; it strikes in the middle of your back when you're eating out at the Château de Dumpling, and you sit there and wiggle because you were taught never to scratch in public.

This itch hit me in five places at once, most of them un-mentionable. At the same time, I was suddenly aware of a pressing need to run into the bathroom. I snapped the briefcase shut and made a quick dash. My hand was on the zipper when I noticed Chamois. I was always the self-conscious type, and, though aware of the foolishness of it (after all, I always watched him when he was doing it), I lifted him out of the tub and shut him outside.

I should have known that he would head straight for his usual spot under the bed. There was a tumult of shouting and barking and, as I expected, a cry of "Rebecca!"

I zipped up and ran out. Dr. Young had a small portable brazier set up, and several leaves dangled from his hands as he tried to hop out of reach. Chamois was running around his feet, nipping at magic ankles in green socks.

"I'll get him!" I called, noticing that Paul had picked up a large bookend. "He usually doesn't behave this way, doctor."

"Can you take him, too?" Paul demanded as I swooped down and just missed the little beggar. "Don't bother with anything mystic; just stuff him in a bottle."

"Be careful, Mrs. Sangesoxe!" shouted the doctor. "Don't spill . . ."

I think he was going to say "Don't spill the brazier" because, before he got to "the," that's what I did. Whatever was in the thing splashed away from me, burning into the carpet, searing the doctor's suit, and sizzling among Chamois's matted hair. The doctor and Chamois howled alike. Paul said something not quite nice. I said something similar, but less arcane.

Acrid smoke filled the room, and Paul said something I didn't follow. A breeze came up (the windows were closed), and the smoke vanished.

With it, apparently, went Dr. Young, the brazier, and Chamois. A large chunk of the carpet seemed to have been bitten away, too.

"Rats!" said Paul.

I looked around the room, not seeing much. "I . . . I'm sorry," I said.

Paul came across the room and put his arms around me. "It isn't your fault," he said, in what, for Paul, is a gentle voice. "It was that damn . . ."

"Paul?" inquired a soft tone.

Paul froze in position, took a deep breath, and turned around. He did not shout, which showed marvelous control. But every word was a separate bark. "What do you want, Aunt Rose?"

She understood that he was vexed about something and stepped back. "Are you busy?" she asked. "I don't want to bother you if you're busy."

Paul took another long breath. "No, Aunt Rose," he said. "What is it?"

"I can't find little Chamois," she told him. "Have you seen him?"

I would not have blamed Paul at all for what I could tell he was about to say. Before he could say it, a little phantom ran up by Aunt Rose's feet and rubbed its head on her ankle.

It was Chamois, of course, a slightly different Chamois. He wasn't as black as he had been, and his hair was less matted and tangled. His eyes were bright and his tongue pink and cheerful.

"There you are, little Chamois," she said, bending over to pick him up. "Good little Chamois."

When she touched him, the little black dog jumped away from her. "Where are you going, Chamois?" she demanded. "Where are you . . . come back here, baby. Come back." But he had vanished.

She looked at us. "Now he's gone off again," she said. "Do you see him?"

"No," said Paul.

I pulled away from him and ran to the closet. "Here, Aunt Rose," I said, handing her a little chain. "You'd better put his leash on him before he gets in someone's way."

She took it from me. "Oh, yes," she said. She was suddenly cheerful, with something to do. "Yes, yes, I will. I'll find him." She turned away from us and disappeared.

We have not seen her since that day. We hope, in fact we believe, that she has at last gone to where little dogs are free to bark and nephews never do. What became of Dr. Young doesn't really interest me.

DAN CRAWFORD *was born in Wisconsin and grew up in Manchester, Iowa. After graduating from Upper Iowa University and the University of Wisconsin, he set out on a career in free-lance writing and indexing. His latest projects have included a history of Upper Iowa University called* Our College Home *and the index for* The Indian in American History: An Introduction.